SEA

&

DESTROY

Seal Team
Combat Missions

SEARCH
&
DESTROY

Mark Roberts &
Chief Jim Watson, U.S.N., Ret.

S.p.i.
BOOKS

A Division of Shapolsky Publishers

Seal Team Combat Missions:
Search & Destroy

S.P.I. BOOKS
A division of Shapolsky Publishers, Inc.

Copyright © 1994 by Mark Roberts & Jim Watson, U.S.N., Ret.

The opinions expressed in this book are solely those of the
author and do not necessarily reflect the views of the
members of the House Republican Task Force on Terrorism
and Unconventional Warfare, U.S. Congress, or
any other branch of the U.S. Government.

ISBN 1-56171-328-7

For any additional information, contact:

S.P.I. BOOKS/Shapolsky Publishers, Inc.
136 West 22nd Street
New York, NY 10011
212/633-2022 / FAX 212/633-2123

Manufactured in Canada

10 9 8 7 6 5 4 3 2 1

Chapter 1

Turbo-prop engines droned in rhythmic monotony as the big, green bird glided over the vast expanse of the Pacific Ocean. After fourteen hours of flight, the men inside had become numbed to the steady vibrations of the scantily insulated bulkheads of the aircraft. Conversation had worn thin. Mostly because talking sounded like chatter on the geriatrics ward. Although splendidly built, with triple redundancy in every system, the C-130-D was a military aircraft and sadly lacked the frills of a commercial airliner. The Navy personnel strapped into canvas and tubed aluminum seats on the personnel deck had to partially stand to see out the round portholes in the outer skin.

When they did they saw nothing familiar. All that came to their eyes was a far, away horizon, where the pale blue of sky merged with the dark blue and green of the water. Quartermaster First Class (QM/1C) Kent Welby had long ago abandoned all of the shipboard activities available to the passengers. Since their last fueling and rest stop on Okinawa, his mind had been on things other than their destination, or how they got there.

Not a soul on board knew what troubled Kent Welby. Not even Lieutenant Carl Marino. "Pope" Marino commanded SEAL Team 2, and would be their OIC for the two platoons in Vietnam. From the first day the team began training, Kent had spent a lot of time in careful study of the handsome Italian-American officer; from the steely, light blue eyes which held the "thousand mile stare" of an Old West gunfighter, to his rock jaw and finely drawn Roman features. Lt. Marino was a mustang officer, one promoted up from the ranks, and early on in their joint training as a team, Kent Welby had copied the confident swagger Pope Marino had inherited as a Master Gunner's Mate, before attending Officer Candidate School.

When the Team had toughened and aged, Kent had foregone that sincerest of flatteries and found himself, he thought, a wife. Yet, Betty had proven to have a side totally strange to Kent. In frustration, Kent ran long, spatulate fingers through his sandy-yellow hair and gritted his teeth as he remembered. He could still hear Betty's voice, as clear now as on that fateful day...

"...I *will not* be here when you come back!" Betty had lashed at him.

Kent Welby didn't know what to make of that. It widened his clear, gray eyes. Did she intend to spend the months of his tour in Vietnam with her parents? He pursed a generous mouth, more often given to smiling, and asked as much. He got a shocking answer.

"We are married, Kent. We are supposed to have a home, and a — family. And we are supposed to live together. If we don't have that, we don't have anything."

Kent took a step toward her, and seemed to tower over Betty at six-foot-one. "You knew when I married you that I was going on active duty. That I could be stationed outside the country at any time," Kent offered, afraid of where this headed.

"Yes. I imagined you being in Europe, or the Mediterranean, or even Latin America. But not where people would be shooting at you."

Kent frowned, and offered feebly, "It comes with the job. That's what SEALS do."

Fire crackled in Betty's hazel eyes. "I'll not be a widow," she snapped.

Unable to face the uncertainty of the situation, Kent asked the fatal question. "What is it you are trying to tell me?"

Betty composed herself, her long, blond hair swaying with her agitation as she clasped small, alabaster hands, made the whiter by the bright red polish on the nails. "Either you get out of the SEALS, and stay here with me, or I'm leaving you, Kent."

Shocked to a tongue-tingling numbness, Kent worked his mouth without producing sound for a long moment. "I can't quit the SEALs. I simply can't refuse to go where my orders send me. And I won't let the other guys down."

Outrage twisted Betty's face into an ugly mask. "That's what it's all about, isn't it? You actually care more for those juvenile cretins than you do for your wife. Who do you think they are? James Bond? Captain Midnight?" Her anger crumpled suddenly and anguish made her cheeks gaunt. "Oh, damn you, damn you, Kent Welby. I loved you so much. So very much. And I can love you still. But I need a life, every bit as much as you seem to think you do.

"Only I don't need it to be filled with bloodthirsty adventures in some god-forsaken jungle, three-quarters of the way around the world." Betty drew herself up and rearranged her features into a serious expression. "I've thought about nothing else since you came home and told me you would be receiving orders to go to Vietnam. It's the only thing I could focus on. You— aren't like those others. Tonto Waters is a— stone killer."

Kent Welby was about to protest that Tom "Tonto" Waters had so far never killed anything other than a mouse, but Betty bore on. "And Archie Golden is a lunatic turned loose in a bomb factory, to hear your friends tell it over beers and burgers on the patio. But you're kind, gentle. Why, you have the makings of a great doctor, if you'd only take the effort to go to college and study."

"Medical school costs too much money," Kent defended himself. "And there's the last two years of undergraduate work I'd have to make up."

"Daddy would help out, I know he would."

And there was the crux of their one, on-going argument. Kent had met Betty at Duke University, where they both shared freshman classes during the sophomore year, those classes always too overcrowded to take when you had intended. They dated, fell in love and were married. Kent, a Navy reservist, opted for active duty to ensure a steady income. Betty's father, who had more money than he could ever spend, had made it in the textile industry. He offered Kent a management position in one of his Tennessee factories. Kent's father had warned him often about working for one's in-laws. So cautioned, he had refused. His argument with Betty began on that day. That Betty often received substantial checks from her father, to provide for far better clothing than most of the other enlisted men's wives could afford, only exacerbated the situation.

Now she fell back on her father's largess to try to get him out of the Navy. Only Kent *liked* being in the Navy, liked the SEAL program even more. He felt truly alive during their training exercises and was still young enough to want to put that confidence into action. "Why couldn't she see that?" he asked himself silently. Betty took his silence for stubbornness.

"I mean it, Kent," she flared. "If you do not stop this foolish endangering of your life, I'm leaving you. I'll be packed and out of here before you come back from Little Creek tonight."

"We have the team gear to load and check. I'm— not coming back." The words felt like steel caltrops in Kent's throat.

"Then I'm not, either," Betty wailed as she stormed through the doorway to their bedroom and slammed the portal between them...

..."Hey, there it is!" Excited voices jerked Kent out of his reverie.

He stood then, in time to catch a flash of sandy beach and dark, green jungle below the starboard wing-tip of the C-130-D as it banked to a more southerly heading. Kent sensed a cold knot forming in his gut. There it was, Vietnam. By the time Kent took a second look, the waters of the South China Sea had replaced the thin slice of land. *It's really happening, he* thought again.

Which opened the raw sore of his second most troubling worry. Through all their strenuous training, Kent had managed to keep it his deepest secret. *How would he do in battle*? The question mocked him. Would he cringe and cower, like some spineless wretch? During his childhood, Kent Welby had not engaged in more than half-a-dozen schoolyard tussles, most without a closed fist blow being struck by either opponent. Betty had called him kind and gentle; his mother favored the term "sensitive."

How would such a temperament stand up to the blood and death, and worse yet, the terrible maiming of men he knew and with whom he shared so close a bond? What about himself? What if he were wounded, or had an arm or leg blown off. Would Kent Welby handle it with the tight-lipped stoicism of John Wayne in the movies? Or would he scream and writhe and make a spectacle of himself? With the sureness of their commitment, made clear to Kent as they neared making landfall on the east coast of Vietnam, vague doubts about his own courage plagued him again.

Thumps and rumbles filled Kent Welby's ears as the hydraulic system kicked in and lowered the huge landing gear from the belly of the plane. A second after they locked in place, the shafts of worm-gears in the wings began spinning. The flaps nudged out of their recessed slots in the trailing edge of the wings and lowered to 30%. Kent chewed the inner surface of his lower lip as the knot of cold in his stomach grew. Not that he had any fear of flying. It was the landings that bothered him.

Even counting the trip across country from Little Creek to NAS North Island, in San Diego bay, and this long jaunt over the Pacific, Kent had taken off in more airplanes than he had ever landed in. That joke had been old decades ago among the thousands of men who had taken airborne training at Fort Benning in Georgia and Ft. Bragg in North Carolina. Kent, along with the rest of Team 2, had become a parachutist, qualified at Ft. Bragg, home of the 82nd Airborne Division and the Green Berets. The Army's elite Special Forces received their basic special warfare training on Smoke Bomb Hill, at the Kennedy Special Warfare Center there.

Considered by the Army, at least, to be the equivalent of the SEALs, the Navy men knew better. The training in Underwater Demolitions Training/Replacement (UDT/R) and after was harder than that afforded to the Army's Sneaky Petes, and more men washed out. In water time alone, the SEALs outdistanced the Special Forces men. All of which did nothing to ease the apprehension of Kent Welby as the C-130-D turned on final and began a steep descent. At least commercial airliners did not bring passengers down from 35,000 feet to sea-level in one single roller coaster drop. When the aircraft leveled out for landing and the flaps went to 60%, Kent's stomach gave a nauseous lurch.

Their pilot spent little time hovering in the ground effect. He dropped the main-gear onto tarmac just past the big, white numerals that identified it as Runway 23. Unknown to a nervous Kent Welby, the Air Force jockey had landed in Vietnam often enough to know what it was all about. Rubber shrieked on the hard surface and the pilot reversed pitch on the turbo-engines to slow their helter-skelter rush down the runaway. Their thunderous roar and brain-shaking vibration gave Kent new cause for uneasiness.

The roll-out ended and Kent saw a splash of tall green race by the windows. Kent raised himself enough to peer out the porthole and see a jeep with a "Follow Me" sign on the back race toward the intersection where the C-130 would turn off onto the taxiway. Kent Welby realized he had been holding his breath and let it out in a gusty sigh.

"Another white-knuckle landing, huh?" Tom Waters remarked from across the crowded space

"Yeah." Kent suddenly found himself wanting to share his hidden fear. "Never can get used to landing in one of these things. I heard one of the crewmen in the PO's Mess at Coronado say that landing an airplane was nothing but a controlled crash. I've never felt the way I used to about them since."

Tonto Waters flashed a white smile. With his dark, curly hair, it gave him a boyish appearance, despite being in his mid-twenties. Deep-set, burled walnut eyes gave Kent Welby a thoughtful study. Then he grinned again.

"Hey, Doc, can you believe it? We're really here."

"Yeah...I've been thinking about that," Kent answered distractedly.

Their steel beast lurched to a halt. Lt. Carl Marino unbuckled his seatbelt and stood on the greasy decking so both platoons could see him. "Can the chatter and the gawking. Unstrap and stand up, make ready to debark. Chief," he directed himself to Tonto Waters. "When we get out on the ramp, form the men in ranks. There'll be unloading to tend to."

"Aye, sir." Tonto responded.

With the groan of more hydraulics, the big ramp door at the rear of the aircraft broke its seal and began to lower. Blue sky and green, growing things filled the space created in the opening. With them came an odor that overpowered even that of oil, hot metal and burned kerosene. Kent Welby's nose tingled and twitched with the impact.

It was the jungle, he realized with a start. It smelled wet, dank, sour and sweet all at the same time. Imagined spices he had never savored came to Kent's mind. His senses stunned, he studied a new idea. He could almost. ..taste it. Then the rear door lay in full horizontal position and Tonto Waters began barking orders. Kent's platoon deplaned first. Kent's first good look at Vietnam left him staggered.

What he saw were two three-quarter ton utility trucks with pedestal-mounted .308 caliber, M-60 machine guns. Beside them, perched on over-size, run-flat tires, a jeep with another M-60 MG mounted on a thick rollbar crouched like a jungle beast. This was it! They were really in a war zone. Was the enemy anywhere around? Kent slanted his gaze to left and right, and beyond the vehicles to the green wall of the jungle.

When Second Platoon crowded out behind them, Kent snapped to in proper squared-away Navy style as Chief Waters barked the command to form ranks. Lt. Marino ambled out in front of the Chief and assumed his position just like on the parade ground. Surely he wouldn't be doing that if the enemy lurked just beyond the high cyclone fence with its dual coils of ribbon wire. Waters came to attention, did an about face and saluted the OIC.

"All present or accounted for, sir."

"Very good, Chief. And that's the last salute you'll be giving me. We heard about that at the officer's briefing on Okinawa. The 'Japs' over here have a habit of looking for officers to shoot."

"'*Japs*,' sir?" Tonto Waters asked dubiously.

Pope Marino smiled wryly. "That's what I've been told the enemy is called. The British used to call them Worthy Oriental Gentlemen, which soon got shortened to Wog. The most common term applied in-country is Charlie, or VC. This short lecture on vernacular came by way of some of Team One's officers who rotated back to Coronado just before we came over."

Tonto Waters let mischief shine in his eyes. "Amazing, sir, plain amazing. You have the men, now, sir." He started to raise his arm in a salute, checked himself, did an about face, and marched to his position.

"In case you haven't noticed, we're in Vietnam." That brought the laugh Lt. Marino expected. "We have a lot of cargo to unload. I'm sure you will lend a hand to these good men from the—aaah..."

"Riverine Force, sir," a burly Chief in the shotgun seat of the jeep provided. "An' your advance party, sir."

"Very well, Chief. Once the gear is loaded in trucks, we will convoy to our base of operations at Tre Noc. We're not officially here, however, until I report in to the OIC of Detachment Alpha, Vietnam. I'll leave you in Tonto's capable hands and do that now."

Lt. Marino made a brisk turn and set off for the headquarters building half way down the runway from where the C-130 squatted on the tarmac. The attache case in his left hand carried their orders and a summary of their personnel records. After he had walked out of hearing range, the thick-shouldered chief climbed from the jeep and walked with a rolling gait to where Tonto Waters stood. His face was lit with a smile.

"How about a beer, Chief?" He offered to Waters.

His armpits already black circles of sweat, that sounded like a damned good idea to Tonto Waters. Beaming back, he gave a curt nod. "Right now I'd kill for a brew, Chief. My name's Waters."

"Butler."

Tonto turned back to the platoons. "All right, men, take ten and grab a beer from those generous fellers over there."

It didn't take any more urging for the members of Team 2 to break ranks and swarm over the Riverine sailors and pop the tabs on the first brew they had enjoyed since leaving Hawaii. While they unwound and made acquaintances, the Riverine force began to hustle to unload cargo and place it in the vehicles. One of them stopped dead on the tail ramp and whistled loud and low.

"You better get a look at this, Chief," he called to the burly Butler. "They got more crap in here than Santa Claus on Christmas eve."

"Oh, yeah," Tonto Waters spoke up, as though remembering something trivial. "I meant to tell you, Chief. You're gonna need at least five duce-and-a-halfs to take the whole load. Also some flatbeds for our STABs."

Chief Butler gaped at Tonto Waters. "Are you serious?"

"Damn right."

"Okay, you heard the man," Butler bellowed. "Let's get them trucks up here while we finish this beer."

Led by the young First Class who had spotted their plane-load of supplies, the Riverines went for the goodies fresh from The World like kids in a candy store.

Lt. Carl Marino entered the headquarters building through a sagging screendoor. He presented himself in front of the Chief Yoeman behind a large, gray, field desk in the proper manner. "Lieutenant Marino, Carl J., to report to the Officer in Charge."

Slowly the Chief's head rose and he peered at Marino over the top rim of his glasses. "Captain Ackerage is away at a staff briefing at Special Forces headquarters in Saigon. The S-Two will receive you aboard, sir."

"Thank you. Where will I find him?"

"Second door to the left."

Lt. Marino walked to the door, knocked and then opened it when bid to. He took a step inside, then stopped abruptly. Color rose up his neck to fill his face. Even to the bored chief clerk it became instantly obvious that there was bad blood between this new officer with the SEAL badge on his chest and their area intelligence officer, LCDR Barry Lailey. He heard no more of it, though, as Lt. Marino closed the door behind him.

"Come on in, Marino," Lt. Commander Barry Lailey growled around the butt of the cigar in one corner of his mouth.

His appearance surprised Lt. Marino. Once hard and tough, like all SEALs, Lailey had grown a substantial gut, and was now slope-shouldered and balding, with a gray fringe around the edges long before his time. He made no gesture to indicate Marino take a chair.

Curt to the point of being rude, LCDR Lailey dispensed with any salutation and spoke sharply, in a rapid, clipped tone. "The OIC is in Saigon and our Executive Officer is in the hospital after picking up some mortar fragments. In their absence, I am in charge." Lailey's small, beady, black eyes shone with malice as he went on. "I want you to know, Mister Marino, that I didn't approve of you being assigned to this AO. In fact, I suggested to Captain Ackerage that a change in personnel be made in Team Two before it deployed platoons here to Vietnam. Now, with that out of the way, I'll accept your orders." Lailey extended his hand premptorilly at arm's length. Lt. Marino handed him the tan manila folder.

"Now, one final thing. I will be accompanying you to Tre Noc," Lailey added in a nasty tone that implied that he did not trust Marino or the men with him.

Chapter 2

Out on the tarmac, the men of Team 2 worked beside the others to unload the aircraft so it could fly out before dark. With that accomplished, while Lt. Marino received his tongue lashing in LCDR Lailey's office, the C-130 used the ground starting compressor to ignite the inboard starboard engine. The propeller blades wound up noisily to a shriek that punished the ears of all of those outside. Then the inboard port engine fired up. The ramp raised and then the outboard engines spun to life. When all four belched distorted heat waves, the empty cargo craft began a slow roll along the ramp, to an intersection with the taxiway and on to the active runway. By the time it lined up and went to full throttle for takeoff, Lt. Marino had returned in another jeep.

With him came a stranger, a Lieutenant Commander with unruly gray hair standing out in whisps under his flying saucer cover, which he exchanged for a helmet swathed in camouflage cloth. All of the enlisted men stiffened to attention.

"You may get started at once, Chief. I will ride behind your jeep, with—aaah—Lt. Rhodes."

Lt. (jg) Cyrus "Dusty" Rhodes, AOIC of the detachment from Team 2, blinked in surprise at that. So did Lt. Marino. This deliberate slight would be noted by the sharp minds of every sailor there. That compelled the OIC of Team 2 to double up in one of the utility three-quarters with his two junior officers, Ensign Walter Ott of 1st Platoon and Peter Brooks of 2d Platoon. The scramble of men to find seats went swiftly and the small convoy of vehicles puked gas and diesel fumes into the jungle air. In a line of ducks, the trucks and jeeps rolled along the access road behind the hangars on the way to the main gate. There an ARVN MP waved them through as the string rolled past, and then closed the rolling barrier.

At once, the contrast struck the newcomers. People, little brown men and women, swarmed everywhere. The SEALs gawked like tourists at this strange land they had come to decimate. Chief Butler headed the convoy north along a narrow dirt road. Tonto Waters sat behind him beside the machinegunner. He had never seen the likes. He wanted to take it all in, his panoramic view like a cyclops, with one giant eyeball in the center of his forehead. A weird-looking vehicle came toward them; part bicycle, part palm-frond thatched bamboo basket. Tonto tapped Butler on one shoulder.

"What the hell are those?"

"Cyclos—pedal cabs—you see them all over out here. They are thick as flies in Saigon and the other big cities."

Waters, like his officers and the men, continued to take in the wonders of Vietnam. More cyclos went by. Very young and extremely old men walked along with laden baskets on their backs, some had them hanging down from shoulder yokes. A flock of young china dolls tripped by in exotic flowing white gowns. Waters remarked on them to Butler.

"They're school girls. Off to somewhere only they know."

Farther along the road, rice paddies appeared. The convoy ground past as old mammasans, faces wrinkled with the years, stooped over their work. Tonto Waters drew a deep breath and smelled the perfume of the Orient; partly the fragrance of flowers and spice, redolent with the stench of too much humanity and rotting jungle. Over it all hung the dark curtain of war.

"Jee-sus!" Waters exclaimed when the one common denominator registered on him. Everybody and is brother walked around with a weapon slung across his back. Tonto quickly identified AK-47s, M14s, M1s and carbines of

Korean War vintage. It caused him to lean forward and speak close to Butler's ear.

"How the fuck do you tell the good guys from the bad guys?"

"Easy," Butler answered through a grin. "The guys shooting at you are bad guys. The guys shooting with you are the good guys."

"Oh. Okay." Tonto spied another fleet of cyclos. All of the operators were young women, some mere girls. "How come those bicycle cabs are all run by women?"

Butler chuckled softly. "The women run them because the strong, young men are either doing their stint with 'Marvin the ARVN,' or with Charlie."

That gave Tonto cold chills, which he shrugged off. "The inscrutable ways of the Orient, eh?"

"Something like that. We'll be at Tre Noc in less than half an hour or so — depending on how many potholes there are, and the number of locals in the way. Lean back and enjoy. After this, you'll be humpin' your ass in the bush, where things aren't quite so friendly."

Tonto tried to make light of that. "That's what we're here for."

Doc Welby had squeezed in with Lt. (jg) Rhodes and the nasty-tempered Lt. Commander, Lailey. He, too, stared in amazement at the teeming life outside the air base. He also listened with growing disbelief as Mr. Rhodes got his ear banged by LCDR Lailey; all about Lt. Marino and all bad.

"I'm willing to bet you are going to have to run this team, Mr. Rhodes. Carl Marino is not cut out for command duty."

"You knew him before, I gather?" Rhodes asked, his Rhodesian accent grown thick under the stress of this down-dressing of his friend and commanding officer.

"Dusty" Rhodes had come to the SEALs by way of enlistment in the US Navy to obtain his citizenship. Considered the black sheep of his family for this indiscretion, he remained a direct blood descendant of Cecil Rhodes, for whom his native land of Rhodesia had been named. He shared his ancestor's tall, lean frame and ramrod posture, long, wavey brown hair, and notched, square jaw. Doc Welby reckoned Dusty Rhodes bore a strong resemblance to Bobby Kennedy.

After serving his first enlistment, Dusty had become a citizen and left the Navy for college. After two years he returned, went through OCS and been commissioned. He then took SEAL training and had been assigned to Team 2. Two years and a promotion later, he found himself in Vietnam. The men liked him nearly as much as Pope Marino. Both being mustangs, it made for a close bond with the enlisted ranks. Now he had need of every bit of the diplomacy in which he had been schooled before coming to America. For all his ability, he could not hide the growing frown that began as Lailey replied.

"Oh, yes. He was in one of my teams when I was with SEALs. Did you know he got a couple of his men killed on a simple op down in Central America? He was a jaygee then, same as you."

"I don't recall ever hearing anything like that about the Pope."

Lailey winced. "Shit. Of all the nicknames to hang on that one. Where was I? Oh, yes, we had this little op going against the Sandinistas. We went in without any problem at all. We got the man we went to see, then things turned to crap. A patrol of the rebels jumped our meeting place. Your pal, Carl Marino panicked. He ran. Two of his men were killed as a result, but we managed to get them out. I took fragments out of a short round from an RPG-7, that ended my career with SEALs. Marino was running the platoon involved, but he abandoned them. Afterward, nothing was done about it."

Dusty Rhodes gave Barry Lailey a blank, guileless look. "If his negligence resulted in two men being killed, and you injured, how do you suppose he got promoted, instead of a court-martial?"

Raw hatred washed across the face of LCDR Lailey. "Why, friends in high places, don't you imagine?" he asked nastily.

In the front seat, Doc Welby clapped a hand across his mouth to prevent himself from laughing in the face of the spiteful Lt. Commander. When it came to guts, Lt. Pope Marino, he knew, had two of everything to spare, and in spades. He looked up to see a glint of water off to his right.

"That's the Big Bend of the Bassac up ahead," Chief Butler told Tonto Waters. "Tre Noc base is just beyond it."

When they arrived, Waters had a hard time concealing his surprise. There were PBRs (Patrol Boat, River) in the water and an APL (barracks barge) that had been converted into a machine shop to support them. A line of little concrete buildings held what looked to Tonto to be small, run-down motel rooms. Or a barrio whorehouse in Puerto Rico. The Bassac, Butler told him, was one of the major waterways of the Mekong Delta. It turned out to be a flowing stream of brown water that looked like thin mud. Huge rolls of concertina surrounded the compound, three piled in a pyramid, with razor wire on top. Beyond it, he got a look at what Butler identified as their fresh water reservoir.

It looked as brown as the river, only it wasn't moving and ducks swam in it. The convoy rolled to a stop near an improvised boat ramp and the low-boys were unhitched. Lt. Carl Waters dismounted from the three-quarter and raised his voice.

"All right, guys, listen up. Our first order of business

is to get our room assignments, put up your personal gear and settle down a little. You'll be assigned six to a room. Evening mess will be before darkness falls. Now, let's get a hustle on. We'll unload the Team gear in the morning."

"Ah—Mr. Marino, will you and your officers accompany me to headquarters?" LCDR Lailey asked, using the indication of lesser rank as a goad for Lt. Marino.

Pope Marino did not rise to it. He went along with Dusty Rhodes and Ensigns Ott and Brooks. In the low, concrete block headquarters, they were introduced to the base commander, LCDR Jorgensen of the Riverine Force. From outside, the voices of the men drifted in as they lined up for room assignments and fell to with the unloading of personal gear from the trucks. Jorgensen had a pat little introductory speech outlining the rules of the road. Still burning inside over the provocations of Barry Lailey, little of it registered on Lt. Carl Marino.

Ham hocks and beans. Kent Welby couldn't believe it. *Navy* beans in the Navy? It never happened back in the States. Only in Vietnam — where he had expected to be inundated with the new MREs (Meal Ready to Eat), which were in the process of phasing out the old C-Rations — would he get a hot meal in the middle of a jungle, featuring the classic, traditional Navy dish. They even had cornbread, a veggie mold of Jello, and ice cream. And the beer the Riverines had brought to the air base had been *cold.* Then, as he left the dining room, Doc Welby had his dreams smashed by the Mess Steward.

"Enjoy it while you can, you slobs. Starting tomorrow you go on C-Rats."

Darkness had not yet fallen and Welby decided on a stroll around the compound. He soon saw that being "behind the wire" had a far more serious, even sinister, meaning than he had imagined. The fence consisted of two, not one, pyramids of stacked concertina, with an open space between. This second serpentine had plenty of deadly attachments. Doc Welby recognized claymore mines, rigged with trip wires. Other trip wires wove through the coil, connected to simple noisemakers — metal cans partly filled with pebbles — or to trip flares, which would burn with a blinding light. Here and there pop-up mines had been placed, ready to explode at a touch. Overlooking this whole deadly mess, Welby observed individual guard towers, stoutly sand-bagged and bristling with searchlights and machine guns.

Spotted at intervals along the wire were sandbag bunkers. One of the first things they had been told, Doc Welby recalled, was which bunkers would be theirs in case of an attack.

That news had been delivered to them earlier in the afternoon, after the platoons had their money changed over to Military Pay Certificates (MPC). They had been told that the purpose of the MPC, or scrip as it was commonly called, was to keep hard money out of the hands of dealers in the black market. Doc Welby would later find out that like most ideas conceived by government bureaucrats, that didn't work. What they got were small, printed certificates in one and five dollar denominations. Not hard to get used to, but to Welby, the paper for dimes, nickels, and quarters seemed odd indeed.

The lecture didn't end there. The newcomers were warned never to pay the local Vientnamese with scrip, they were always to be paid in piasters. But that they were always to be paid for services rendered. The limit was given for the amount of MPC one could exchange for piasters. They were given the current exchange rate, and where they could go and when. All of the rules of the base were laid out for them.

One hell of a lot to remember in so short a span, Doc Welby thought. Then they were told they would be the defense force. "You're kidding," came a voice from a rear rank of 2d Platoon. "We just got here."

"You can shoot, can't you?" came the laconic reply.

An officer in crisp, short-sleeved suntans chose to ignore the byplay. "Now for the big Numba One rule. You don't leave the base at night. After sundown, all of the land belongs to Charlie."

That made everyone somewhat uneasy. It came back to Doc Welby with a jolt when a siren wailed a few minutes after he completed his circuit of the perimeter fence. Time to head back to the barracks area.

After evening chow, the officers of Team 2 had again closeted with their counterparts of the Riverine force. The topic was an area familiarization that would begin the next day. Lt. Marino, Dusty Rhodes and the two Ensigns took careful notes on the pages of small plastic-covered pads. When the program had been laid out, questions were called for.

"Will we be employing our boats in this training, sir?" Pope Marino asked, thinking of what would have to be done to make their STABs (SEAL Team Assault Boats) operational.

"Not at first. We have plenty of PBRs to transport your men, by platoon, to the areas you will survey, and the transition range that's been set up is only a couple of klicks up the road," the Riverine captain replied.

Dusty Rhodes asked in his Rhodesian drawl, "We are accustomed to work on the squad level, sir. Will that be the case here?"

"Of course. You're here to do whatever you do, however you do it best."

More questions came, about the climate, the terrain, the enemy. The conference had not ended when the curfew siren sounded.

Several of the new men stood outside the concrete build-ings, smoking and getting caught up on a situations brief-ing of sorts of their own. Of most help were the guys from Team 2 who had been on the advance party and in-coun-try a couple of weeks. In exchange for tidbits of local poop, they got filled in on the latest gossip from back at the Creek. Everything seemed quite normal and relaxed, un-til a new sound entered the lives of the Team.

A whuffling flutter grew out of the gathering night, to be followed by loud, violent *kaboom*! Whirrrrr, whirrrrr… kaboom, karang-boom! Chief Butler cut steely brown eyes to Chief Waters. "This is it, guys. It's dark-30. Time for the fucking war."

His words danced on empty air. All the rest of the men of the new platoons had dived under flatbeds, into bun-kers, and those inside their concrete cubicles sought safety under bunks, tables or whatever they could use as scant cover.

Chapter 3

Lt. Marino and Dusty Rhodes remained behind at the request of LCDR Barry Lailey when the mortar rounds whizzed into the compound. After the first explosions, a stunned silence filled the room, while concrete dust sifted down from the ceiling.

"Welcome to Vietnam, Mr. Marino," LCDR Lailey said acidly.

More dust joined the earlier spill as the second salvo hit. Lt. Carl Marino blinked and watched the light, a bare bulb in a screw socket at the end of a rubber-covered cord, sway in the sharp force of the shock waves. "Is it like this every night?"

"Yes. Except when Charlie has a party," LCDR Jorgensen replied soberly. More rounds kept lobbing in pairs, at a rate of about ten a minute. "Charlie Cong owns the night," the Riverine CO continued his explanation between bursts.

Pope Marino cut his eyes from one officer to the other, shrugged and squared away his shoulders. "What say we get started on taking it back?"

My kind of fighter, Jorgensen thought with satisfaction and anticipation.

Smart-ass punk , LCDR Lailey reflected uncharitably.

When a short lull came in the mortaring, the men in exposed positions made a dive for the bunkers. Many joined them from inside the barrack quarters. This being their first time in a combat situation, the staggered mortar fire made some of the new Team 2 guys edgy. They felt no embarrassment, however, in scrambling for the sand-bagged bunkers.

Following the lead of the more experienced men on the base, they hunkered down under the low roofs, made of a layer of hardwood and palm logs, which supported rock, dirt and more sandbags. After a tense twelve minutes, the rounds dropped in on them in lesser number, about two or three at a time, two or so minutes apart, which the neophytes soon found even more nerve-racking. Tonto Waters looked around the makeshift fortification and noticed more than one pale, sickly face among the first squad men of 1st Platoon, who occupied the dimly lit space with him. He nodded to the Radio Telephone Operator (RTO), Chad "Repeat" Ditto, who gnawed at his underlip, one hand straying to his thick thatch of curly, blond hair.

"Hey, Repeat, what's to sweat? We've been under mortar fire before," Tonto quipped to keep the mood light.

"Yeah," Doc Welby answered for all of them. "But those were going over us, these are coming right at us."

Chad lost his usual sweet smile that gave him the appearance of a little boy. He merely nodded and swallowed with difficulty. He turned deep cobalt eyes, made blue-black by the paleness of his cheeks, on Doc Welby. For all Chad's stocky build, he looked helpless as hell to Tonto Waters.

A soft chuckle came from Chief Butler. "The pucker factor really gets to kicking in the first couple of times this happens to you. A guy can slice washers off his bung-hole with a dull knife. Once you realize Charlie ain't tryin' to hit anyone in particular, just lettin' us know he's out there, you get over it."

"Maybe you do," Chad muttered quietly.

Doc Welby silently agreed. The butterflies in his stomach had turned into vultures. The heavy fluttering of their wings reminded him of the sound of incoming mortar rounds. He suddenly realized how badly he needed to take a leak. He'd had no idea how insistent that could become… before now.

The demand grew overpowering. Doc Welby tried to speak, surprised at how rusty his voice had become in so short a time. "Is there—uh—a—ah—jerrycan in here?"

"Why?" one of the old-timers asked.

"I—ah—gotta piss like a racehorse." Soft chuckles answered him.

Someone produced a five gallon cooking oil can. "You're not the only one to be caught in here under the same circumstances."

Gratefully, Doc took the square-topped container and worked his way to a dirt wall. His back to the others, he let go a long stream. To his ears, it sounded like hail on a tin roof when the urine hit bottom. Time dragged as more of the ugly, finned bombs dropped all around them. After half an hour, the mortar attack stopped. Somewhat sheepishly, the new men returned to their quarters. Tomorrow, or so rumor had it, things would start hopping around Tre Noc.

There being no designated place for physical training, and the roads being watched by too many unfriendly eyes, Lt. Marino directed that morning PT be conducted on the makeshift parade ground. Riverine sailors looked at the SEALs as they ran in place like lunatics dropped from the sky, along with the mortar rounds, the craters of which they labored to fill in.

"Platoon, halt!" commanded Chief Waters after the equivalent of a two mile run had been accomplished. "Spread out. Jumping Jacks. Ready. Commence. One— two—three—one. One—two—three—two. One—two— three— The count went to fifty.

"All right, drop to the leaning front rest. Push-ups. Ready. Commence. One-one, one-two, one-three, one-four…" That count went to 100.

Everyone sweated gallons in the hot, humid, jungle air. Dust grimed into mud on the utilities worn by the SEALs. Everyone in the platoon participated, including the officers. Quite a novelty for the Riverine sailors. The last time they had seen an officer do anything that vaguely resembled PT was back in The World, before being sent to this godforsaken country. When the routine ended, Lt. Marino took CBM Waters aside and spoke softly to him.

"Everyone has regulation swim gear along, right?" he asked. To Waters' affirmative, he went on. "From now on, we'll do our PT in swim trunks like back in UDT/R, then hit the showers before we chow down at breakfast."

"Numba One, Pope," Tonto Waters responded, grinning at his easy use of the local slang.

"Good. Now get these people cleaned up. We need to unload our technical gear. I want a radio check, then have Repeat and True Blue survey our STABs for serviceability."

Even though Chad Ditto was the platoon RTO, he and Truman Oakes had been selected for that task, Waters knew, because they were a First Class Boatswain's Mate and Machinist's Mate respectively. Cross-training went only so far, and the technical gear was the province of the experts.

By eleven o'clock, every piece of equipment had been stowed in its proper place, the radios worked, new batteries in place, and the engines had been run up on the STABs. That's when a jeep rolled up and the driver off-loaded two large, metal-bound fiberboard cases. Lt. Marino called for the platoons to break down into squads and familiarize themselves with the 1:50,000 terrain maps of the Delta.

"Make sure you can recognize what landmarks there are from that map, "Lt. Marino told each squad as he walked among them. "And relate them to the smaller area maps. Starting tomorrow, we're going out in that country."

After the humiliation of the previous night's mortaring, Doc Welby and Tonto Waters noted the eagerness with which that was received. These guys really wanted to go out there and get a piece of Charlie. Pope Marino continued then, and faces lit up with expectation.

"Also, there's a train-fire course three klicks from the compound. We're scheduled to go there after noon mess. Each man will take his primary weapon and a hundred rounds, also another small arm that you want to refamiliarize yourself on, with fifty rounds."

Those orders sustained the men through their noon meal. Immediately after, armed to the ears, they set out at a fast double-time pace along an arrow track. Charlie might rule the night, but those black pajamas they wore stood out too well during the day. They reached the range without incident. Everyone swiveled heads from side to side, hoping for a look at those who had shelled them from afar with seeming impunity. Had any of the "Japs" been sighted, Doc Welby believed, they would have been literally sawed in half with a thunderous blast of small-arms fire.

This train-fire course turned out to be nothing like the usual. Instead of the standard transition firing range, with colored and black-and-white pop-up targets in buildings, in vehicles or behind them, around corners, and other familiar places, this one featured tree perches, spider-holes, and head silhouettes that bobbed up and down, back and forth, in clumps of cabbage palm, and lace-like ferns. Pope Marino personally went through the course with each squad. He, like the men, fired a single magazine of rounds.

When he got ready to take Tonto Waters' squad through, he repeated the now-familiar instructions. "Fill magazine to capacity, load and lock. When you move out, set your selectors on single fire. We will assume standard squad patrol formation. Point man, step out."

Tonto Waters took his usual position as point man for

the squad and led off through the red-topped, yellow-painted pipe stakes that marked the entrance to the range. He'd made only ten long paces when a spider hole popped open and he was looking straight at the hand-drawn likeness of a grinning VC. The shotgun in Tonto's hands roared without conscious effort on his part and the face of the "bad guy" disappeared in a slash of buckshot holes. Automatically, he plucked another round from his utility jacket pocket and thumbed it into the loading port after ejecting the spent round.

He advanced again, some three meters, and a raucous buzzer sounded as two more hidden VC snapped into battery behind him and were eliminated by the men who followed him. "Minus one, Tonto," Lt. Marino sang out. "Plus one for you and Archie, Ditto."

So that's how it works, Tonto Waters thought to himself. He made a silent vow to not get caught out again. Five long strides took him around a curve and he came face-to-face with a fallen log that blocked the trail. The place just screamed ambush. Tonto swept the area with the muzzle of his Ithaca. He sensed movement a fraction of a second before the target began to swing. A load of No. 4 Buck splashed the paper villain before it reached the full upright position.

At once he cycled the weapon and fired as another Charlie showed behind the log roadblock. No sooner had he trashed that one than Tonto Waters spun on a boot heel and made the signal for Enemy in Sight. Then he faded into the bush at the side of the trail.

"Bring up that one-forty-eight," Tonto called out. He referred to Archie Golden, who carried an M-16, outfitted with an XM-148 grenade launcher tube.

Grinning fiercely, his carroty hair sticking out in spikes from under his boonie hat, 1st Class Master at Arms (MA/1C) Richard Archie Golden wormed his way through the clinging vines, ferns and thorny bushes until he had a clear view of the target area. He adjusted his weapon and fired.

The XM-148 made it's characteristic *ka-chunk* and a 40mm grenade spat out the muzzle, spiraling on its way to being armed and ready.

It struck an upright tree trunk beside the ambush core and showered the paper targets behind the fallen log. Tonto went on the move the moment the bang of the grenade faded. He skirted the ambush and checked the targets. Then his face and slouch boonie hat appeared over the rough bark of the barricade.

"All clear. Let's move out."

So it went, with the guys in the squad getting wiser and sharper as they progressed through the 1K train-fire course. Confidence soared, while the sweat poured. When both squads in the platoon had completed their run, they cycled to the rear for a briefing on their performance, while the second platoon began the grueling exercise. When it had ended, the SEALs started back to camp.

"Eleven big ones!" Archie Golden brayed, gloating over the eleven point advantage by which first platoon led second.

"We'll get your ass tomorrow, Archie," a dark visaged, barrel-chested SEAL in second platoon challenged.

"We'll see, we'll see," Archie chortled. "I've got me some ideas on how to max this fuckin' thing."

"The purpose of that exercise was to acquaint all of you with the fact that warfare in a jungle is not like anything you have trained for before," Lt. Marino summed up.

Archie Golden spoke up from his seat in the briefing room. "Do we get another crack at it?"

"We'll be going out tomorrow, but don't expect the same scenario." Groans answered that, and Lt. Marino accepted that he had banged their ears enough. "Dismissed."

The showers got a big play. Especially those with only

tepid water from linked 55 gallon drums. When the SEALs of 1st Platoon turned out in fresh uniforms, a number of River Tigers from Riverine Force approached. Butler explained their purpose to Tonto Waters.

"Time to see what passes for short liberty around here," he announced. "We're gonna take you to the best joint in that shanty town outside the wire."

"Where's that?" Tonto asked.

"The Mi Flower laundry," Butler answered simply.

Instantly dubious of that, Tonto Waters was on the point of refusal. He wanted some beer, not to have his clothes washed. He decided on the platoon bar, a knocked-together affair in one of the barrack rooms. A couple of beers would go down good. "I was going to hit the Platoon Saloon."

"C'mon, you'll like it," Butler urged.

Mi Flower turned out to be a low dive, like any one of a hundred that lined the main street outside Little Creek. That prospect appealed to Tonto Waters like fresh water to a man stranded in a desert — it didn't even matter that the mammasan who ran the place did indeed take in Navy laundry. Outfitted with two bottles of the local beer each, the noisy band of sailors settled down around two oval tables jammed together. To Tonto, the beer tasted as though if someone sent it to a lab for analysis, the report would have comeback reading, "Your horse has diabetes." But it *was* cold. And, what came with it had a certain, if obvious, advantage.

A young woman, small, with all of the right curves and hollows in place, almond-shaped Oriental eyes, her face made up with subtle care, took her place on a dime-sized stage and began to sing a couple of Vietnamese ballads, to the accompaniment of an old wind-up Victrola. The words, in an alien language, were meaningless to the SEALs and their friends, though the emotion projected by the lovely performer touched them all in various ways. When she completed a set of six tunes, she stepped down and worked her way through the throng of Americans to a small, detached table where Kent Welby sat with Hospital Corpseman First Class (HC/1C) Filmore Nicholson.

Seeing the two sailors together would give even a stranger an understanding of why the handsome, genial-looking Kent Welby got the handle "Doc," while Fil Nicholson's features cruelly belied his kind and gentle nature. Where Doc Welby looked like a Norman Rockwell college freshman, Nick wore a bulldog face, fitted on a short, thick neck that made him look like a professional wrestler. Both men tended to be loners, and generally wound up together on short liberty calls like this, which only served to heighten the disparity between them. To their SEAL friends, the young woman's beeline to that table had only one purpose.

"Uh-oh, looks like Doc's gonna score again," Archie Golden remarked to the others crowding the large table.

"Hey, he's got a wife," Repeat Ditto squeaked. "I have twenty ass-wipes says he turns her down flat," he added, using a term for MPCs that was becoming popular among the enlisted ranks.

"You're covered, man," Truman Oakes offered, slapping down four five-dollar MPCs on the beer-sodden table.

"Cool, True Blue. "I'll be happy to take your money."

True Blue split his ebony face with a dazzling white smile. He rolled his eyes until the whites showed and waggled his hands at shoulder height like a black-face in a minstrel show. "Sho' nuff, massah. Bless mah grits if'n I don' think you gwine do dat."

Tonto Waters made a sour face. "Bein' from New Jersey, I don't know why anyone would want to bless his grits. But, ain't you layin' it on a little thick, True Blue?"

Oakes recalled the lecture they had been given back at Little Creek about the ethnic sensitivity of the Asian peoples, although he wondered just what in hell "ethnic sensitivity" really meant. Being one of only three black men in the SEALs at the time, he remained inordinately proud of his accomplishments, and of the warm camaraderie of his brother SEALs. It hadn't been that long ago, he reminded himself, that the only place for a black man in the Navy had been sweating his buns off in the galley of a ship of the line.

"My, how times have changed," he alluded to his thoughts as he responded to Tonto's remark. He gave Tonto a big wink. "I'll watch my pees and ques, Chief."

Silence became instantaneous as the young Vietnamese spoke in excellent, if accented, English. "You are new here. Have you come with the men we heard about?"

Unable to evade the fact that the question had been directed to no one but him, Doc Welby answered softly. "Ye-yes. We just got here from the—The—ah—World."

The beauty produced a small, though attractive frown. "I have heard that term often. What does it mean, please?"

"Well-uh—it's what people over here call back home."

She gave a curt nod. "I see. I am Francie Song. May I join you?"

"Uh—oh, of course. Yes, sit right down." Doc Welby sensed that he had started to babble, and tried hard to stem the flow of words. "This is True Blue Oakes and I'm Do—er—Kent Welby."

A trill of laughter answered him. "I am glad to make known of you, Kent Welby, True Blue — is that really your name? — Oakes," Francie responded warmly.

"No, Fran—Miss Song. My given name is Truman."

Francie perked up. "After the American president?"

"Well, uh, yes. My father was a dyed in the wool Democrat. I was born the year Harry Truman was elected president."

"How interesting. And, please, call me Francie. What about you, Kent Welby?" She leaned an elbow on the table and rested her slightly pointed chin on an open palm, her torso inclined toward Kent with unmistakable body language fairly shouting.

"Nothing much. I was a college washout, joined the Navy... and here I am. Let me buy you a drink."

"That would please me, thank you."

Although she came on strong, from the vantage point of Tonto Waters, Kent Welby seemed oblivious of it. He did buy her several drinks before the siren went off in the compound and the SEALs and their hosts had to leave. This just might prove interesting, Tonto thought, amused, as they walked toward the gate.

Chapter 4

After breakfast the next morning, the platoon drew arms to take to the range. Doc Welby had discovered how unwieldy the big 700 Remington sniper's rifle could be in such situations and asked permission to draw a different piece. Lt. Marino answered him simply with the reminder that he had chosen to become expert on the sniper's weapon. So, when they went into the bush, he would be carrying the Remington, and he had better get used to it. In addition to his shotgun, Tonto Waters selected a compact Mac 10 Ingram in 9mm parabellum, with two full magazines. Along with his privately purchased .357 Colt Python, it gave Tonto awesome firepower. He formed the platoon on the parade ground and Lt. Marino addressed them briefly.

"We're splitting up today. First Platoon will run the course this morning, Second in the afternoon. You'll understand why when we get there."

Leaving the SEALs with that enigma, Pope Marino led them out of the compound. They learned the reason behind the divided training when First Squad, accompanied by Lt. Marino, encountered the first target.

A full-color silhouette of a grinning VC popped out from behind a mangrove root. No sooner had it snapped into position than a flash and report came from the target. It all happened before Tonto Waters, on point, could react and fire. When he did, 27 pellets of specially hardened, No. 4 buckshot shredded the paper man. From back in the squad, came a complaint from Repeat Ditto.

"Aw, shit, they're shootin' back at us."

From beside him, Lt. Marino prodded, "You think the Cong won't be?"

"Of course not, Lieutenant. But what comes next?"

"I don't know," Pope Marino answered plainly. "We'll just have to keep going and see."

They saw soon enough. Intent on seeking targets, Tonto Waters' gaze kept sweeping the strangler figs, lianas, and bamboo thickets. He didn't feel the trip-wire until it pulled tight across the instep of the jungle boot he wore. Too late! With a snap, the Whip, made of a stalk of green bamboo, fitted with spikes at its outer end, swished forward and slammed into the barrel chest of Tonto Waters. Although made of strips of truck tires too worn for repair, the rubber points did their damage all the same — to Tonto's self-esteem. He vowed never to make that mistake again.

From now on, he would wear some foot gear more sensitive to the slightest contact. Perhaps canvas coral shoes, like Doc Welby and Ensign Ott. Then his self-image reached a new, all-time low at Pope Marino's curt remark. "You're out of there, Tonto. KIA. Take his place, Archie."

While Chief Tom Waters fell back to the starting line, MA/1C Richard Golden snaked forward to take point. Not until Tonto had cleared his weapon and sat down to assuage his constant thirst with a sip from his canteen did he realize how quickly they were learning under these conditions. He'd be ready the next time, Waters promised himself.

It took the squad an hour to cover the .5 k transition course, and less than ten minutes to return to the starting line. Lt. Marino briefed them on their performance, while Ensign Ott took Second Squad through. After a suitable pause to re-adjust the range equipment, First Squad had another go at it.

For the first two hundred meters, they missed not a target. Then, unexpectedly, a sudden burst fired from their left and 7.63x39mm slugs snapped overhead. Not blanks, like on the previous run-through, but live ammunition. Without conscious thought, everyone dropped and faded

Without conscious thought, everyone dropped and faded out of sight into the underbrush. Again, without direction, Archie Golden popped off a round from the XM-148. It dropped into place overhead of the firing station. The wooden stock of the remote-fired PPSh43 shattered in the burst of shrapnel.

"Good kill, Archie," Pope Marino praised softly.

Tonto Waters nodded silent agreement and moved out on point again. He identified a trip-wire for another Whip and steered the squad around it, then pushed on. He nearly stepped on the compression plate of a land-mine, avoiding it only by sensing the slightest hint of motion. He uncovered three more boobytraps and guided the men past them without incident. Then ,from an oblique angle, the heavy *chug* of a Soviet-made DShK-38, 12.7mm heavy machinegun vibrated in the air. The fifty caliber weapon spat thumb-thick slugs at a slow rate of 550-600 rounds per minute.

Recalled from a classroom session the previous afternoon, Tonto's growing experience of warfare in Vietnam provided the fact that although designed as an air defense weapon, the Viet Cong preferred to use the DShK-38 for perimeter protection. That would mean that there was supposed to be some sort of bunker system or compound over there. Perhaps even a POW camp. He eased back from his exposed position and joined Pope Marino.

"Lieutenant, we've got an enemy concentration to our left. Might be a holding base for prisoners of war."

Pope Marino smiled with satisfaction. He liked the way the men had gotten into the "roles" that the train-fire course scenario called for. "Circle it and be ready to kick ass," Pope issued an order that sounded vague, but was ,he knew, all his men needed.

It took half an hour. When the situation grew ripe, the squad laid down a heavy base of fire and Archie lobbed in grenades from the XM-148, prior to their assault. They found it to be a roadblock type bunker, made of coconut logs and sandbags. The rest of the problem ran without a hitch.

Seated on the benches in the rest area of the range, the squad listened as Lt. Marino talked them through the exercise. "You did well. Much better than the people who designed this course ever expected anyone to do. The most important thing you must remember is that this is not a set-piece battle. This is three dimensional warfare. In fact, you could say it is four-dimensional — time is a factor, too. The enemy can be anywhere, anytime. He can come from below the ground, out of the river, from the trees, in the bush, and in numbers a hell of a lot bigger than ours. It's his country, very likely his home province. He knows nearly every inch of the terrain. Some of them, the cadres who fought with the Viet Minh, have been at it for almost twenty years.

There isn't anything they don't know about jungle warfare. I'd wager some have forgotten more than we can ever learn." Pope Marino paused then and took a backhand swipe at the runnels of sweat that poured down his forehead.

"There's one thing they don't know," Tonto Waters offered.

"What's that?"

"They don't know anything about SEALs."

That brought a broad, white flash of smile to Lt. Marino's face. "Damn right. And the only ones we want learning about us are those who are about to die. That's why this afternoon's classroom work will be devoted to a review of camouflage techniques. We're going to start painting our faces for tomorrow's exercises. We are to have some real, live ARVNs to act as the enemy. They're supposed to spot us before we can spot them. I don't intend that they see a single man from our platoons. Now, form in a column of twos and we'll head back to the base."

After much-needed showers, the SEALs of First Platoon descended on Mi Flower. This time they carried seabags of muddy, stained, smelly uniforms, skivvy shirts and shorts. These they gratefully turned over to the old, wrinkle-seamed mammasan, Rose Throh, who ran the place. Their dirty clothes disappeared behind a bamboo curtain into clouds of steam. Momma Rose came back as they settled around tables. First, she tweaked the chubby cheek of a round little two-year-old who sat on the counter. The kid seemed to go with her everywhere. Then, she clapped her hands and chattered in Vietnamese to the bartender, who began to open bottles of *Bamibah* and put them on serving trays.

These he distributed among the thirsty SEALs. Momma Rose stood against the bar and clapped her hands again. "This beer is — how you say? — on the roof."

"On the house, Mammasan," Tonto Waters sang out. "But what's the occasion?"

"First time in bush, first drink on house."

A chorus of thank-yous ran through the seated SEALs. Doc, who had been unusually quiet all day, remarked on this generosity, and turned silent again. Francie Song joined the platoon then and sat pointedly close to Doc Welby. Distracted by the thought that whenever their mail caught up to them he should be seeing divorce papers, Doc didn't even acknowledge her presence.

At least not until she gave him a friendly dig in the ribs with an elbow. "Hey!" the young SEAL yelped. "What was that for?"

"Ten piasters for your thoughts," Francie responded in her musical English. "You look so sad, Doc Welby. I sing a happy song for you."

"Aw, it's nothin'…nothing you can do anything about anyway," he added in a mutter, more to himself than the lovely young woman beside him.

Francie's face took on an impish expression. "How do you know until you try? I have been unhappy many times in my life. My music always helps me."

Her eyes held a twinkle that Kent Welby read as sincere compassion. He'd be lower than whale shit if he failed to respond to her effort to cheer him. "I suppose we could give it a try," he offered lamely.

"All right. I sing for you. Only... only if you take me to dinner tonight."

All of a sudden, her presence as a woman weighed in on Kent Welby. He put his concern into words. "I don't think that would work. I'd have to stay out after curfew."

Francie gave him a beaming smile. "No problem with that. Some sailors do it all the time."

"Those sailors aren't SEALs," Kent answered indignantly.

"Oh, cut yourself some slack, Doc," Tonto Waters interjected from the other table. "We ain't never held the reputation of bein' angels. We'll cover for you, don't worry."

Kent Welby gave that some thought. It was obvious that Francie had a big thing going for him. She was beautiful. And she wanted him. While Betty, he thought darkly, had her mind set on getting rid of him. Francie had said she had known unhappiness in the past. It might do some good to talk with her. In private, of course, not with all these bozos around. He shrugged in acceptance, and felt his cheeks grow warm.

"Okay with me. We can give it a try anyway," he agreed to her plan.

"Atta boy!" Tonto brayed through his laughter.

Francie sang for them, turning her attention directly on Kent Welby. Partway through her first set, he began to have second thoughts about violating curfew and taking the risks that came with it. Then Francie poured on the heat in a romantic French ballad and he melted. Kent and Francie left the Mi Flower shortly before the siren went off.

She led him down the muddy dirt street of the haphazard village that had become an extension of the Naval compound. A tiny yellow light, from a kerosene lantern shone over the unmarked entrance way to what Kent discovered to be a restaurant. Not in the usual sense, he quickly found out. This place was as far removed from Vitali's Fine Italian food, or even McDonald's for that matter, as Kent was himself.

It sported half a dozen rickety tables on a pounded dirt floor, a pulpit-sized bar, and the cooking was done in one noisy corner of the single room. To Kent's surprise, genuine rectangular ratan fans — moved with hand-power against their springs by small boys who squatted against the walls —shoved the humid air around in lazy fashion. Candles and even some oil lamps guttered on the tables, providing the room's only illumination, save for a modern Coleman white gas lantern that hung over the steaming woks and charcoal ovens. It was right out of a 1930s, Claude Raines movie. His astonishment showed clearly on his face.

"It is *Phon Bai*, the best place in town," Francie assured him, misreading his reaction.

"I wouldn't want to see the worst," Kent responded frankly.

"The food is very good."

Kent grunted. *We'll see*, he thought to himself. To add to his surprise, Francie ordered a bottle of wine and they got it. They sipped the cold, white spirit while Francie suggested that she should order for both of them. When the food came, the savory aromas delighted Kent Welby. Although he peered under the lid of a clay pot and the high-domed cover of another dish, Kent could only recognize one item.

He made an effort to make his voice lightly self-critical, so as not to offend. "I'm glad you did the ordering. I know only one thing we've got. Those egg rolls. We ordered them from Wing's Carry Out Chinese at Little River."

Francie seemed slightly amused. "Those are Imperial Rolls. They have alot more things than the Chinese put in egg rolls."

"What's the lettuce leaves for?" Kent asked, puzzled at their presence on the plate.

"You wrap an Imperial Roll in a leaf and dip it in *Nuoc Mam Nhi* — fish sauce. It's very good for you."

Unlike many who had been in-country for a while, Kent had not as yet seen any of the small, back-yard factories, that dotted the Vietnamese countryside, where Nuoc Mam sauce was made. So he willingly mimicked Francie's movements and dove into the pungent, salty condiment. Francie used it on everything, as she served first him, then herself, identifying each dish as she ladled it onto his plate.

"You can call this a typical Vietnamese feast. This is Duck in a Hot Clay Pot. Real spicy. And this is Lemon Grass Prawns. And, of course, rice." She sat back and surveyed his heaping plate. "Enjoy."

Kent blinked and produced a rueful grin. "Jeez. I thought onlyi mitation Orientals back in the States said that."

Francie's trill of laughter danced in the room. "It is simply the best English translation of the salutation given in most Asian languages before one takes a meal. But, why do you call them 'imitation?'"

Kent's frown of concentration left his youthful forehead almost before it formed. "I'm thinking of the native born. It's inconvenient saying; Chinese-American, or Vietnamese-American, or Japanese-American every time you talk about someone. Technically, they are Americans, not Orientals." He stopped, frowned again. "I suppose that sounds arrogant, or rude. If so, I'm sorry." Kent placed a hand over one of hers.

"No, Kent Welby, not really. We are mostly one people, living in our countries over here. It is hard thinking about living among so many different people, in a place so foreign as America."

Kent tried for a joke. "That's funny. I don't think of America as at all foreign."

He succeeded and Francie's laughter turned heads in the restaurant. When she quieted, they gave their attention to the food. Kent licked his lips and ate a disproportionate amount, answering the demands of his young body for fuel. All the while, he marveled at how this out of the way place could come up with such good chow. It surprised him that he developed a tiny, niggling suspicion born of this observation.

After dinner they lingered over cups of a powerful rice wine and small bowls of lotus root, sweetened in coconut juice. Guilty conscience, something rumored to have been trained out of SEALs, began to goad him regarding the violation of curfew and Kent made noises about really having to go.

"Nothing will happen to you, wait and see," Francie urged.

Kent remained adamant. "I have to be back soon, anyway. It's—it's been a terrific evening, Francie. But, if I want to enjoy any more like it, I'd better not tempt fate."

He relented partly when Francie asked that he walk here to her home. They paused outside the narrow doorway that opened on the stairway to her second floor apartment over a grocer's shop. Unaccountably, Kent felt as off-balance and hesitant as a high school sophomore on his first date. Francie solved that awkwardness for him by taking the initiative.

She rose on tiptoe and kissed him firmly and warmly on the lips. "Good night, Kent Welby." Then she disappeared into the pool of darkness in the stairwell.

For an instant, Kent reeled with the electric contact of those soft, yet demanding, lips. Then he turned on one heel and started off toward the main gate to the Tre Noc base. His first impressions of the small village altered abruptly. Not a light shone in the street. Only after covering a block at a brisk pace did it strike him. The nightly mortaring had not come as usual. Maybe Charlie would leave them in peace? Or maybe, they would launch a real attack. He had gained another half-block when two dark figures appeared from an alley between ramshackle huts.

Kent Welby tensed, without giving visible sign, as a thin sliver of ice ran along his spine. Although more closely cropped than regulation, the hairs on the back of his neck tingled and came erect. Quickly he ran a mental inventory of his options and possibilities. Like the others, he had gone out armed. The comforting presence of his .357 Magnum and a SEAL utility sheath knife gave him a solid advantage over anyone not armed with an automatic weapon or shotgun. All the same, deep inside, Kent sincerely wished that this wasn't really happening.

Francie Song may have said that he would be in no danger, but the presence of this sinister pair made her words sound a hollow boast. Kent gritted his teeth and took another step forward. The silhouetted men responded in kind. Kent worked one hand down to the loose hem of his shirt, worn outside his belt and felt for the butt-grip of the Colt Python. If this turned out to be a couple of VC, Kent vowed not to be taken without one hell of a fight. Suddenly, the enormous tension of Kent Welby exploded into relief as he recognized a familiar voice.

"You get laid, Doc?" Tonto Waters asked out of the darkness.

"Dammit, Chief, you scared the crap out of me," Kent blurted before he could cover himself.

"You didn't get laid," Tonto answered his own question.

"We waited to cover for you." Now, Kent Welby could make out the figure of Chad Ditto.

"I appreciate that, Repeat. Only now we're all gonna catch hell."

"Not really. I squared it with the guard," Tonto Waters advised.

"Then let's get back," Kent breathed out in relief.

Gratefully they made it to the compound without incident. Five minutes after they entered their barrack room, the mortaring began.

Chapter 5

After a grueling week of intensive exercises, including live-fire engagements with ARVN troops, the SEALs of 1st Platoon waited in irregular formation expecting yet another day of more of the same. That changed abruptly when Lt. Marino appeared in the doorway to the Riverine Force headquarters. With him was the base CO, LCDR Jorgensen. At once the "old hands" of Team 2 knew something important had changed. Pope Marino didn't keep them in suspense for long.

"You've been weighed and found fit and ready. Today we do it for real. First Platoon will be taken in separate PBRs to a minimal activity area to lay out an ambush for the purpose of kicking ass and taking names on Charlie."

Innate discipline kept the men from letting out a bellowing cheer. It didn't keep them from making silent, thumbs-up signs, shooting fists into the air and grinning like cream-fed cats. Lt. Marino gave them a few moments to blow off steam.

"Nothing new about this. We've been rehearsing it for the past three days. There'll be a quick briefing, we draw equipment and then move out. Get 'em going, Chief."

Tonto Waters drew himself up. "Damn betcha, Pope."

It had been mutually decided that despite the insistence of LCDR Barry Lailey that the SEALs use the STABs for high profile psy-war purposes, that it would be in the best interests of the platoons to move among the enemy without being noticed. To do that, the PBRs would be used for insertion. Foremost water-borne operations that provided a certain anonymity. The PBRs were on the water every day and night, running up and down. To the VC, they were like a single helicopter. They could be about anything; a mail run, transporting supplies, a liberty party. Night time cloaked the activities of Charlie Cong and added a certain terror factor. No sense, they reasoned, to expose themselves in daytime for such an unimportant target.

Accordingly, the briefing was short and loose. "This entire part of the Delta," Pope Marino told his men, "is south and west of the Rung Sat Special Zone. Since the earlier success of the detachments from Team 1, Viet Cong activity has been increasing steadily throughout the network of rivers, with the major activity concentrated on the Mecong and the Bassiac. We know of four major trails used by the VC to transport supplies and move personnel. We are going to this one, the southernmost. It is an area of light activity, compared to the other three, and any we haven't found yet. Word has come that Charlie will be moving an approximate company size unit, heavy laden with ammunition and medical supplies tonight or tomorrow night. Our job is to get in their faces and mess them up." Lt. Marino tapped the map with a pointer.

"We'll move inland from our Initial Point for a distance of about one klick, until we encounter the trail at approximately here. Note this small, steep knoll. It's the highest piece of ground near the area. We'll set up our first ambush at its base, with the corner of the Ell up against it. Anyone coming up the trail from the river will walk right into it. First squad, this will be your responsibility. Best case scenario is that they'll be carrying supplies. Second squad will support the ambush by enfilade fire... from here." Marino drew an imaginary line with the pointer.

"What happens if there's a whole company of them?" Chad Ditto asked.

"Intelligence says that the Viet Cong are not presently concentrated in such numbers in the Delta. If we do find they outnumber us by too many, we trip the Claymores and fade into the bush. Then all we have to do is work our way to the river for extraction. Questions?"

"Do we have any secondary ambush sites?" Tonto Waters asked.

"Yes. Here and here, closer to the river, in the event that the VC send a patrol after us after we hit the main force. It's more a rear guard action, but we may as well use it to ambush them again."

After answering a couple more questions, Pope Marino dismissed them to draw equipment. In addition to weapons and ammunition, Archie Golden packed away four Claymore mines and stood with a broad grin while he handed out grenades to each squad member.

"You get smoke, frags, and Willie Peter," he announced gleefully. Archie especially loved the white phosphorous. "Use them wisely and well."

"Are you taking any C-4, Archie?" Tonto Waters asked.

"Oh, yeah. A couple of blocks. Never can tell when we might need some."

In addition to their usual gear, this time each man received four C-Ration packets. That brought the usual comments as the men stuffed them into pockets.

"Oh, joy. I've got ham and lima beans," Repeat Ditto groused. "I'll have the runnin' squirts for a week."

"I'll trade you for one of mine," Doc Welby offered eagerly. "I've got your basic two ounces of sawdust sausage patties in six ounces of grease."

"Keep them!" came a chorus from the squad.

A moment later, the number of field rations they had stowed away reminded them better than Pope Marino's briefing that they were staying *out there* for at least a day and a night. Charlie owned the night. The low rumble of newly started engines on the PBRs reinforced that thought. With the last of their gear packed in a tense silence, the word came to move out to the boats.

Already the industrious machinist mates of the Riverine Force had attached the SEALs' Honeywell MK-18, hand-cranked 40 mike- grenade launchers to the port side of a pair of PBRs. They had also fixed a swivel stansion to the starboard gunwhale, into which True Blue Oakes fitted his M-60LMG. With the three .50 caliber machine-guns on board, it all provided awesome firepower. Yet, as their instructors had reminded them from the first day of weapons familiarization, "There's more air out there than meat."

Doc Welby found himself dwelling on that after the PBRs edged away from the pier. It would be up to him and True Blue to seal the ambush kill zone. True Blue Oakes would initiate the ambush with his M-60, while he closed the back door with his Remington. He had quali-fied expertise with the Model 700, as well as several other rifles. But that was punching holes in paper. What would happen when the target in the cross-hairs of the Redfield was a living, breathing human?

Of course he had thought about that before. Everyone in the squad had wrestled with the morality of killing a man. Yet through his training, most of his mental energy had been focused on keeping up with the rest and not quit-ting the program. Simply becoming a SEAL had become the most important thing in his life. Now they were on the way to find the enemy and kill or capture as many as they could. He would be up a tree. What if the ambush failed and the Charlies broke through? He would be trapped, perhaps taken prisoner or killed. A deeper tone from the engines interrupted his gloomy reverie as the coxswain increased the throttle.

Oily brown water slid past the PBRs as they glided down the Bassiac. Kent Welby's thoughts slipped away also, back to that fateful last week before they left the base at Little Creek, Virginia for the UDT/SEAL base on Coronado Island, in San Diego Bay...

They had known that part of Team 2 would be sent to Vietnam for a month. Excitement mounted as the platoons were evaluated to determine which ones would go. Then, when Kent Welby reported on the base that on Monday morning, Lt. Marino had made the announcement. First and Second Platoon would be going, while 3rd and 4th would remain at Little Creek.

"Not to say that they lacked any in skills," Pope Marino hastened to point out. "As you know, it's policy that the Teams are never deployed as a whole unit. The detachment remaining here will be employed in training replacements in the event they are needed. And you might as well accept that they'll be needed. The enemy over there doesn't use blank ammo."

Pope's little pep talk did little to defuse a certain grudging resentment among the men in 3rd and 4th Platoon. Nothing stood out about the SEALs as much as that they were motivated. They wanted to get into a fight, to prove that their agony and sacrifices in training would pay off. Throughout the day, silent speculation went on as to where they might be stationed. To Kent, everything seemed changed.

He saw the sunlight as brighter, the air smelled crisper, he heard everything sharper. When he got home, he discovered an entirely different outlook awaiting his news.

"I don't believe it," Betty stated in a voice that sounded hollow to her ears. "You can't possibly be going there. East Coast teams are designated for duty in Europe, the Middle East, Africa. Why don't they send some Team from the West Coast?"

"They're already there," Kent explained patiently. "Have been for nearly three years. But, right now, it's the only war going and the brass think we should get a little experience."

"I don't want you to go."

"I know that, Betty. It's not like I put in a request chit for this. Yet, in a way, I guess I did. Being a SEAL is a volunteer thing. Going to jump school was a volunteer thing, same for Ranger school. I can't simply quit volunteering now when the going gets dangerous."

Betty's lovely, heart-shaped face twisted into an expression of anguish. "Don't you see? All of it is dangerous. Jumping out of a perfectly functioning airplane is dangerous—no, it's insane. Sliding down steep mountains on a ridiculously small rope is dangerous. Playing with explosives, or whatever it is you do, is dangerous. Kent, darling, you've become a danger junky. I can see it in your eyes.

"You're looking forward to this. You're eager to go to Vietnam. Well, I'm not. I don't want you to go. Not now, not six months from now, not a year from now." Betty paused in her rush of words to gasp in a deep breath and push a stray lock of her blonde hair from in front of her left eye. "Can't you transfer out?" At the look of sudden, baffled anger on her husband's face, she amended her remark. "To another Team, I mean."

"What's gotten into you, Bett?" Kent turned partly away, to hide the hot fury he felt burning in his face. "That would be like running out on my buddies. I'd look a coward in their eyes."

Bitterness curled Betty's lips. "Better a live coward than a dead hero."

"It wouldn't work, anyway. If I tried for a transfer, even to Third or Fourth Platoon, I'd be busted out of SEALs altogether."

Betty seized on that at once. "Third and Fourth aren't going?"

"No, of course not. A part of the Team always stays behind."

"It's not fair that you have to go and they stay behind."

Kent tried to lighten the mood. "I'm sure they agree with you. They're all unhappy that we got picked and they didn't."

"That's not what I mean. I don't like what you're doing. I don't like it at all."

"You like the muscle that I've built up being a SEAL. And the year-round suntan. You tell me about them often enough when we're in bed."

"Yes! When you and I are together, here in bed, where it's safe, I do like those things about you. Can't you see, I'm afraid of losing all of them, and you, too."

Kent could no longer contain his anger. He had to break this off. "I don't want to talk about it now. We have a week. We can work it out. We. ..have to."

Betty's response came in a sob as she rushed brokenly toward the bedroom door. Their later talks did little to get beyond Betty's fierce determination to keep Kent safely at home. Their sex life ended on Wednesday. After that, bitterness kept a wedge between them, until that final morning when Betty told him she would not be there if he went with the detachment...

Throaty rumbles from the exhaust of the PBRs, as the coxswains reversed the screws, brought Kent Welby back to his deadly surroundings. The nose of the lead boat edged toward a muddy strand and the SEALs got the good news from Tonto Waters.

"Over the side. We walk from here."

Pope Marino led the way. The SEALs wound up in knee-deep mud the consistency of sludge in a sewer plant. The water surface came up to the armpits of Chad Ditto. Progress was slow the few yards to the bank. Like walking through freshly poured concrete, Kent Welby thought. Once he had pulled free of the sucking morass, Doc Welby hunkered down to search a sector of the jungle that surrounded them. Doc became aware of the leeches a moment later when Chad Ditto whispered breathily from beside Lt. Marino.

"Shit, oh, shit! Somethin's got ahold of my dick."

HC/1C Phil Nicholson forced his way out of the muck while Doc Welby became aware of gentle, though insistent, tugging on the inner sides of his thighs. "It must be leeches," the platoon medic spoke in a low tone. "We're too exposed here to strip down. We'll have live with it and move further into the jungle."

Pope Marino nodded his agreement and motioned the

squad forward into the undergrowth. Tonto Waters took the point as Second Squad came onto the slippery bank behind them.

Eyes constantly on the move, Tonto stepped out. He brushed aside a clinging liana and edged around the low fronds of a cabbage palm. Walking on tip-toe, his canvas coral shoes made the only breathy sound. While he advanced, he ran an idea through his brain. What this kind of fighting called for was some means of changing a shotgun's shot column from a rounded shape to a horizontal spread. He'd like some sort of attachment that could do this. Maybe he should lay on some beer and talk it over with the Riverine CMA and a machinist when they got back to Tre Noc. A sudden flicker of motion to his left froze Tonto in place.

Had that been a man? If it was, it had to be Charlie. He raised his freehand in the signal to halt and faded into the pale green filigree of a giant fern. His heart beat faster. Tonto could sense it in the surf-like roar in his ears. Was he about ready to kill his first man? Or be killed by doing something stupid?

Chief Waters caught sight of the movement again. A bright blur of colored feathers. With a squawk of protest, a big, blue-green yellow bird raised from a spoiled fruit it had been eating and fluttered into the lower branches of a mangrove tree. Relief formed an inaudible sigh and Tonto turned back. He followed a slightly different course than on his approach and came in sight of the squad after some thirty paces.

"Thought I saw someone," he whispered beside Pope Marino's ear. "It was a bird."

"Better safe than," Pope replied. "If the birds are going about business as usual, I think we can be sure Charlie ain't anywhere near. We can do something about these leeches. Pass the word."

"Aye-aye, sir," Tonto gave in a relieved tone.

Half of the squad stripped down and began inspecting

one another for the presence of leeches. The other half faced outward, alert for any sign of human presence. When Phil Nicholson had checked a man as clean, he redressed and relieved one of the others. Tonto Waters wished for a big cigar to use to dislodge the five ugly creatures that clung to him, sucking his blood. A loud gasp from beside him told Tonto that Repeat Ditto indeed had a leech attached to his penis.

Long and black, it clung to Repeat's organ, which had shriveled in reaction to this assault. Ditto touched the glistening parasite, closed his eyes and screwed his lips into a pucker. Then he slowly pried the leech away from sensitive, vulnerable flesh. Phil Nicholson pulled two more from the small of Chad Ditto's back, above one kidney. Chad dropped the one he held and crushed it under the heel of a canvas sneaker, then pulled up his Levi's.

"Mother-humper, that was one big sucker," he whispered.

"Done looks like he swallowed more than his fair share," True Blue chuckled.

"Fuck you very much, Mr. Oakes," Ditto retorted.

"Can it," Pope Marino cut off their banter. "We're not out here alone."

With the last man freed of the voracious parasites, the squad moved out. Repeat Ditto hung close to Pope Marino with the radio. Doc Welby walked right behind, eyes on the confusing sameness of the jungle. After a while he could have been easily convinced that they had walked in circles. Walk thirty minutes, rest five became the order of the day. For a little variety, insects descended in clouds.

All of them hummed or buzzed, found every opening on a man's face and crawled inside to inspect. They bit and stung, too. The SEALs endured with stoic silence. He would remember next time to put on more insect repellent after getting out of water, Kent Welby reminded himself. Then he recalled that some of the old hands among the River Tigers had said that the VC could smell the scent of the repellent from a goodly distance and zero right in on a man. Somehow Doc doubted that, but better to put up with the bugs than wind up dead. How could he put the theory to a test? He jerked to a sudden halt when Tonto Waters signaled that their objective was in sight.

Another thirty meters along the trail and Doc Welby spotted the low, conical mound. A small, treeless meadow stretched out to the southeast from its facing slope. Back that way lay the river. The squad remained inside the cover of the jungle until 2nd Squad caught up. Then they skirted the meadow. Doc Welby picked a suitable tree some twenty meters up the knoll and made for it. From his Alice pack, he removed his sniper's platform, actually a simple, commercially made hunter's stand. He tied a piece of coiled line to it, and another to his Remington 700, then shimmied up the trunk.

He found a nice position, shielded from direct view by the leafy branches, and drew the platform to him. Once he had it fastened in place, he settled in and brought up his rifle. He gave the weapon a quick going over and set it on the planks between his legs. Next he took two frag grenades from the webbing straps of his pack and laid them in the depressions cut into the surface of the platform for a hunter to put his thermos and cup of coffee. Then he shrugged out of the pack and arranged it as a back rest. Nothing to do now but wait for Charlie. Out of professional curiosity, he raised the Redfield scope to his eye and began to search for any sign of 2nd Squad.

He knew they would be back a ways in the jungle on the eastern edge of the meadow, at right angles to the main ambush. Their task was to enfilade the kill zone, while avoiding friendly fire. Below Doc's perch, the rest of 1st Squad spread out.

Archie Golden emplaced three of his claymores along

the trail, aimed to fire from both sides, and overlap slightly. The fourth one he placed in the deep shadow of a fern, rigged to detonate straight down the pathway. So far, Doc considered, it had all gone like just one more training mission. He eased back and let his eyes rove across the terrain in order to prevent eye-strain.

Like a kid picking at the scab of an old sore, Kent Welby could not keep his mind from returning to images of his wife. He relived again the bitter, icy showdown that left him with nothing to hope for but divorce papers.

Afternoon straggled into twilight while Doc still prodded himself as he tried to find some right way to handle it, the proper words that even now he could say and save their marriage. Mechanically, he detached the Redfield and put his Starlight night scope into place. With any luck, he had not jarred any of the settings and his aim would be dead on. He still ran practice phrases through his head when the crack of a small branch and a muffled curse in Vietnamese yanked him back.

Suddenly tense, his mouth dry as the southern Colorado desert, Kent Welby eased the butt of his Remington into the hollow of his shoulder and turned on the night scope. When his eye adjusted to the wavery green images, he recognized a single file of little men walking along the same trail they had used to reach the ambush site. All of them carried heavy loads. Only the point man and the three immediately behind him had weapons at the ready. Heart thudding Doc waited for the last man to show, or at least for the majority to enter the kill zone.

He knew the moment that point had been reached when True Blue's M-60 opened up and sprayed 7.62mm death into the startled VC. The 700 Remington bucked backward with a solid thump when Doc Welby sighted in on the chest of the rearmost visible man. Although equipped with a flash-suppressor, the muzzle bloom — seen through the Starlight — all but blinded Doc. Then all hell broke loose when Archie tripped his Claymores.

Chapter 6

Tracers marched through the night, the outgoing blended with the magenta of twilight, while those seeking targets among the SEALs wobbled and glowed an unearthly green. Those dried up quickly as the Cong exhausted their supply of Soviet made ammunition. The chatter of a MAT-49 came to the attention of Doc Welby. The Team had several of those back at Little Creek. The French submachinegun was among the worst for accuracy. Right now, this one's muzzle flashes located its user for Kent and he lined up his sights. The Remington cracked and the MAT-49 went silent.

Welby's ears still rang with the blast of the Claymores. At least eleven VC had been scythed down by the slashing spray of bearings blown out in fans by the shaped charges. Only six muzzle flashes remained. Doc Welby swung his muzzle a couple of degrees to the right and fired again.

An insane woodpecker went to work on the tree trunk above him. Shredded wood filtered down on his head. Someone was shooting at *him!* From farther to the right, 2nd Squad opened up on the surviving Cong. They quickly suppressed all in-coming fire. Two grenades shattered the following stillness, then white phosphorus burst in eye-hurting brightness.

Two little men in black pajama suits briefly strobed in place, hands raised to shield their eyes. Repeat Ditto's AR-15 crashed out a short burst and one VC got stitched from crotch to throat. He went down without a sound as the second enemy made to break and run. He covered ten meters before Tonto Waters let go with his Ithaca. The eight shot scatter gun blasted two fast rounds. The buckshot impacts sent puffs of dust and a mist of blood into a halo that surrounded his suddenly hunched shoulders.

Silence settled over the clearing like a wet, black blanket while the WP grenade burned out. A long pause followed. Then Pope Marino's voice came from the darkness. "It's over."

A moment later he spoke again. "Raintree, this is Eagle One. Over."

So complete was the quiet that Doc Welby could hear an indistinct, tinny garble as the radio operator back aboard the lead PBR acknowledged the call. "R—nt—e. Copy you, Eag— —ne. O—er."

"We're ready for extraction, Raintree. Engagement complete. Over," Pope Marino stated tightly.

"Ro—er, Eag— On—. ETA one-hour, Po—t —an— o. Over."

"Say again, ETA and location, Raintree."

The radio squawked again, clearer. "One hour, Point Tango. Do you copy?"

"Five-by-five, Raintree. Eagle One out." Lt. Marino gave the handset back to Repeat Ditto and called to the squad. "Gather up their weapons and the supplies they carried. Pile them here and Archie can use some C-4 to wax it all. And, Archie, make it a long fuse this time."

"Aye-aye, Pope," Archie replied with a soft chuckle. "God, we really creamed them."

"Yeah," Pope Marino said softly. "And if they have any little brown friends out there they can cream us if we don't get out a perimeter guard. Tonto, check with Second Squad and make the arrangements. By the way, you guys did real good work. Perfect ambush."

Kent Welby suddenly couldn't remember having climbed down from his perch in the tree.

First Platoon reached the extraction point five minutes ahead of the PBR that swerved out of the main channel and slowed for the pick up. Under covering fire laid down on the patrol of VC who had rallied and followed them from the ambush site, they leap-frogged the last hundred meters to the bank of the river.

Filmore Nicholson yelped when a spent round slapped into his medical pack. Two more jolted him off his feet. "You son of a bitch!" he bellowed while he unlimbered his 9mm Carl Gustav "Swedish K" SMG and blasted a five round burst into the belly of the charging Cong. Although as a medic, HC/1C Nicholson was technically a neutral according to the Geneva Convention, like his Special Forces counterparts, as a SEAL, Fil went armed at all times.

Fil was next to last to board the PBR, followed by Pope Marino.

"Everyone accounted for, Pope," Tonto Waters reported.

"Let's haul outta here," Pope told the coxswain.

Back at Tre Noc by noon, they cleaned themselves and then their weapons and gear. Some of them talked about heading for the laundry ASAP. Lt. Marino, being part of the 10% who hadn't gotten the word, did not as yet know what else the Mi Flower laundry sold. He shrugged off this new diligence of his men for care of their clothing. A young yeoman approached Pope Marino where he cleaned his M-16 on a bench under the widespread branches of a mangrove.

"Message for you from Group Gulf, sir."

"Thank you, Yeoman." Pope didn't like the sound of that. Looking on the bright side, it might be directly from the OIC, CDR Stuart Ackerage.

It didn't turn out to be, though. He glanced at the sig-

nature before reading the message. Barry Lailey. *Damn*!
In essence, after all the formal, military verbiage, it got
down to one thing. Lt. Marino was to report to the S-2 at
0900 hours the following day. For what it didn't say. Sighing, he wiped the last dab of mud from his fourth M-16
magazine and slid it empty into the last pocket of a cloth
bandolier.

Boonie cover under his left arm, Lt. Carl Marino reported
to LCDR Barry Lailey at the headquarters on Bhin Thuy
airbase at precisely nine the next morning. Still display-
ing his sour attitude, Lailey did not invite the young SEAL
officer to take a seat. Rather he began in a voice heavy-
laden with sarcasm.

"I recall you saying it was time to start taking back
the night, Mr. Marino." He puffed a foul cloud of cigar
smoke Pope's direction and quirked his full lips in a parody
of a smile. "Are you ready to get on with it?"

"Aye-aye, sir. Glad to. And—ah—by the way, sir, if
you hadn't noticed, I've been promoted. I'm a full lieutenant now."

Lailey might have bitten a green persimmon. "I am
aware of your advance in rank, Lt. Marino. Just force of
habit, from the old days, you know."

"I know only too well, sir." Lailey winced. "Now, I
would like to report our first success in the field. We had
our first field op over the past two days. Not a casualty,
and thirty enemy KIAs, about three tons of supplies and
weapons destroyed."

"Your men are good, Marino. They can be counted a
credit to the whole SEAL program."

"Thank you, sir," Marino answered, although it grated
on him to bandy words about like that with the toad of a
man across the desk from him. "I'll tell them you said
so." Marino straightened a nonexistent crease in his

tigerstripe trousers. "May I ask, sir, why I was summoned here?"

"I—er—rather, the Det OIC has an assignment for you."

"Good," Pope said with enthusiasm. "We're ready for it."

From a folder on his desk, LCDR Lailey produced a somewhat fuzzy color photo of a stout, thick-waisted Vietnamese in the uniform of a North Vietnam Regular. "This is General Hoi Pak, of the NVA. He is in command of the southern provinces of the People's Republic of North Vietnam. He is also charged with the responsibility of exercising control over the Mekong Delta. General Hoi is personally committed to this mission at any cost."

"Is there any particular reason for his zeal?" Marino prompted.

"Ever since UDT Eleven and Twelve began to operate in the RSSZ, the VietCong presence in the Delta has declined. General Hoi is rumored to have taken this as a personal affront. Word is he intends to open a major front in the Delta. He's moving large quantities of supplies, particularly ammunition and spare weapons, mines, grenades and medical equipment to launch this offensive." Lailey paused and with a minute show of reluctance, went to a covered map on the far wall. He turned back the canvas screen and pointed to the chain of islands in the Mecong and Bassiac rivers.

"These supplies are supposed to be hidden in deep bunkers on islands in the two major rivers of the Delta. For your first independent mission, you are to take your platoons, by squad, out to survey the area in question and determine if this is true."

"What about their food supplies?" Lt. Marino asked.

"Other than storage silos of rice, the VC usually take what they need by force from the people. Of course, any rice caches you find are to be located on the map for future disposition."

"What and who will we be working with?"

"You'll be inserted by the Riverine Force, extracted by helicopter. You will have six PUC assets, also six assets who are men loyal to a Big Ticket local asset, Linh Kao, code name Buddha, who is run by the CIA."

"Now, isn't that just dandy," Lt. Marino said with sarcasm matching LCDR Lailey's initial remarks.

Lailey cocked an eyebrow, sensitive to this change in his nemesis. "I gather you don't approve of converted VC working with us?"

"I have no problem with PUC assets, sir. I don't approve of having the spook house mixed up in it. Those cowboys make too many mistakes. Besides, they and the men they train can't keep up with SEALs. Hell, Commander, the most they ever run during training is five miles, and that only in their final qualifying exam."

Barry Lailey sounded like it pained him terribly. "You have a point there, Lt. Marino. I have no more love for those wild hair spooks than any field commander. They seem to fuck up more operations than they carry off."

Marino nodded thoughtfully. "I had one of them tell me once that the only ones we hear about are the ones they fuck up. He said that for every one that screws up, there are a hundred that worked."

"Hummmm." Lailey crossed the room and poured water from a bottle of Perrier. He made no offer of a glass to his visitor. "That could be. Not our problem, though, is it?"

"I have a little problem with this Buddha, Commander. Who says he's reliable?"

"I do, among others. He has provided perfect, pin-point product. Even General Belem, the COSPECWAR-MACV-SOG, sings his praises."

"What's the story on him?"

"Buddha is a former Viet Minh district cadre. He never bought into the Communist aspect of Poppa Ho's "glorious revolution," and changed sides after the defeat of the

French. He had a hard time of it for a while, until he moved south into Cambodia. He soon learned then that if he extended his umbrella of protection over the people, fed, sheltered, and treated their sickness, he could count on them to protect him in turn. He did it first with his fellow Viet Minh, then with the Cong." Lailey paused to swallow the mineral water, using it to chase an antacid tablet.

"He established an open door policy. The first time they came to him for food or medicine, or a weapon for personal protection, he welcomed them, no questions asked, fed them and took their photographs. When they came back for more, they became his creatures. They followed his orders, did his bidding, covered for him with their fellows in the VC and in North Vietnam. He trusts them and you can trust him totally."

"I hope something doesn't come up to make me believe differently. Very good, sir. When do we leave on this operation?"

"You have two days to get ready."

Lt. Carl Marino found himself dismissed without ceremony.

Seen from the crushed seashell road, the opulent French Colonial villa outside Vinh, in Vinh Province, People's Republic of North Vietnam, that housed the headquarters of General Hoi Pak, appeared to be still the country residence of a wealthy planter, with business connections in the northern part of Vietnam. The only indication of its true nature came from the uniformed guards at the tall wrought-iron gate, where the road passed through a high arch in a low stone wall, and the flag of the People's Republic of North Vietnam on the staff atop the cupola over the main entrance. Inside, the hustle and bustle of any military command center left no doubt.

On the second floor, removed from all of that, General

Hoi Pak sat in a large rattan, fan-back chair, its soft and luxuriant cushion supporting him easily. He languidly sipped at a cup of tea as he stared off into the distance. A small smile curved the thin lips of his spare mouth when he reached down to tousle the lush black tresses of the young woman who knelt before him.

Barely out of her teens, if that old, she inclined her head forward to the opening in the general's green uniform trousers, bobbing rhythmically up and down. The gentle tugging action she created produced the soothing sensation that filled the body of Gen. Hoi. The area commander for the southern provinces of North Vietnam sighed contentedly as he enjoyed her ministrations and his eyes took on a far-off stare. An abrupt knock at the double doors to the suite interrupted his afternoon recreation.

"What is it!" Gen. Hoi snapped testily.

The bird-like visage of Colonel Nguyen Dak — small, narrow head, with an early lipless mouth, set on a long stalk of neck, bright, beady eyes —popped through the opening between panels. "Sorry to disturb your siesta, General Hoi," Nguyen chirped.

Gen. Hoi made an abrupt gesture, signaling his G-2 to enter. "I left specific orders that I was not to be disturbed. What is it that brings you here?"

Col. Nguyen darted his small beak of a nose toward the clipboard in his right hand. He had tucked his mottled green pith helmet under his left arm. "Again, I apologize for disrupting your day. But urgent transmits have arrived from the South. I have only now finished decrypting them."

"So? What makes them so urgent?"

Col. Nguyen nodded toward the crouching girl. Gen. Hoi reached down with both hands on her shoulders to stop her oral pleasuring. "That will be all for now, Yeuin." He gestured with a cant of his head toward the door. His young plaything restored his clothing to order, rose on bare feet and padded out of the room.

After clearing his throat, Col. Nguyen continued. "They come from our Soviet friend, the Spetznaz Lieutenant."

"I assumed as much. Go on." Gen. Hoi gestured toward the tea pot and Col. Nguyen shook his head in rejection of the offer.

"The United States Naval contingent to MACV-SOG, designated NAVSPECWAR, has received additional personnel. It is believed by Senior Lieutenant Kovietski that they are from one of the units known as SEALs."

Gen. Hoi's face clouded. So far, tactical units of these SEALs, and their comrades of the Underwater Demolitions Teams had wreaked considerable mischief in the South, and in provinces of the North as well. Using the trained lackeys in Lien Doc Nguoi Nhia, of the so-called Navy of South Vietnam, they had blown up bridges, destroyed some 50 metric tons of rice in a single raid, cut rail lines and taken prisoners for interrogation. Given enough of their kind, it could create new problems.

"How many are they?" he asked coldly.

Nguyen again consulted the papers on the clipboard. "The number, as reported by Lt. Kovietski's principal agents in the South, is believed to be twenty-four enlisted men and four officers."

Gen. Hoi snorted and reached for his tea cup. "That hardly comprises a formidable force. Tell me about them."

"They arrived two and a half weeks ago. So far their activities have been confined to training, or our Spetznaz friend, Kovietski, believes, rehearsing for an operation. Two nights ago, a work party moving supplies into the Delta was ambushed. It is believed these new SEALs conducted that operation. All of the supplies were destroyed on the ground."

"This is not the time for that to be happening. It cannot be tolerated. Our timing is too delicate." He cut off further comment, always conscious of the requirements of security. "Are these SEALs, as you call them, a serious threat?"

Col. Nguyen produced a wry expression. "They are trouble in every way. To date there have never been more than forty-five of them in the South, yet their operations in what the enemy has called the Rung Sat Special Zone have created panic among our comrades in the Viet Cong. They have captured several ranking cadres and killed many more. They have earned the name among our comrades of 'the Men with Green Faces.'"

"Recall for me how they operate," Gen. Hoi invited.

"No doubt the methods will remain the same as elsewhere in the Delta. They will work with the river patrols, perhaps other SEAL detachments, and with their counterparts in the LDNN of the Republic of Vietnam Navy. Given their distance from the major areas of engagement, they will likely use local assets as well."

"I see. Please, old friend, to keep me informed. Now," Gen. Hoi said as he cast a sigh and cut his eyes to the door, "I must return to my—ah—meditations."

Face immobile, Col. Nguyen ground his teeth in exasperation. His general had made it clear that he had not been impressed by the presence of twenty-four more enlisted men and four officers. His mistake! Col. Nguyen knew that implacably to be true.

Chapter 7

With two fingers, BM/1C Chad Ditto smeared a wide streak of pale green across the ridge of his cheekbone and down toward the side of his jaw. It overlapped the black he had applied earlier. He repeated it for the opposite cheek. Another touch around the corner of his right eye, then on the tip of his chin. Now to catch the bare spots. He wiped his fingers and reached for the tan stick. After all this time it still surprised him that True Blue Oakes also put on the green face.

"At least you don't have to put on any black," he quipped at the Squad Automatic Weapon (SAW) man.

"You think so, huh? Hey, skin oils make you shine, no matter what color's behind it. This war paint flattens that out. How 'bout that? Braves put on war paint, take heap many scalps."

"This is a sneak and peek op, remember?" Doc Welby piped up from where he sat with a hand-held mirror while he turned his face into a green horror.

Most of the squad had shaken down well, he allowed. They had all found foot gear that suited them, Chad Ditto even went barefoot some times, said it helped manage the weight of the radio. Many wore boonie hats, in tiger stripe or forest pattern, while canvas shorts and blue jeans outnumbered BDUs or cammo uniforms. A lot of green T-shirts and tank-tops had shown up as the weather turned warmer and more humid. A camouflage jacket over the top served for better concealment.

True Blue peered slantwise at Doc Welby. "You look like five days at sea in a typhoon."

"Good. It'll scare the be-jezus out of any Charlie I run

into." Welby finished his decorations, wiped his hands and turned to his weapons.

This would be a night insertion so he packed his Redfield into its case and put in his pack. He had five full magazines for the Remington, the 40 loose rounds taped to a web belt, which he would sling over one shoulder like Pancho Villa. Always weight conscious, most of the squad had taken to leaving their side-arms behind. They could lug a couple more grenades for the weight of am- munition and gun. What bothered Kent Welby most was the eight C-Ration packets they had drawn.

They would be out two and a half days and two nights. A long, risky patrol. Only they weren't supposed to en- gage in a fire fight with Charlie. They were to observe and make notes. Well and good, Doc Welby thought. He wondered if the Cong had been told that. Sighing to cover his unease, Doc sat back to wait.

Pope Marino and Tonto Waters collected them twenty minutes later. A heavy overcast blocked out what could be seen of the sky through the trees. It left them in total darkness as the squad, followed by second squad, pro- ceeded to the pier. They would take the PBRs most of the way, transferring to their SEAL Team Assault Boats (STABs) for the final run into more shallow water. Once aboard the river patrol boats, the SEALs had nothing to do but wait. Hurry up and wait. Hell, that's what the army always complained about, Doc Welby thought as he felt the vibrations of the big engines through the bulkhead he leaned against.

During the long trip to the canals that would hope- fully give them an unobserved approach to the suspected area of the supply caches, Doc Welby had ample time to reflect on what it took to be a SEAL. It took, he recalled, a hell of a lot of agony, several tons of determination, and endurance beyond any limit it had always been thought impossible for human beings to exceed.

Kent Welby had been in excellent condition when he

reported to UDT/R training. Or so he had thought. From the very first day, the increasingly longer swims became pure murder. His calves and lungs gave sympathetic mental throbs even two years away from the program. The long runs in alternating wet and dry sand had sapped Doc and his classmates.

Puerto-Rico had been seen as total agony. Not because of the climate, or the people, or the cockamame "revolutionaries," but because of the longer swims, in tugging, cloying currents, and the endless runs. Kent Welby winced as he visualized the heavy boats they ran with. Inflatable Boat, Small (IBS) they were called. It took the place of earlier log PT, they had been gleefully told by the instructors. And even before Puerto-Rico, they were introduced to the Around the World evolution.

Their instructors wanted this class to take a traditional Around the World at Little Creek, and then again in Puerto-Rico. Being instructors, they got what they wanted. Around the World turned out to be a scheduled problem in which each seven-man boat crew had to complete with its Inflatable Boat, Large (IBL). The IBL, as Kent Welby knew so well, was over fourteen feet in length, and almost eight feet wide. It weighed more than four hundred pounds. "Just a little something extra for youse boat crews," as one laughing instructor put it. Their Little Creek evolution turned out to be pure hell.

Each crew was given a handout chart that showed the route they would take. The uniform of the day was fatigues, boonedocker boots, helmets, and heavy kapok life vests, which were worn over inflatable UDT vests. As the PBR rocked gently from the wake of a passing motorized junk, Kent recalled that a kapok vest weighed six pounds dry and around twenty-six pounds wet. They had been wet most of the time. On top of all this came the IBL.

For this Around the World, Kent's class took their IBLs through hundreds of yards of Chesapeake Bay swamp and muck. They had to pull, carry, or paddle as needed, while protecting their boat from harm and logging in at instructor-manned checkpoints. After the swamp and mud flats, they crossed over a seawall jetty bordering a channel entrance from the Bay. Kent Welby winced as he relived the punishment to his ankles from the riprap of the seawall, mostly a big pile of large, loose stones constantly doused with saltwater, slippery and laborious to move over.

After they had crossed the first one, Kent's crew had to paddle across the channel and navigate another identical seawall. But it didn't end there. Next they paddled their boat over a long stretch of open water along the bay, guided by landmarks they could hardly see in the gloomy darkness.

Back on land, at the end of that, they went even further, guiding over obstacles, barbed wire, more mud flats, open ditches, and canals, then off to the final checkpoint. Sodden with salt water and sweat, the UDT/R class slogged toward their objective.

An instructor waited for them on the top of a giant sand dune on Beach dSeven, named Mount Suribachi. One final surprise waited, Kent had soon learned. Being made of loose sand, Mount Suribachi proved too yielding to crawl up dragging the IBL, and too steep to walk up with the IBL on their heads. Thinking fast, the boat crew decided on crossing the gap in a sort of half-crawling walk, the heavy IBL wobbling on their heads.

In retrospect, Kent realized that if they had not cooperated and worked as a team, a boat crew could not complete the course. As a reward, the class had been told that the winning crew, the first to complete the evolution, would get an extra thirty minutes of sleep. To the best of Kent's knowledge, no one in his class actually received that blessed extra sleep.

Then they went back to Puerto Rico for another Around the World. It seemed twice as bad to Kent Welby, because right after arriving at the base in Roosevelt Roads, it was announced that they would also do their Hell Week there.

Thinking back on those hours he and his classmates had spent lugging those boats around on their heads brought a soft curse to Kent's lips as the PBR engines rumbled drowsily. Yet, he could not deny the pride they all drew from simply *doing it*, and not quitting. He looked away from his fixed stare in the direction of the invisible jungle and sighed heavily as he reflected on how many they were the first day at UDT/R and how few the last.

"You thinkin' about school, Doc?"

"Yep. Could you read it on my face?"

Tonto chuckled softly. "Naw. Not that clear. It was that far-off stare and the sighs. Also, you said 'goddamn' about seven times. Yeah, school was a bitch, but we made it, buddy. Say, what about Jungle School in Panama? All that snake-eatin', George of the Jungle shit?"

"Ya-know, I'll bet you there's not a single blanket head who goes through there now who would believe that the changes made in the course are a result of a SEAL evaluation of the program. Who needs to know how to find and use arrow poison frogs?" Kent's chuckle got lost in the exhaust throb.

"It doesn't fit our mission, is all, Doc. Special Forces blanket head shave to live off the land, do things the way the natives do. We're in and out of there like Speedy Gonzales, 'Wham-bam, thank you, ma'am.'"

Doc slanted a questioning gaze at Tonto. "You standin' up for them, man?"

"Uh! Well—ah—yeah…to some extent. Most of them are pretty good boys. Remember those guys who came over from Fort Bragg to take underwater training? SFs just have a different mission."

"Speaking of missions, what do you think we're gonna find out there?"

"Piles and piles of crates of ammunition, boxes of rifles, medicines. All the shit it takes to make war. Pope said our intel was numba one. So we should find something."

Right then the distant, heavy thump-thump of Browning .50 caliber machineguns cut off conversation. White light flickered from behind far off trees like dry heat lightning on a Kansas summer night. Static crackle from the earphones clamped over the ears of the boat's RTO. He listened, spoke into the mike, then turned to Pope Marino.

"That's Bluestreak Three. Them and another Mike Boat have jumped something big up-river beyond Tre Noc."

"Are we going to abort?" Pope asked tensely.

"Nope. Not that I've heard."

"Good. With that stirred up, things ought to be quieter where we're going."

Well beyond the point where the sounds of the fire fight up-river faded out, the PBRs throttled back and edged out of the main stream of the Bassiac. A powerful premonition impressed itself on Lt. Carl Marino. It seemed so real that he almost blurted out the word, "Ambush!" He restrained the urge, though, and spoke instead to the chief of the boat.

"Keep the STABs in tow, Chief. And then, can you take us into the mouth of the largest canal near the Initial Point?"

Shrugging, the chief nodded his helmeted head toward the bank. "Sure, sir. There's a big one right at the IP."

Insertion of the platoon went without incident, shortly before 2240 hours, in spite of Pope Marino's overwhelming hunch. Once on the sloping banks of the canal, he called the men together. "Second Squad, take the next canal over. We'll walk the sides and get a general reecee of the area. Take both banks, in squad assault formation. Point men, if the water is not too deep, take your path right down the middle. Let's move out."

From his left, Tonto Waters spoke softly. "We need another radio for this kind of operation."

Pope Marino had been thinking the same thing. "Right you are. I'll see what I can cumshaw when we get back."

With a nod, Tonto took the point and waded through the murky water of the canal. Soft silt on the bottom clung to his canvas sneakers and gave him a drunken lurch as he pressed forward. About a hundred meters of that and he signaled for a halt. After a careful check of their surroundings, he returned to the center of the formation where Pope Marino hunkered down beside their RTO.

"The muck's gettin' thicker. I'll make enough noise to alert them in Hanoi if I keep to the water, Pope. Besides, I can see better from near the top of the bank."

"You got that right, Chief. We'll have to send someone to tell second squad."

"Chips is smart enough to figure it out for himself," Tonto advised. "Besides, Mr. Ott will get wise as soon as we did."

"You've got a lot of faith in these men," Pope allowed.

Tonto Waters chuckled softly. "Yeah. Or I wouldn't be here, right?"

Pope stifled a groan. "Move out, Tonto."

With the eyes of the point man clear to range beyond the confines of the canal, the squad advanced with much better speed. It didn't take long for Tonto Waters to note a brief flicker of motion above the lip of the second canal bank. Chips Danner, the point man, had figured it out sure enough. Using the pace they had decided best suited for a jungle — walk half an hour, rest five minutes — they covered three clicks with ease. Also without discovering any sign of Charlie.

At 0300 hours, Pope Marino called for a chow halt. The squad deployed for security of the area and settled in to munch at the small cans of mixed fruit, cold beans and wieners, and other "delicacies" provided by Uncle Sam for his men in uniform. They used the ubiquitous P-38s to soundlessly open the cans. The little folding-blade can

openers had been around since WW II. Rumor, and that's
all that existed about them so far, had it that the new MREs
were in tear-open bags. Some day they might find out,
Kent Welby thought philosophically.

First Platoon spent the rest of the night making a general sweep of the mission AO to a depth of three klicks.
Only nocturnal animal life stirred beside the SEALs. Doc
Welby began to think it would be like that all the way
west to the terminus of the Ho Chi Minh trail and Cambodia beyond. Good enough by him, he admitted as he
massaged a sore spot on his shoulder, caused by the chaff-
ing of his battle harness. Four grenades, his K-Barknife,
and pouches filled with spare batteries he carried for the
radio dragged on a man in even the best physical condition after a few hours. Not far away, Pope Marino and
Tonto Waters studied a handout map by the shielded light
of a hooded flashlight.

"We should reach the patrol ROD site about half an
hour before first light," Tonto advised his leader.

"That'll give us time to dig in. Provided we don't run
into Charlie beforehand," Marino surmised.

Tonto's reply came weighted with irony. "Yeah, there's
always that."

Dawn found the platoon settled into their Rest Over Day
(ROD) positions. Those not on perimeter security grabbed
what sleep they could, then relieved the others. They ate
and drank sparingly of their water. The first night had
turned out a total bust. They hadn't made any contact and
saw no sign of any of the bunkers or supplies intended for
the enemy. When the volume level of daytime birds and
monkeys made it impossible to hear any stealthy approach,
Tonto Waters roused himself and stretched with the grace
of a Bengal tiger.

"For a piece of real estate so damned small," he put it,

thinking of their lack of contact, "it's a wonder we aren't riding in one another's hip pocket."

Archie Golden cast a mischievous glance Tonto's way. "Those black pajamas don't have hip pockets, Chief."

With the jungle alive with noise around them, unlike areas closer to the base at Tre Noc, Lt. Marino decided that they might as well swing back toward the river and look along there. He put his thoughts into words and met with instant agreement.

Not that they abandoned caution when the platoon set out to the east. The point and rear guard kept especially alert in daylight, as did all those along a meandering trail they encountered. For the most part it led in the right direction, so they followed along. Doc Welby noted that the glow of "being there" held through the day as they worked closer to the Bassiac's banks. The men crossed the dikes of several canals without complaint, and swatted ineffectually at buzzing insects in silence. Still no sign of Charlie. Doc wondered how long that would last.

In mid-afternoon, an electric tingle ran through the men of First Platoon. From his position at far point, Tonto Waters made the sign for Enemy in Sight. Exactly as in practice, everyone faded into the jungle. Pope Marino worked his way forward.

"What have you got, Tonto?" His question crackled with tension.

"Might be some Japs, Pope."

"Where do you get 'might be?'"

"There's definitely some bunkers up ahead. I count three, could be more. They don't look too big, and they have grass planted over the sandbags to hide them. Give me Archie Golden and we'll go have a look-see."

"He's on his way," Pope promised.

Tonto and Archie worked their way in a wide, distant

Tonto and Archie worked their way in a wide, distant circle around the low mounds that broke up the otherwise uniform flatness of this section of mangrove swamp. Not once did they encounter any sign of a human. By hand signals, Tonto conveyed that they should wait fifteen minutes.

At the end of that time, not a sound had come from the bunkers since Tonto had first spotted them. He edged over to Archie. "Cover me with the Stoner. I'm gonna go have a close-in peek."

"You got it, Chief."

Tonto suddenly found his mouth dry as desert dust as he filtered through the bush, from tree to tree, until he came within five yards of the first bunker. Only a single black line denoted the closed hatch. Tonto waited another five minutes. Those few yards could be the last he would ever walk.

"Get on with it," he muttered to himself.

Crouched low, the muzzle of his 8 shot Ithaca leading the way, Tonto Waters crossed the small clearing to the revetment. He knelt to one side of the door and reached to open it. He took a deep breath, flung the cover wide and poked in the barrel of the shotgun.

Tonto sighed out the breath he had been holding and peered inside. Empty. Low and cramped, the interior smelled of unwashed humanity and Nouc Mam sauce. Quickly he moved to the next.

Oily beads of sweat popped out on Tonto's forehead as he repeated his approach and opened the bunker. Another empty one. The third yielded the same results. He located a fourth, dug into a slight rise, that faced the river. Still not a VC anywhere around. He remembered something he had seen in a Western movie before shipping out for 'Nam.

An Eastern greenhorn from a wagon train had remarked to the trail-wise scout that they had not seen a single Indian. "That don't mean they ain't out there," the scout had said. "They only let you see 'em if they want you to." He wondered if the Viet Cong were the same way. After easing the tension kinks out of the muscles of his legs and back, Tonto returned to where Archie waited.

"Go bring up the platoon. Nobody at home."

When Pope Marino reached the spot, he gave careful study to the compact shelters and arrived at the same conclusion as Tonto Waters. "These look like people-hiding bunkers, sure not for supplies. They've been used recently, so we had better be ready to rub up against the ones who stayed here some time tonight."

Chapter 8

Starshii Lortynat Alexi Gregorivich Kovietski sat behind an olive-drab, folding field desk manufactured at some Gulag in his homeland, the Union of Soviet Socialist Republics. Lazy afternoon sounds of the Cambodian jungle filtered into the room of his temporary operations center near Svay Rieng. He gave careful and complete attention to the flimsy sheet of paper before him. It had been delivered only moments before by a courier. Kovietski, alone now, unfastened the button of his high, uniform collar and undid the first three on his chest.

That felt better. The wings of his uniform collar held his insignia of rank and the crest of the Soviet Spetznaz (Special Forces) troops. Normally he would have been wearing the *de rigeur* outfit of their gray, black and green camouflage fatigues, but he had been entertaining some ranking Cambodian communist cadres at an early luncheon when this message arrived. His left hand reached for the flute of vodka as he re-read the decrypted message.

It had come from one of his prize agents in place, who operated within the area of the American bases along the Bassiac River in Vietnam. Quite an asset, that one, he reflected. In more ways than one, a wry thought prompted him. What it contained bothered him.

The report stated that one element of the new SEAL platoons had gone out on a large operation. Only his best local asset had no idea of what or where it might be. So far, he had learned from his sources inside the headquarters of General Hoi, the general had not taken too seriously the presence of more SEALs in the Delta. Perhaps this would awaken him to the threat, one that was no longer potential, but entirely real. He would have to report it to his superior, the director of Department 5 (Asian Affairs).

To that end, he took a small book from his safe and laid out a page on which to draft the message. Bound in red leather, the slim volume bore across its center the cyrilic characters for Encryption Manual, and below that:

ОТДЕЛ 5
ВОСТОЧНЫЙ ДЕЛО

Emblazoned into the leather at the top was the Soviet star with hammer and sickle in the center, and below that the crest of the dreaded *Komitet Gosudarstvennoi Bezopasnotstie* — the KGB. The crew-cut, blond giant with wide, square shoulders might be Senior Lieutenant Alexi Kovietski to his Vietnamese and Cambodian comrades, but in fact he was Major Payotr Maximovich Rudinov of the KGB, station chief for Cambodia and the Delta region of Vietnam. And right now he had every intention of putting an end to the menace represented by the presence in Vietnam of the SEALs of Team 2.

At 1700 hours, the platoon halted, ate again, then divided into squads. There had been islands spotted to north and south of their position. None seemed occupied at present. That didn't mean they would remain that way during the night. Doc Welby selected his position well. He settled into the rotted out bowel of a huge mangrove along the river bank. A section of old dike formed a low berm that concealed all but a small part of his head and his rifle barrel. It also provided excellent cover. He settled in and waited.

He still waited when time crept up to 2340 hours. Nothing had moved so far, except a small sampan. The single occupant, a boy who could not be more than ten. The youngster looked so frightened through Doc's Starlight scope, as he sculled the craft down-river, it left no suspicion he could be a VC. Caught out after dark, he no doubt feared the Cong as much as most of the locals. Doc Welby's bladder began to ache around midnight.

Doc had to relieve himself. And he didn't want to do it in his jeans. Gradually he shifted position until he knelt in the cave-like depression inside the tree. Doc opened his fly and let go a long stream that splattered in the mud at the base of the mangrove roots. An air-root plant bobbed in the yellow jet.

"What the hell's all the noise for?" The voice of Pope Marino came in a harsh whisper from a foot behind Doc Welby's head. Damn, the man could move silently.

"Had to leak," Doc said lamely.

"Should do it in your pants."

"I know... but..."

"I suppose there's no harm done. Don't seem there's anyone out here but us and the mosquitoes."

"I considered that, Pope, before I made my move, sir."

"Okay, Doc. Stand fast. We'll pull back and link up with second squad in half an hour."

After a second no-contact night, Lt. Marino made an inventory of remaining rations. They had at least two meals each. Ammunition was no problem. Everyone had a full issue. Based on what he considered an ample supply of food, and reluctant to return without any positive information, Pope Marino called Chad Ditto to him and reported in to Tre Noc.

To his surprise, his report got bumped up to Det Gulf HQ at Binh Thuy and came back down the line in less than half an hour. "Eagle One, this is Whitehorse. You are cleared to remain in the field. In fact, the exact wording is to stay as long as you need. Over."

"I roger that, Whitehorse," Pope Marino responded with eager relief. "We will call for extraction tomorrow when ready, Eagle One, out."

He turned to his SEALs and saw for a moment what he would see in the near future. To the last man, they had become fire-eaters. "We've got another day," he said simply.

During the long, boring day, Doc Welby had come up with a way to keep from dwelling on the impending bad news that he believed would come with the next mail. He finally banished that painful week with Betty by making a conscious effort to concentrate on Francie Song. He had learned a lot during the whirlwind relationship that had developed over the two weeks he had known her.

Her father had been a healer, an herbal doctor, half Chinese, hence her family name. Her mother had been a Christian Vietnamese, a Catholic. That accounted for her first name, Frances. Dr. Song, Francie had told him, had been murdered by the Viet Minh when she was nine years old. She hated them, hated the Viet Cong, and everything about the Communists, she told him tearfully the first time she had invited him upstairs to her rooms.

Doc had held her tightly and felt a stirring he had not experienced with Betty since he had been graduated from UDT/R. It shocked him to realize that he and his wife had actually been drifting apart for more than a year. With brutal frankness, he had stripped away the gauze of self-deception in which he had swathed himself, while he embraced the thin trembling form of Francie Song. For all intents, his marriage to Betty had been dead for a year before she announced she was leaving him. How could he have gone on day after day and not known that?

It came with a start that he had already answered that. Self-delusion. He was a SEAL, the most elite of all of America's fighting forces. He never quit anything, never failed, surely that applied to his private life as well, right? Wrong! All at once it became as though he had never truly known or loved Elizabeth Reardon Welby. For the first time in his life, Kent Welby believed, he had truly fallen in love... and it was with a beautiful China doll named Francie Song. Gently, he pushed her away from his shoulder until he could reach her lush, nubile lips. He kissed her shyly at first, then with rising ardor.

Francie clung to him, kissing back, laughing, weeping, and making small, cooing sounds. Not surprisingly, they did not become lovers in the intimate sense that first night. After all, Kent didn't know for sure if Betty would go through with her threat to get a divorce. Filled with such distractions, the day went swiftly for Doc Welby. After the rapid sundown of equatorial regions, he sought the same topic to ward off the dulling effect of long, empty nighttime hours.

It worked rather well. Before long, Doc had his mind filled with images of Francie and himself. It was night as well. They lay full length in her bed, nude, a light sheen of perspiration covering their bodies. They had just finished making delicious love. Doc could not believe the delicate, wildly erotic methods Francie revealed to him. She had drained him.

She had begun simply enough, prolonging the sensual experience, coaxing him along, urging him to fight back the onrush of his imminent climax, sustaining him, fondling, kissing, using her tongue to heighten his response. He plunged into her receptacle, a ride on an electric bull in a boot-scootin' bar. She held him back until he knew he would explode the next second—and then an uproarious climax that went on and on forever.

"You will think me shameless," she whispered softly into his ear.

"I will not. I'll only think you caused me to be very late getting back. They've made it harder on guys who duck around curfew."

"I please you then, Kent Welby?"

Doc raised his head, inclined toward her, kissed her eyelids. "You please me more than I can say."

"I want to make you happy. You all the time look so sad."

Doc considered that a moment. "I have been. At least until the other night. I realized that nothing I...left behind mattered. All that counts is here and now. Does any of that make sense?"

"Oh, yes. Oh, yes. It say that you and me make happy every night from now on."

"Except when we have something going on the base."

Francie frowned and made a mock pout. "Don't let that happen too many times, Kent Welby," she said teasingly.

"I'll try not." Doc Welby started to envision their second amorous encounter when the dull *tink* of an exposed metal surface on a thorny bush jerked him back to the present. So intense had his erotic visions been that Doc Welby nearly missed the arrival of the Viet Cong on the river bank.

They came in single file, down the same trail the platoon had used, and crossed the shallow channel to the island Doc Welby watched. The moon, nearly full, hung high overhead and added its silver glow to the frosty stars. What light filtered through the leaves of the deciduous forest of the Delta allowed Doc to see in detail without the use of his Starlight scope. The VC divided into pairs and spread out, backs to the mound of dirt in the stream, and kept watch on the dense jungle on the outer banks.

Charlie had come for something, Doc considered. He

felt a tenseness in his gut. Confident that the others also watched, he made no attempt to signal them. It soon became clear to Doc Welby that the VC were waiting for someone. After twenty minutes of growing tension, Doc heard the soft, rhythmic splash of sculling paddles.

The sampan materialized out of the darkness and two Vietnamese in the stern sculled it expertly to the sloped bank of the island. Two of the guards came forward to retrieve it and drew the bow up on the mud. They helped fold back woven palm mats and Doc turned on his night vision scope to study the details of what had been brought. The first thing he recognized was the narrow, flat rectangles of rifle cases. The four VC quickly off-loaded and carried four of them to shore. Next six squarish wooden boxes with rope handles that Doc determined to be ammunition. Five thousand rounds each, he surmised.

These Cong had to have something big in the making. Doc Welby heard more gurgles of bow waves and the splash of sculling paddles. Another junk glided out of blackness and proceeded on beyond the one already unloading. It grounded on a small island thirty feet off the narrow upstream end of the one he watched. The hummock of earth looked like an overgrown hootch. Two of the VC guards waded over to it. Using his Starlight, Doc watched while the flat boxes that denoted cases of grenades came from the inside of the sampan.

The situation turned into a regular parade as more sampans coasted up to the dots of land in midstream. When each sampan had been unloaded, one of the crew remained behind while the other headed off downstream. Within an hour, Doc counted six sampans. More came, and passed on beyond the collection of islets, into the area covered by second squad. By the time the last native craft had off-loaded its cargo, Doc had counted an even dozen leaving supplies at the islands directly in front of him, and an equal number that had gone farther up river. When the last one sculled out of sight, the guards resumed their watchfulness while the work force set to stowing the arms and munitions in underground bunkers.

Doc Welby had long ago forgotten about his cramped physical condition as he watched the Cong work. Now, a throbbing in his right thigh and calf reminded him of his body. Slowly he eased his leg outward to lie parallel to the river bank. He wanted to sigh with relief, yet knew he dare not. It took another hour for the VC on the islands to secure the supplies and conceal the entrances to the bunkers. Then they waded the eastern channel and disappeared down a trail into the jungle. Good, Doc Welby concluded, now maybe he could get out of there. His intention to put thought into action ended abruptly in the sharp, loud chatter of automatic weapons fire.

A VC security patrol had stumbled into Chips Danner, 2 Squad's point man, at his position on the northern extension of the surveillance formation. The first Charlie had all but stepped on Chips, before he opened up with his Swedish KSMG. Yellow-white flashes erupted from the enemy patrol and slugs slapped into trees and cut vines all around Chips.

"Get a flare round over here," Tonto Waters heard Chips shout. An XM-148 blooped a moment later and the jungle took on an eerie simulacrum of high noon.

Caught in the open, black pajama-clad VC quickly became the receiving end of a terrible onslaught of jacketed bullets. Nine millimeter, 5.56 mm, .45 ACP and 7.62 mm rounds. The survivors, counting among them several wounded, dove for the darkness outside the sphere of light. Already, Pope Marino had the handset of the AN/PRC-25 in hand, talking low but earnestly into the mouthpiece. "That's right, Whitehorse, we need an extraction ASAP. We've come under fire by Charlie in large numbers. None of us has taken a hit so far, but there's two dozen more bad guys not a klick away on the east side of the river. Over."

"Roger, Eagle One. We have a Mike boat on the way already. Your PBRs will rendezvous with it half a click north of your position. Mark your location with flares when they arrive. Hang in there, Eagle One. Whitehorse out."

Pope nearly had the handset jerked out of his grasp as Repeat Ditto spun on one heel and cut down two Cong with a five round burst from his AR-15. Bark chips slashed at Marino's face as one Charlie reflexively cut loose a dying burst from a MAT-49. Flat thuds joined the battle as Tonto Waters stroked his Ithaca in a controlled motion.

"Pass the word," Pope Marino spoke softly to his RTO. "Everyone pull back, center on that big mangrove on the river bank." He doubted Kent Welby would appreciate that, but it was the largest landmark for the boats to find.

In the fading light of the flare, the egg shape of two Soviet type RGD-5 hand grenades sailed through the fringes of brightness toward the SEALs. "Grenade!" Mule Carlson yelled unnecessarily.

One landed with a plop and did nothing. The 2.42 ounces of TNT in the other detonated with a sharp crack and bright flash. Fragments of shrapnel whizzed through the air. "Sumbitch," Archie Golden grunted and returned the favor with two hastily thrown M-26 frags.

He followed that with a WP grenade. All three went off. Slave labor made for poor quality control on the Eastern Block stuff Charlie got a hold of, Archie reasoned as he winced at the shrapnel cut close to the small of his back. Trust Uncle Sam's ordnance every time. With a Stoner and an M-60 inaction, plus the two XM-148s, the squads held the heads of their enemy down long enough to pull back to a tight defensive ring around the tree occupied by Kent Welby.

Doc soon proved Pope right about their reception. "Did

you have to drag all of them over here? I've got enough to worry about across the river."

He moved the barrel of the Remington 700 a scant two inches and sighted in on a VC with a PPS-43. Doc fined down his sight picture and took up the slack in the trigger. The big .30-06 rifle bucked and the VC went down. His burp gun discharged into the leafy cover over his head.

"There's still three over there, with more on the way," Doc Welby said over his shoulder to the back of Pope Marino's head.

More grenades crashed as Archie Golden let fly with them. Incoming fire dwindled. Charlie was trying to figure a way around this nasty nest of firepower. Pope Marino didn't want to give them the chance.

"Get the automatic weapons on the flanks. They're not going to come on us head-on."

None too soon did the gunners move into position than the VC charged the southern flank. Two of the enemy went down in the first burst. Another died screaming, his gut ripped open by three rounds from a Stoner. Over the rattle of gunfire, Doc Welby made out the deep throb of the powerful engines of a Boat Support Unit (BSU) Mike boat. A moment later its blunt prow nudged around a curve in the Bassiac and Chips Danner popped a day-night flare to mark his end of the SEAL position.

On the far end, True Blue Oakes did the same. Almost at once the 40mm Honeywells opened up. Three .50s followed, drowning out the M-60. The 81mm mortar in the front troop well coughed and a parachute flare illuminated the enemy. HE rounds followed, adding to the slaughter wrought by the machineguns and grenade launchers.

From behind this blaze of terrible retribution the PBRs zoomed in toward the platoon's position. Covering one another, the SEALs jumped into the water to meet the boats. The loading went quickly. Their own .50s belching destruction, the PBRs made wide turns and headed back north. With a final fusillade, the Mike boat also withdrew.

Their first sizable engagement with the enemy concluded, First Platoon came out of it safe and sound... at least for the time being.

Chapter 9

Colonel Nguyen Dak entered the office of General Hoi Pak through the louvered, wooden French doors. He quietly closed the white-painted portals behind him and crossed the parquet floor to a position in front of the large, ornately carved mahogany desk. After a long moment, the general looked up from the stack of documents he was reviewing for signature.

"Yes, Dak? What is it?"

"I have the after-action report of Comrade Captain Thuy Mi. He concludes that the contact with enemy forces two nights ago was of no consequence. His subordinates are experienced and levelheaded. They all agree that the troops encountered on the river bank came from the Riverine Force. The—ah—River Tigers as they are called. On the surface there is no reason to doubt that. Yet, I have appended to this an analysis of the action by Sr. Lt. Kovietski that completely contradicts that estimate of the situation." Col. Nguyen pulled a wry face. "I am inclined to agree with our Soviet Comrade."

Gen. Hoi's black eyes twinkled as he regarded his friend. "Why is it that I suspected as much?"

"Here, read for yourself," Nguyen extended the sheaf of paper to his superior, then waited in silence while the general perused the contents.

When he finished, he laid it down and cleared his throat. "It is hard to argue with the logic of Captain Thuy." He struck a small gong on the desk with a tiny wooden mallet. When a servant appeared, he ordered a bottle of Phon Wei, a potent Chinese wine, and two cups. "I have purposefully withheld reading the report from Sr. Lt.

Kovietski. Let us first examine what our good Comrade Captain has to say.

"Thuy concludes that since it was Riverine patrol boats that covered the retreat, and that they arrived so soon after contact was made, that it had to be these River Tigers. A routine patrol. That holds up to the closest scrutiny," Gen Hoi added with satisfaction. "Further, the commanders of the security force and the workers both swear that they found no indication of an enemy presence before, during or immediately after the arrival of the supplies, it stands to reason that the Riverine Force patrol had been landed in the ten minutes or so after the workers left the east bank of the river. Capt. Thuy and the remainder of his security force came upon them in their final sweep of the west bank."

"All very logical, as you say, but..."

"But you don't believe it," Gen. Hoi completed the sentence as the servant returned with their wine.

He used a small pen knife to remove the thick, red wax seal and a folding corkscrew to pull the cork. Wordlessly, he poured the first cups and withdrew. When he was well away, Gen. Hoi picked up the report and thumbed to the appendix written by Sr. Lt. Kovietski.

"Now, I want to see what Comrade Kovietski makes of this." He read with growing interest.

Particularly Kovietski's conclusions. "'Given the ferocity of the fire fight, and the number of killed and wounded incurred by the security patrol, it is obvious that the new contingent of SEALs from the enemy's Team 2 was involved,'" Gen. Hoi read aloud. "'Their presence in the marshaling area for your planned offensive constitutes a threat that must be addressed immediately and forcefully.'

"He seems quite positive about that," Gen. Hoi observed. "And, of course, you concur?"

Col. Nguyen hesitated a moment, then plunged ahead. "Yes. More or less. The elements he stresses do tend in that direction, given what we know of the fighting skills of the SEALs. However, if it turns out to have been troops from the Riverine Force, I contend that they must have been in place long enough to have observed the activity on the islands. In which case we face a problem of even greater magnitude. Whichever condition prevails, we must act to counter it at once."

"Toward that end, have you any progress to report regarding placing agents in the American compounds?"

"Not much," Col. Nguyen responded. "The problem is that as more Americans arrive, many of the jobs that used to be held by indigenous peoples are being taken over by them."

"I want you to proceed with all dispatch to that end. Particularly those bases in the Delta. Also, I want a staff meeting for sixteen hours, after the Ministers leave."

"Are you going to bring this up to the Ministers, General?"

"What? Of course not. For all they dress up in uniforms, they are still civilians, and politicians at that. First thing you know, they'd let something slip, it would be blown out of all proportion, and we would have a panic on our hands."

Eager not to be seen as a "political" type officer, Col. Nguyen hastened to clarify his intention. "I mean, sir, that if they are advised of all this, it might cause them to loosen their purse strings when it comes to upgrading our weapons and equipment."

Gen. Hoi laughed sardonically. "I am afraid that in order to do that, I would have to offer proof that I was the second coming of the Buddha. And, as good communists, we are not supposed to have any religion. No, I must positively say that the good Ministers remain in ignorance of this situation until we can hand them a victory. Now, drink up, old friend, and have another. I have to attend to putting matters in motion."

After Col. Nguyen departed, convinced that his old

companion did not consider this situation as seriously as he should, Gen. Hoi reached for a thin sheet of paper. On it the crafty old personal friend of Chairman Ho drafted in a neat, clear hand a set of orders that increased surveillance activity throughout the Delta and around the SEAL compound at Tre Noc in particular.

Quite a stir developed in the SEAL compound in mid-morning of that day. A Huey settled on the pad and immediately drew a huge crowd of curious SEALs and other sailors even before the skids touched the ground. Seated next to the open port door was the easily identifiable figure of a young woman. Tonto Waters was one of the first to join the general movement in the direction of the chopper. He got there in time to watch appreciatively as the trimmest set of ankles and loveliest pair of legs ever seen around Tre Noc de-planed. Tonto got close enough to hear her name when she introduced herself to Lt. Carl Marino.

"Eloise Daladier," she said simply.

She identified herself as a journalist sent out by *Le Monde*, the Paris news magazine. For guys who had seen nothing except little Vietnamese women for nearly a month, and the old-timers who had gone even longer, Eloise was enough to drive them ga-ga. Two moon-struck sailors willingly toted along her luggage. After she departed with the officers, to get a preliminary interview on the situation at Tre Noc, the eager SEALs swarmed around Tonto Waters to hear the latest poop.

Some of the beauty-struck sailors remained by the helicopter to inhale the faintly lingering scent of her perfume, which hung in the passenger compartment despite the odor of exhaust fumes and fuel. Tonto and the men of 1st Platoon moved away in the wake of Eloise Daladier and the officers. Waters halted well clear of the helipad and chuckled at the antics of the idlers around the helicopter when the pilot wound up the main rotor in preparation for lift off.

"She's a journalist," he related, after giving them her name, a bemused smile on his face. "Works for some Frenchie outfit called *Le Monde*. She's here to make us all immortal in glowing words."

"If that's the case," Archie Golden piped up, "we'd better get her away from those officers, or she'll get a one-sided view of things. She needs to know it's the Petty Officers who run the show."

Tonto gave him a big wink. "You got that right, Archie."

Repeat Ditto pushed in close to the Chief. "We've gotta make her know what great guys us SEALs are."

"Too true," Tonto allowed, with a light punch on Chad's shoulder. "And for those reasons, I have taken the initiative to ensure she is properly briefed. We have an appointment for drinks in the Platoon Bar at seventeen hundred hours."

Archie Golden produced a pained expression. "You might know. Our star cocksman is the one to score."

"Yeah," Chips Danner agreed. "Too bad she don't work for the Salvation Army. They give to the needy, not the greedy."

The reputation Tom Waters had earned as the ladies' man of Team 2 had not been lightly bestowed. Although not the source of real jealousy, some minor resentment surfaced occasionally. Tonto always took it in stride.

"Hey, is it okay if some of us join you there?" Chips Danner asked expectantly.

"I'd counted on it," Tonto replied unruffled. "I wouldn't have it any other way."

"Oh, sure," Archie growled. "The shy and modest nature of Tonto Waters is known to SEALs of every generation."

"And legendary among the ladies," Doc Welby chimed in.

"Right you are, my man. I really do need some of you along to tell her hair-raising tales of my adventures."

Laughing, Tonto Waters pushed through the throng of SEALs and River Tigers back to the table where he had field-stripped his shotgun and worked with toothbrush and cotton patches to rid it of the least speck of powder grime or dirt. The elevator, he noted, had a new brightness about it. He'd put enough rounds through it that it ought to positively glow, came his first thought. Then his attention turned to the promise represented by his later meeting with Eloise Daladier. Oddly, he found himself eager as a high school sophomore awaiting his first date. Somehow that sort of pleased him.

Eloise Daladier had changed from her revealing skirt into more fitting costume for the Delta jungle. When she met Tonto Waters outside the barrack room that served as the platoon bar, she wore a light cotton jumpsuit, done in the camouflage pattern used by the French Foreign Legion. Disappointed, Tonto noted that it hid all her remarkable attributes, though he now got a better appreciation of her face.

Heart-shaped, it featured a wide mouth, with full, sensuous lips, a slight hint of Gallic in the nose, and wide-set, somewhat almond shaped eyes. The faint olive cast to her complexion gave a better hint as to her origins than the hazel, green-brown blend, of her irises. She greeted Tonto warmly, calling him by his given name.

"Thank you for inviting me, Thomas. I hope I won't be out of place?"

"Not at all," Tonto answered, then received a jolt.

For the first time since coming to Tre Noc, he sincerely wished they had a proper CPOs Mess, or Petty Officers open mess in which to entertain so lovely a young woman. Instead, they had only this. The raw wood of the bar, made of packing crate planks nailed on top of ammunition boxes, showed stains from many a spilled beer or soda. A single, bare light bulb hung from a rubberized cord in the center of the ceiling. In the constant dampness of the jungle, the cinder block walls had taken on a patina of mold and other living things. Grenade cases and landmine boxes had been made into miniature tables, half a dozen scattered around the room, with more of their genre serving as chairs.

Tonto steered Eloise to the least rickety of these and offered her a seat. "What'll you have? A beer or a soda?"

"I have some really nice Chateau Neuf Rothchild in my luggage," Eloise suggested.

Tonto struggled not to make a face. "I've never gotten into drinking wine. My old man was a big beer drinker and I sort of grew up with it."

"A beer will be fine, Thomas."

Tonto left the table and took two cans of Miller's from the refrigerator, careful to put a hash mark beside his name on the roster taped to the front. The bar ran strictly on the honor system. Every man was expected to put a mark beside his name for each beer or soda pop he consumed and then settled up come payday. He returned and popped the pull tabs. Those he dropped in a cut off 105mm shell casing that served as an ashtray. As was his habit, Tonto remained standing. After their first, satisfying swallows, Eloise took note of this and urged him to sit with her.

Once he had obliged her, she leaned toward him, radiating intense interest behind what she asked. "Now, tell me, please, all about Thomas Waters?"

"There's not really much to tell," Tonto dismissed.

Eloise took another sip of beer and waggled a finger his direction. "I don't wish to pry. I won't ask you anything too intimate, or embarrassing. Nor do I want any State secrets you might be holding. I would just like to know about you, about your childhood and youth, how you came to join the Navy, how you became a SEAL, and how you were assigned to Vietnam."

"Like I said, there isn't much to tell. But, here goes. Little Tommy Waters was born to working class parents in 1937, so I'm too young to have any clear memory of War Deuce."

"'Deuce?'" Eloise asked.

"World War Two. My father worked at the bus company in Jersey City until '42. By then the country was gearing up for defense production, so Pop moved the family to Pennsylvania. We lived with my grandparents in Sharon Hill, outside Philadelphia. Before long most of the family had moved in. Luckily, my grandparents had a big old, three story house with pillars on the front porch. Sort of a picture postcard sort of place.

"I started school right there in Sharon Hill. All that had little lasting effect. I was a rowdy kid, and preferred sports to long division. Most of all, I loved football. I remember I was in and out of trouble at school, mostly for not doing my homework. Mainly, I tried, but if there was a ballgame, English and all that crap was out the window and I was down on the sandlot with the other guys. It was during that time my Dad got a job as head test driver for the army tanks Baldwin Locomotive Works was making. Toward the end of the war, Dad moved the family back to Jersey City. In a way that was great. Just across the river from our house, you could see the Empire State Building sticking up into the sky. That sight could give a kid big dreams.

"The war ended while we lived there. When VE day came, all the bells in town began to ring. People came out in the streets and there was just one hell of a party. The biggest I'd ever seen. Then, a few months later, came VJ day and the war was completely over. That party was even bigger. I went on to Junior High, and High School, and got interested in music. I played the horn."

"That's interesting. Do you still play?" Eloise asked to lead the narrative.

"Naw. I sort of gave it up after I joined the Navy. I did make it to some national Drum and Bugle Corps contests. We won a couple and I won the Tri-State Baritone Bugle Individual contest in 1953. In High School I decided I wanted to be a doctor. Since college for a kid without rich parents came through scholarships, I intensified my athletic activities. Everything went fine until an injury sidelined me from football or participating in track events. It wasn't long after that I lost all interest in school."

"That's too bad," Eloise commiserated.

"Naw, not really. As it happens, I like what I am. Hey, I'm sayin' too much about me. Let me get us another beer and we can talk about you."

When he returned, Eloise skillfully cut off his attempt to probe her past. "You haven't told me yet about how you came to join the Navy."

"Oh, yeah, that. Well, you might say it was because of a movie I saw. But, that comes later. I quit school at the end of the term and kicked about in several odd jobs. In February of 1955 I had a job as truck driver's assistant that Dad had arranged for me. It was hard, honest work, but by fall I decided it was time to take on something else. It was kinda funny — an' here's where the movie comes in. A few summers earlier I had gone along with a group of friends to catch the Saturday-afternoon matinee at the Five Corners Orpheum Theatre in Jersey City. The main feature was *The Frogmen*, starring Richard Widmark.

"No other film I have ever seen impressed me as much as that did. It was about these Navy sailors, trained as UDT swimmers and taking on the Japanese during World War Two. The teamwork and close companionship among the swimmers reminded me a little of the best parts of being on an athletic team—a winning team. So right then in 1955, I decide I'm going to join the Navy and be a frogman."

While he paused, Eloise sipped sparingly from her beer

and studied his face to see if he was trying to spin her a tall tale. She found only burning sincerity. She decided to nudge him a little more. "And that's how you got here?"

"Well, not exactly. I joined the Navy right enough. I put up with the BS in boot camp, and it was off to UDT school, or so I thought. Surprise! UDT is a qualification, not a specialty. One did not volunteer and get accepted to Underwater Demolition Team Replacement training without having a specialty."

"What is a specialty?" Eloise asked right on cue.

"It's a job, such as boatswain's mate, quartermaster, or even cook. Only I hadn't been to any school and I didn't have a specialty. Now, here's where my music came back to help me, or so I planned. Our boot camp had a recruit training drum and bugle corps. Right down my alley. Not only was I certain I would do well in the corps, I had learned that musician was a specialty. If I could hack it with the corps, I could be more quickly assigned to UDT-Slash-R."

Tonto paused to drain off the last of his beer, checked by eye with Eloise and left the table to retrieve another round. "Only bad thing about being in the corps was that when I graduated boot camp, I was assigned as an instructor.

"So there I was," he resumed his story, "still without the necessary qualifications. To make a long story short, I could have been stuck at Bainbridge as a friggin' instructor until I turned white on top, and still never be rated in a specialty. Well, that wasn't for me, so I put in for a transfer. I wound up assigned to the USS *Gwin* attached to the deck force, which meant a lot of painting and scraping, sweeping and line coiling. Luck finally fell my way, not because I was able to get a rating, but because I was always neat and careful. The chief quartermaster…" Tonto broke it off and peered over his beer can at Eloise. "You sure you want to hear all this?"

"I'm fascinated. Please go on."

Tonto sighed. Contrary to the banter of his team mates, he was not given to being a braggart. "Where was I? Oh, yeah, the chief quartermaster came to me and asked if I would like to be a quartermaster. In my immense knowledge of things naval, I asked, 'What the hell's a quartermaster?' Instead of ripping my head off and booting it over the side, he gave me a straight answer. 'We work up on the bridge, around all the officers. Now do you want to stay down here and swab decks and scrape paint all the time or come work with me?' I blinked and acted dumb, but said sure. The outcome was I wound up with a specialty after being rated as a quartermaster, and I put in for UDT Slash R."

"Tell me about the training. I hear it is very difficult."

"Hey, woah, there. Enough about me. What is the Eloise Daladier story?"

She colored slightly and covered her embarrassment with a swallow of beer. "I have to echo you here. There's not a lot to tell. I was born right after the war, so I don't know anything about it that I have not read or been told. My father was an officer in the Foreign Legion, my mother was Vietnamese. A Eurasian, actually. I was raised here in Vietnam, attended the convent school, learned to be a proper French girl. After my father was wounded in the early fighting against the Viet Minh, he was posted to Algeria and later to France. My mother refused to leave Vietnam. At least not until both of our lives were threatened. I attended journalism school at the University of Paris. I lived in the Maison du Provance Francais on the Sorbonne campus. After college, I took my first and only job with *Le Monde* and they sent me here."

"Interesting, tell me more, then we'll go to dinner."

Tonto learned that in addition to excellent English, Eloise spoke fluent French and Vietnamese, and could hold her own — her words — in Cambodian. They had risen to leave when Kent Welby showed up. When he learned their destination, he unabashedly invited himself along.

"Francie and I are eating at Phon Bai, too. Why don't we all go together?"

Tonto shot Doc a glower, and a questioning glance to Eloise. "Why not?" she asked. "It should be interesting."

"All right. Eloise Daladier, this is Doc—er—Kent Welby. He's not our hospital corpsman, that's his nickname. Doc, Eloise."

The amenities taken care of they left the compound for the Mi Flower laundry. At first, Francie exhibited a coolness unlike her usual self toward Eloise, until the latter remarked, "My father was a soldier in the Foreign Legion, my mother was Vietnamese. I work for my living and this is more home to me than anywhere else I've ever been."

From then they got along famously. Tonto noticed, with a touch of appreciation, that Eloise had not mentioned that her father had been a Foreign Legion officer. Once settled in the Phon Bai restaurant, the women chattered incessantly and sipped white wine. Tonto and Doc ordered beer. At Eloise's suggestion, she ordered for all of them in as rapid-fire Vietnamese as that used by Francie. She also managed a fine bottle of wine to go with dinner. When the meal ended, Tonto left a tip on the table and paid the tab. Doc slipped up beside him while they waited for the ladies to leave the powder room.

"I'll split that with you tomorrow, okay, Tonto?"

"Sure, kid, no sweat."

They walked Francie to her rooms over the small shop and her feelings showed clearly on her face when Doc indicated he would not be staying. Then they strolled down the street and back to the Tre Noc compound. Inside, Tonto saw Eloise to her quarters and instructed her as to the use for the bunker when the nightly shelling began.

"They're late tonight. Maybe Charlie is having a party and we'll get skipped."

"I hope so. Those two, Kent and Francie? They are lovers, *non*?"

"I suppose you could say that."

"I wish them all the luck in the world," Eloise said with feeling.

"Good on you. They'll need every bit of it."

Tonto wanted so badly to take this lovely woman in his arms and passionately kiss her until they gasped for breath. He settled for a ligh touch of her fingers against one cheek. He walked with a lighter tread all the way to his bunker.

Five minutes later, the first mortar rounds dropped into Tre Noc.

Chapter 10

At Quarters the next morning, Lt. Carl Marino dropped a tidy bombshell on 1st Platoon. "We're going back. Based on what we brought in, and some new intel recently delivered, there's no doubt that Charlie has a major stores build up under way on the Bassiac. After morning chow, you are to report to your readybunker, with notebooks, for a briefing. Any questions can be asked there. Dismiss them, Chief," he told Tonto Waters.

Damn, that really blows it, Doc Welby thought as he walked away from the formation. He was to meet Francie Song and vouch for her to get her through the wire. Over the past week she had become even more insistent about seeking employment on the base. The previous night, swimming in a sea of voluptuous ardor, he had given in and agreed to do what he could to help. He'd have to meet her at the gate, tell her they were on standby or something and arrange for another time. And all of that before breakfast. Nothing but bad news. Grumbling, Doc headed for the main gate.

Francie waited for him there. He greeted her with an expression of guilt on his face. Her own visage reflected that she sensed something had changed. Doc took her to one side and put both hands on her shoulders.

"You look beautiful this morning," he began awkwardly.

"It is my dress for church," she stated simply, a tightness in her voice.

Doc Welby forced a smile. "You could convince any interviewer dressed like that. I'm sorry you had to get out your good clothes for nothing." He raised a hand to still her flood of protest. "Something has come up. We've been put on standby," he deftly evaded the truth. "It will only be for a few days. Then we can try again."

"You know how much this means to me, Kent Welby. It is—it is the most important thing in my life."

"I know, and I said I was sorry. What's two or three more days?" He felt miserable and she knew it.

Francie rose on tiptoe and kissed Doc lightly on the lips. "After waiting for three years, I suppose nothing. I will miss you. Will you be at Mi Flower tonight?"

"No. I don't think so. When we're on standby we can't leave." Doc hated lying to her, yet he could think of nothing else to do.

They kissed again, briefly. Then Doc Welby left her, to head for chow. All the way he could not keep from calling himself a louse.

"It's the same drill as before," Pope Marino told the attentive men of 1st Platoon. "We're going to sneak and peak and log any enemy activity. The name of the game is to see without being seen. Avoid contact if possible." Pope took them through the high points of the AO and pointed out recognizable landmarks, then gave them conditions in the area. He held back the last startling information given by LCDR Lailey. They would be contacted somewhere in their AO by assets of Linh Kao.

"We're being inserted by helicopter during this afternoon's siesta, just north of where we ran the op two nights ago. We'll be out three nights. We work our way northward along the river for that time, then we'll be extracted by the PBRs. That's all. Any questions?" There were none. "Go draw your equipment."

Doc Welby remained distracted by concern over Francie as he drew his rifle and ammunition, fixed grenades to his battle harness, and taped them in place so the safety spoons would not be released inadvertently. Damn these rations, he thought as he stuffed them into pockets and pouches. Three day's worth got heavy in a hurry. Tonto Waters came to him as he finished.

"Does it smell to you like Charlie has something big coming up?"

"Sort of," Doc replied. "Do you think he could be getting ready to try to push us out of the Delta?"

"It wouldn't surprise me that much," Tonto responded with a nod. "The question is, how long before he makes his move?"

They left the compound for Binh Thuy by truck, fully armed and ready. When Francie Song recognized Kent Welby in one of the vehicles, she stared thoughtfully after him for a long while, then she straddled her bicycle and peddled away from the compound.

Dust, leaves, and bits of saw grass whirled high in the air as the SEALs of first squad jumped the short distance from the skids of the Huey to a small clearing ringed by tall trees. Second Squad quickly followed, to make it a perfect insertion. Chances were that Charlie had no one around watching, and the VC generally ignored a single, unarmed helicopter as much as they did the river patrols.

Their pilot had flown a standard operational altitude until the last moment. Then he had zoomed down quickly and his crew chief had given the signal to use the bird. That put a small, cold, hard knot in the belly of Doc Welby. Flying bothered Kent Welby every bit as much as swimming effected Tom Waters. Doc could never figure that one out. Tonto was damn good at his swimming. He outdid more than half of the platoon. Yet, anything more than ankle deep put the burly Chief off his feed. Doc looked around and saw the squads moving out with practiced ease. Even before the chopper had lifted clear, the last man disappeared into the bush. They would make for the Rally Point (RP) individually, in a wide, fanlike arc.

A month plus in-country and still no word from Betty about their future, Doc thought as he pushed through the clinging growth. After five weeks, he'd give anything to see some hills. Even the low, rounded mountains of North Georgia and Tennessee would be a relief to all this flat, swampy ground. He had heard that not far to the north and west were some respectable highlands, and some little brown men known as Mont-anyards. Maybe so, Doc allowed, but for now they had a lot of jungle to slog through. He reached the RP to find Lt. Marino and Repeat Ditto already there. Pope had just completed a report to Whitehorse.

"Anything new, Skipper?" Doc asked.

"Nope. When both squads are gathered, we're supposed to continue as ordered."

"I'd say we'll make the river before nightfall," Doc opined.

Marino nodded thoughtfully. "I counted on it. If something is really brewing, Charlie will be out early tonight."

This time they didn't draw any blanks. Charlie came out early and in force. From their positions, in two-man teams along the river bank, with Lt. Marino and his RTO in the middle, between squads, they watched as the swarm of "Japs plied the water. The SEALs had been briefed that outside of themselves, anyone out after dark with or without a weapon had to be VC. One new thing had been added to the routine.

After their initial contact on the first mission, at least one of the men in each sampan carried a weapon. Although the shape of the crates they unloaded suggested AK-47s, most of the security force appeared to be armed with Czech 7.62x45mm Model 52 semi-automatic rifles, a few with the Czech ZH 29, and even fewer with the Model 58 Czech assault rifle. Observing through his night scope, Doc Welby noted that something new had been added.

Each squad, which had stripped down to blousey black trousers and left their arms close at hand, was covered by a PRC Type 56 LMG, with drum magazine. This Chinese copy of the Soviet RPD light machinegun had not been seen much this far south in the Delta, Doc knew. It definitely looked as though something big was in the wind. Although he could not see fine detail, Doc was ready to bet that these would be the earliest, more crudely machined models. The general area briefing informed the SEALs that the Chinese communists were notoriously stingy with their client states. He ceased his idle speculations when more sampans sculled to the island he watched with True Blue Oakes. Doc could read the thoughts of the black SEAL as though Oakes spoke next to his ear.

"These dudes are makin' up for some real hot war."

From 2100 to 0330 hours, the sampans came and went with their cargoes of death. Lt. Marino summed it all up when they met at their ROD point for breakfast an hour after sunrise. "It they keep it up like this every night, it won't take long for them to have enough supplies to keep a division in heavy action for at least a week, more likely longer than that."

"Which ain't good any way you slice it," Tonto Waters expressed his opinion.

After morning chow, the squads made ready to move out. Pope Marino halted them with a suggestion. "Before we go, I'd like to get a look at some of those bunkers. Tonto, you and Archie come with me. The rest of you set up a tight perimeter to secure the area."

"We're gonna wade over to that island?" Tonto blurted.

"Sure. The water is only four feet deep or so," Marino told him with a straight face.

Tonto Waters didn't look too happy about that. He made a sour face. "I was thinkin' it's too bad we don't have one of the STABs along. We could bring back some evidence that way."

"We can do that anyway. Physical and photographic." Marino turned to the RTO. "Repeat, do you have that camera handy?"

"Aye-aye, sir." Grinning, Chad Ditto produced a Leicha with a small strobe unit attached.

To the surprised faces of the SEALs around him, Lt. Marino explained," Courtesy of Det Gulf's S-2. We're to take pictures of whatever we uncover."

Tonto Waters didn't like this. He didn't like any part of this from the moment he stepped off the sloping bank of the Bassiac into the four foot water and sank to his arm-pits in muddy ooze. So much for the accuracy of that sounding. For all its sluggish appearance, the brown river tugged with insistence at his body. As usual, he had the point with Pope Marino and Archie Golden holding in-side the screen of brush on the bank until he reached the island. Shotgun in the lead, Tonto kept alert to any possi-bility the enemy had left someone behind.

Idly he wondered if he would ever find the time to discuss his idea of a shot-disburser with the Chief Master at Arms and the machinist of the River Tigers. When he felt a rise in the gradient beneath him, Tonto pushed harder to get out of the water with all the speed he could manage and still be quiet. On dry ground, he crouched low and swung a careful look around the low mound. Still no sign of anyone, enemy or otherwise. He signaled for the others to cross.

Pope Marino held the camera above his head, well clear of the water. In his right hand he gripped the pistol grip of his AR-15. Archie Golden, with only a sweat band on his head, his freckled face aglow with anticipation of ex-amining the enemy's explosives, looked even more like his namesake, Archie Andrews. What did that make him, Tonto thought with a wry snort, Jughead? The pair of SEALs came out of the river dripping brown streams.

On close examination, they quickly learned how the storehouses could hold so much material. The islands had been laboriously built up with layers of dirt, over the coconut palm logs and sandbags of each bunker, then painstakingly landscaped with jungle plants to make it appear natural.

"Clever little *schmucks*, ain't' they?" Archie remarked while he studied the handiwork of the VC.

"Let's take a look inside," Lt. Marino prompted.

Tonto Waters found the hatchway first. He and Archie pried it open with entrenching tools. Lt. Marino smeared the raw scars with mud. Inside, they found the place stacked from floor to ceiling with cases of grenades. Pope took flash pictures, had Tonto open a case and did a close-up of the Soviet made hand bombs. Hastily painted out, the cyrilic characters could still be made out in places. Especially ОСТОРОЖНО, ГРАНАТЫ, which spelled out the words in bold, black letters for DANGER, GRENADES.

"We could make one hell of a bang with this, sir," Archie observed eagerly. His eyes shined with the images of a colossal explosion that would rip the island to its roots.

That brought a droll tone from Pope Marino. "Unlike our counterparts in SOG, we *are* supposed to *study* and *observe*, not make enough noise to raise the dead. We also want Charlie to remain ignorant that we ever saw this stuff."

Chagrined, Archie abandoned his dream of a shattering blast. "Aye-aye, sir. Whatever you say. But it would sure be great," he added with the unholy fire back in his eyes.

During the up-close survey through that long morning and afternoon, the SEALs found a wide variety of arms and ammunition. Of particular note were a hundred cases filled with yellowish blocks of Symtex plastic explosive. The item that raised the most anger in the squads was a diabolical device that had been named the "grasshopper mine." Designed and manufactured in the Soviet Union, they could be delivered by air, or in hollow artillery shells, or dropped off by retreating troops. Cleverly camouflaged, they lay inert on the ground until someone came along and disturbed one of them. Then they bounded up to about waist high and detonated.

Although effective only on a one-to-one ratio, the nasty devices tended to maim more than kill. And the obvious object of maiming was the genitals. The SEALs had received information and demonstrations of the mines at the Special Warfare School at Ft. Bragg. What seemed even more disturbing to these men who loved their families was that these nasty horrors made no distinction as to age or gender.

"Rotten sons of bitches," Filmore Nicholson grumbled when he saw the devices.

"Hey, loosen up, Hospitalman," Lt. Marino advised. "We've got beehive rounds for our big guns, and Tonto has six flechette cartridges along for his shotgun. Both sides are going to use what they have to decide the outcome. This is war, man. We're all out here to break things and kill people."

Visions flooded the mind of the young medic. The reality of what Pope Marino said made him momentarily bitter. "Yeah, I gotcha, sir. It's not how you play the game, but whether you win or lose that counts."

Sensing that he faced a turning point in the life of this young man, Carl Marino reached out and took Fil by the shoulder. "You've got that right about out here. You damn betcha we're here to win. The other alternative is too awful to consider. Check it off to these people not being wired the same way we are. Life is cheap in Asia. We value it enough, at least, that we save our nasty stuff for people who are trying to kill us. Let me get some pictures, take a couple of samples, then cover it up again. This is the last island for today."

Back on the river bank, the squads made ready to move out. Two little brown men appeared out of the bush, one with a scrap of white rag. "We come, take you to Buddha."

"They don't look like priests to me," Archie Golden muttered to Blue Chip Reno.

Lt. Marino understood at once. The contact that might or might not happen. "Mr. Ott, move the men on to the next mission site and settle in. Tonto, you and Archie come with me."

Doc Welby nodded in approval. Just like that. No hesitation. Two little gooks show up and the old man takes off with them without skipping a beat. Pope did take Archie, his explosives and his Stoner, Doc reminded himself. He turned the way Ensign Ott indicated and walked off into the bush. They'd learn the outcome sooner or later.

If anything, the three guides moved even more quietly than the SEALs. Tonto Waters felt uncomfortable not being on point, yet had to admit to himself that these guys knew the territory and never missed a thing. He tensed and almost fired a round when a small, wild pig burst from its hiding place in a dark blob of shade that could have been the mouth of a cave.

At the same instant Tonto relaxed his finger on the trigger of the shotgun, the lead native signaled the all clear. The little man's gaze settled on Tonto and he nodded in acknowledgment of the big American's restraint. Tonto thought he might have smiled briefly. They had gone about three klicks when the lead Vietnamese signaled them down. He went forward and returned after five minutes to beckon them ahead.

They came out on a narrow roadway carved into the jungle. It seemed entirely incongruous to Tonto. Yet he saw where wheeled vehicles had traveled it recently. Bicycles, he judged, and some hand powered carts. Another klick further to the west and they came upon the crumbling remains of a former colonial villa. More of the little men gathered in the door yard and watched the Americans with suspicious eyes. All were heavily armed.

"You come," the ex-VC point man invited.

He led them inside through a tunnellike passageway that gave onto an open courtyard. Here, behind the facade of decay, the three SEALs saw the walls to be strong, with doorways opening onto carefully restored rooms. A large man, nearly a match for Tonto's 5' 11 $\frac{1}{2}$", appeared in the center opening. Tonto checked and saw the same surprise register on the face of Lt. Marino and Archie Golden.

From the little they had been told, they expected another small, typical Vietnamese. Linh Kao turned out to be huge, by the Asian norm, with a barrel chest, big belly, muscular arms that bulged from a sleeveless khaki shirt, slab thighs below short cammo pants. He wore cut down boondockers on large feet. He made a welcoming gesture and bowed deeply at the waist. He turned his attention to Pope Marino.

"You are Eagle One, yes? I am Buddha," his bass voice rumbled. "Welcome to my poor, humble lodgings. Let us sit on the lanai. I will send for refreshments."

A youngster of ten or eleven brought a tarnished silver tray of tropical fruit, cut in sections, which he passed around. A young woman in her late teens came with a pot of tea. At last came a man somewhat older than her with a wheeled service table containing bottles of liquor. He walked with a pronounced limp. Linh Kao noticed the Americans watching him.

"Thran had an encounter with one of your American trip mines. His comrades in the Viet Cong abandoned him before he was fully recovered. He came to me." Buddha waved an arm to encompass their surroundings. "First, let me apologize for the poor lodgings. My main base in Cambodia is much more splendid."

After what became to Tonto Waters a tedious fifteen minutes of polite chatter, Pope Marino cut to the chase. "You sent for us?" he prompted.

"Ah, yes. My loyal friends tell me there is a buildup of supplies. They also say there is to be a major offensive launched in the Delta."

Pope nodded. "We have heard similar things."

"No doubt. I am curious as to what you are going to do about it."

"Well, Buddha, we sort of figured on spoiling their game."

"I wish you good fortune in that. There is to be a meeting of the ranking cadres. As soon as I learn the place and time I will inform your Commander Lailey."

For another twenty minutes they talked about the known and suspected activities of the enemy in the Delta and what it might lead to. When Buddha rose, to signal that the interview had ended, Pope Marino thanked him and the SEALs followed their guides out.

They proceeded in silence to the dead end of the road. Half a klick beyond the turnaround, they suddenly came under attack from a small patrol of VC.

Chapter 11

Nine millimeter slugs snapped over the heads of Lt. Marino and his subordinates a fraction before they heard the harsh chatter of a MAT-49. Instinctively, they dropped and melted into the bush. The ex-VC guides had disappeared at the same time. A voice clamored in agitated Vietnamese. More shots, from a Chinese Type 58 joined in from the right of Tonto Waters. Archie's Stoner snarled and screams answered from that direction.

Archie made to move and came up head-on with two more VC. Casings from the 5.56 mm LMG sparkled in the air as he burned one down. The second Charlie dove behind a tree. Archie stripped a grenade from his harness and pulled the pin. He let the spoon slip, counted two and tossed it toward the tree.

"Grenade!" he shouted belated warning to his fellow SEALs.

Tonto Waters put his 8 shot, pistol-grip Ithaca into action and scored a shoulder wound on another Cong that blew off an arm and put the man out of action. Moaning, the enemy crawled out of sight. Tonto slipped two fresh rounds into the loading gate and sought another target. He soon found he had a whole lot of them.

Muzzle flashes winked from a dozen places in the shadowed jungle undergrowth. He picked a pair close together and let fly. From the flat sound of the discharge, he knew it was a flechette round. One series of flickering light stopped. He cut his eyes to left and right, then behind. Without conscious use of his arms, Tonto whirled and fired in one smooth action. His buckshot load caught a charging VC in the gut and doubled him over. The Charlie's feet churned a moment longer, until he fell over, victim of massive shock.

"Hell, they're all around us, Pope," he called out to Marino. "Musta been a set-up."

"I don't think so." Then, a moment after a metallic crack came from his position, Lt. Marino bellowed, "Aw, shit!".

"What now?" Tonto called out.

"I took a round that shattered the forestock of my 'fifteen. Cut a gouge on my hand, too."

"I'll cover you while you patch up." Tonto hosed the jungle with No. 4 buckshot beyond the position Marino held.

With only one round in the magazine tube, Waters reloaded swiftly and moved behind a fallen coconut palm. Five slugs slapped the grayish bark a second after he sank out of sight. Archie lobbed another grenade. It dropped deliberately short. Two screaming bodies lifted off the ground not five meters in front of Tonto Waters when it detonated. Unfortunately, some shards of shrapnel slashed into the tree trunk behind which Tonto Waters had taken shelter.

"Goddamnit, Archie. That's too close."

"You'd rather have your friends out there up close and personal? Just doin' my job."

They ain't leavin', Tonto thought uneasily as the minutes wore on and the fire fight degenerated into hurried potshots. He sensed, more than saw, motion to the right of a dome of earth. He put two loads down range in rapid succession. There came a brief shriek, then Tonto saw the conical palm frond hat first. Skewed at a crazy angle above a bloodied face, it slowly came from behind the knoll. A shoulder, covered by black pajama cloth came next. Then the body leaned out toward Tonto. The right hand rising revealed a Chinese Type 50 SMG. The muzzle seemed to line up directly on the center of Tonto's chest. Right here, right now, he was going to buy it. Fire spurted from the muzzle.

Tonto didn't feel a single bullet impact. At that range, how could the guy miss? Tonto's trigger finger twitched and he blew away the rest of the Cong's face. In the next instant an enormous heat and overwhelming pain radiated from a point to the right of Tonto's heart. Numbed instantly when the slug struck, he had not sensed it until now. He looked down to see the frayed edges of a hole in the thick webbing of his battle harness. Behind it, he knew, he had only his utility jacket and a stashed packet of C-Rats.

Fingers shaking, Tonto sat aside his weapon and fumblingly undid two buttons on his jacket. He reached in and withdrew the C-Ration package. Melted grease ran from the hole in the top of a can. Tonto could smell the sausage patties. Quickly he turned the can over. The bottom had split and a bright copper glint came from the ogive of the .32 caliber pistol slug that had been trapped there. Numb relief washed through Tonto.

He knew that the Model 50 Chinese pistol cartridge was considered a sub-caliber with little impact power, but he never realized that at a range of 30 meters it hadn't punch enough to go clear through his web gear, BDUs and a can of C-Rat sausage. *By God, he'd found a use for that shit after all.*

Suddenly Tonto wanted to laugh and shout, to get up and do a war dance. Training, and the gun-happy VC, gave him the restraint to remain down. He sobered quickly. He'd have one hell of a bruise, no doubt, and perhaps a cracked rib. Small price. The world felt brand new.

A second later, his elation ended, when Archie gave the attacking VC one of his grenade sandwiches; two M-26 frags with a Willie Peter grenade taped between them, all hurled at once. It went off with one hell of a flash-bang and set the three SEALs to ducking and dodging small pellets of smoking white phosphorous.

That broke the nerve of the remaining Charlies, and nearly that of his team mates. "*Didi mau! Didi mau!*" came a wail from the jungle.

Firing dwindled and the VC set about dragging off their dead. Silence, except for the constant buzz and hum of insects, returned to the jungle. Lt. Marino and his men remained in place for a long fifteen minute count, then gathered up on the small trail they had been following.

Tonto gulped greedily from his canteen. Archie stuck a stick of gum in his mouth and chomped on it as though his life depended on it. Pope Marino broke smoke discipline to light a stub of cigar. Hell, Charlie already knew they were there, he reasoned to himself.

"You guys aren't gonna believe this," Tonto prefaced his account of the round that had caught him. "But I got my ass saved by a can of those stinkin' C-Rat sausages."

"You're shittin' me," Archie stated flatly.

"No, I'm not." Tonto went on to describe what happened and to show off the mortally wounded can of sausage patties.

While they chilled out after the fire fight, nerves still a-jump, the three guides showed. They simply melted out of the bush with big grins. The oldest one, who the SEALs had considered in charge all along, spoke for them.

"We come, tell you no double-cross. Not know VC there until too late." Then, grinning even broader, he lifted a greasy thong from around his neck. "Those who get away from you don't get past us," he announced proudly as he displayed a string of fresh-cut ears.

That was definitely not the SEALs' style of fighting. Lt. Pope Marino swallowed his flash of revulsion and patted the leader on one shoulder. "You have done well. Your loyalty does you honor. We do not suspect you. The trustworthiness of Buddha and his men has been told to us by no lesser than Blue streak Two."

Immediately Tonto Waters and Pope Marino noted that although the former VC appeared flattered by this, they seemed to be less than pleased by who gave the endorsement. All the same, they set off in a happy mood to lead the SEALs back to the rest of the platoon.

Tonto Waters could taste the tension, a cloying thickness on his tongue, as they neared the Rest Over Day point. The jungle was too quiet. SEAL training and experience got them beyond that problem. Someone was stirring up the bush. He stretched out his long paces in order to get farther ahead of his companions. Around a slight bend he found the three assets from Linh Kao squatted down, motionless and intent on a spot in a tangle of vines.

A tiny flash of light speared into Tonto's eyes. It winked rapidly. Morse code. Mr. Ott was thinking, sure enough, Tonto thought with relief. Only what in hell is going on? E—I—S. Three characters. E—I—S. Hell yes, *Enemy In Sight*. Tonto made hand signs to tell the guides to remain in place and returned to where Marino and Golden waited.

"There's some Cong around here somewhere. Mr. Ott put someone on watch for us and signaled with a mirror. Three letters, EIS, enemy in sight. We've got to be extra quiet and let them guide us in. No sense in blundering into a lot of bad guys."

"Right, Chief. We'll move in individually, five minutes apart. The guards Buddha sent can cover us."

"I'd say it's important you go first, Pope. You need to get on top of what's going on."

Marino considered that grimly. "You're right. Though I'd rather go last, make sure you all got there. Okay, from where do we start?"

Waters took them to a small clearing, filled with slender, young bamboo, that waved gently, ten feet tall. "From here the mirror flash was at zero-niner-three magnetic. Just hang on that bearing an' you'll find the platoon."

His wrist compass held up before him, Lt. Marino ghosted off into the bamboo. Tonto counted down five minutes and gave Archie a tap on the shoulder. "You're next. Zero-niner-three."

"Gotcha."

It had to be the longest five minutes in his life. Tonto Waters had soaked through his cammo jacket and jeans, his toes itched from wetness and his eyes felt like two piss holes in the snow by the time the second hand clicked into place and he set off to join up.

His blind journey through the bamboo took less time than Tonto expected. Fully twenty meters short of where he believed the jungle would begin again, he stepped through a tangle of lianas and came upon Repeat Ditto and Ensign Walter Ott. Wally Ott had an excited expression on his boyish face.

"Somethin' stumbled onto us, or damn near. I was just tellin' Pope about it. It's over on one of the islands. I'll show you."

They wormed their way through the crowded underbrush toward the river bank. When they reached it, Tonto's eyes popped wide and his jaw sagged. He had never seen so many VC big shots in one place at one time.

At least fifteen important-looking VC stood on the island with seven ranking NVA officers, their uniforms stark against the drabness of the VC. Oblivious to the observation by the SEALs, they bent over open crates, inspecting the contents. With them was a blond giant, a stranger that none of the SEALS could identify. One of the ARVN Special Forces troopers assigned to the platoon for this mission came to where Lt. Marino and Ensign Ott crouched.

"What they say is interesting, *Dahwi*."

"How many times do I have to say this? I'm a lieutenant, not a captain."

"Same difference. You in charge, you *dahwi*," the young ARVN lieutenant responded blank-faced.

"All right—all right." Their earlier fire fight still

weighed heavily on Pope Marino and this sudden, new situation did little to lessen it. He took a grip on his riding anger. "What is it they are saying?"

"Before you come, the little, old one, the cadre from Vinh Loi, asks how many men he will have to provide. His real boss, a colonel from the north...." he pointed. "That one there, say he must bring a hundred men. He get mad, just now says that take long time to get together. The Russian says it will be another month of hard work to distribute these supplies to the bunkers. And a week after that to dispurse them, before the offensive can begin. Not to worry about time to round up men. Now he say the man from Vinh Loi will produce the number of men needed or be tried as a reactionary traitor."

Lt. Marino whistled soundlessly. "That's some heavy stuff. Thank you, Lt. Bhan." Marino took Wally Ott, Tonto Waters and the two squad leaders apart. "That's one more confirmation that there's a major offensive being laid on in the Delta. We've got to get this above decks fast, and in person. Can't trust it to the radio. In case we don't all make it out of this place, here's what we've got," he went on to brief them on what Buddha had revealed.

Shortly before noon chow, the small, black telephone on the edge of the desk at Binh Thuy Airbase tinkled fitfully. LCDR Barry Lailey shifted the three inch stub of cigar from one side of his mouth to the other and reached for it.

"Commander Lailey, sir."

"Commander Lailey..." The hiss of static told Barry Lailey that the call came from off base, by radio. "It's Dan Evers, Barry. The General has been reading your reports with considerable interest."

Colonel Dan Evers (RA), adjutant to General Ian Belem (RA — West Point), Area Commander of Special Forces Operations, Vietnam, assigned to MACV-SOG.

Barry Lailey privately considered Evers an ass-kisser, and Gen. Belem the pompous ass that got the most kissing. He suddenly realized that Evers was still talking.

"You've been keeping real busy down there. Good work. The General has decided that you must have some people in need of rotation for R and R. Some of your small boat force and at least some of the SEALs. He's asked that you draw up a list and submit them for passes—er—liberty cards."

"Exactly who does he have in mind, and to where are they to be rotated?"

"Well, that's why I called you," Col. Evers responded cheerily and proceeded to tell LCDR Lailey.

Lt. Marino directed the platoon back from the riverbank before the inevitable happened. He contacted Raintree by radio and set up the extraction. Then, with Tonto Waters on point, Mr. Ott with third and fourth squads, they headed for the extraction point. They had a two hour wait. When the PBRs swooped in from the main stream, a tidal wave of relief washed over the entire platoon. They quickly lined up to board.

Huge in-line engines rumbling, the PBRs sped up the muddy brown river. Lt. Marino sat with his back to the hatch combing over one engine, with Ensign Ott, Chief Waters and the squad leaders around him. Tonto Waters summed it up for them all.

"The shit's gonna hit the fan, ain't it, Pope?" It was the first time they had had to discuss it since the hasty meeting on the river bank.

"You got that right, Tonto. And no later than six weeks from what that Russian was saying. By the way, who is he and what the hell was he doing there?"

"They'll probably send us out to find out," Wally "Clever" Ott observed sourly.

Pope Marino cocked an eyebrow. "You know, I'd a hell of a lot better do it that way than turn it over to the spooks. Half the time they can't find their ass with a ten man work party. Or to give it to Barry Lailey, for that matter." Their rapt silence was all the encouragement he needed. "We're getting overworked, right? Second Platoon has hardly done crap since we go there. And we're getting all the shit details. I'm afraid the bad blood between Lailey and me is behind that. My only regret is getting that dumped on your shoulders."

"We can carry the load, don't worry, Pope," Tonto Waters spoke for the mall.

Marino sighed. "We'll know soon enough when we get back. But be sure of this. If there's some way he can figure to put us on the shit end of this stick, he'll do it."

Chapter 12

On their return to Tre Noc, the SEALs caught sight of the most outlandish character they could ever imagine. He wore black pinstripe, gray Western trousers, with matching jacket, a frilly-front white shirt, cowboy boots, a 4X, pearl gray Stetson, and wraparound, reflecting sunglasses. He bounded along the dock to the lead PBR and had his hand out for a shake even before the SEALs debarked.

"Jason Slater, pilgrim," he boomed at Lt. Carl Marino in an abrasive New York accent, made even more disagreeable by his attempt to do John Wayne. Everyone took it for granted that wouldn't be his real name. "I'm one of the—ah—civilian advisers to these fine Vietnamese folks." The butt of a Colt .45 single action (SA) revolver protruded from the shoulder holster under the left side of his jacket. His issue service arm, a 9mm Browning High power, was tucked away out of sight behind his belt at the small of his back.

"Lt. Carl Marino," Pope replied, taking the hand. *The Spook Out of Hell*, he instantly labeled the CIA man.

"I came down here to have a little chat with you fellers. Can we sort of mosey over to the isolation compound?"

"We don't have an isolation set-up here," Lt. Marino told Slater a bit more coldly than he had intended. "All we've got is a ready bunker."

Banishing the puzzled expression that had washed over his face, Slater produced a broad grin. "That'll do fine, just fine."

"You want the whole platoon?"

Slater thought on that a second. "Just the ones who saw any action."

Recollection of what they had encountered on the river

bank prompted Pope Marino to modify that request. At least this way he would not have to worry about leaving such sensitive material in the hands of Barry Lailey. "You might want to talk to a couple more. We—ah—came across something out there."

"Whatever you say, Lieutenant. Think of this as just your garden variety debriefing."

Of necessity, Lt. Marino led the way to the ready bunker. Once there, he sent third and fourth squads off for their regular after-action debrief, except for Ensign Ott, the squad leaders, and the ARVN interpreter. Inside, they seated themselves while Slater extracted an area map from a slim attache case and followed with a telescoping pointer.

"I knew it," Pope Marino whispered confidentially to Doc Welby, seated beside him. "The Spook Out of Hell."

"You got that right, Pope," Doc agreed without hesitation.

"Your AO for this op was bounded north and south by the Mekong and Bassiac rivers, right? And to a point three klicks west of the tributary that runs by Vinh Long? Okay, we've got that much," Slater stated crisply. "From the radio traffic I gathered you came under fire from hostile elements of the VC?"

"Yes," Lt. Marino answered hesitantly.

He warmed up though as Jason Slater's probing, intelligent questions revealed that the CIA agent possessed a lot more substance than the SEAL officer had expected. Slater took him through the fire fight smoothly and professionally, which decided Pope to conclude with his major revelation.

"As it turned out, it is my conclusion that this was a security force for a far more important activity that was going on at the time, back at the Bassiac."

Slater tilted his head to one side, pursed his lips. "And what was that?" His expression indicated that this was something entirely new. It had not been on the radio.

Pope Marino glanced at Wally Ott. "Ensign Ott should

give you the background on that. He was there when it went down."

"Do so," came a spare reply from Slater.

"We were securing the next observation site, which became our extraction point, with third and fourth squads. All of a sudden, some big shot Charlies showed up in a motorized sampan. All their bodyguards had AK-47s. Then some jokers show up in a larger vessel, Chinese make or maybe Russian. NVA regulars."

Slater raised an eyebrow. "You're kidding."

"No, I'm not. They were in full uniform. About half an hour later, more VC cadre showed, along with this big, blond guy. Bak here, told us later that the was a Russian."

A frown deepened on Slater's brow. "Tell me about him. Everything you can remember."

Ott thought back over it. "He was better than six foot tall, broad shoulders, moved like a dancer, or a *karateka*, graceful, always in control. He had almost white-blond hair, cut real short. From where I was, his eyes seemed either dark brown or black. The gooks, even the NVA, bowed and scraped over everything he said."

Paranoia being the mother's milk of the intelligence game, Need To Know ruled every agent with the iron fist of secrecy. In a rare breech of that dictum, Jason Slater spoke musingly. "Our friend Senior Lieutenant Alexi Kovietski of Spetznaz." His lapse did not extend to the private conviction that Kovietski, under another name, was Station Chief of the Delta Region and Cambodia for the KGB.

"Who, sir?" Ott had not been long enough removed from the Naval Academy and surrounded by SEALs to have gotten over the habit of referring to anyone whose rank he did not know by that honorific.

"The Soviets, as I'm sure you know, Mr. Ott, have made advisors available to the enemy, much like our earlier role in South Vietnam. Sr. Lt. Kovietski is one of those. To put it as you SEALs might, he's been a pain in the ass in the past and is sure to be so again."

"He said something about an offensive, but I suppose Pope—er—Lt. Marino should tell you about that," Ott stammered out.

Slater got that out of Pope Marino, confirmed by Bak, the ARVN lieutenant. He posed a few more pointed questions, all rolled into one. "These supplies. Tell me about them. I'll ask more when it comes to me."

"Every one of those islands in the Bassiac has been converted into a storage bunker," Marino informed him. "At least nearly every one we've come upon so far. This Kovietski said it would take a month more to get all of the supplies here. That says one hell of a big, long offensive to me."

Slater nodded. "What you've come upon here, gentlemen, is one hell of a humungous operation. I'll want transcripts of this debrief and copies of your after-action reports, then I'm off, back to Saigon."

That raised an eyebrow for Pope. Tonto Waters could have read Pope Marino's mind. Not just some cowboy spook, then. *This sumbitch has to be the head of station, or his right hand man,* the Chief thought. *We've stepped into some heavy pucky*.

For all the action, and preparation for more, 1st Platoon had started to get antsy. From Tonto Waters' observation that they seemed to get a disproportionate amount of the risky assignments, to the idlers' chatter in the platoon bar, to BS sessions at Mi Flower, the word went around that the SEALs of Two-One would appreciate a little time off.

So the message they received was met with relieved surprise. Nobody ever got what they wanted, not in this man's Navy. "I don't fucking believe it," was how Blue Chip Reno put it. "We're really getting liberty?"

"True thing, Blue Chip," Tonto Waters assured him over the rim of a can of beer. Came down straight from the CO Spec War MACV-SOG. Some general by the name of Belem."

Archie Golden, the oldest man in the platoon, rose from his grenade crate seat to get another beer. "Ian Belem?" he asked. "He was with Seventy-seventh at Bragg when I took the Army Special Warfare course."

"That's him," Doc Welby asserted. Then he frowned. "He'd have to be awfully young to be a general, or too old for the school, wouldn't he, Pope?"

"No. He was a colonel then, commanded one section of the Group. A damn good man."

"Where are we going?" Repeat Ditto had hopes for Japan, or even Australia.

"We're to leave tomorrow on the mail chopper, for Saigon," Tonto told the RTO.

"And for only four days," Doc Welby glumly added.

"At least we know our efforts are appreciated. Not much, but appreciated," Pope Marino quipped.

"It sounds just jim-dandy to me," Tonto Waters asserted with a smug grin. "Mademoiselle Daladier will be there, staying at the Hotel Internationale."

"Watch the hanky-panky, Tonto," True Blue Oakes quipped.

"Now, now, be nice," Tonto came back, waggling a finger under the broad, mahogany nose of True Blue. "I have higher things in mind than that."

"No you don't, you sex maniac," Chips Danner growled good naturedly.

"Before she left here, we made plans. They include dinner at a fancy French restaurant, and a visit to the museums and places of interest," Tonto defended his intentions. "Now, find some hanky-panky in that."

"I can hold on the pad for only half an hour, then I have to haul buns outta here," the chopper pilot told Lt. Carl Marino.

"That's long enough to sort the mail. The guys going can read theirs on the trip to Saigon," Pope offered in encouragement.

"Okay. But not a second longer," the Army warrant officer accepted.

Their long delayed mail had arrived. Bags of it. Most would be left behind, Pope Marino worked out as he walked off the helicopter pad at Tre Noc. Dusty Rhodes could sort it and see to having it distributed. One quick go-over for 1st Platoon mail, then off to the big city. Already the gun cleaning tables had been covered with packets of white oblongs, and a mound of packages. It took twenty minutes for first squad to separate out the mail for 1st Platoon.

"Kent Welby," Pope Marino called out.

Ice hardened around Doc Welby's stomach. Here it was. He stepped forward and accepted a small pile. "Thank you, sir."

He took a quick glance at the half dozen letters. From his parents. And another from Stubs Perkins in 3rd Platoon at Little Creek. Stunned, he discovered that they didn't include any thick envelope of legal documents. No letter had come from Betty, but no divorce papers either. The bad news came to Archie Golden. He didn't know about it until he got on the chopper. He opened and read the letters from his wife and children in chronological order, starting at the first one written. The bad news showed up in the last one.

"I hate to bring worries to you, *bubi*, I'm sure you have enough of your own," Iris had penned in her fine, clear script. "But here goes. Davey is in trouble at school. Now, before you go on about breaking things or sassing his teachers it's none of that. It's for fighting in the boys' room.

"Some of the boys who go to the same school," Iris continued, "whose parents are activists leaders in the Anti-War movement..." Archie could read her suppressed anger in those words by the deep, dark impression on the paper. The tip of the ball point had almost pushed through the other side of the paper. "In the Anti-War movement," Archie reread, "have been giving Davey a hard time because you are in the Navy. God knows what they would say if they knew you were in Vietnam," Iris put in as an aside. "Anyway, Davey finally had all he could take and punched out the lights for a couple of them. He's on suspension for a week." The rest of the letter meandered through lighter subjects and was signed "with all my love, from Iris."

It gave Archie something to brood about all the way to Saigon.

One minute after the skids touched the tarmac of helipad 31 at Ton Son Nhut airport in Saigon, Archie Golden was out of the chopper, ditty bag in hand, and on his way to the long rank of telephone booths beyond the incoming gate. Without thinking of the date and time difference between Saigon and Little Creek, Virginia, he quickly got an operator and gave his home number.

"It's one o'clock in the morning there," the operator protested, "yesterday."

"I don't care what time it is. Just call, call," Archie said forcefully.

The phone on the other end rang seven times before being answered by a sleepy voice. "Yes? Golden residence." Iris, all right, but scratchy and indistinct.

"Iris, it's me, Richard."

"Richie? Gewalt! Are you all right? Is everything okay? Are you hurt?"

"No—no, nothing like that. It's your—your letter. The last one? I got them all today. I'm worried about Davey. Is he...back in school?"

"Oh, yes. He's not happy about it, but, well, the principal took sides with those nasty agitators and their brat kids."

"The schmuck!" Archie barked. Then, "Naw, that's a part of a *man*. That whining asshole, Herbie Butts, is a *putz*. Is Davey there now? Can you get him up?"

"Of course he's here, this is his home. But, getting him out of bed, Richie? That'll take so long. This call must be costing you a fortune."

"Naw. These are free calls for GIs." It was just a little lie. "I wanna talk to him."

"But, Richie, he's only twelve, he needs his sleep," Iris continued to stand in the way, worried her husband would heap more hurt on their son.

"Right now he needs his old man. Get... him... up... Iris."

"All right, yes, I'll get him. I'll hurry, promise."

Two minutes later, a sleepy-voiced, dopey-sounding Davey Golden chirped into the phone, "Pop? Is it you?"

"Davey. In poi-son, as Jimmy Durante used to say."

"Who's he?"

"Never mind. Your mother tells me you got into trouble at school. Fighting? Nice little Jewish boys, on the verge of their *bar mitzvah* don't fight."

"This was different, Pop. They're a bunch of stinkin' horses touchases, real *yentzen gonnifs*." Archie noticed the mixing of languages in forming the plurals. The kid didn't know his grammar in Yiddish. "They said we were fightin' an immoral war in Vietnam."

"Maybe we are, maybe we're not. It's not for them to say unless their ass is on the line," Archie replied tightly.

"They were bad-mouthin' the Navy, Pop," Davey tried his most persuasive argument.

"Well, now, that's a different matter. What happened?"

"I gave Chuckie Fulton a black eye and split lip, and Eddie Marquesa a bloody nose."

"Son, son, I don't like to hear about you fighting. Especially when it interferes with your schooling. Getting an education today is everything. Hell, I wouldn't be where I am if I'd gotten a good education. I'd be running the friggin' war from a desk in Washington. I want good things for you," Archie went on with the expected fatherly lecture. "Better than anything I had a chance at. You get a reputation as a brawler, you won't amount to a hill of crap. Take my word for it. Now, is your mother close enough to hear what I'm sayin'?"

"No."

"Good. What I really want to tell you is this; the next time those ass holes mouth off at you, you should get the little putzen off where there are no witnesses and pound the living shit out of them."

"Yesss! Right, Pop. I'll remember that," Davey enthused.

"Great kid. Now, good-bye. Let me talk to your mother again."

When Archie finished his conversation with Iris, he walked off to join the others, feeling good. Damned good.

Kent Welby looked up to see Archie Golden returning, his bantam rooster strut restored. A big grin spread on his face. "What's up Archie?" Doc Welby asked.

"My youngest punched out a couple of punks at school. He got suspended for a week."

Genuine concern rang in Doc's voice. "Did you tell him how serious that could be?"

"Oh, yeah, yeah. I told him all the stuff about college

admissions boards and how they saw such things. Then I told him that if it happened again to make sure there ain't any witnesses." Laughter spread among the SEALs. "The hard part was calmin' Iris. It made me thirsty. Let's go find a beer."

"I was talkin' with that Fleet Marine sergeant over there. He says there's a great place to do liberty here. It's a street called Truman Key. I'll meet yez there," Tonto Waters advised.K

"Where are you going?"

"Have you forgotten already? I have an engagement at the Carousel Lounge."

A couple of low whistles answered him, then Doc Welby took the lead. "Okay, then, we'll meet you in the best joint on Truman Key."

Chapter 13

After descending from the back-tilted seats of the cyclo cabs that had delivered them to Truman Key, the SEALs of 1st Platoon stared around themselves in amazement. True Blue Oakes summed it up for them.

"I don't fucking believe it. Every other place is a bar. The rest are geedunks or noodle shops."

"You're wrong, Blue," Repeat Ditto told him laughingly. "There's a tailor shop. And another one down there. 'Custom Fit Tiger Stripes,'" he quoted from a hand-lettered sign in English in the window of one establishment.

That deserved a belly laugh, Archie Golden decided. "Oh, my, don't these ground pounders have it sweet?" he clutched his gut while he made fun of such extravagances. "We won't be able to live with ourselves until we have some of those in the Delta."

"Okay, guys," Doc Welby rallied them and pointed at the nearest bar. It's garishly colored neon struggled feebly to compete with sunlight. The signs claimed the bar actually stocked *Tiger* beer from Singapore, and *Sapporo* from Japan, in addition to the old standby; 45 (*Bahmibah*). "What are we here for?"

"Beer!" came a chorus.

"And?"

"Chow!"

"And?"

"Women!"

"But not necessarily in that order," Chips Danner brayed.

"We can get a good start right now," Doc Welby prompted.

They headed for the doorway to the bar as one man. The SEALs of 1st Platoon had changed their limit of scrip for piasters before leaving Tre Noc, and again at Ton Son Nhut. That gave them double the piasters allowed at any one time. They'd not have to go back for more until the next day. Or at least that's the way they saw it. They had yet to see the prices in Saigon.

"Thirty piasters for a lousy beer?" Archie Golden grumbled. "Hell, that's almost a dollar. I can get two for that price back home."

"Well, this is Saigon, my friend, not The World," True Blue advised him.

That still failed to console Archie. "Unless they've fixed the prices, it has to be better somewhere else. Let's drink up and go."

First and Second Squads split off from Third and Fourth at the next watering hole they stormed into. The reason being it was too small to hold all of them. The icy bottles of *Bahmibah* they were served came at a reasonable 18 piasters. That still didn't please Archie, though he stayed to drink three rounds. The SEALs divided further outside that place, the second squad opting for some chow in one of the noodle shops.

They had spied large bowls of the rice threads on display in the window. One sample had sliver-thin slices of roasted duck, scallions and bok choi floating in the clear broth. First Squad went on for more beer.

In the third joint, they were engaged in a rousing old time, the ageless military game of stacking cans, when the brightness from outside dimmed as a young woman filled the entrance way. Doc Welby glanced up and his features rearranged into a dumb-struck expression. He half rose from the table.

"Fran—Francie, what are you doing here?" he asked unbelieving.

She crossed to the table unsteadily. "Kent Welby, I did not think to see you here."

"That's what I just said. What are you doing in Saigon?"

"I have an aunt who lives here. She has taken ill. I must come to take care of her and her house. She has small children. I did not know you would be here."

Bedazzled by the radiant presence of the lovely young woman, Doc fumbled for words. "I'm glad you're here, though. Will you join us?"

"I must not. I only came on an errand for my uncle. He wanted some beer, and some noodles for my aunt." She beamed at him. "You can walk me back to my aunt's, though."

"That's something, I guess." He turned to his squad mates. "I'll catch up to you later."

"Watch out for bicycle bombs," Archie, the explosive expert warned.

Doc Welby put on a concerned expression. "What are those?"

"Charlie uses them. It's real simple. I got it out of a manual on Viet Cong booby traps. They take plastic explosive and stuff it in all the tubular parts of a bicycle frame, then set up a detonator. Kids wheel them around and leave them close to Americans. They especially like to catch one of us alone," he exaggerated, enjoying Doc's discomfort.

"That's a comforting thought. Might be it's you guys who should keep a sharp eye." With that, he and Francie departed.

While the platoon reveled in the distractions available on Saigon's infamous Truman Key Avenue, Tonto Waters made his way to the Hotel Internationale. He found the Carousel Lounge packed, although it was well after the lunch hour. Most of the customers were loud, drunk, and American. They wore a mixture of civilian clothes, with here and there bits of military garb. Journalists, Tonto judged them from the absence of visible weapons.

The only popular item of martial clothing, he noted, was a sleeveless kapok vest, in Tiger Stripe cammo pattern, which in a still photo or on television would look, to the uninitiated, like a flack jacket. A sourvignette struck Tonto.

"Our heroic war correspondent, dodging bullets alongside the soldiers of umpti-ump battalion to bring you the latest from the front." Right then Tonto spotted Eloise Daladier and waved to her. He shoved his way through the shouting, gesticulating reporters to the small corner table where she sipped a glass of white wine.

"There you are, Tom," she said brightly. "I got the message in our news bureau first thing this morning. You're lucky you got through on such short notice."

Tonto grinned knowingly. "Friends in high places." He sat down. "Tell me about your work."

"I've just finished a whirlwind tour of Vietnam, interviewing your Army's Corps Commanders for an article I will do from here in Saigon."

"Sounds dull."

Eloise made a face. "It is, but I can put some spice in it, if only I had a good hook."

"A what?"

Light laughter answered him at first. "That's a journalism expression. 'Every good story needs a hook to hang itself on,'" she quoted. "In my case, I need a really good hook. Everyone is so closed-mouthed. Especially with what they consider the foreign press. The commander of Eye Corps would not even admit it was Eye Corps until I pointed out the corps insignia on the wall over his desk."

"You mean that red shield with a sword and the Roman numeral I on it?"

"Yes. Silly, don't you think?" Eloise suppressed a giggle.

Their waiter came. "What will you have, m'sieu?"

"Beer. But none of that local stuff," Tonto admonished him.

"We have Heinekins, Beck's, Amstel."

"Beck's will do. And bring the lady another-" he made a face, "wine."

"At once."

"Nothin' exciting on your plate? Like maybe another trip into the Delta?"

Eloise considered it a moment. "It's possible. Once I complete this article on an overview of the big picture."

Waters canted his head, tapped one ear with an open palm. "That's gobbledegook. You didn't talk that way when I first met you."

"I've been listening to too many Americans with too much rank, I suppose. They all talk that way."

"Armchair soldiers. Completely out of touch with reality. Not a one of them could find his butt with a ten man working party."

Eloise let the giggles come this time. "Now, that's really funny. May I quote you?"

"So long as you don't identify the source," Tonto bantered back.

"How can I quote you without attribution?"

Tonto peered into her lovely hazel eyes. "More gobbledegook, or another tidbit from journalism school?"

Eloise produced a wry smile. "A little of both, I think. Tell me what you've been doing?"

Guarded shutters dropped over Tonto's walnut brown eyes. "You'll get what I *can* tell you. Where shall I start? We've been eatin' a lot of C-Rats, and chasin' around in the boonies."

"Chasing anyone in particular?"

"Noo-o," Tonto replied after a moment's hesitation. "Just Charlie in general," he evaded. "Some big shot decided we had earned a little rest, and that's why we're in Saigon."

"Who is 'we?'" Eloise inquired as she leaned toward Waters.

"All of First Platoon. They've been runnin' our legs off for the better part of the month. Out nearly every night."

"That must be hard on you," Eloise prompted.

"Yeah, well, nothin' we can't handle. It's all sort of routine now."

"Have you had any engagements with the enemy?"

"A few."

"Has anyone been injured?"

"Nothing big time. Scratches mostly."

"Tom, loosen up for me, please. It's not just my job, I'm concerned for you, for all of you SEALs. I've taken considerable liking..."

Tonto held up a hand to stem the flood. "All right, all right. You remember Lt. Marino?" At her nod, he went on, "He got a bullet crease across the back of one hand last time out. Archie—that's Richard—Golden picked up a piece of shrapnel from a VC grenade." Their drinks came and Tonto cut off all comment while the waiter remained close by. "Oh," he resumed with the obsequious table server departed with their orders for a shrimp salad and a roast beef sandwich. "I had my life saved by a can of C-Ration sausage patties."

"You... what?"

"It's nothin'," he depreciated. "I took a spent bullet in the chest. It happened I had a C-Rat package under my BDU jacket. The slug didn't get all the way through."

Eloise paled suddenly. "That's interesting, and a bit frightening. But I'm afraid it's not the hook I need to hang my story on."

He hadn't been telling it to her for that purpose, Tonto thought, a bit miffed. "Ah! This ain't a secret to anyone, except maybe people out there in The World. The Cong have stepped up their activity in the Delta."

Eloise brightened. "I wasn't aware of that. And I

haven't interviewed the Corps Commander in the Fourth Zone yet."

Tonto laughed softly, relieved to have a light ending to all this interrogation. "There you are. You can go south, use that to lead your story and have an excuse to stop off at Tre Noc."

Joining his laughter, Eloise radiated satisfaction. "What about the rest of your day?"

Tonto shot his cuff and checked his diver's watch. "I'd better check in with the other guys, make sure they haven't torn a new a—er—torn up Saigon too much."

"What about dinner?"

"Suits? What time and where?"

Eloise considered that a moment. "Meet me here at 21 hours, and we'll go to the Maison Dupris. Very ritzy, and my treat."

"No, I'm payin', and is that the same as twenty-one hundred?"

"Yes. Or nine o'clock."

"Good. Now that's settled, let's eat up and I'll go round up those yahoos."

Chief Tom Waters would soon find good cause for his concern over the status of the SEALs of 1st Platoon. First and Second Squads had linked up again and held forth in one of the larger beer halls on Truman Key. A round score of highly drunken Marines lined the bar and had been tossing good natured insults at the "Squids." After one return barb that centered around the procedure for diapering a Marine, the insults became markedly less good natured.

One burly, bullet-headed gyrine squared off, facing the SEALs, his back pressed against the bar. "You squids oughtta watch your mouths. This is a Marine bar an' youse from the lesser branch of our service are only tolerated."

Roused from his own fog of alcoholic fumes, Mule

Carlson shoved to his feet. "Where you get that? You goat-fuckin' jarheads are nothin' but sea-goin' bellhops. You guard the gangways and important places on board our ships, and occupy space at the gates to Naval bases. It's our Navy and you're just a teensy part of it."

In a blur, the hefty Marine launched himself away from the bar, fists clenched. "I'm gonna knock that shit-mouth of yours around to the back of your head!"

Mule Carlson stopped his intention with a display of the source of his nickname. He delivered a solid karate snap kick to the bulging belly of the desk-bound Marine. Instantly doubled over, the Marine's lips spewed first air, then a long, ugly, discolored stream of beer. Mule continued his spin into a full roundhouse and nailed his tormentor on the side of the head. The puking cut off as though Carlson had thrown a switch. With a soft flutter of lips, the unconscious man fell face first in his own vomit. Instantly, a general melee erupted.

With a roar, Marines and SEALs fell on one another. Sheltered behind the mahogany, the bartender, who resembled a twelve-year-old beside these American behemoths, blew frantically on a brass whistle. He ducked lower as a beer bottle whizzed past his head, and kept on blowing. Shrieking bar girls jammed the doorway, shoulders of the first pair tightly wedged together. The pandemonium spread beyond the barroom.

Inside it remained a scene of wild, flailing confusion. Doc Welby found himself in the center of what had to be only his life's third brawl. A Marine about his size popped up in front of him. Months of intense training took over. Doc smacked the jarhead in the solar plexus, which put the unfortunate fellow out of the contest, eyes bulged, mouth gaped, face scarlet. Another Marine grabbed Doc from behind. A big mistake.

Doc Welby flexed his knees, then dropped suddenly, with a bend and twist of his body that sent the leatherneck flying. At the last moment, Doc took one of his opponent's hands in a "chicken wing," bent down, and let the other's falling body apply the pressure.

An ululating wail of agony came from the surprised battler. He squirmed around on the dirty floor like a dog chasing its tail. "Be nice now," Doc leaned close to his face to say, then kicked him in the temple. The wailing stopped. *By God, I can really do it*, Kent Welby thought elatedly. He took a quick look at the progress of the fight.

Pope Marino held a Marine gunnery sergeant motionless with an Aikido technique designed to deliver excruciating pain if the person so held struggled in the least. His back to Marino, Ensign Wally Ott blocked and swatted away a steady flurry of blows. He was grinning wildly. Truman Oakes rode the back of a bruiser a third again larger than the black SEAL. Methodically, True Blue slapped bare palms against the huge Marine's ears. Archie Golden exchanged boxing jabs with another redhead in Marine khaki. Doc blinked when he caught sight of a sprawled pile of three Marines in front of Repeat Ditto. The little guy was one hell of a scrapper. True still rode the back of the dazed Marine when heavy boots pounded on the walk outside and the bar girls fled shrieking from the approach of the military police.

Their arrival distracted Archie, who caught a good one on the point of his chin. He grunted, staggered, then unleashed a roundhouse right that decked his adversary in a flash. Naturally the MPs were all over Archie and True Blue in a swarm of black and white armbands and churning, surging batons. Hickory met bone half a dozen times and bone lost. With a soft sigh, True Blue slid from the back of his opponent. Archie went rubber legged, with the scrawny neck of an MP tightly grasped in one hand. In seconds, silence returned to the bar.

"All right, I want you people to line up by groups. And I want the ranking man from each group to step forward," a beet-faced MP sergeant bellowed.

Pope Marino released the gunney, who scurried over to his men at the bar. He recovered himself and turned to step out smartly. "Gunnery Sergeant Clifton! First of the First!" he bellowed.

No-one came forth from the SEALs, all of whom were dressed in civilian clothes. The MP sergeant cut his eyes from one to another, settled on Kent Welby. "What's your rank?"

"Yeoman First Class Kent Welby."

"I guess you're the ranking man."

"No, I'm not."

"Well, then, who the fuck is?"

"I am," Pope Marino said quietly. He unzipped his poplin jacket to reveal his suntan uniform shirt. Above the pockets were a black on tan strip with U. S. NAVY and his name. On the collar gleamed the double silver bars of his rank. "Lieutenant Carl Marino, First Platoon, SEAL Team Two."

Master Sergeant Tucker of the military police exchanged an astonished glance with SFC Ramirez. "Jesus! Officers brawlin' with enlisted? What the hell's going on here—uh—sir?"

Droll humor abounded in Lt. Marino's reply. "These Marines, Master Sergeant—ah—" he glanced at the name tag. "Tucker, apparently became befuddled with too much to drink. They reached the mistaken conclusion that the Navy was a branch of the Marine Corps, not the other way around."

"So you're tryin' to say this was a form of education... sir?"

"Re-indoctrination, more like it. I think if you ask Gunny Clifton, he'll tell you that one of his men launched the first attack."

"We'll get into that down at the Provost Marshal's office. Meanwhile we still have the problem of the damages to this place, the upset of the proprietor, and the distress of his girls."

"No problem. Mr. Ott will you start a collection among the guys?"

Taylor's eyes swung from one man to the other, then settled on Ramirez. "Another fucking—another officer?"

"Looks like it, Sergeant," Ramirez replied. He was no more amused than his superior. "I don't like this at all. There may be some other violations besides disorderly conduct."

"Yeah, I hear you, Ramirez," Taylor went on, ignoring the SEALs. "We might have some other infractions of military law. Like fraternizing with enlisted men."

"That's all bullshit," Pope Marino said sotto voce to Ensign Ott.

"Yeah. You got that right."

Pope Marino extended his remarks to include Sergeants Taylor and Ramirez. "That's bullshit, Sergeant, especially in a combat zone like Vietnam. Having a few drinks with the troops doesn't constitute fraternization. Besides, there's nothing like that in the UCMJ. That comes from the *Officers' Guide*, the leadership manual. We've been out with these guys nearly every night for the last month."

"Don't make it any worse than it is, sir," Taylor advised.

"We happened to be in the bush, Sergeant, getting shot at by Charlie. Where were you?"

Suddenly flustered, conscious of the plush drinking accommodations he visited nightly, Taylor opted to change the subject. "You're gonna walk for now, Cap—er—Lieutenant. Along with most of your men here. These two are goin' with us." He indicated the unconscious forms of True Blue Oakes and Archie Golden. "Disorderly conduct, public drunkenness, and maybe a couple other charges we can hang on them."

Fire sparked in Lt. Marino's eyes. "I'll go with you."

"Sorry, sir. Not enough room in the jeeps. Get them on their feet, Ramirez."

After the MPs had departed with Archie and True Blue, Pope Marino turned out a lexicon of obscenities for a solid five minutes, with his opinion of military police, the Army, and books of regulations in general. "The main thing is to prevent True Blue and Archie from getting put in the local lock-up. Or, springing them if it's already too late. I'm going after them right now."

"I'll go with you, Pope."

"No, Wally. You'd best stay here and keep the lid on." With that Pope was out the door.

Chapter 14

He moved within her, and the world seemed to move in lazy spirals along with their joyous coupling. A heady aroma of clean young woman, consummate sex and a faint miasma of garlic-anchovy Nuoc Mam emanated from Francie Song. Kent Welby groaned involuntarily as he thrust again. Passion's dampness put a thin skein of perspiration over their naked bodies.

Deep within himself, Kent sensed the explosive buildup of their nearing completion. Francie's black hair lay in a fan around her gracefully shaped head, which she thrashed from side to side, her small, white teeth pressed into her lower lip. Three hours earlier they had eaten a light lunch, bought a bottle of rice wine, and found this room in a side street hotel.

Since then they had made delightful, languorous love, the wine left untouched. To his credit, Doc Welby had not expected it. Had not even made preparations for this to happen. In a bizarre way, he looked back on it as a scene out of *The Graduate*; the mature, experienced older woman — though Francie was a good three years younger than Kent — seducing the high school senior. After the first hesitant minutes, the demands of his long, celibate weeks washed away any inhibitions he retained.

He went joyfully into their amorous coupling. And he found it good, oh so good, the best sex he could ever remember. No complications, no strings, no hang-ups. Demandingly, the rush to the pinnacle drove them both into a greater frenzy than either of the previous two engagements. Colored lights burst behind Kent's eyes and he found nirvana in a rose-hued haze of dizzy oblivion.

When reality returned, they lay, still joined, arms and

legs twined in abandon. Kent bent and kissed the hollow of Francie's throat. "You are wonderful," he whispered.

"Thank you, Kent Welby," barely a sigh of sound.

"I believe you are—you do that the best of any woman I've ever known."

A deep, throaty chuckle rose from Francie Song. "And how many are they, Kent Welby?"

That jolted Doc Welby upward onto one elbow, brow worried into furrows. "Just…three. Two girls from school, and my wife." His answer shocked him in its surface inadequacy.

Francie's eyes widened. "You never said you were married, Kent Welby."

"I'm getting a divorce," he blurted and wondered if it sounded as contrived to her as it did to him.

She seemed to ignore it, her mind on other things. "Kent…" Her mode of address alerted Doc that something serious would be forthcoming; Francie only dropped his last name when she had important things on her mind. "I hope you will not be unhappy with me. I am wondering about our future. Where we go from now on? It is not possible that we marry, even if you…divorce your wife."

"Why is that?" Kent surprised himself in asking so forcefully.

Francie lowered her eyes, the long lashes spread on her high cheekbones. "It is…something in my past. You would not be happy to know it." She gave a little toss of her head. "It does not matter, really. Only, if—if we have a child…" Anguish twisted her face momentarily. "Life is hard here, with the fighting and everything. A woman, a mother, must look out as well as she can."

"But, I'll be here to help you," Kent urged.

Francie shook her head. "When your—ah—tour is done, you will be gone. You might not come back. And if you do, it might be to another part of the country. Then I would be — how you say? — devastated." She sighed, gathered her resources and forged on. "That is why it is so important to me. You can help make my future secure. All you need to do is introduce me to someone who can place me in a job inside the compound. You have influence, so does your friend, the big Chief."

"You mean Waters?" Kent had not considered that before. "I suppose he does. He's our platoon chief."

Brightening, Francie tried a fleeting smile. "You see? I so need your aid, so I can help my country and my American friends. Also, I can save enough from what I make so that my future will be secure."

Doc Welby wanted to change the subject. "Tell me about your aunt. How serious is her illness?"

Francie frowned and marshaled her thoughts in order to elaborate. "She is sick enough that they sent for me to come here. It is the—the lung disease."

"Cancer?"

A brief frown deepened lines on her smooth forehead. "No. It is the coughing thing."

"TB."

"What?"

"Tuberculosis."

Francie brightened. "Yes! That is the word the doctor used."

"How did you get here so fast, Francie? We were together at Mi Flower only two nights ago."

She thought on it. "I walked a ways, caught rides with people on the road, and I rode my bicycle the last twenty kilometers. I was very tired when I got here."

Somehow it didn't ring entirely true to Doc. He tried to file it, to worry about later, but it wouldn't go away. Francie began to try to arouse him again and he found his niggling suspicion got in the way of continuing their amorous encounter. At last, before exasperation overtook both of them, he gently disengaged them and sat upright on the bed.

"What about we shower, take an early trip to a bar, then a late supper?"

"That is marvelous, Kent. I would enjoy that very much."

Lt. Carl Marino, admittedly not his best in such situations, ran into the bureaucratic mindset at the Military Police precinct in Saigon. Located near the Binh Wa outdoor market, a sprawling affair, busy from daylight to dark, the Provost office occupied a high-walled, block-sized compound of an old colonial town house. American ingenuity had added a triple concertina of barbed wire to the broken glass that adorned the top of the wall. Inside the cool , dimly lighted interior, Pope Marino quickly watched his remaining restraint dissolve when he confronted the burly, beet-faced desk sergeant.

"What do you mean, no visitors?" Pope asked tightly when refused the chance to talk with his men.

"Those swab jocks are being held on serious charges, Lieutenant. Only their unit's legal officer may interview them."

Steaming, Marino made a snap decision. "Then I just appointed myself my unit's legal officer. I want to see my men."

Aware that the old Army prejudice against the Navy had kicked in, Pope Marino fumed further when the pudgy, soft-handed, short-breathed Senior Master Sergeant produced a nasty smirk. "Can't authorize that myself. You'll have to see the Assistant Provost Marshal."

"Then let me in to see the Assistant Provost Marshal."

Another cat-and-mouse sneer. "Can't do that. He's occupied right now."

Marino didn't even hesitate. "Then goddamnit, get him unoccupied."

Icy anger hardened the plump features of the sergeant's moon face. "That wouldn't be a good idea... *sir*. Major Harkness don't like being disturbed when he's busy. Lots of important cases comes through this office every day. He has only so much time."

"Well fuck that, Sergeant." Lt. Marino had thought his voice to be under control, but it came out even louder than her previous outbursts.

A door opened down the hallway and a pigeon-breasted man of medium height poked his long-lobed head out, an expression of petty annoyance fixed on the sallow complexion of his face, which was puffy with sleep. "Who is responsible for all that racket?" It came out in a querulous high pitch, almost a whine.

The sergeant came to his feet. "A Navy lieutenant, sir. Here about those squids Taylor and Ramirez busted."

Thin, overly-red lips pursed disapprovingly. "Fifteen minutes. I'm busy now."

"You heard the man, Lieutenant… *sir.*" It came late enough to be considered insubordinate.

"I think now would be a good time, Major," Marino grated out.

Meanness showed in the deep, close-set eyes. "What gives you that idea?"

"I'm their platoon leader, also their legal officer." He omitted the obligatory "sir."

Maj. Harkness gaped at such an affront. "What's a Navy full lieutenant doing commanding a platoon? That's a job for second lieutenants in this man's Army."

"I'm OIC for our Team's detachment in-country and Executive Officer of SEAL Team Two, stationed at Little Creek, Virginia." Marino put extra heat in his words.

Maj. Harkness cocked his head to one side. "SEALs, huh? I've heard about you. Come on in. I'll make the time for you."

"You're quite considerate." Marino's sarcasm rolled off the MP officer.

Lt. Marino had seen no one leave the office of the Provost Marshal, and the room was empty except for himself and Maj. Harkness. He saw a half-filled, steaming cup of coffee on the table and an open comic book. How in hell did this guy make field grade? Pope Marino asked himself. Harkness waved toward a chair near his desk and stepped behind it. Marino noticed that the Army officer bit his fingernails.

Harkness drew a slim file from his IN basket, opened it and glanced down the numbered paragraphs. "Now, what's this all about?"

"The two men you have in custody are no more guilty or innocent than any of the men in the two squads involved from our platoon. Nor, of the Marines. Yet, they are the only ones arrested. Can you give me a good reason for that... sir?"

"They were observed still assaulting two Marines after my MPs arrived. Also, one of them assaulted one of my MPs. That's why they were first arrested. They also resisted arrest."

"I beg your pardon, Major, but I was there. I saw what happened."

Maj. Harkness took on another prissy expression and laid three fingers along one cheek, like a Hollywood interior decorator. "Suppose you tell me what you saw that differs from what my sergeants say happened."

"First off, the Marines started the fight by attacking one of my men. They soon had the situation in hand, and the Marines learned that SEALs aren't part of any idlers' deck party. Your MPs burst into that place blowing their whistles and jumped my SEALs before they could even begin to stop what they were doing. They used nightsticks to club both of my men to their knees before they even found out what was going on."

"It says here that when they arrived on the scene, a fight was in progress. That two men were assaulting two Marines and refused to desist when ordered to. After that, my MPs were required to subdue the suspects."

"They took a whole hell of a lot of pleasure in doing so, Major."

"Highly motivated. You seem to have overlooked one important thing. So far, I have declined to press charges against you and the rest of your platoon. You're all walking around free. That can change."

Marino had all he could take of the smug, superior attitude of this two-bit policeman. He was out of his chair in an eye-blink, face ashen with suppressed anger. "Is that a goddamned threat, *sir*?"

"Take it any way you want to, Lieutenant. I'm merely making you aware of the situation."

"Son of a..." Lt. Marino caught himself before he completed another epithet. He drew himself together and calmed his voice, to speak in forced tones of respect. "Permission to interview my men, sir."

"Denied."

"On what grounds?"

"I need the paperwork designating you as legal officer before I can allow that." His nasty smile conveyed the spite behind his words.

"Then I demand a complete list of the charges against them."

"I've already told you. They are being charged with disorderly conduct, public drunkenness, willful destruction of civilian property, and assault of a military policeman, two counts."

"You'll never make it stick," Marino growled.

"Oh, I think I will. Which reminds me, your unseemly outburst has convinced me that SEALs lack self-discipline, and as an object lesson, the two in custody are also going to be charged with impersonating an officer."

"That's ridiculous."

"They were at a table with two officers, socializing and drinking, all in civilian clothes. To me, that's impersonation. You have not been named on any charges as yet. If this case is allowed to proceed through normal channels, and your men take their punishment in an acceptable manner, it is possible that everything else will be forgotten."

Marino stiffened to attention. "Very well, sir. I will see that the paperwork is completed in a timely manner, sir, so the processing can goon in the usual manner, sir." *Like hell it will*, Lt. Marino promised himself.

With a smirk a hair's width short of patronizing, Maj. Ralph Harkness returned the parade ground salute Lt. Carl Marino offered. "Excellent. Now that you see things the Army way, I wish you luck in preparing your defense. Dismissed."

Fuck you too, Pope Marino thought as he set off to join the rest of the platoon and bring them up to date.

Soft music came from a quartet, tastefully seated on a small, spotlighted stage, draped in white and scarlet silk wall hangings. Two violins, a cello, baby-grand piano, and harp. They played a mixture of French country airs, native Vietnamese compositions and selections from the classics. Tastefully masking the low buzz of conversation, it gave the Maison Dupris an elegant air. A leftover from the French Colonial days, the restaurant had maintained a good reputation and steady clientele.

Tom Waters and Eloise Daladier sat in rattan chairs at a small, round table in the salon-bar, sipping drinks. Although reservations had been made and confirmed, they had been shunted off into the bar as were nearly every party with recognizable Americans among the group. Tonto and Eloise spent a pleasant half hour getting reacquainted. Since their meeting in early afternoon, Tonto had sensed a certain urgency about Eloise. If he didn't so strongly doubt a reason for it, he could swear she was in heat.

Eloise sat with her legs crossed, and constantly twitched the toe of one spike-heel shoe. She fidgeted with a bracelet, and stared deeply into Tonto's eyes as into limpid forest pools. They had reached the point of anecdotes about his life before he came to Vietnam when the maitre d' flowed up to their table and interrupted the conversation.

"Mademoiselle Daladier, my abject apologies," a prissy, rotund little man in formal dress gushed in French as he reached their table. "We have at last located your reservations. If you will please come this way."

"*C'est bien*, Gaston, *merci*," Eloise responded. "Isn't he a delight," she addressed to Tonto. "He came to the new owners with the restaurant."

He led them to a slightly larger table in an alcove off the main dining room, bowing and scraping to Eloise and chattering away in French. Once seated, they ordered another round. While Eloise sipped a chilled glass of white wine, and Tonto had a beer, the SEAL Chief watched while Gaston, the maitre d' ran his scam on two more parties of American reporters. He had suspected as much when their reservations had been "lost." Now he had confirmation. Eloise noted his highly amused state and inquired about the cause.

"It's your friend over there, Gaston. He's scamming the customers."

"'Scamming,' what is that?"

"He's conning them. It's a variation on the old bait and switch game. Watch when another group of Americans comes in. They'll insist that they have reservations, which Gaston will regretfully tell them do not exist. They will complain, urge something be done, and end up offering him another large tip for working them in, which Gaston will reluctantly accept. Then he will steer the marks to the bar to wait."

"How can you be sure? You said Americans. I made our reservations and that very thing happened to us."

"Oh, yes. Remember, I asked for our table while you went off to powder your nose? There's no hiding that I'm an American. Good old Gaston went into his act and shoved me off to the bar. Then, when you joined me, he got all ruffled and out of sorts. Nervous as a whore in church... excuse me. Anyway we got our table a lot faster than some of them. No doubt he shares in the extra revenue from more drink sales, maybe even in the tips to bartender and table waiters. It's a neat little racket head waiters use all over the States."

Eloise pulled a face. "That's simply terrible. Why ever do they do such things?"

Tonto gave her an expression of infinite patience. "Because they are in the right place at the right time to get away with it."

Eloise pouted prettily. "What a terribly cynical outlook on life, Tom."

"Hey, I just calls 'em as I sees 'em," he defended with a shrug.

After a sumptuous meal of Veal Stew Provincial, sopped up with thick, crusty French bread, with side dishes of an Asian vegetable that resembled and tasted like Brussels Sprouts, and broiled, stuffed mushrooms, all ordered by Eloise, they enjoyed a demi-tasse with Camambert and water biscuits. When she drained the last of her strong, French roast coffee, Eloise laid long, slender fingers lightly on one of Tonto's wrists.

"I've been thinking. Why don't you come back with me to my room in Press Country at the Internationale? We can have a nightcap."

Having come by his reputation as a Don Juan naturally, Tonto Waters read everything into the invitation that Eloise Daladier intended. He hid a quick grin with one big hand and helped her from the chair. He laid a sizable tip in piasters on the table, paid the tab and they departed.

Outside, the streets of Saigon teemed with humanity, although already ten o'clock at night. They made the four short blocks to the hotel without incident. Up in her room, a cozy cubicle with a sort of half-sitting room appended to the separate bedroom, Eloise poured them balloons of cognac and they drank deeply. She offered a tentative smile, though neither spoke, as Tonto turned out the lights and Eloise started to unbutton her blouse.

Chapter 15

Ensign Wally Ott sat at a table with the men of 1st Platoon in a bistro with the appropriate name of The Navy Bar. How it existed in Saigon, an area of Army dominance, he had no idea. Not that he cared all that much. An angry Lt. Carl Marino joined them there. He quickly enlightened them on the fast shuffle the Army brass was trying to pull.

"What say we pull a jail break?" Repeat Ditto suggested.

"Naw, that wouldn't do," Chips Danner dismissed.

Thoughtfully, Blue Chip Reno offered his option. "Hadn't we ought to get a hold of Mr. Rhodes at Tre Noc? He needs to know what's going on."

"I considered that," Pope Marino replied. "But this is my problem and I want to take care of it right now, from here. And the first thing to do is get a hold of Chief Waters and let him know. Any idea where he is?"

Chips Danner glanced at his wrist watch and wiped a smirk from his face before answering. "Right now, I'd say he is in bed."

Lt. Marino looked at him oddly a moment, then remembered that the Chief had a date with his French reporter. "Yeah. I think you're right. Repeat, you and Fil run him down. You might start at the Hotel Internationale."

A soft knock on the door to the suite of Eloise Daladier brought Tonto Waters instantly awake. For a moment he experienced the confusion of awakening in a strange place. Then he saw the spray of black hair on the pillow beside him and the planes of Eloise's face. He threw back the sheet and swung bare feet and legs out of the bed. Careful not to disturb the sleeping woman, he slid into skivvy shorts and padded out of the bedroom and across the small sitting room to the door.

He opened the little flap on the grill-covered observation port and looked into the hall. His eyebrows rose involuntarily when he recognized BM/1C Chad Ditto. He shut the port and opened the door. Immediately alert to possible trouble, he hissed, "What the hell are you doing here?"

"We've got troubles, Chief," Repeat told him tightly.

Inside the suite, Ditto explained in hushed tones about the fight, the arrests, and the Provost Marshal's plans to throw the book at Archie Golden and True Blue Oakes. Tonto Waters heard it with a growing frown.

"Hell, they can't do that. There's nothin' in the UCMJ about officers choosing to drink with their enlisted men."

"That's what Pope said." Repeat continued up to being sent to find Tonto.

When Tonto got it all, he went to the bedroom and dressed quickly. Then he awakened Eloise.

"Sorry to disturb you, hon, but a problem has come up. I'm going to have to leave."

"What is it?"

Tonto told her what he had learned from Repeat. She responded with indignation. "I'm sorry about Archie and True Blue. Perhaps I can help." Tonto started to protest the impossibility of that, and she hushed him with a finger over his lips. "I know a thing or two about that Major Harkness. He used to be in some staff position in Eye Corps. Battalion Adjutant, I think. There was a big attack, the VC overran the battalion headquarters. Major Harkness deserted his post. That's right, he ran. Only, he has some friends among the American leaders. They arranged to cover it up and had him transferred here to Saigon and put in the Provost Marshal's office. He's not in charge, there's a Colonel Dawson commanding the Military Police. But, Maj. Harkness is a power in his own right. There, does that help you?"

Tonto was grinning while he nibbled at her lovely finger. "You bet it does. Between Pope and me, we can use that some way. Now, good-bye."

"Will I see you tomorrow?"

Tonto glanced at his watch, saw it was still before midnight. "Yeah, sure. If we get this worked out. I'll call you here at the hotel."

"First thing we should do is get a hold of the Old Man. He should be the first one to know, outside of the platoon," Tonto Waters offered when he had rejoined the men of First Platoon.

"You mean Capt. Ackerage?" Repeat Ditto asked.

"No, Repeat," Lt. Marino answered for the platoon chief. "He's talking about Commander Hardy back at Little Creek. I agree, Tonto, but you know what he'll say… that I should take care of it myself. He needs to know, but do we go through channels to do it or call him from here at the air base?"

They all worried that one around a while, still no one had an answer. At last, Ensign Ott risked sounding as green as he felt in this situation by speaking up. "I'd say we had better go through channels. At least that way we get our version across to the Commander first off."

"Right enough," Pope Marino agreed. "That Major Harkness would like nothing more than to send an official notice of the arrests to the Old Man, with his list of bullshit charges."

"Maybe I should be the one to do that. Considering that MP dork's threats, you should lay low, Pope." Ott urged.

Reluctantly, Lt. Marino agreed. The members of first

and second squads finished their beers and made ready to leave for their billets at the Special Forces compound on the edge of Ton Son Nhut air base. That would require navigating the streets of Saigon in cyclos, operated by girls, and a few boys, barely in their teens. It was decided that Pope would spend the night at a small *pension* at the end of Embassy Row. What the morning would bring, none of them knew.

Strident ringing from the telephone across the room from his bunk in the Bachelor Officers Quarters (BOQ) at Binh Thuy air base aroused LCDR Barry Lailey shortly after 0300 hours. Bleary-eyed, his head fogged from too many cigars and too much bourbon, Lailey dragged his way from bed and stumbled over the bare floor to silence the noise.

"Who the hell's calling at this hour?" he muttered aloud.

It didn't make him any happier to learn that it was Ensign Ott from First Platoon, Team 2. Nor did it please him, at first, to hear the nature of the call. "Sir, we're in Saigon," Ott started after identifying himself.

"I know that," Lailey growled.

"There's been some trouble, sir." He went on to describe the provocations by the Marines, the attack by one of them, and the resultant arrest of MA/1C Richard Golden and MM/1C Truman Oakes."

Fully awake now, LCDR Lailey snarled into the mouthpiece, "Where's Marino? Hell, he should be taking care of this."

"He knows that, too, sir. Only, there have been some threats made by the Army's Provost Marshal." Wally Ott gave an account of the shenanigans the ground pounders had in mind for Pope Marino, effectively rendering him helpless.

A broad smile spread on the face of LCDR Lailey as

he heard the details. How fortunate he had given orders that any messages from 1st Platoon, Team 2 be routed through his office at any time of day or night. And what a good way to get that snake Marino into some deep shit with the brass hats, he thought gleefully. That way, his hands would be clean, and it would appear Marino's ineptitude finally caught up with him.

"Sir? Are you still there, sir?" Ott squawked over the crackling wire from Saigon.

Lailey jerked his attention back to the conversation. "Yes—yes, Mr. Ott. What was it you were saying?"

"I want to get a report of the incident through channels to Commander Hardy at Little Creek, sir. As CO of Team 2, he should know at once, right, sir?"

"Certainly." Lailey thought rapidly. He would have to somehow see that the Army version of events got to the Team commander. "I'll take care of everything. Don't you worry about that. All you have to do is look out for our Lieutenant Marino. Now, let me get what sleep I can for the rest of this night." LCDR Lailey hung up, then immediately raised the handset and the switchboard call burred in his ear.

"NAVSPECWARV headquarters, Binh Thuy, sir. Yeoman Second Willis. How may I help you, sir?"

A new kid, LCDR Lailey speculated. He didn't recognize this as an internal call. "This is LCDR Lailey, Willis. Get me the flight line, helicopter ready room."

"Aye-aye, sir."

"Chopper hut. Sergeant Gargan, sir."

"This is the S-2, NAVSPECWAR. Do you have a bird ready to fly?"

"Yes, sir," more alertness in Gargan's voice now. "We always do."

"How soon can you arrange a flight for me to Saigon?"

Purple clouds made an orange lattice of the eastern horizon as the Huey bearing LCDR Barry Lailey flew crabwise across the threshold at Ton Son Nhut air base in Saigon. The constant vibration of the tired old insectile craft had given Lailey a hellish headache. Right then, dawn held no promise at all for him.

"Face it, it's a fucking hangover," he grumbled to himself.

The crew chief saw LCDR Lailey's lips moving and wondered if the chubby desk sailor was praying for a safe landing. Ahead on the elevated flight deck, the pilot continued toward the series of landing pads, directed by the traffic controller in the tower. A strobe winked whitely on the middle one. In a swift, sharp maneuver, that had LCDR Lailey's stomach threatening to rebel, he yanked the chopper around and flared out over the indicated landing site. Slowly he settled to the concrete.

"You can unfasten now, Commander," the Marine sergeant told Lailey as the main rotor spun down to lazy turns at 20 rpm.

LCDR Lailey wanted desperately to go somewhere private and puke his guts out. He hated flying, and helicopters in particular. He'd not likely get the chance he acknowledged dumbly when he saw that there was not a jeep waiting for him. First he would have to walk what looked to be a quarter goddamned mile to the nearest buildings. He climbed in ungainly fashion out of the chopper and noticed at once that the creases in his suntan trousers had been shot to hell. The wrinkles made him look like a bag of dirty laundry. He could feel the wetness of a large patch of fear-sweat in the middle of his back.

When the pilot emerged, Lailey turned to him. "Does your ready-room here have clean-up facilities? I need a shower and shave, get squared away before I report in."

"Yes, Commander. And there's a gook, hurry-up laundry just outside the fence," the Marine Corps warrant officer informed him pleasantly.

"Marvelous. You fly-boys have all the comforts of home."

The pilot didn't like the epithet, but what the hell. This pudgy desk jockey outranked him by more stripes on the sleeve than he'd ever see. "You've got it pretty nice at Binh Thuy, too, sir. With all the gear the construction guys brought in, I like it well enough. Remember, there's enough of us now that we don't rotate back here to Saigon any more."

Lailey nodded curtly. He knew that, should have remembered it. Never mind, he chided himself, as he struck out for the small building beside the nearest hanger, the one with a red-globed light over the door. Lailey wondered if that had been done out of a sense of irony. Well, he had time. A check of the luminous dial of his wristwatch showed him two hours before he would present himself at 0800 hours to the Army's Provost Marshal of central Saigon precinct.

While LCDR Barry Lailey busied himself with washing away his fear of flying, a courier delivered an intelligence report to KGB Station Chief Kovietski. The major from the Komitet was drinking strong mint tea from a tall glass. A plate of blinis (blintzes to the Jewish people the Soviets so thoroughly hated), smothered in sour cream, with genuine Beluga caviar dotted on top, sat on the table near his elbow. Those items constituted his usual breakfast, along with a bowl of assorted sliced fruit.

"Thank you, Comrade Phong. It will be some while before there is a reply."

After dismissing the courier, Kovietski opened the security envelope and extracted a flimsy sheet from a One

Time Pad. The chemically treated paper, developed in the KGB laboratories under the Lefortovo Prison on Dzerzhinsky Square, had so low a flash point that a common clothes iron would turn it to a ball of flame. From his safe he took his code book and began to decrypt the message. A smile spread on his face as words formed on the page.

"So," Kovietski said aloud, "the SEALs from Team 2 will soon no longer be a problem. Two of them are under arrest with serious charges leveled. That's interesting. So is this," he addressed to the lithe, lovely young woman lounging in the bed across the room. "Their OIC is under a cloud. My source in Saigon is even more efficient than you, my dear. Almost as good as my primary agent in place in the Delta. This has brightened my day considerably."

"What about me, Alexi?" the young Asian woman asked pettishly. "Did I not brighten your day?"

"Of course you did. Now, I have work to do. Get out. You have your orders. See that Cambodian idiot pours all his brains out through his *moojskay polovay chlee*." He doubted that she understood the Russian for penis, but she should get the idea.

Kovietski pretended to ignore her completely while she pouted and dressed. A good agent, yes, and a tremendous experience in bed, but she lacked both imagination and ambition. If not for her 98% eiditic memory, her value would be reduced to seducing government ministers for the cameras in order to compromise them. When he heard the latch click behind her, he completed his messages and headed to the communications room to send them to General Hoi and Moscow Central.

YO/1C Kent Welby returned to the SF compound in time for morning chow. He was greeted glumly by the members of first squad. When he heard the reason why anger flared in his slate-gray eyes.

"What are we doing about it?" he demanded.

"Standing by and waiting. Mr. Ott sent word to Little Creek. It'll be up to what Commander Hardy decides how we take it from there," Tonto Waters told him.

"But that's not good enough," Doc Welby protested. "We've got to get Archie and True Blue out of there. Damnit, from the way you tell it, those jarheads attacked the squad first."

"True. But the MPs are achin' for an excuse to put us all in the brig," Tonto reasoned with him, then changed the subject. "How'd your night go?"

Doc still lacked enough in experience with women to blush. "Great. Really a terrific night. How about you?"

Tonto shrugged. Unwilling to add to the legend, he answered evasively. "I got interrupted by this mess before much went on."

Doc Welby shrugged. "Well, there's always the next time."

Rubbing his palms together, Tonto produced a leer. "Yeah. And with this thing at a standstill, that's gonna be this afternoon."

Lt. Carl Marino awakened in a strange room, with a jumble of foreign languages flying through the open window, and the odor of long untended, wet diapers seeping under the door. Kidneys being boiled, he recognized from a trip to England. Then he remembered the previous afternoon and evening and knew the reason for all this oddness around him. He sighed heavily as he reviewed the difficulties he faced. At least by now, Mr. Ott would have spoken to Cmdr. Hardy. He had better get squared away and head out to the Special Forces camp.

He crawled out of bed to tend to a shower, shave and dress in fresh clothing. Again the haunting acceptance of how and why first squad had gotten into trouble gave him a powerful goad to return to the Provost Marshal's office and try again to reason with Maj. Harkness. To do that, he knew, he had to have a trump card to take the trick. From a small, giddy corner of his mind came the suggestion; perhaps a big club.

But that, Pope Marino knew would be a fool's errand.

LCDR Harry Lailey reached the military police compound at 0800 hours. He was informed by the master sergeant behind the desk that Major Harkness arrived at 0900. He was welcome to wait, or he could go grab coffee and a roll at one of the vendors in the open air market. Lailey chose the latter.

Women with net bags or wicker baskets thronged the huge square. While Lailey gingerly sipped coffee strong enough to climb out of the cup and walk for itself, they selected from among a plethora of fresh fruits, vegetables, fish, ducks, chickens and the pink carcasses of plump puppies. When he recognized the young dogs, it turned Lailey's stomach. He returned to the Provost Marshal's compound in time to see Maj. Ralph Harkness enter his office.

"If you don't mind, sir, give him five minutes to pour coffee and get settled and you can go in."

"Thank you, Sergeant," Lailey replied, barely restraining his impatience.

"When LCDR Lailey entered the office, he received everything but a cordial welcome. "Commander Lailey," Maj. Harkness grated icily. "You're here to try to talk me into dropping charges against your sailors, right?"

"SEALs, Major. They are SEALs. Very elite troops, expensive to train, too. So, what I came for is to assure you that so long as the enlisted men involved do not face a General Court, nothing will be done by the Navy to thwart your prosecution. In particular, it would be viewed favorably if some charges could be brought against Lt. Carl Marino."

Surprise raised the shaggy brows of Maj. Harkness. "I'll admit I am curious. Tell me why not?"

LCDR Lailey had quickly sized up Maj. Harkness as a kindred soul. He felt he could talk frankly. First, the "official" version he had contrived on the way here, then he'd see how Harkness reacted. "Marino is an unfit leader, a loose cannon. If he could be busted out of the SEALs, it might be called 'for the good of the service,' if you catch my meaning."

Maj. Harkness grew a shrewd expression. "There must be more. Tell me."

Lailey framed his features in sincerity. He sighed heavily, as though reluctant to elaborate. "Marino is a considerable thorn in my side." He paused. "May I be frank?" At the curt nod from Harkness, he went on. "I would consider it a personal favor if the book could be thrown at Marino, and his two men, to a lesser degree."

Maj. Ralph Harkness found himself hearing the unbelievable, if not the unheard of. Intramural feuds and politicking went on all the time, but inter-service cooperation in such a vendetta? According with his doubts, he carefully framed his reply.

"Supposing, just supposing, this could be accomplished, I can honestly say I would have no objection. However, my responsibility is directly to the area Special Warfare commander, General Belem. The outcome will rest with him."

Lailey knew that to be not true, yet did not contradict. He put on a cat-full-of-cream smile and spoke with lowered voice. "Well, then, there's nothing can be done, is there?" He'd won and he knew it. "I think we understand each other perfectly. So I'll bid you a good morning."

"Do you have transportation?" Maj. Harkness asked solicitously.

"As a matter of fact, I don't."

"I'll see you have a jeep, Commander."

LCDR Lailey left the Provost Marshal's office with a lightened step. Half way down the steps he caught himself humming a snatch of a popular tune. Sure as that Army stuffed-shirt hated sailors, Carl Marino was about to get his, and good.

Chapter 16

While LCDR Lailey rode out to the air base in an MP jeep, Lt. Carl Marino strived to keep out of sight, or so he believed it, by taking breakfast in the Special Forces officers' mess. He had just shoveled a thick wedge of juicy ham and a fluff of scrambled eggs into his mouth when a familiar voice assailed him from behind.

"Carl Marino, isn't it?"

Lt. Marino turned in his chair and saw a familiar face. "Bud? Bud Eccels, right?" A genuine smile lighted Pope's face for the first time since the dust-up in the bar.

"In the flesh. You remember Randy Andy, don't you?" Another young officer came forward, a green beret, emblazoned with the turquoise arrowhead patch with upright sword and three gold lightning streaks of 5th Special Forces, cocked at a rakish angle on top of a head of curly, yellow-brown locks.

Pope Marino placed them then. Bud Eccels and Bill Andrews. The three of them had gone through Ranger School together. Make that suffered through, Marino amended.

"May we join you?" Bud Eccels asked.

"Sure, there's plenty of table."

Andrews looked at the black-on-green collar tab on Marino's shirt. "I see you made Cap—ah—Lieutenant, that's what you guys call it right?"

"That's right, Bill. You can't tell the difference in these field insignia, but I assume you're both first lieutenants now."

"Oh, yeah. And soon to be captains, if the rate of attrition continues like it's been going," Bud Eccels told him.

"I gather you've been getting hit pretty hard," Marino offered quietly.

"That we have. Say, what brings you to our bailiwick?" Bill Andrews asked.

"We're here on some R and R."

"You've been in-country long?"

"A month and a half."

Bud and Bill exchanged envious glances and decided to laugh at it. "You Navy guys have got it made, Marino. The closest we've been to rape and regurgitation in six months is this joint right here, and then only a day or two, every other week."

"I told you you should have joined the Navy," Marino said through a chuckle.

"You don't exactly look like you're enjoying your liberty," Bud prompted.

"I'm not." Pope Marino debated whether to launch into an explanation, only to have the decision taken from him.

"You step into some deep shit?" Bill Andrews asked.

From the far-off look in their eyes, Pope Marino could tell that these guys had been to the mountain, seen the elephant, and watched too many guys buy the farm. When he ran out of cliches, he shook his head in self-reproof over the inconsequential nature of his own difficulties, then rearranged his thoughts to tell them about it in the least dramatic way.

When Pope finished the tale, Bud Eccels eyed him levelly. "You should take this directly to General Belem."

"Oh? Why's that?" What possible interest could the COSPECWARV have in a run-in with the MPs?

"Belem thinks the sun rises and sets in SEAL asses," Bill Andrews advised him. "When he did an information tour of the school and later observed some of your training ops, he came away impressed. He's also aware that SEALs in airborne training, Ranger school and E and E consistently come out in the top ten graduates. You really ought to talk to him."

"Bill's right. This Harkness is a nasty little prick. He's fucking you over for sure. Hell, we mingle with our enlisted men. We work together, drink together, fight together, call one another by first names, it's no big deal and Harkness damn well knows that," Bud Eccels volunteered.

"That bastard Harkness is a coward, too. He bugged out when his battalion headquarters got temporarily over ran. He's the original brown nose, with loads of friends among the REMF officer corps."

"'REMF?'" Pope Marino asked, unfamiliar with the acronym.

"A Sneaky Pete term," Bud Eccels explained. "It stands for Rear Echelon Motherfucker. Anyway," he took up Bill Andrews' enlightenment, "instead of a General Court, he got transferred here to Saigon and put in as assistant provost marshal. A little more ass kissing and the whole incident was covered up."

"Sounds like someone I know only too well," Pope offered, an image of Barry Lailey fresh in his mind. If those two ever got connected up, his ass would be thoroughly fried.

"Anyway, finish your breakfast and go see the general," Eccels urged. "If nothing else, he'll be glad to get to talk to a real, fire-breathing SEAL again."

Pope Marino took their advice. The last crumb wiped from his chin, he left the officers' club and crossed the compound to the headquarters building. Inside he stopped before a clerk's desk, gave his name and stated his purpose in talking to the general. The Spec-2 (Specialist Second Class, a technician, as opposed to Corporal for a combat arm) sent him to the Brigade Sergeant Major.

"Sergeant Major," Pope addressed himself to the burly green beanie with enough rockers, hash marks and a diamond in his chevrons to give added weight to the sleeve. "I need to speak with General Belem."

"Sorry, Lieutenant. The general is in an intelligence

briefing and can't be disturbed for the rest of the day. If you come back at 0830 hours tomorrow, I'll see if he will receive you."

Nothing else for it. "I'll do that," Pope pledged. Without delay, he left the headquarters to look for his men.

This is as exciting as watching concrete harden, Tonto Waters thought as he forced an expression of interest and a smile onto his face. Nothing as yet had come through channels from Commander Hardy at Little Creek, so the platoon had nothing to act upon to benefit Golden and Oakes. He had allowed Eloise to talk him into taking in the sights — such as they were —in Saigon. They stood across the street now from the high wall that surrounded a rectangular, three story structure, its facade ornately decorated in Oriental bass reliefs.

"This is, or was, the colonial administration building. The Directory had offices here, as did the trade commission, the provincial Chamber of Deputies, and the courts. It was all subservient to the French Colonial Government in Hanoi, of course, but it served well to establish the structure of self-government when the French left. It is now occupied by an annex of the United States embassy."

"Of all the things we have a surplus to export, it's bureaucrats," Tonto observed.

"Maybe someone in there could help your friends?" Eloise suggested.

"Naw. It's a Navy problem and it'll have to be handled the Navy way. Is there a place around here where we can grab something to eat and a cold beer?"

"There's a food shop near the river docks that has marvelous fresh prawns and hot and sour soup. It's not far."

"Good. Lead the way."

After a three block walk, Eloise steered Tonto around a corner and stopped at a hole in the wall eaterie that consisted of a doorway and window joined together and converted into a counter top. It featured stand-up tables built around upright posts which supported a large awning. Pedestrian traffic steered around the outer fringe, or threaded obliviously through the clusters of diners, who ignored them in turn. The tangy, salt-sweet aroma of steaming seafood reached their nostrils from half a block away. Huge copper woks steamed and bubbled on charcoal fires, tended by boys of 12 or 13, who looked and dressed alike in sweat-grayed T-shirts and short khaki pants.

A balding man with the permanent sun-darkened skin of a fisherman perched on a high stool behind the counter. His perpetual grin revealed three prominently missing teeth. Beside him a girl in her late teens oversaw the cashbox and added up the tabs on an abacus, which she double-checked on a calculator. Eloise ordered for them in singsong Vietnamese and the proprietor sprang into action.

He came off his stool with fluid grace and snatched two deep bowls from a stack beside the nearest wok. Into them he ladled some clear noodles, and topped them with a generous portion of heads-on prawns in the shells. He topped that with a garnish of chopped scallions and fresh Chinese parsley, added a wedge of lemon, and slapped them down on a serving tray. He added small, covered bowls of rice, then ducked below the counter to come up with two long neck bottles of *Tiger* beer from Singapore.

Tonto Waters eyed the latter with sincere appreciation. No question that the blackmarket was alive and well in Saigon. He began to salivate in appreciation. The girl picked up the tray and led them to a vacant table.

Following Eloise's lead, Tonto pulled the head and shell from a huge prawn and took a bite. His eyes closed involuntarily while he chewed and savored. His face took on a beatific expression. Eloise stifled a tiny, unladylike giggle.

"Didn't I tell you they were delicious?" she prodded.

"They have 'em like this in New Orleans, steamed I mean. Only...the taste isn't the same. These are unreal. The best I've ever eaten."

"Enjoy, then we'll go on to the botanical garden."

It took less than five minutes for Tonto Waters to discover that he could do without the botanical garden. Every day he saw dozens of varieties of the plant life exhibited when they went into the bush. The only difference, he had to acknowledge, was that at least here it was in orderly arrangement, and he didn't have to worry about Charlie jumping up and taking a shot at him. He did find the display of the hundred varieties of rice that grew in Vietnam to be of interest. He was also getting thirsty, and he could not stop worrying about what was being done for Archie and True Blue. After a gaggle of school children drifted away from the rice display, he took Eloise aside.

"Look, hon, we've had a great day. I've enjoyed everything so far. But, I'm getting worried about not knowing what is going on. I need to check in with the guys and see if there's any progress on getting Archie and True Blue out of the brig."

Eloise put a hand on one of his wrists. Her face clouded for a moment, then cleared as she made an effort to be supportive. "I understand. You can't have too good of a time while being constantly distracted. Go on. If you can, we'll have dinner together tonight?"

"Of course." He bent down to her upturned face and kissed her lightly on her soft lips. A light squeeze of her shoulders and he was gone.

Chief Tom Waters found Kent Welby and Chad Ditto in the Special Forces NCOClub, huddled over beers. He reversed a chair, his preferred way of sitting in one, and folded forearms over the back.

"We've gotta have a strategy meeting," Tonto announced to the pair.

"About what?" Repeat Ditto asked.

"About this mess the Skipper, Archie, an' True have gotten into. The way I see it, those bars on Pope's shoulder could get in the way of an easy solution. Which means, as usual, it's gonna be up to us ratings to get things done."

Repeat produced a puckish expression. "Any bright ideas?"

Before answering, Tonto let his gaze roam over the room, took in the off-duty Green Berets drinking, playing pool and tossing darts. "Maybe we could get some help from these guys," he suggested.

"How do you figure that would do any good?" Chips Danner asked as he approached the table and took a seat.

Kent Welby had picked up on Tonto Waters' direction and waved a hand to encompass the other occupants of the club. "You know how different we found things at Coronado? All spit and polish, and a mile wide gulf between officers and enlisted, right? Take a look at these Sneaky Petes. They're alot like us. Their officers dress down and socialize with the men."

"Then, why can't the rest of the army be like them?" Repeat asked plaintively.

"You're right on target, Doc," Tonto advised. "To answer your question, Repeat, I been thinkin' that it's sure as hell that those MPs aren't bustin' any of these SF guys for petty shit like they did our guys. So I was thinkin', why not ask some of them, find out how they get away with it."

Repeat Ditto's eyes sparkled. "Maybe they know a way to put some pressure on that Major."

That got Tonto to thinking again. "Hey, maybe you're right. Remember that it was the Special Forces commander who got us this liberty. What we ought to be askin' them is how approachable this General Belem is. All it'll cost us is for a few beers. Let's get at it."

Half an hour of buying beer, glad handing, and slapping backs brought the four SEALs welcome information. General Belem was considered *very* approachable by the men who served under him. Although a West Pointer, he went out in the field with the troops, jumped with them whenever he could, and, much against advice and regulations, had even gone out on several ops up around the DMZ.

Highly pleased with the results, Tonto Waters suggested the outline of their campaign. "We've gotta look up Mr. Ott first off. Then we lay out what we want to tell the general."

Ensign Wally Ott looked up from the three day old copy of the *New York Times* he was reading when the four enlisted men entered the lounge of the Special Forces officers' mess. "Well, then, you look a serious lot." Reading the precise language of the *Times* gave him a flare of British accent.

"We are, sir," Tonto Waters spoke for the quartet. Quickly he outlined their idea for helping Lt. Marino and the pair in jail. Wally Ott nodded and listened patiently, then spoke up.

"We're ahead of you on that, Chief. Pope has an appointment to talk to General Belem in the morning."

"Leave it to Pope to figure this thing out," Waters observed with relief. Now, they'd damn well get something done.

Sr. Lt. Alexi Gregoravich Kovietski sat in a comfortable chair in his Cambodian headquarters. To his immediate left was his assistant *resedentura* of the KGB, Captain Feodor Viktoravich Dudov. Short, thick, burly, and cotton-haired, he looked every bit the Ukranian peasant his father had been. Seated across the low coffee table from them was a slender man of small stature. The shape of his head, with its almond eyes and light olive complexion, and the little, precise mouth marked Maxim Maximovich Yoriko as an Asiatic Soviet citizen, with more than a touch of Mongol in his bloodline. As such, he easily passed for a Cambodian or Vietnamese. Kovietski sat down the tulip glass half-filled with vodka.

"Feodor, old friend, I am placing in your hands the logistical planning for distribution of the supplies for the offensive Gen. Hoi is planning. I'm confident you can bring some order and efficiency to this demented scramble of small sampans and men strange to the territory. Likewise, I have something quite out of the ordinary for you, which I will mention later." He turned his attention to young Maxim Yoriko.

"*Tovarisch* Yoriko, I am pleased with your progress so far," Kovietski praised. "With the information we receive from dear little Quan, you have been able to penetrate deeply into the Cambodian government." The smile lines around Kovietski's eyes tightened. "Now, I have a new, very special assignment for you. It is absolutely vital that Agent *Koar* penetrates the operations office at the American Navy base at Tre Noc. I want you to go there and work with her, make sure she evades their security measures and relays useful information to you. You are to transmit it from the west bank of the river across from the base. I want everything, even if what she tells you sounds trivial."

"I understand, Comrade Major," Yoriko responded. "What cover shall I use? Rice farmer again?"

"No. There is little rice grown in the area. A sampan will be made available to you. You can work as a ferry service. It might be you will even make a little profit from the lazy Americans. Whatever you do," Kovietski cautioned, "keep a low profile."

"That should be easy. The Riverine sailors are used to seeing sampans."

Kovietski shook his head tightly. "Maxim, my friend, it is not the River Tigers I worry about. Tre Noc has become the newest base of operations for a platoon of Navy SEALs. They are very smart, very dangerous men. It would be wise for you to stay out of their sight as much as possible."

Chapter 17

At 0830 hours the next morning, Lt. Carl Marino, Ensign Walter Ott, and Chief Thomas Waters entered the headquarters orderly room at the Special Forces compound. The Brigade Sergeant Major passed them on to a major, who turned them over to a Lt. Colonel, who listened as politely as the other two and escorted them to the office of General Ian Belem.

Gen. Belem greeted them warmly. "It's always nice to meet some of the Navy's finest, gentlemen. Come in, sit down, would you care for coffee? I can even offer some Jamaican rum to spike it with."

Tonto Waters winced. The squad had celebrated the previous night to the expense of his throbbing head. "Coffee's fine, sir," he announced after the officers had responded.

"I hope you like it. It's also from Jamaica, Blue Mountain as a matter of fact. Crebs here grinds it fresh from beans for each pot."

After the orderly, Crebs, had poured for those assembled, and departed, the general sipped appreciatively and set his cup aside with some reluctance. "Now, tell me, what brings you to my office?"

Not bad coffee, Tonto Waters thought as Lt. Marino began his explanation. "A couple of my men were arrested as a result of a brawl with a group of Marines in the American Eagle bar, down on Truman Key the other day. They were the only ones arrested out of two of my squads and a dozen Marines. When I went to try to talk the military police out of charging them, I found that the Assistant Provost Marshal, a Major Harkness, had made up a long set of charges from whole cloth."

"Where were you, that it took so long to get there so Harkness had a chance to exercise his creative talent?"

"I was at the bar. I went directly there, behind the MPs who took my men in custody." It had all been too convenient. In retrospect, it looked to Pope Marino as though the MPs had come with the express purpose of arresting some of the SEALs, and that the charges had been trumped up in advance. To voice such thoughts to the general would sound paranoid, so he withheld comment. He went on to explain the list of charges, ending with that of impersonating an officer.

Gen. Belem's scowl deepened as Marino named each accusation. When Marino concluded, he exploded with a slap of one big palm on the arm of his swivel chair. "That's a lot of bullshit! Hell, better than three-quarters of my officers drink with their detachments. We live... and work too close for it to be any other way. Harkness knows that. But, Ralph Harkness has a couple of major flaws. One, he absolutely hates the Navy and anyone connected to it. The other is that I personally think he's an arrogant, self-important little prick. Yellow as the underside of a channel cat, too," the general added, his mid-West origins slipping out. He paused, looking from one man to the next.

"That's all? Nothing to add to this?" Again Gen. Belem hesitated, head cocked to one side, an expression of deep calculation on his face. "Harkness screwed up big time at Eye Corps. He's here on the good graces of the CO at MACV. They were classmates at the Point. Considering that Harkness has been passed over twice for promotion, he's going to retire in the grade he's now holding. It would be nice to get something on him that would send him back to the States. However, that might put him in a position to do greater harm than he does in-country.

"I digress, gentlemen," the general declared as he stood to his full, lean, mean, crew-cut six foot two height. "Something can be done about this, and I'm going to do it right now. I want you to stand fast, while I make a phone call. I think you'll like it."

Gen. Belem reached for a standard, civilian telephone and dialed zero. "This is General Belem. Get me the Central Saigon Provost Marshal's office. Major Ralph Harkness." He drank off the remainder of his coffee while he waited, then his face suffused with scarlet when a tinny voice rattled in his ear.

"I don't give a damn if he's having a major coronary. I want him on the line now!"

Another, higher, voice squawked through the ear piece. "What's the meaning of this? I left word that I was not to be disturbed."

"This is General Ian Belem, Harkness. I'm certain you didn't mean to have that apply to me."

"Oh! Well, no, not at all, sir. May I inquire what you called about, sir?"

"I understand you are holding two sailors in your jail, subject to charges under the UCMJ. Is that correct?"

"Yes, sir, a couple of SEALs. Ill-disciplined louts if I must say so, sir. The charges and specifications are being drawn up as we speak, sir."

"Were any others charged? Say, any among the Marines who were involved, or the other SEALs?"

"Ah—er—no, sir. There are some possible charges against the SEAL commander, a Lieutenant. ." His mouth snapped shut as Gen. Belem interrupted.

"Lt. Marino, Carl," Gen. Belem growled. "May I ask why none of the others were taken into custody? From what I have learned, the Marines started the fight."

"No, sir, not that I could a certain, sir. When my men came on the scene, the only ones fighting were the two SEALs, attacking two Marines."

Howling down from Antarctica's Mt. Ross, a winter's gale held not a degree less frigidity than the voice of General Belem. "You are aware that as SEALs, they are members of the *United States* Navy, and as such, that

Navy is our ally, not the enemy, Major Harkness?"

Stunned by this sudden change in the general's attitude, Maj. Harkness stood gape-mouthed a moment before stammering a reply. "Wh—why—why, certainly, sir. It's just that their infractions were so blatant, and they are so obviously guilty, sir, I wanted it handled in a timely manner."

"You sound like a fucking lawyer, Harkness. Now, as to those Statements of Charges. They are not to be completed."

"I—beg your pardon, General? May I ask why?"

"Because those men are not to be charged with anything."

"Why not?" Harkness rallied his flagging determination. "I believe that those SEALs, as an organization, need an object lesson."

"Hear me clearly, you blithering idiot. You are going to personally release those two SEALs, and give them an apology from the Army to the Navy, which had better come from the bottom of your heart. Furthermore, all notes and records of the incident are to be—and I'll give you another asshole lawyer word — expunged."

"Sir! I must protest, sir. There are regulations..."

Gen. Belem cut him off. "Screw your regulations, Major. There are also regulations about desertion in the face of the enemy, during combat. Perhaps you'd like me to file some charges of my own?"

Everyone in General Belem's office could almost visualize Maj. Harkness turning white. His violent gulp was audible over the phone. "Sir, please, that's in the past. The entire affair has been laid to rest."

"Only so long as I chose not to resurrect it, Harkness. Now, stop acting like a moron and do as you're told." He slammed down the handset and turned to a thoroughly impressed Lt. Marino. "Now that this matter has been attended to, I would strongly suggest that you pick up your men and get the hell and gone out of Saigon, ASAP."

Pope Marino drew himself up and saluted smartly. His subordinates did likewise. "Aye-aye, sir. Right away, sir. And…ah—thank you, sir."

Lt. Carl Marino had left the Provost Marshal's office with Archie Golden and True Blue Oakes in tow only an hour before Eloise Daladier made an appearance there. When told of her presence, still smarting over his humiliation at the hands of Gen. Belem, Maj. Harkness at first thought of refusing to see her. Then a tantalizing waft of her perfume reached him behind his desk. Sure couldn't be a hatchet-faced bull dyke and smell like that, Harkness considered, relying on his faulty impression of female journalists.

"Send her in, Sergeant," he rumbled, hand reaching for a fresh pack off lip-top Marlboros.

"Major Harkness," Eloise purred as she entered, the glove from her right hand clutched in the left, while she extended the bare one in greeting.

"Mademoiselle Daladier," he said, almost breathless. Harkness rose and took her hand with self-conscious grace, and bent to kiss it in a gesture of imagined gallantry. "What a distinct pleasure to meet you. I have ready our articles. I must say I am impressed."

"*Parlez vous francais?*"

"Uh—no, I don't speak French. I have read you in the English edition of *Le Monde*. It's popular here among the staff officer corps. At least we get an unbiased view of the war." He gave an affected chuckle, to show he was a man of the world. "But, I digress. What brings you to the office of a mere policeman?"

"More like a Poirot than a mere policeman from what I've heard," she unashamedly flattered him. "To be frank, there is a case in which you've become involved of late that has caught my interest. I was recently in the Delta.

There I encountered some of your Navy's elite special warfare personnel. The—ah—SEALs? Now I understand that some of your military police have arrested some SEALs. Is that correct?"

Stinging from the demeaning manner in which Gen. Belem handled the situation, Maj. Harkness sought a sympathetic ear. To achieve his goal, he realized he would have to lay a trap. So he couched his reply accordingly.

"I'm sorry, I'm not certain of what arrests you refer to."

"The incident in the American Eagle bar," Eloise answered levelly. "It was my impression that some Marines were involved, along with the SEALs."

Harkness tried to keep control of his voice and hold a neutral expression when he replied. "There have been no charges brought. The men involved have been questioned and released."

"And that is all there is to it? All you know?"

Harkness spread his hands, pudgy palms up. "No, Mademoiselle, it is not all I know. A moment ago you referred to the SEALs as elite Naval special warfare forces. I am sorry to say they are far from that. These so-called elite warriors are nothing more than loose cannons. They disgrace the uniform and make all Americans lose face in front of the Vietnamese. If you were favorably impressed by them in the Delta, I must say that they could not be the same individuals who came to the attention to our MPs."

Unable to contain herself, Eloise Daladier's hackles rose. "They happen to be the exact same men I met in the Delta. As a matter of fact, their platoon chief and I were having a drink in the Carousel Lounge at the time the fight happened. Perhaps I could fill out my article if you would be so kind as to explain a similar incident that involved Army personnel and the Marines three weeks ago, in which no charges resulted? Or a large brawl in the Jade Curtain Lounge on Truman Key a month ago between Air Force and Army troops. Only the Air Force men were charged with anything, as I recall." At Harkness' increasingly grim expression, Eloise make her voice nasty and biting.

"And there was that little scandal involving a staff officer of Eye Corps. Seems he ran in the face of the enemy. You wouldn't know anything about that, would you, Major?"

"*Out!*" Harkness shrieked, his face ashen. "Get out of this office. The interview is at an end."

"I'll go, Major. I require my press pass too much to try to directly —how you say? — bump heads with you. Only this isn't the end of my interest. It's just the beginning."

Archie Golden clapped his hands together then reached into his ditty bag for afresh can of PX beer. It was Millers' and still cold. He popped the tab, flipped it toward the open door of the Huey and leaned back for a long, soul-soothing swallow. Then he sighed and began to expand over the intercom on their incarceration.

"Well, as brigs go, it wasn't so bad. Only thing, the Army seems to be full of junkies. They had more guys in there for shootin' heroin into their arms, and smoking wacky tabacky than for any other crime. Most of the ground pounders treated us like celebrities. No love lost between them and the jarheads. The food was lousy. I mean real rotten. Right True?"

"I've swilled hogs with stuff smelled better than that tasted," True Blue Oakes agreed.

"Did they use rubber hoses on you, Archie?" Repeat Ditto asked.

"Naw. They didn't even question us. Why bother? They had their little *drecky* minds made up, so what good would it do? You know, fightin' with those gangplank anchors reminded me of one time when Tonto here took on a Master Gunnery Sergeant who had become over-insulting of us 'squids' as you know they call us. Whoo-boy, was that one donnybrook."

Even with Archie Golden's voice distorted by vibration, his words drew Tonto Waters back in memory. It seemed like just the day before…

…It had been a month to the day after Tom Waters had reported aboard to Team 2. He and Archie Golden had become fast friends, despite the difference in age between the two. They had gone out on the town in Little Creek for a few rounds of beer and some giant hamburgers at the Vesuvio, located on the Strand, down the street from the old UDT hangout.

After wolfing down three each of the half-pound, handmade burgers, they had a final beer with Red and Tony, two retired UDT Chiefs who owned the SEAL hangout. Then they had settled down in O'Doyle's Emerald Isle to do some serious beer drinking until they had to report back aboard the base. An hour into their dedicated tippling, five big Marines from the permanent guard force swaggered into the pub. Right away, they spotted the SEALs. The biggest of them, a Master Gunnery Sergeant, started in with the bad-mouthing even before he had a beer in his hand.

"Look what the rats drug in," he brayed. "Must be a dozen squids foulin' up the air in here. Does your mommie know you're out, Squids?"

"Ignore them," Archie, the family man, urged.

"Fuck them," Tonto Waters growled. "I'm thinkin' of breakin' that shit-mouth's arm off and stuffing it down his throat."

"Could get you some brig time, Tonto," Sam Furgeson advised. "Sure as hell a Cap'n's mast. The Old Man's death on public brawling. Gives the SEALs and the Navy a bad name, he says."

"Couldn't be one any worse than he's calling us," Tonto persisted.

"Whatcha doin', Squids? You cookin' some way to suck up to us and get out of here without takin' any lumps? That ain't gonna happen. This is a Marine bar." The Gunney Sgt. flashed a big grin that revealed two gold teeth, downed the whole glass of beer in one breath and returned to baiting the SEALs. "But, I got something you can suck on. Jest come over and get in line."

Tonto came to his feet so rapidly that his captain's chair tilted over with a loud bang. "That does it! No goddamn sea-goin' bellhop is gonna fuckin' tell me to suck his..." With that, Tonto started across the floor.

One of his companions had taken a better look at the SEALs. "Take it easy, Hank. They're wearin' UDT badges."

"So what? They're still nothin' but Squid fruit loops." Then he saw Tonto advancing on him. "That's the way, you little Squid fuckers. Come on over and get a dose of yer medicine, you ball-less fru—." Tonto had reached him by then and ended his taunts with a hard fist that made thick, ugly lips even more unpleasant to look at. Blood squirted and Tonto followed up with a hard left to the Gunney's gut.

Light on his feet, Tonto danced back a couple of steps and went to work on the exposed face. His knuckles cut skin under both eyes, put a bloody crescent on one cheek. He paid for it, though, when pain exploded in his hand and ran up through his wrist to his elbow.

Then Hank recovered enough to snap a hard right to Tonto's chest. It rocked YO/1C Waters back on his heels. He backpedalled and kept up his guard as the Gunnery Sergeant let out a bellow and charged. Tonto went in under the big, burly arms, raised both hands and grabbed a wrist.

With a quick downward snap, he did a hip throw and spun to stomp a heel into the exposed throat of his opponent. ! The command came from his mind a fraction of a second before he crushed Hank's larynx and ended his own career at Portsmouth Naval Prison. Too drunk, or too enraged to consider such an outcome, the Marine grabbed one of Tonto's ankles and began to furiously gnaw on it with his expensive dental work.

Spears of pain burned up Tonto's leg. He redirected his free foot and kicked Hank in the head. Stunned, Hank's grip released and Tonto pulled away. He started for the mouthy jarhead again when another Marine grabbed him from behind. Tonto spun and put the toe of his black shoe in the man's crotch. The leatherneck went down howling. Tonto bent down and balled a fist in Hank's shirt front. With a soft grunt, he yanked the groggy gyrine upward and pounded a piston-like fist into a slack face. Again, then again.

When Hank's body went limp, Tonto stopped. Not even panting hard, he rose and shot a fiery gaze at the other Marines. "Anybody else want some of what I've got?"

Sheepish glances went from one jarhead to another and they eased back against the bar while Tonto…

"…the difference in age between the two of us. We'd gone out on the town in Little Creek for a few rounds, and wound up ol' Tonto tore that Gunney Sergeant a new asshole," Archie concluded.

Oily sweat had broken out on Tonto Water's forehead and back and he breathed hard at the vividness of his recollection. Had it taken no longer than a second to happen? At least they had sprung Archie and True Blue. No doubt, considering what had gone on in the general's office, it would be back to the bush again with a vengeance.

Chapter 18

Once returned to Tre Noc, Tonto Waters' forecast proved only too true. For a week, first squad went out every night, to run patrols. They interdicted sampans coming up the Delta and made life in general most unpleasant for Charlie. To say nothing of the effect it all had on the SEALs.

Constant operation frazzled the brain. Kent Welby devoutly believed that. On the fifth straight night of ambush activity, he named the characteristics that indicated growing stress for each man in the squad. Tonto Waters stopped laughing. Just as well, because Archie Golden had stopped cracking jokes. Chad Ditto had what appeared to be a personality regression to what Doc Welby considered the age of a high school freshman.

Fourteen year olds were known to shed an occasional tear for no apparent reason. Doc had embarrassed himself and Chad when he discovered the young RTO doing just that on the return run from the previous night's patrol. Now, as he used the vibrations of the rumbling engines of the PBR to ease the ache in his strained muscles, Doc recalled the conversation he had overheard between Lt. Marino and Tonto Waters.

"Do you get the feeling that Lailey is saving the nastiest operations for us, Chief?" Marino had asked.

"You coulda plucked dose woids right outta my head," Waters had responded, letting himself slip into his New Jersey accent.

That had been before their R&R trip to Saigon. What they had been handed since their return made it all seem like a cake walk. It shocked him then, twenty minutes later as they climbed from the boats, to hear a similar exchange between Pope Marino and Dusty Rhodes, who had come down to meet them.

"How'd it go?" LT. (jg) Rhodes asked as the weary men clumped onto the planks of the dock.

"Rough," Pope Marino said through a soft sigh. "Dusty, I can't get over the suspicion that Lailey has picked us especially to be exposed more than he rest of the platoon."

"That has grim implications. What would be behind that?"

"You know there's no love lost between us. It could be he's gotten word somehow of our little problem in Saigon. If so, he'd get off on sweating us until I break."

Lieutenant Commander Lailey sat behind his desk, the grin of a feeding shark on his face. The intelligence data on his desk had come from Buddha, and it was good product. The Viet Cong district commander, Trey Fon Lok, had put a bounty out on the heads of each of the Men with Green Faces.

"Orders have come down from General Hoi Pak that the SEALs are to be disrupted and hounded out of the Delta," the report stated. "In accordance, Trey Fon Lok has placed a reward of 5,000 piasters on the heads of each of the Men with Green Faces. Needless to say, this has highly motivated the lesser cadres and their men. Only those loyal to me will not participate in winning this bounty. On other matters..." Buddha continued with a information on the arrival of supplies.

"Couldn't have happened at a better time," Lailey muttered to himself. Never mind that Gen. Belem had interfered with what he and that major, Harkness, had planned. Now he had a chance to get what he wanted most of all.

Highly pleased, he decided to put 1st Platoon in the field once again. Tonight would be their seventh straight in the bush. Perhaps a couple of days off, let third and fourth squads run some probes. Then put first and second squads out there, with Marino, and leave them out.

"Did you hear the latest?" Doc Welby asked the rest of first squad at Tre Noc as they luxuriated in the welcome inactivity they had so unexpectedly acquired.

"What's that?" Repeat Ditto asked.

"Charlie's district commander has put a bounty out on our heads. Five thou in piasters for every SEAL they can capture or kill."

"Oh, wow! Sends cold chills down my spine," Archie Golden quipped sarcastically.

Boredom radiated from Tonto Waters. "I must admit I am totally under-impressed by it all. I'll tell you one thing, though. I'd like to see the little fuck try to collect it personally."

General Hoi Pak stood at the end of the long, highly polished mahogany table that served for staff meetings. He had advised them that the river war had cooled to an all-time low. No engagements were being initiated by any of the Viet Cong units in the Delta.

"Why is that?" a major in supply asked.

"You are in charge of supplies, are you not? Do you have to ask, Comrade Vahng? Our primary mission at this time is to complete the emplacement of necessary supplies for our offensive. We are three weeks away from an all-out effort to seize the Delta."

"And if the American Navy brings in more SEALs to the Delta, Comrade General?" Nguyen Dak asked with an arched eyebrow.

General Hoi smiled at his friend and confidante and

sipped from a cup of fine Oolong. "You, yourself, answered that for me. It seems highly unlikely that more of these elite troops will be inserted before we launch our major series of attacks. Although the SEALs remain the fair-haired boys of the Special Forces commandant, General Belem, they are not in such a good light with commander of Four Corps, or with the U.S. Army military police. Our Soviet friends," he assured them, "inform me that there is talk of appealing to the American Naval leaders to remove the SEALs from the Delta and place them elsewhere. Some place where more control can be exercised over them.

"Also," he added with a crooked smile, "I have recent, reliable information that a certain Major Harkness of the Provost Marshal's office in Saigon considers the SEALs to be loose cannons." Gen. Hoi paused a moment at the puzzled expressions on the faces of several of his staff officers. "It is an American expression. It means highly unreliable. Given enough examples of the SEALs' unconventional nature, and I am sure the American high command will act in the way we want them to. Now, I would like your reports on progress for the offensive."

One by one the staff reported their status. The G-1 stated that all personnel had been notified of their staging points, and that when they arrived they would be briefed on their area of operation and the mission. Col. Nguyen related the current intelligence profile on the American troops, concluding that nothing they had done so far indicated knowledge of the impending massive assault. The G-3 indicated that the operations orders were being cut as of this morning. All cadre would be gathered for a major briefing a week prior to the offensive. Vahng, the G-4, advised that the supply line had not been cut or negatively interrupted on any permanent basis. Gen. Hoi took it in with growing excitement. At last he rose and braced both hands on the table.

"From what you have said, Comrades, I conclude that

we are exactly on schedule and that the major troop movements can begin as indicated, two weeks from today. Continue the good work, Comrades. Dismissed."

Francie Song had returned to Tre Noc. With a full day of restricted area liberty, Doc Welby met her in the lunch room of the Winds of the East Hotel, a ramshackle establishment with a pretentious name and a decidedly unpretentious appearance. They sat at a small, sun-dappled table beside a high, narrow window. Chipped and faded green paint showed on the shutters, which had been secured, their louvers left open to admit shafts of sunshine. The window panes and casements had obviously been scavenged from some former French planter's home.

Doc wanted to take Francie in his arms and kiss her long and passionately the moment he saw her in the marble-faced entrance way. He restrained himself and rose to greet her as she crossed to where he waited. A waiter appeared as Doc helped her into a chair. Francie ordered bottled mineral water and Doc had a beer.

"I missed you, Francie," Doc blurted after the waiter departed.

"And I missed you, Kent Welby. The nights were especially empty."

Doc wanted to change the subject. "Your aunt? Is she improving?"

"Oh, yes. Enough that she can get around on her own. Her eldest daughter and her sister are tending to the house now." Francie ducked her chin and lowered her gaze to the tablecloth. "I came back."

"I'm glad you did."

They talked inconsequentials for a while, and then ordered their meal. Due to reduced enemy activity, more food stuffs reached the village and the vegetables proved fresh and sweet. In keeping with general instructions on eating native foods, Doc avoided uncooked fruit and veggies. Over coffee and cheese, Francie brought up an old and sore point between them.

"Kent Welby, it is absolutely important that I get an introduction to someone in the compound, so I can get a job there."

Her hurried request, pressed so urgently, set off the niggling uneasiness in Doc's mind. "We've been over this and I've agreed to help. Right now is not a good time. I don't see why it has to be so immediate."

Francie shrugged. She could only fall back on well-belabored reasons. "Lots of Vietnamese work there. Only, when new men come from your country, not so many keep their jobs. I have terrible need for the money I would make."

She had not admitted that much to him before. Worried for her, Doc tried to puzzle out the reason. "Why? Are you in trouble? Do you owe someone a lot of money?"

Francie shook her head, would not meet Doc's eyes. "No. Nothing like that. The trip to Saigon..." she faltered. "That did take a lot of what little I had saved up. But, I do need the money, badly. Rose Throh does not pay a lot for me to sing at Mi Flower. The job I had before the Americans came is no more. There is nowhere to go back to. Only to look ahead. Won't you please do something today, right now while you have the time? I need your help so much."

"I told you, now is not a good time," Doc returned lamely.

"When will it ever be the right time?" Francie challenged in impatience.

Their disagreement had escalated rapidly and now reminded Doc Welby of his conflict with his wife. Stung by the similarities, he became defensive.

"I said that I will help, and I will. Only... don't... ask me... now."

Francie produced a pout and her eyes went lackluster.

"I'm not so certain of that," she grated. "Not... any more."

"Francie! I'm not going to be rejected a second time," Doc blurted before he realized what he had said. "Oh, God, I didn't mean... I didn't mean to say anything to hurt you."

"You didn't mean for that to come out, is what you mean." Icily now, already on her feet. "Do you not believe me? Do you not *trust* me, Kent?"

"No—Yes. I don't know," he babbled, too late to cut off the flow.

Tears sprang to Francie's eyes and she spun on one heel to run from the lunch room. Staring, obsidian eyes of the Vietnamese diners pinned Doc Welby to the window like a specimen on a microscope slide. He made a helpless gesture and stalked off, not waiting for the bill. He would pay the cashier.

It had been called a routine patrol. It went that way during the last three hours of daylight and the first two of darkness. Then Tonto Waters, out on point as usual, picked out a faint sound from among the night noises of the jungle that turned his bowels to ice water.

Voices, muted and irregular, from several positions on the left flank of the squad. What made it worse was that they came from behind him. The relaxed chatter came closer. Tonto could not turn back and warn the squad and he dare not go on forward. All at once, the under sides of the overhanging leaves washed from white to pale yellow-orange and the stutter of automatic weapons fire shattered the hum of insects and hunting howls of monkeys.

While Tonto watched, helpless, the fire fight swept through the area where he estimated Pope Marino, Archie Golden and Repeat Ditto should have been. The firing went on for a while, then faded out. An angry chatter in Vietnamese rose, then cut off short. Doctrine had it that he should wait at least fifteen minutes to see if the enemy would return, or if any had remained behind. Tonto could not have it that way.

He waited a long three-count and then retraced his steps. To his relief, he found no dead SEALs. He took a deep breath and continued along the line of march the patrol had taken. After some twenty cautious paces, a voice called out softly to him.

"Is that you, Tonto?" Chad Ditto.

"Naw, it's the VC, Repeat. Where is everybody?"

Relief flooded Repeat's voice. "I don't know, Tonto. I got separated from the Skipper. He an' Doc and Archie got pushed to the right flank by those Japs. Where'd they come from?"

"To our left."

Another rattle of gunfire to the north of their position froze the two SEALs in the fern leaves. "Oh, shit, are they still chasin' the guys?"

"I don't know, Repeat. Right now we've got to find the rest of the squad."

They spread out and made a silent search of the bush around their line of march. One by one the rest of the squad came out of the undergrowth. Tonto gathered them and made a quick head count. Pope, Archie and Doc remained the only ones missing. On to the next thing, Tonto ticked off mentally.

"Can you bump second squad on that radio?"

"Sure can. I'm glad Pope managed to requisition some handsets with the same frequencies. Now we can keep in touch."

"He didn't 'requisition' them, Repeat. He reconnoitered them, then went back and stole them."

"Uh—well, we needed them didn't we?"

"Any way we could get them, kid. Now go ahead and raise Mr. Ott or Chief Sturgis."

Due to the tenseness of the situation Repeat raised second squad on the first try. He handed his handset to Tonto.

"This is Eagle Two. Eagle One and two chicks are out of the nest. I say again, Eagle One and two are missing. We're hold in' our own at the point of contact. Where are you relative to us? Over."

"Eagle Two, this is Nimrod One," Mr. Ott's voice, a bit high and edgy, reflected his mental state. "We're about three hundred meters behind where the fire fight broke out."

"I suggest we hold what we've got, Nimrod. Can you link up? Over."

"That's a roger, Eagle Two. Can you confirm status on Eagle One and the others? Over."

"Negative. We need more warm bodies for that. All I can say is they weren't KIA on the site. Eagle Two, out."

Gunfire erupted again on their right, closer now, louder, individual discharges discernible. *Those fuckers are coming back*, Tonto thought, a full jolt of adrenaline surging through him, making the hairs on the back of his hands rise.

The little red call light winked on the AN/PRC-25. Tonto tapped Repeat on the shoulder and the kid answered it. "Talk to me, Eagle Two. What's going on? Over."

Tonto took the handset. "Charlie's comin' back, Nimrod. Over." *Nimrod*? Who the hell thought that one up? Sounds too much like Numb nuts. He was getting giddy, Tonto Waters brought himself up tight. Have to watch that.

"Better pull back on us, Eagle Two. Over."

"Negative, Nimrod. We've got guys out there. You know we never leave them behind. Over."

"We'll get them, Tonto, don't worry. Now, fall back. Nimrod One, out."

Lt. Carl Marino motioned his two men down into the underbrush. The faint light of the moon and stars that filtered through the overhead jungle canopy barely allowed them to see the movement of his hand and arm. They obeyed at once. Pope Marino gave it a long five minutes, then worked his way back to them.

"We've circled their route of march all right. Only thing, if this compass didn't get knocked haywire when I took that header over that log, we are further east of where they hit us."

Archie Golden groaned softly. "Just what we need. Wonder what the other guys are doing? The way I see it, they've got two options."

"Yeah. They can come along the trail and try to link up with us," Pope enumerated, "or they can wait for us to go back and find them."

"Either way, it's the pits," Doc Welby put in.

The quiet of the moment shattered in a burst of gunfire. Faintly, in the distance, they could see the muzzle flashes. The direction they came from didn't please any of the trio. Ice formed a knot in Doc Welby's gut as Pope Marino spoke the obvious.

"Charlie's come back."

"It makes sense," Archie Golden admitted grudgingly. "They had to know there's more of us out here. And they didn't find anyone the way they went."

"Too true. Only now, we're cut off from the rest." Pope Marino didn't sound any too happy about it. "My bet is they'll figure the patrol rushed forward, rather than turn back, and they'll be comin' our way. What do you have with you, Archie, to spoil their day?"

Archie Golden's grin crinkled almost audibly. "Well, I've got a couple of sandwiches made up already. There's a claymore, and some captured Symtex I removed from the boobytraps Tonto found. Given a little time I can rig some real nasty surprises for them."

Twenty minutes later, Archie had most of his ugly toys laid out in a manner to protect their front and flanks. He had started on another when Pope Marino raised his AR-15 and cut down the enemy point man. Three others, close behind him dove off the narrow trail onto the tripwire for the claymore set up across from them. It went off with a bright flash and an ear-piercing bang, and shredded them beyond recognition.

Archie Golden laid his explosives aside and took up his Stoner. With short, precise bursts, he welcomed the Viet Cong to their night of reckoning.

Chapter 19

Tonto Waters and the rest of the two squads found themselves isolated on a small point that stuck out into the Bassiac. True Blue Oakes came to the platoon chief a moment after they had settled into suitable firing positions. The left side of his green tank-top shirt bore a dark stain, which dripped black in the frosty light from above.

"I took me a little scrape back up the trail when Charlie hit."

His voice stern to hide his genuine concern, Tonto braced the black SEAL. "Why didn't you report it to me at the time? And why didn't you take yourself to Nicholson to get patched up?"

"Didn't want to slow us down, Tonto. Besides, it ain't no big deal. It stings and irritates more'n anything else."

His sincerity could not be doubted. Tonto Waters snorted in exasperation. "Our pan handler's down there in those mangrove roots. Report to him now and get that fixed before Charlie comes to call."

"Right, Chief. Uh! You ain't gonna tell Mr. Ott, are you?"

"Lunkhead, I have to tell Mr. Ott," Tonto growled.

"Oh."

True Blue came back some fifteen minutes later, with Filmore Nicholson in tow. The medic confirmed what True had said about his wound. "Nothing life-threatening. The bullet ran along the outside of his ribs, barely under the skin. Went clean through. It'll burn and itch a lot, but he can still handle that one-forty-eight."

"Yeah," True Blue added, "only thing I don't like is that all this blood is drawing more than my share of bugs. They's buzzin' around me in a regular cloud."

Tonto shrugged, nearly unseen in the dim illumination of stars and half-moon. "Take your place on the line, True."

"You got it, Chief."

He would have to report this to Mr. Ott, Tonto thought, worming his way out of his own spot. When he reached the young ensign, at the center of their defensive line, he saw Repeat Ditto on the radio-phone, in animated conversation. Tonto quickly advised Ott of the situation with True Blue. By then, Chad Ditto had turned to them with a report.

"Mr. Ott, Whitehorse says there's no chance of an extraction for a while. There's a big Riverine operation to the northwest of our position and no available boats or choppers to pull us out. Whitehorse advised that we stand fast and hold what we got."

Wally Ott's scowl could have been seen in a coal mine at midnight. "Let me have that thing." Repeat quickly raised the base at Tre Noc and passed the handset to Ensign Ott. "Whitehorse, what the hell is going on? You already know that Eagle One and two ratings are out there somewhere. Charlie has come back for a visit and is spread out between us. We'll need a Slick to come in and pull those men out of there. Nimrod One, over."

"We copy, Nimrod. The only birds not in use are with an ARVN outfit. And they won't release even one for a night op in that region of the Delta. It will be at least two, three hours before we can send anyone. I have your AOIC here, do you want to talk to him? Over."

"Roger that," Wally Ott said with relief. Right then he wanted very much to talk to Dusty Rhodes.

"Nimrod, this is Eagle Two. What's your situation? Over."

Quickly Wally Ott laid it out. He ended with the return of the VC. "So we're cut off for now. Better the Japs come this way. We have the fire power to hold them until Eagle One can hit them in the rear. Over."

"Any chance of linking up with Eagle One? Over."

"Negative, Eagle Two. At least not until daylight. Over."

"Then hold fast until then. It'll probably take that long to bring in boats for an extraction. Eagle Two, out." Then a moment later, the voice of the RTO in Tre Noc. "Whitehorse, out."

Wally Ott turned to the men near him and explained the situation. "We're going to have to hold this piss-ant point until daylight. If Whitehorse has convinced Dusty that there's no available transport, it has to be true."

"What about Pope and the others?" Anxious concern rang in Tonto's voice.

"They're going to have to hold what they got, keep their heads down and hope Charlie doesn't find them."

Right then a stutter of gunfire interrupted anything else Wally Ott had to say. The distant flash of a claymore followed, the sound of the detonation trailed it by a second.

Drinking iced *Sovietskia* vodka, thickened to the consistency of syrup in a freezer, Sr. Lt. Kovietski and his guests lounged in the comfort of his quarters inside Cambodia. The intimate dinner party had been given for one of his top agents in place in the Delta region. The KGB *resedentura* sat on a plush love seat, with one arm around the bare shoulders of the guest of honor.

She in turn lounged back against the cushions, a long swatch of thigh and foreleg exposed by the slit in her chamsong. She was laughing at a joke, told in Russian by Feodor Dudov. The two Cambodian girls with Dudov and Yoriko held blank expressions. They didn't understand the language. The lovely Vietnamese agent had the advantage there.

She had been educated at the Leningrad spy school, and later at the farm the KGB maintained, hidden deep in the Ural Mountains, and known as the Charm School. There she had learned flawless, idiomatic American English from American prisoners of war, taken at the outset of Vietnam, and earlier in Korea, whose cooperation had been forced. Now she spoke in the same language Dudov had used.

"That is nasty, Feodor Viktoravich—but funny. I am so glad you came to this little fete to honor my unworthy accomplishments. And thank you, dear Alexi for being so thoughtful. The food was exquisite, the company congenial, and the vodka..." She hoisted her glass in salute. "The best in all the world. Now, I fear I have to excuse myself. I must get back."

Disappointment clouded Lt. Kovietski's face. "You're not staying the night, my dear?"

"I cannot." She turned to the others to explain, "From what the good Comrade Major told me before you arrived, it is vital that I return and complete my assignment." Mischief danced in her eyes as she turned them on Kovietski again. "That will require considerable sacrifice on my part, as I'm sure you are aware."

"Yes—yes, of course," Kovietski responded. "I know how much you loath the Americans."

"Almost as much as the French, sweet one," she purred.

Kovietski made a sour face of disgust. "Presenting yourself to one of them must be terribly..." He fought for the proper word. "Must be revolting."

Her eyes rolled upward a moment while she recalled blissful hours of unrestrained passion. How delicious. Not at all like making love with this stolid Russian. Communist dogma must have driven every last spark of imagination from him. Or were the lives of all Soviets filled with such strict prudery? Flat on your back, legs wide apart, while he crawled on top to thrust and grunt away until the inevitable end as he squealed like a pig. And don't ever, *ever* give the slightest sign that you might be enjoying it.

"Right you are, dear Alexi. It is all I can do to keep my skin from shrinking away at his touch. Now, I must go."

"I'll show you to the door."

At the outer door, still in the shadows of the short hall, Alexi gave her a long kiss. A passionate one for a change, which she returned with surprised vigor. Then, clutching to her chest the small evening bag, which held the flat, narrow box with the Order of the Red Banner she had been awarded, and the 50,000 piasters, she hurried to the dock to board the powered sampan which would take her back to Vietnam.

Gritty eyed, LCDR Barry Lailey poured more coffee and added a dollop of bourbon before returning to his desk. A low-wattage, green-shaded, brass lamp put out minimal illumination in the room. When darkness had fallen, he had returned to monitor the radio traffic from the Delta. Long past his usual bedtime, his head drooped frequently. He jerked awake instantly, though, at any mention of the Eagle call sign.

He had listened with growing excitement to the first report of contact with the enemy, and of Marino being separated from his second squad and the remainder of the first. Oddly, pride flared in his chest when he heard the exchange between Ensign Ott and the Tre Noc base. The boy had a good head on his shoulders, made a good SEAL, Lailey had silently praised. He had followed procedure exactly for the situation the prevailed; Regroup, set up a strong point, and call for extraction. He had the urge to contact Tre Noc and issue a direct order not to send a chopper for Marino and the other two. He'd word it as "do not risk a helicopter and pilot for three men already killed or captured".

That wouldn't work, he realized the next second. There

would be a record, someone would know he'd intervened to the end of abandoning the first SEALs, anywhere, ever. Although he bitterly resented the way the brass had cashiered him out of the SEAL program, their *esprit de corps* and the legacy of never leaving a man behind called to him. If Marino got overrun, so be it. But he would make no effort to prevent an extraction, even of a corpse.

He took a swallow of his spiked coffee and listened avidly as events developed. No exfiltration until daylight. His body jerked and jolted in anticipation, as though jabbed with a cattle prod. Surely now, this time, Marino would finally get his. Yes! And how Barry Lailey would savor that moment.

Shortly before 0400, the men grown restless from inactivity, the night sky lit up with yellow-orange flashes and the eerie spectacle of tiny, intensely bright dots of white, wavering upward. Contrails of alabaster smoke followed behind. It came from slightly more than one klick to the southwest. The thuds of initial explosions got lost in the sharp detonation of a Claymore.

"Looks like Pope and the boys are laying it on," Tonto Waters observed casually to Mr. Ott.

A steady stutter of automatic weapons fire came next. Ensign Ott cocked his head to one side. "Damnit, that means Charlie got smart and went in the right direction."

"Maybe not. Sounds like the Cong walked into a hornet's nest. Pope's forgotten more about under strength ambushes than we'll ever know," Tonto offered fulsome praise. "I think we'd better look for some of Charlie's people to head our way before long."

Silence returned, all of the animal life driven in fear from the area of the fighting. It did little to improve the mood of the SEALs waiting on the sliver of land in the Bassiac. In particular, Tonto Waters didn't like it one bit.

As time stretched out, without an attack on their position, or even a cautious probe, he began to suspect that his friends and the Skipper had been defeated. Another hour passed and the eastern sky took on a sickly gray-green tinge. Dawn would arrive soon.

When it came, those SEALs who had nodded off neatly cleared the ground in reflex response to the eruption of another fire fight. More grenades and white phosphorous went off. Then came a tremendous, ear-torturing explosion of the Symtex. A lull followed, then more firing, moving their direction, and panicked voices shouted back and forth in a jabber of Vietnamese. Here they come, Tonto had a moment to think.

He was not mistaken. Within fifteen minutes, the demoralized VC had come close enough for individual voices could be discerned. Seven of them rushed into the open, to stop in consternation when they found a bristling hedgehog of weapons facing them. They had not expected any more of the terrifying fighters they had so recently faced. Paralyzed a fatal moment too long, they got their Chicom 56 rifles into action far too late.

The SEALs opened up with everything they had. Slugs cracked high over their heads, while theirs poured into the chests and bellies of the enemy. A pall of smoke and dust rose from the tiny finger of land in the Bassiac. Chad Ditto fired sporadically while he yammered into the radio, calling for instant extraction.

Covering him and Ensign Ott, crouched beside the RTO, True Blue Oakes opened up with his Stoner as a dozen more VC poured into the grassy swath between the river bank and the jungle. A swarm of 7.62mm bullets bit air all around the SEALs. A grenade sailed high over the Cong advance and burst ten feet in front of the hastily erected parapets of the SEALs. With a soft bloop, the XM-148 answered. The HE, antipersonnel round detonated with a tiny puff of smoke some eight feet off the ground and slashed broken bits of crimped wire shrapnel into the heads and upper torsos of four Charlies.

One fell forward, one went back, and two simply sat down in an awkward lotus position and remained that way, dead where they sat. Still more VC rushed to the attack. Tonto Waters shot a quick glance to Chips Danner.

"If there's this many left, how many did the guys with Pope take out?"

"Not enough," Chips answered. "I'm gonna swing my section up to the right, cover that flank."

"Good thinkin'. See ya."

"I fuckin' hope so," Chips growled.

With the enemy close now, Tonto sang a deadly chorus with his 12 gauge Ithaca. His hand felt sweaty on the pistol grip of the weapon as he realized he could read every shift of expression on the faces of the enemy. He'd never seen them on so personal a basis before.

Specially hardened No. 4 buckshot splashed two of the Cong in front of Tonto. He started to swing the muzzle when a blast from behind him savaged his right ear. Three rounds from the Stoner in the hands of True Blue blew off the back of a VC's head. The dead Cong fell three feet from Tonto's chest.

"Thanks, I needed that," he bit off for his own benefit, more than for True.

Then he slipped his special convincer into the loading port of the Ithaca. The psychological *piece de resistance*, a flechette round, would bring scalding pee on the swarming Cong. He hastily brought the shotgun to waist level and cranked off a round. Buckshot splattered one Charlie while Tonto cycled the action and touched off the flechette charge.

Ten of the nasty little buggers found a place in flesh, decorating the throat and face of the VC platoon leader with the soft, gray fins on the fletched ends. The whistle he had been blowing hysterically shot from his mouth, pierced by one of the nasty barbs, and he went down in a gush of his own blood. Instantly seen by many of the survivors, it proved enough for the VC. The enemy quickly faded into the green undergrowth, dragging their dead and wounded with them. Some of the more controlled among them gave covering fire.

"They're gone," Repeat Ditto sighed with relief.

"No, they're not gone," Tonto Waters corrected. "And they'd damn well better not be forgotten. If there are enough of them, they'll come back. If not, they'll pull out eventually. Either way, we'll have to fight our way through them to reach the others."

Without being told, the SEALs began to give their weapons a cursory clean-up and reloaded. Tonto passed a canteen among the men of first squad, and munched on a chocolate bar from a C-Ration packet. Mr. Ott went among them, offering encouragement and passing out tidbits of gum and candy held back from his rations. He kept at that until summoned by Repeat Ditto.

Wally Ott took the handset of the AN/PRC-25 and spoke his call sign. When the other end handed back, he spoke hotly. "Where the hell's that extraction? We just came under fire from a platoon strength unit of VC. Over."

"Why are you still talking to us, then? Over." came a sarcastic, doubting question.

"Because we beat them back, you idiot." A sudden through struck him. "Say, who are you, Whitehorse? Over."

"This is Signalman Second Miller, sir. Over."

"Well, SS-Two Miller, you find me someone who can answer questions intelligently, starting with where in hell are those boats? Over."

"I can tell you that, Nimrod. ETA is five minutes. Two PBRs and a Mikeboat. You are to be ready to board instantly. Over."

After all the effort to get this laid on, Ensign Ott suddenly recalled the tradition of the SEALs. "Negative, Whitehorse. Not unless we can get our detached personnel out at the same time. That's the final word on that. Over."

"Nimrod, there is a Slick on the way to extract them, with a Kiowa for cover. All that is needed is to get the word, or a radio to the rest of your patrol so they can call in the rescue. Whitehorse, out."

Quickly, Wally Ott related all of this to the squads. Tonto Waters could not believe what he heard. "That's all? Just take *them* a radio?" he blurted. Then with a shrug and a grin, he added. "Nothing for it but to do it, I guess."

Chapter 20

Five minutes seemed to streak by. These river sailors had no concept how far a click and a half was on land. Or how long it could take to cover that in a jungle. Furious with himself, Ensign Ott consulted with Tonto Waters and Buck Sturgis of second squad.

"They ain't comin' out, Mr. Ott, 'less we go in and git them," Sturgis rumbled in his Oklahoma drawl.

"If we take a radio to them, whoever goes will have to extract with Pope and the guys on the Slick," Tonto clarified Buck's observation.

"If we can get a radio in, why can't we come back out the same way?" the youthful Ott asked.

"Take too long," Tonto stated simply. "What we ought to do, sir, if you don't mind, is load out on the PBRs, head up river a klick or two and then head for where we heard that fire fight. Let the rest go out on the boats, whoever takes the radio extracts like I said."

"How many men would you recommend go, Chief?"

Tonto considered it a moment. "Three. No more than four. It looks like Charlie gave up on Pope and them. However many are left out there in front of us, we can mark our position and get Raintree to unload on the VC. Should discourage them from following."

"I don't like it, but I think it might work. Ditto, get me Raintree."

By the time the Mike boat and its attendant PBRs arrived, the plan had been discussed, elaborated on and everyone involved knew what to do. The Mike boat showed first, its bow wave a creamy *café au lait*. The moment the twin fifties in the forward troop well cleared the screen of trees, they opened up.

Tracers probed glowing fingers into the ferns and fan palms that masked the position of the VC. The mortar near the fantail coughed with authority, the tube nearly vertical, and lobbed a fat 81mm round into the bush. White phosphorous and screams erupted. The Honeywell chugged rhythmically. An instant later, the PBRs added their fury to the onslaught. Engines reversed, and turning just enough rpms on the screws to hold station, the awesome collection of armaments unloaded its worst on the enemy. Time to haul ass.

Every other SEAL ceased pouring small arms fire into the unseen enemy and took to the river. They waded out and rolled aboard the PBRs. Immediately they cleared their weapons and laid down cover for those still on shore. They came with alacrity, Mr. Ott and Chief Sturgis being last to leave the river bank. Once aboard, still dripping, they watched while the armada released one final volley.

Then the coxswains put the engines in forward, curved sharply and sped up river. Tonto Waters had volunteered to lead the radio party. With him would come Repeat Ditto, Mule Carlson and Blue Chip Reno. They tended to their weapons and made ready. All of them sensed the change in vibrations through their feet as the engines throttled back. Time to go. Chad Ditto traded off his primary weapon for an XM-148 and twenty rounds. The exhaust barely a whisper, the coxswain of the lead PBR coasted into the bank. The bow touched and bounced, while he spun the wheel and put the small, armored vessel parallel to the bank.

Off they went, Tonto Waters in the lead, Repeat Ditto close at his side. All four made it without incident and faded into the jungle without a backward glance. This was going to be one sure enough bitch. The joker in the deck, Tonto knew, was that the radio was the key to it all. If it got damaged, they'd be stranded. And it was one hell of a walk back to Tre Noc.

Three hundred meters from the river bank, Tonto Waters came upon the faintest trace of a trail. It led generally in the direction they wanted to take. Sight of it, coupled with every instinct, and the knowledge of what they might find up ahead, made him want to run along this narrow track. Training and experience cautioned against it. Relying on his skill as a point man, Tonto led his companions along the path in a silent, gliding advance.

Vines and ferns impeded their progress. Air-root plants danced before Tonto's face, threatening to disorient him. Every second, he and the others expected to come under fire. So intent was Tonto's concentration that he nearly blundered into a punjee pit. Only the slight flex of the covering bamboo poles warned him of its presence. He froze instantly and eased back.

In his mind he saw the spikes of green bamboo driven into the bottom and up the side walls to the height of an average Vietnamese's shoulders. Others, above those, pointed downward. All of them smeared with human excrement. He fought off a shudder and skirted around the boobytrap, alert for any tripwires that might lead to mines. No wonder he had seen only the faintest signs of human use of the trail. Once certain the other side held no nasty surprises, Tonto signaled to Repeat, Blue Chip and Mule.

Using hand signals much like those he used as a driver's helper to back a big rig, Tonto directed them around the pit. Then he faded off on the point. Only the normal jungle sounds came from around them. Birds squawked and trilled, insects hummed, monkeys scolded and little rodent critters slithered through the ferns. Tonto made another hundred meters and froze in place. He swiveled his torso at the hips and signed for the others to go to ground. A foot from the toe of his sneak was a tripwire.

Tonto bent and marked it with a twig jammed into the

soft ground, and stepped over it. Six feet along the trail he came to the trap door that concealed a nasty, barbed, rusted, wrought-iron head and the wooden shaft of an Angled Arrow Trap. Buried in the ground at an acute angle that would set the impact point at chest-high, it was propelled by a length of tightly stretched inner tube stripped from a bicycle tire. He went to one knee and gingerly plucked the projectile from its bamboo tube container. With that disposed of, he motioned for the others to come on.

By dead reckoning, Tonto estimated they had come the better part of three-quarters of a klick when he identified the faint outline of a Sideways Closing Trap. The wicked device relied on nothing so sophisticated as a concealed tripwire. Split strips of bamboo, had been studded with large, flattened nails, their ends fashioned into hooks and driven into the bamboo of both long sides of the trap. Kept apart by a central prop, powered by strips of inner tube, these deadly devices would lay inert until an incautious intruder stepped onto the spreader. A poisonous mixture of human feces, cobra venom and other deadly substances coated the tips, designed to rake the legs, groin, abdomen, which would result in a slow, painful death.

With Tonto's guidance all of them avoided it successfully. They made it to a point Tonto estimated to be a klick into the jungle. He called the other three to him.

"Time to stop. Take ten for a breather. Go easy on your water, Pope and those guys are going to be thirsty."

Another two hundred meters along the pathway and Tonto stepped out onto the familiar main artery they had been following the night before. A quick study of the faint, intermingled footprints told him it was hopeless to try to make anything out of that mishmash. It was evidence enough, though, for him to determine that the VC who had hit them had indeed been part of the force that had jumped the patrol up the way a bit.

"Let's pick up the pace. Nobody could have had time to rig boobytraps after we came along here last night."

Much faster now, at about a slow to normal walking gait, the SEALs began to close the last few hundred meters to where they hoped to find Pope and the others. Everyone scrupulously maintained noise discipline. Charlie could have left a few friends behind to keep the isolated element of the patrol boxed in.

Tonto estimated they had covered 180 meters when they came upon the first bodies. Little brown men in black pajamas, a few with remnants of dark green uniform pieces, which reminded Tonto of technicolor movies he had seen about the Japanese in WWII. The NVA used the same basic color, he reminded himself. His eyes made knowledgeable sense of the scene of death.

Here lay men who had leaked to death. Wounded who had stumbled along this trail that led to the Bassiac until will and determination alone would no longer sustain them. God, these little bastards had guts, he thought to himself. Some had simply stumbled to the side of the trail and sat down to die. Others sprawled in grotesque postures of death, struck down as they jogged along side their comrades.

"They wouldn't be here if there were many Cong around," he advised the others, though he knew they had to be out there somewhere or Pope would have joined them at the river. "Best keep humpin' it." He gave the signal for caution and glided a canvas-clad foot forward.

Approaching a bend, Tonto found more corpses. Their wounds made ugly red-brown splashes against pale skin. Flies and other scavengers had gathered to feast. He averted his eyes from their desecrations and pushed on. In the next instant, he froze, ears and eyes searching. After a long, tense minute, he turned slowly and signaled to the three SEALs, Enemy in Sight.

Normally in icy control of his emotions, Sr. Lt. Kovietski hurled the glass of hot tea against the concrete block wall of his Delta area command post. " *Kak kotorohye solip'shim* SEALs! That's who it is. Those sons of bitches," he repeated. "I warned General Hoi. Now is the time for a little *dusha— dushe'* with him." Yes, he fumed to himself. A little pointed soul-to-soul with that overconfident NVA pig is definitely in order. Something to shake him out of his complacency about the importance of these SEALs.

What lay behind the KGB *resedentura*'s fury lay crumpled in a corner where he had hurled it upon reading the content of the message. The night before, a reinforced platoon of Viet Cong had been wiped out utterly, with the exception of the platoon sergeant and nine men. They had broken-off contact, but still surrounded what they estimated to be between three and seven enemy survivors. The sergeant had dutifully reported to his cadre superior and the information came to Kovietski before reaching anyone else.

It could be no one else, he raged in silence. "Explain how this is possible, Comrade," he charged his paid informer from within the cadre's staff.

Trembling from the powerful rage of this giant Russian, the *stucach* (informer—snitch) brought a flicker of a smile to lips twisted in anger for Kovietski. "I—I—I do not know, Comrade Kovietski. Lieutenant Xien-Gow's force far outnumbered any patrols the Americans have sent along the river before this."

"Has the late Lieutenant Xien-Gow ever encountered the SEALs before?"

"N-no, Comrade."

"I thought so. Very well. You will receive the usual consideration for this information, even though it's implications greatly displease me. You may go." Kovietski wanted to cover his face with both hands and wipe away the hardening-plaster feeling that his tension triggered.

Now, to Gen. Hoi. "*Mladshiy Serzhant* Borkoi!" he bellowed, "Bring me more tea. And send in *Yefreytor* Sugorov. The good private has a nice session of cranking the portable generator for our radio."

Frowning, Junior Sergeant Borkoi fixed a glass of tea for his superior, and carried it into the inner room of the CP. The first thing he spotted was the shards of broken glass on the floor and the wet splatter on the wall. Not a good day, he thought in sighing resignation. Not a good day at all.

Francie Song sat at a small table near the partition that divided the laundry portion from the bar in Mi Flower. She jiggled and fondled a small, thoroughly naked baby boy on her lap. She made the Vietnamese equivalent of baby talk and the child cooed and gurgled as if in intelligent response. Since her dispute with Kent Welby, she had felt a heavy weight pressing on her shoulders. One that grew with each day.

How could she accomplish what she knew she must do? She could not just walk away, go somewhere else and disappear. She hugged the baby, the same one Rose Throh kept in a wicker basket up by the cash register most of the time. Then she gently kissed the fine, silken, black hair that spread evenly over the round shape of his skull. She moved slightly and quickly kissed the small bald spot. Too much depended on her getting a job inside the compound. Too many people depended on her. Somehow she had to make it up with Kent Welby.

Her mind drifted from the baby as she tried out scenes in her mind that would reconcile her with her American lover. Sensing her absence from his tiny world, the child let out a plaintive wail. Jolted back to the present, Francie hugged and rocked the baby, speaking softly into its ear.

"No, my baby, no my sweet son. Momma loves you," she repeated over and over until the little boy lost the red flush to his face and his temper tears dried on his chubby cheeks.

Instantly the SEALs with Tonto Waters had faded into the jungle. In the blink of an eye Tonto disappeared off the slight track they had been following. He breathed softly, shallowly, though his mouth to avoid any noise and held absolutely motionless, blended into a waterfall of green vines at the base of a huge tree. Only his eyeballs moved. Thirty seconds passed, then four VC litter-bearers materialized out of the thick undergrowth ahead.

They carried a canvas stretcher, slung between two bamboo poles. Two had MAT-49s slung, butt up, over their shoulders. The other pair carried Type 54 semi-automatic rifles. Tonto watched without a twitch while they came on. Abruptly they stopped and bent over a corpse, not three feet from where Tonto stood.

They jabbered animatedly in Vietnamese, gesturing disjointedly back up and then down the trail. The decision apparently made, two lowered the poles of the litter and stepped over the dead man to bend and lift him. One of the others froze suddenly and slowly looked up at the green smear in front of his face.

Gradually his expression changed as he made out the hard, cold eyes looking at him above the muzzle of a shotgun.

"Look out! Look out! Green Faces!" he shrieked in his native tongue as he made a desperate grab for his MAT-49.

A long tongue of flame from the Ithaca licked at his

face as Tonto blew his jaw off and peppered his chest with buckshot. From enfilading positions, two of the other SEALs opened up. Bullets slashed into the remaining VC. Swiftly they cut down the enemy, leaving twitching, blood-soaked corpses in the wake of their murderous assault.

"*Son loi, son loi,*" one of the VC pleaded for help. Then his appeal turned to a liquidy gurgle and then silence.

When the sound of the shots died out, along with the final sigh of the last VC, a voice called from close ahead. "Tonto? Is that you?"

"Damn, it's good to see your ugly face," Pope Marino told Tonto Waters when the chief stepped into the hastily erected defensive position that held the lieutenant, Doc Welby and Archie Golden. "No time for a reunion now, we have to get moving."

"They've got a Slick orbiting out there somewhere for us," Tonto explained tersely.

Lt. Marino motioned Chad Ditto forward and extended a hand for the radio. "This is Eagle One, we're on the air now. Over."

A moment's static answered Marino, then, "Eagle One, this is Birdseye Two-niner. Can you pop smoke to mark your position? Over."

"Negative, Birdseye. We are in a hot spot. There's about a dozen unfriendlies around us. Over."

"Minus four," Tonto told him with a grin.

"Can you locate by landmarks? Over."

All of the SEALs gave a careful study to the visible terrain. Their study lasted a long, tense three minutes. Through the trees to their north, Tonto Waters spotted one of nature's genuine oddities. Looking like an upside-down Mayan pyramid, a termite nest showed clearly about a klick away. Not impressive from this distance, but awesome up close. He pointed it out to Pope Marino.

Pope nodded and gestured to what looked like a wooly green snake, that twisted sinuously parallel to the distant river. Quickly they took bearings on these terrain features and compared notes. Then Pope got on the horn again.

"Birdseye Two-niner, this is Eagle One. We are about a klick from a termite mound, bearing zero-zero on us. Also two klicks east is a pressure ridge that must have been shoved up eons ago. Looks like a green snake. Bearing zero-niner-one. Over."

A long silence followed, one in which Chad Ditto and Doc Welby began to give up on any hope that the choppers were anywhere near them. Then the radio sputtered to life again. "Got you, Eagle One. Okay, you're about half a klick from a suitable LZ, on a heading for you of zero-four-zero. Make it fast, because it'll probably be a hot LZ. Oh, and I'm sending my Injun friend over to play with your friends. When you see him, mark your position with smoke and panels, if you have them, and get your heads down. Birdseye Two-niner, out."

Tonto Waters felt it first, a thudding in his chest like an increased heartbeat, the steady *whop whop* of rotor blades. Then he saw a mind-boggling sight; slowly rising above the tree line, only the main rotor of the Bell 206B Kiowa eased into view. It hung there a moment, then moved off an oblique angle to their position. Suddenly the fusilage of the deadly machine popped up above the forest.

"Eagle One, this is Kiowa Four-three X-ray. Let's see that smoke, you swabs. Kiowa X-ray out." Pope had already changed frequencies, Tonto noted.

Quickly the SEALs marked the four corners of their defenses with red smoke grenades. When the scarlet billows rose high enough the airborne meatgrinder swung around and began a circular run. From the nose, a 7.62mm mini-gun opened up. Spent casings spewed down the discharge chute. Door gunners added their rain of jacketed slaughter and from pods abaft of the center of balance, puffs of smoke and streaks of light announced a volley of air-to-surface 57mm rockets. The jungle began to erupt.

When the Kiowa completed its sweep, it commenced a second run. This time, when the murderous circle had closed, it streaked upward and dwindled to a tiny dot in the sky. Pope Marino was already up and moving. "Let's get the hell out of here."

Chapter 21

With Tonto Waters on point, the remainder of first squad set off toward the landing zone. They pushed through unspoiled jungle, in a rough squad diamond formation for better security. The point man and tail-end Charlie faced the most risk. In the center of the elongated diamond came Lt. Marino and YO/1C Ditto, the RTO. Given the conditions of the terrain, the distance between each element was considerably less than in open country. At about thirty meters from their start point, Tonto came upon the first bodies.

Mangled and tossed about, ragged toys at the mercy of a careless giant child, they sprawled grotesquely in wet, red heaps. Ten yards beyond, a Type 56 rifle sprayed bullets around Pope Marino. Archie Golden silenced it with a burst from his Stoner. They kept going. Pope contacted Birdseye again and gave him an ETA.

"Roger that, Eagle One. We'll be here. Heck, ain't no place else we can go. Birdseye, over."

"I'll bump you again when we get within fifty meters. Eagle One, out."

Despite obstacles, they kept dead on the correct bearing. Tonto Waters split his attention between his compass and the ground ahead. Occupied with the compass, it came as a surprise, then, when he looked back at the jungle and saw a short, brown man in a conical, woven palm hat and black pajamas directly in front of him.

Swift reactions put the Ithaca 12 gauge in action at once. Tonto fired and missed. Without taking time to react, he pumped up another round and fired again.

Sgt. Nguyen Nguyen (the Vietnamese equivalent of John Jones) had survived the pounding from the Kiowa gunship. He and only four living members of the platoon had broken out of the deadly swath of fire and stumbled off without conscious direction. When he heard the brief exchange of gunfire from back in the direction from which he had come, he knew his blind route could still pay dividends.

He had posted a man to watch, in the event the Americans happened to come the same way. Keeping a strict silence, he motioned for his other three men to take up positions that gave them a good view of their back trail. Then they waited. Nguyen had about reached the conclusion that the Americans had veered to one side or the other, after encountering his man, when he saw the big man with the green face headed directly at him.

Nguyen Nguyen held back until the last possible second, then stepped into the open, his rare, highly prized AK-47 at the ready. The American saw him and reacted with such speed that it shocked Nguyen into numb immobility. As in a dream, he saw the shotgun fire. The shot column shredded leaves above his head and he forced his trigger finger to move.

The first round spat from the muzzle of the AK-47 a fraction of a second before a powerful fist slammed into Nguyen Nguyen's chest and rocked him backward. Multiple impacts assaulted his nerves until they went into overload. Numbed, he sensed the AK still ticking off rounds, though now aimed at the sky. Faintly he heard the dull roar of the shotgun again and his world turned to a splash of red. Blackness quickly followed.

Buckshot had slashed Nguyen's cheeks and sent a spray of blood upward a moment before other pellets slammed into his eyeballs and blinded him. He released the AK-47 and fell backward, to the left. Unconsciousness claimed him before he hit the ground. He lay there, oblivious to his twitching body, until death claimed him.

Archie Golden hosed down another of the VC, his Stoner burring steadily in short bursts on full-auto. Chad Ditto saw that from the corner of one eye and then picked up movement to his right. He swung his AR-15 and let go with a 40mm grenade from the XM-148 under the barrel.

Grotesque shrieks rewarded his effort. An arm's length ahead of him, Pope Marino had gone down on one knee and fired five neatly spaced shots from his AR-15. A big cabbage palm in the receiving end of the assault rifle thrashed and rattled for a moment, then went still. Silence followed. Everyone held their own. From the point, Tonto searched the ambush site and swiveled at the hips to signal the others.

"All clear. Looks like that might be the last of them. This one must have some rank. He's humpin' a Kalashnikov."

Curious, the SEALs came forward. Few of the VC they had encountered had this well-made Soviet rifle. Pope Marino wiped the back of one hand over a dry mouth and croaked softly. "We'd better keep moving. Repeat, it's about time to check in with Birdseye again."

That accomplished, the SEALs covered the last fifty meters to the LZ without scaring up any more of the enemy. They came to the edge of a little grassy space, barely long enough to allow for the tail rotor of the Huey which was comin' forward to carry them home. Pope announced their arrival and moments later the Slick nosed over the trees, swooped down and hovered with the skids four feet off the ground.

Tricky birds, Tonto Waters knew from past experience, it was difficult for the pilot to maintain a static hover.

Every movement threatened to dash the tail, and its vulnerable rotor, into the trees that surrounded the opening. With half of the SEALs covering the other, the dash for deliverance began.

Stubbornly, Tonto Waters insisted on being last to leave. When the others had snagged the skid and rolled over the lip of the door into the interior, Tonto finally followed. Archie Golden stood above him, Stoner to his hip, intent on the tree line. With a whining surge, the chopper lifted off and crabbed through the sky. They'd made it, Tonto noted, and with only a dozen bullet holes in the skin of the Slick.

Jason Slater met the chopper when it landed. A surprise for those aboard. Slater wasted no time. "What the hell did you run into out there, Carl?"

Oh-ho, first names now, Lt. Marino cautioned himself. Carl Marino had this private theory that whenever a Company man got on a buddy-buddy, first name basis, he was getting ready to slide a ten inch stiletto between one's shoulder blades.

"Not sure, Duke," Pope Marino shot back. When he saw the flare of fire in those normally cold, gray, gunfighter's eyes, he regretted the barb. He spoke quickly to cover his *faux pas*. "One hell of a big unit of VC, for certain. There's getting to be more of them in the Delta. Both platoons have noticed it. Funny thing is, they haven't been active against the river patrols or engaged us in any serious fire fights until last night. It must be part of that buildup the Russian was talking about."

Slater laid his steady, storm cloud-colored gaze on Marino and spoke without inflection. "You were hit by a reinforced platoon. Say, thirty-five to forty men. Your two squads took out all but four of them. And you're right, it is part of the buildup. You also stirred up a mighty large hornets' nest. Blew minds all the way to hell and gone right up into North Vietnam."

Lt. Marino's light blue eyes narrowed and took on his well-known thousand mile stare. "How'd you learn all that?" He doubted he would get a straight answer, but considered it worth the try.

Slater spoke softly, barely above a whisper. "My people keep their ears to the ground. Besides, my old friend, Kovietski's been burnin' up the airways to General Hoi and to Department Five."

"Oh? What Department Five is that?"

"*Otdiyah Pyaht* of the *Komitet.*" Slater flashed a warm smile. "Always figured that fucker was KGB. Now you've gone and uncovered him for me. Thanks, I owe you one for that."

Favors from a CIA station chief could be two-edged. Pope decided to file that one for later reference. "Don't get in a hurry to do me any favors."

Jason Slater put a splayed hand to the center of his chest in a mock gesture of hurt. "You wound me. But, you would be surprised what sort of rabbits the Company can pull out of a hat for deserving guys like you."

"Right now, I'd prefer it fried, with mashed potatoes, a stack of Johnny cakes, a bowl of greens, and... well, you get the idea. We're hungry."

"A quick debrief and you can chow down to your heart's content. I'll even see if I can't scare some steak and eggs out of those pot-wallopers in the mess. If they're holding any of them prisoner, I'm sure they can be convinced to release them to me. Bring everyone who was out there with you. And, that won't count against what I owe you. And... by the way, I do greatly admire Mr. Marion Michael Morrison."

"Who?" Pope Marino blinked and asked.

"The Duke, John Wayne. I've seen every film he's made. All of this..." Slater made a depreciating gesture that encompassed his clothing and the outlandish single action revolver he carried. "Out here. ...this has been the only opportunity I've had to emulate him."

Pope Marino's jaw sagged. "Goddamn! First time I've been right about someone and not pleased to be so." He nodded to Slater's left armpit. "Can you hit anything with that?"

Pride shown on the face of Jason Slater. "Qualified Expert just before coming over here, and again last week in Saigon. It ain't fast, and it's got a damn good recoil, but it's dead on when you know how."

"I'll be damned. Let's get on with that debriefing."

LCRD Barry Lailey looked up at the short, stocky men standing respectfully before his desk at Binh Thuy. The two assets working with Buddha had arrived half an hour ago. Neither spoke any English and their purpose had to wait until an interpreter reached the office. Now, LCDR Lailey listened with growing excitement.

"Buddha has received information that the VC cadres are talking about a big buildup. It is coming within a week. One of the cadres, Phon Bai, is to be at a meeting with his contemporaries three nights from now. It will be held near the small village of Rach Gia, near the Cambodian border." The interpreter paused when the ex-VC did, then resumed when the musical words spilled from the informant's lips.

"Phon Bai will travel by boat both ways. He says that Phon is the one with the most knowledge. He will be heavily guarded, and Buddha recommends that he be allowed to come and go unmolested."

Excited by the prospects, LCDR Lailey had other ideas. He would have this Phon Bai yanked out of there and interrogated. Word had come down from NAVSPECWARV that intelligence on the anticipated offensive was so critical that all means were to be employed in order to obtain it. If indeed they considered it that important, Lailey decided, he should go along on the Snatch Op. He turned his attention back to the former Cong.

"How many bodyguards would he be expected to have?"

When the question and answer had been relayed, the interpreter responded. "Probably six. Five armed with AK-47s, as will Phon. The sixth man will most likely have a Chinese Type 30 light machine gun."

Lailey frowned. That 7.92mm LMG packed a lot of punch. It had nearly the range and power of the 8mm machineguns favored by the Germans in WW II. A slower rate of fire, though. He asked a few more pointed questions, thanked the messenger, and told him to thank Buddha as well, then handed the ex-VC a fat, oversized, letter type manila envelope. The fifty thousand in piasters inside would tide the benevolent warlord over for some while. After the informant and the interpreter departed, Lailey took a yellow legal pad from his desk drawer and began to lay out his plan for the kidnapping of the VC cadre, Phon Bai.

He would use first platoon of Team 2, with Marino in command, first and second squads for the actual black bag operation. Grudgingly he had to admit they were the best, and he wanted no second placers around him when he had his ass hung out in Indian Country. He consulted a stack of papers on a clipboard, labeled "Working Ops." The two squads would be coming off an op at 0700, according to that. With strangers in the room, naturally Lailey had not been able to indulge himself in his pastime of monitoring 1st Platoon's radio traffic. So he remained unaware that they had run into trouble and been extracted at 0630. Had he known it, it would not have mattered.

They would be given a day to rest and restore equipment, and a day to rehearse the approach, the actual kidnapping, and extraction. How to do it? It was a hundred klicks down river, then inland another thirty or so. Helicopter most of the way, then go in by boat. Sampans would be best, using some of Buddha's people, something decidedly native and familiar. This was all Charlie country. A wicked smile creased his thick lips and an unholy fire glowed in his small, beady eyes. It could happen that Marino would buy it this time out. Could it be... arranged? He dismissed such thoughts and returned to laying out the operation.

Approach the target, twenty klicks from the village — Rach Gia —overland for the last two klicks by foot. Spyplane overflights had provided excellent photos of every gathering of more than three hutches. There would be good ones on file for Rach Gia. They would provide a good source for cobbling together a mock village for the rehearsal. He had better find them fast and get carpenters to working on the secure range at Tre Noc. Now: Bang—bang-bang, grab Phon Bai and *didi* out. Back the same way they came to the first suitable LZ. Final extraction by chopper. Better and better, LCDR Lailey congratulated himself. Might even get some fast-movers off the *Hornet* to fly cover. At least some A-6s, he modified the plan. He would see to the photos, then get with the S-3 and have the Op Orders cut.

After the debriefing, Jason Slater proved his word to be good as the best. Grinning line-servers slapped thick, juicy steaks on each mess tray for the men of first section, first platoon, added eggs cooked to order, hashbrowns, french toast and all the condiments needed. Only one glum face could be seen. That of Chief Mess Cook Brian O'Doyle. He had been saving back those luscious K.C. strips for a beer, poker, and steak fry party with his fellow Chiefs among the chefs, bakers, and short-order cooks, from throughout the Delta AO.

Amazed at the extent to which Slater had gone, in a minimum of time and threats, Marino wolfed down his food right along with the rest of the men. He took time to sincerely thank the Agency man and then put his men to cleaning and repairing their equipment. When 1st Squad had tended to their gear and weapons, and stacked a sufficient number of Zs in the corners of their rooms, they gathered in late afternoon on the parade ground.

"Let's go to the laundry," Repeat Ditto suggested.

"Yeah, I could stand seeing a *friendly* gook face for a change," Blue Chip Reno approved the idea.

Tonto Waters could taste the beer. He licked his lips and nodded his willingness. Doc Welby could see the tantalizing figure of Francie Song. Archie Golden formed images of his Iris and wanted to be alone to write to her, so he encouraged the others. Before long, all had set off in twos and threes toward the Mi Flower. Archie turned back to the barracks, his mind busy trying to recall where he had left that flimsy air mail stationary.

When Francie Song entered Mi Flower, the beer can pyramid had reached the fourth tier. Momma Rose had recently become affluent enough to buy on the black market and now offered American brands as well as Vietnamese and Japanese. Following the principals of capitalism, an increase in choices led to a growth in business, which in turn allowed her to purchase more items from the entrepreneurs of the shady side, which in turn made her even more money. And none of it had anything to do with cauldrons of steaming, soapy water and other people's dirty clothes. Cartons of cigarettes, jars of instant coffee and gayly wrapped American bath soap lined the shelves built into one wall, perpendicular to the tiny bar. When Francie saw Kent, she wanted to run to him and beg him to forgive her.

Doc Welby didn't know exactly how to react when he first saw Francie Song in the doorway. Part of him wanted to run to her and beg her to forgive him. Another portion urged him to remain aloof. The majority of him longed for the marvelous, silken body that had the power to enchant him, even when fully clothed. As a result, he rose from his chair and made a nod into a gesture of warm invitation.

Francie came to him on uncertain feet. Doc led her to a small table beside the minute bandstand. "I've missed you, Francie."

"Yes. And I have longed to see you again, Kent Welby."

"Does it matter that I still can't introduce you to someone important in the Riverine office? Or anywhere for that matter."

Not understanding, Francie put a hand on Kent's bare, sun-browned forearm. "Am I still angry with you? Is that what you mean? I am not, you should know that."

Doc Welby's features changed into an expression of defeat. "The truth is, I don't know anyone important. I'm just a First Class Petty Officer. As such, I don't talk to officers, except in the line of duty. I wanted to help you so much. I—I was relying on hearing some scuttlebutt, maybe pick up on someone who needed office help." He looked miserable.

"Surely there is a way. Try for me. Please, Kent Welby, try hard for me."

Plummeting once more into the depths of those beguiling eyes, Doc answered with ringing sincerity. "I will, Francie. I promise you I will."

Chapter 22

They sat shoulder to shoulder in the belly of the chopper. Through the open door, Doc Welby could see the nose of another helicopter, which bore Second squad. The lieutenant commander who had bad-mouthed Lt. Marino rode with them. *Well and good*, Doc thought. Pope Marino was good people in his book. He had led them into some hairy situations and come out with no-one panicked and damn few injuries. More than that, he had gotten Archie Golden and Truman Oakes out of the brig and the whole incident erased from official records. And he fought like a tiger. No matter what Lailey said, there was no yellow in Pope Marino.

Doc Welby wasn't so sure about LCDR Lailey. When he went to board the Huey, the potbellied officer had a greenish-white tinge around his lips. And he sweat bucketsful. The hundred kilometer flight couldn't go fast enough for Doc. They had never pulled a kidnapping of a ranking VC leader before. For all his usual nervousness at the outset of a mission, he actually looked forward to this one.

He wanted to be on the ground and moving toward the objective. Doc wasn't too sure about the trip by sampan. Something could go wrong and they would be sitting ducks. A subtle change in the pitch of the rotor blades warned him that they were about to descend. He would know about the sampans before long.

"Two men to a sampan," Lt. Marino instructed when the SEALs had reached the river bank from an LZ composed entirely of sawgrass. Pope Marino turned then with a wintery smile to LCDR Lailey. "Commander, you'll want to be at the center of our little flotilla, I'm sure. We'll depart two at a time, ten minutes apart. Once we get close to the objective we'll close that distance to within sight."

"I know what the op order says," LCDR Lailey grumbled pointlessly.

Tonto Waters took the lead sampan, along with Archie Golden. They lay down on rattan mats across the bottom strakes of the sturdy little vessel. Weapons angled across their bodies at the ready, daylight faded out for the two SEALs as the boatman covered them with more woven mats. At once he pushed off and began to scull up the narrow tributary of the Bassiac. All sound faded and Tonto was left with his thoughts.

He didn't much like having LCDR Lailey along. He was obviously scared shitless of flying. Worse, the man was out of shape, dangerously so. Tonto seriously doubted that the desk sailor could maintain silence during the last klick to the target. All they needed was someone flailing around like a wounded elephant to let the Cong know of their presence. He dismissed that thought and concentrated on the snatch.

Phon Bai would come up river after they had arrived at the hut where the cadre would wait to be taken to the meeting site. Their first job would be to neutralize anyone waiting there for the VC chief. Then, back to the river to grab their subject and haul him off. He hoped these boatmen, sent by Buddha, had their shit together. If they took a wrong turn at the confluence of another stream, that could put them miles from where they should be. Such concerns faded rapidly for Tonto when he heard voices calling a challenge from the river bank.

"Where are you going, Citizen Boatman?"

"To my home. I have been fishing," the ex-VC sculling Tonto's sampan replied.

"Did you have good fortune?"

"Oh, yes." Some of the matting rustled as it was thrown back to reveal a wicker basket filled with fish.

"Umm. Tell me, Citizen Boatman, do you believe in

Father Ho's great plan to redistribute the wealth on an equal basis?"

"Yes—yes, I do, Comrade Soldier."

"Then...don't you think it would only be fair and proper for you to share your catch with us? My comrades and I have not broken our fast as yet, and fish would taste real good."

A heavy sigh. "It is as you say, Comrade Soldier. Here..." The sampan rocked violently and Tonto Waters thought for a moment they would capsize. "Take these two. No, take three, you look very hungry."

"You are most gracious, Citizen Boatman. Pass on in peace."

Tonto Waters had not understood a word, yet he recognized a shakedown when he came upon one. He rolled his eyes and contacted those of Archie Golden. The grinning SEAL had one middle finger extended rigidly. The sculling began again.

When the boat containing Doc Welby came upon the shake-down artists, the boatman exposed two large stalks of bananas. He peeled off two big hands and passed them over to the greedy Viet Cong. They, too, passed by without incident. While the small boat navigated the river, Doc let his mind wander back over his most recent mail, which had begun to arrive at least weekly. In a letter from his mother, she had written:

" *My dear son, I cannot understand it. We have not heard a thing from Betty. It is as though she has fallen off the ends of the earth, Kent. I would suppose by now she would have contacted us about disposing of the house and sending us your belongings. You know I do not approve of divorce. Would that I could have it any other way. That would greatly please me. Although, I have never believed that the girl was the right one for you.* "

She went on with her usual list of Betty's faults, as seen only by a mother-in-law.

For that matter, Doc had not received even a post card. What was Betty doing about the divorce? Had she changed her mind? He wanted it over with, a quick, clean cut and get on with his life. Or did he? That would require some sort of commitment to Francie Song. Did he love her enough to marry her? And, what about her obsession with getting a job at Tre Noc? Would a husband, a home, and a family relieve her anxiety about her future? Kent Welby sincerely hoped that would be the case. Another hail from the river bank took his mind off such worries.

"Where are you going?" a harsh voice demanded.

"To visit my brother who is very sick," the boatman lied smoothly.

"Who is this brother of yours?" Suspicion dripped from the foreign words, which set a knot to tying in Doc Welby's stomach. He had no idea what was being said, but the menace was real enough.

"Nguyen Gap," the boatman responded.

"I know of no one named Nguyen Gap."

"Do you know everyone who lives along this river then?" An edge of defiance in the boatman's tone turned Doc Welby's blood to ice.

"Peasants and lazy river trash," came a sneering reply. "I have no time for such. What is in your sampan?"

Again the matting rustled. "Bananas. I was taking them for my brother to sell to make money for the doctor."

"He does not need to sell so many to get well. We of the People's Liberation Army of the South will tend to his healing... provided he joins us afterward. Here, give me three or four bunches."

"Please, Comrade Soldier. If there are many like you along the river I will not have any for my brother by the time I get to his village. And, they are called hands."

"What?"

"Bananas. When they are grouped together they are called hands."

"I've never heard that before. I suppose they do look like fingers. How far do you have to go?"

"Three lai more. I will be there by midday."

"Get on with you, then. And don't forget to give me the bananas."

Kent Welby waited until the sampan rounded a bend in the river before he let out a long, relieved sigh.

Sr. Lt. Alexi Kovietski sat on the midships thwart of the motorized sampan that bore him down the Thran Gia river. He had received information that the SEALs from Tre Noc were involved in some sort of heavy duty action in the area of the planned offensive. Already he knew that NVA units of battalion strength were on the move south, along the Ho Chi Minh trail. Newly trained guerrillas from Cambodia waited on the border, anxious to get blooded before joining the workers' struggle in their homeland. If the SEALs managed to compromise that operation, there would be trouble enough all the way down the line to him, and beyond. General Hoi should be advised.

He had considered that before leaving his office in Cambodia. Then he reasoned rightly that were he to do so and the general changed his plans for the offensive, it would compromise his own major source of information in the Delta when the Americans found out about the delay. In the end, he concluded that the interests of the Soviet Union and the KGB were of greater priority than those of General Hoi Pak and the People's Republic of North Vietnam. He would withhold the intelligence until it would be too late to change, which should protect his agent in place and still cover him with the NVA.

It didn't stop him from coming to have a look, if possible, at the SEALs in action. What perturbed him now was their location. He turned his head to bark at the boatman. "Why are we this far southeast of Rach Gia?"

"A report came in of unusual activity on the river, Comrade Lieutenant," the man answered placidly.

"What sort of activity?"

"Many sampans on the water, Comrade."

"Of course there are. There is a meeting of cadres at Rach Gia. I am supposed to be there."

Misreading his passenger as being more concerned about his own self-importance, than the possibility of an infiltration by the enemy, typical of all foreign devils, the boatman added, he responded accordingly. "You will be back in ample time, Comrade Lieutenant."

"I had better be. Tell me what you know of these boats that have been sighted."

Uh-oh, he is interested. "They are ten in number so far, Comrade. Each with but a single person in them. Odd wouldn't you say?"

Scorn colored Kovietski's words. "Do they usually go about with people stacked to the gunwales?"

"No. Of course not." Said stiffly.

"What about the arriving cadres? No sighting of them?"

"None so far. They will not be here until late in the afternoon, I think. Except for Phon Bai. He is coming early."

Phon Bai. Kovietski wrinkled his brow. The name should have some meaning for him. Who, or what, was Phon Bai? Then he had it. He was the leader of the cadres in the Committee to Liberate the Delta. That Phon Bai. What a juicy target for the SEALs. Only they would know nothing of his presence. Of that much he could be certain, Kovietski assured himself.

A motor sampan blocked the narrower channel around the small island in the Thran Gia River. Tonto Waters and Archie Golden had been advised of it in broken English while their sampan remained a good two hundred meters from the obvious patrol. The boatman doffed his conical palm frond hat and gave the armed men aboard the power craft a friendly wave as he stopped sculling and his boat lost weight.

"Come over here," one of the black pajama-clad VC commanded.

"But I am late already, Comrade Sergeant."

"You flatter me, I am but a corporal. But we must inspect your boat."

Under the matting, out of sight of the Viet Cong, Tonto Waters closed his hand around a suppressed S&W .38 Super auto loader. Beside him, Archie Golden did the same. Too damn bad if they had to use the "Hush Puppies," Tonto thought. They would have to double up in order for some of these former VC to take the place of the guards killed.

"Oh, I cannot take the time. I am late by so much my wife will not feed me when I get home. She might not even..." He pulled a long, sorrowful face, "sleep on my mat tonight."

Laughter came from the patrol boat. "Someone so concerned about the true essentials of life cannot be a traitor, eh? Tell you what, Citizen, scull past us and we will take only a small, quick look in your sampan."

"I...er...If I must," he relented.

A couple of minutes went by in mounting tension for Tonto and Archie, then the two boats bumped together. A portion of the matting made its familiar rustle. A grunt of distaste came from the patrol sampan.

"What have you got in there?"

"Some fish, that I caught before dawn today."

"They are sure getting ripe, aren't they?"

Glancing first at the large mackerel, then at the VC guards, the boatman gave a big wink. "It doesn't matter. I caught them to make Nuoc Mam."

Tonto visualized the typical Nuoc Mam factory; the grooved boards exposed to the hot, tropical sun, nails struck through them, the flayed mackerel hanging from those by their heads, the juices running down into collection buckets. The flies gathered in clouds. His stomach gave a powerful lurch. And Kent Welby went for that stuff like a kid did for chocolate milk.

"Go then. Quickly."

"Yes. Thank you. Thank you, Comrades."

When the distance had widened sufficiently between the wooden craft, Archie whispered softly, "Close."

"Wasn't it?" Tonto answered, relaxing his grip on the Smith autoloader.

Two hours later the two squads gathered inside the screen of riverside jungle. The last boat to arrive carried four SEALs from Second Squad. "We had to waste a couple of VC on a motorized sampan. They threatened to shoot our boat boy if he didn't let them search."

"The kid's got nerve. He didn't blink an eye when we blew them away. We waited for the last boat and left its owner there to take care of the other sampan and the dead men," Chips Danner added.

Pope Marino frowned. "I don't like that. Although I'll admit I thought of doing it if anything went wrong when we went by." He stood to his full height, stretched, trying his land legs again. "Well, First Squad gets all the fun jobs. Let's go neutralize that hutch where Comrade Phon is supposed to go. The rest of you hold what you've got and don't be seen."

Without exchanging a word with LCDR Lailey, Lt. Marino and first squad faded into the jungle. They skirted wide of the faint trail, in order to avoid any guards which had been posted. It turned out to be less than a klick to the low hut.

Three VC lounged in the shade of a cabbage palm to one side of the crude structure. No sign of any ranking Cong officers. So far everything had gone as Buddha had predicted. Tonto and Archie took opposite ways around the small clearing. They approached the lazing men stealthily , suppressed pistols at the ready. At a range of less than ten feet, Tonto halted and took careful aim. The big can hung on the muzzle of the .38 Super contained most of the sound when he fired. Only a wheezing *phut*! came from the parted end-wipe when the slug spat out.

Two of the Cong dropped like stones before the third realized something had happened. Then he too took a round in the chest. The gelatinous Hydroshock material in the hollow point of the bullet created such a violently drastic shock that it shattered his heart like an explosion. Archie Golden stepped out into the open.

"You might say he died without knowin' it."

"You're a lot better shot than I am, Archie. I sure wouldn't want to go for two so fast."

"Yeah, Tonto. You'd probably miss one, or both."

"Well, fuck you very much, O dead-eyed one."

"Now what?" Archie asked.

From close behind him came the irritated voice of Pope Marino. "You drag those bodies off and get the hell out of sight."

"Aye-aye. You think they've got any little brown friends hangin' around, L-T?"

"Let us hope not. I for one am ready for those birds to get us out of here. Meanwhile, we hold this place until it is time for the snatch."

Murphy's Law had been put in high gear for the SEALs that day. If anything could go wrong, it went wrong. The sampan transporting Phon Bai arrived near 1600 hours. The short, bowed, wrinkled man in his early forties, with jet-black hair, a long, whispy droop of mustache and vandyke beard climbed out sprightly enough and started up the trail with only three of his bodyguards. That left LCDR Lailey holding an empty bag. He and second squad were to have made the snatch before Phon got out of the boat.

An unexpected jink by the operator of the motor sampan prevented this. Then with three alert and observant guards left behind, including the man with a light machine gun, they were unable to quietly jump the subject before he struck off at a fast clip along the trail. They would have to silence the guards, Ensign Ott realized. Accordingly, he directed two of the squad to each guard. The men, all with suppressed weapons, took time maneuvering through the bush until they reached positions close enough to their designated target to be effective.

Then they took careful aim and fired as one. So accurate was their countdown that the six bullets struck within a quarter of a second, two of them placing theirs simultaneously. The boatman stared dumb struck as the trio of guards went down in bloody, tumbled heaps. He didn't even wait to determine what had happened. Instead, he yanked frantically on the pull-rope of the outboard motor so it roared to life. In a fog of blue smoke, he spun the sampan into the current and sped off up river at full throttle.

Behind him, second squad started off after Phon Bai. They caught up to him as he reached the clearing with the hootch. One bodyguard went down before any of Chief Sturgis' men could open fire. He had been dropped by a

.30-06 round from the 700 Remington in the hands of Doc Welby. The long, fat suppressor on the end of the barrel chuffed a second time to put another round into the target just as Chips Danner cut down another bodyguard. Tonto Waters took out the remaining one while two other SEALs rushed forward and grabbed Phon Bai.

Lt. Pope Marino came into view in the doorway of the hootch and started forward. "Not the way we rehearsed it, but a good job anyway. Now let's *didi* the hell out of here. Repeat, let me have the radio."

When he reached the waiting Hueys, he was brisk with his report. "This is Eagle One. We have a bird in hand. I say again, we have a bird in hand. There's a clearing here big enough for an LZ. The coordinates are… " According to standing procedure, he read them off backward. "Eagle One, over."

"Roger, copy that, Eagle One. ETA is five minutes. Over."

"Roger, Kingpin. We'll pop green smoke to mark the LZ. Eagle One, out."

So far, so good. And only one living Cong knew they were there.

Which lasted only until the frightened sampan operator blundered into the patrol boat bearing Sr. Lt. Kovietski downstream. He blurted out the news, showed the bodies to the Russian, who observed them with cool detachment, and then ordered the boatman to lead him to the spot.

Chapter 23

When they reached the spot indicated by the frightened boatman, Sr. Lt. Kovietski studied the terrain carefully, with the aid of a pair of Ludoyi 5x75, inert gas binoculars. He found not the least sign that the SEALs had indeed landed here or ever been deployed in the jungle around the landing site. It came first as an impression on his subconscious. A rhythmic throb that quickly grew into an audible presence, which he could not ignore. He knew that sound only too well.

It came from the rotor blades of one or more helicopters. They were winding up to lift off. And not far away. Sr. Lt. Kovietski raised his field-glasses to stare over the treetops. He had no sooner focused on the increased distance than the blur of revolving rotor blades, their pitch set for maximum lift, filled the field of his glasses. Three of them, and less than a kilometer away.

Fury burst like a hand grenade in Alexi Kovietski's chest. "*Leshad locha!*" he exclaimed in baffled surprise, then repeated, "Horse piss!"

How had they gotten here so soon and completed their mission so fast? He made a futile wish for an SA-7 Strela (the ones the West called Grail) missile tube. He could knock those troublesome SEALs right out of the air. They had a range of nearly 10km. And for all the weaknesses they showed in taking on jet aircraft, helicopters were their borsht. All he had was an ancient DShK-38 mounted on a pedestal on the forward, covered deck of the motorized sampan. Even so, it was good to 1000 meters. The fat, 12.7 mm slugs would tear a helicopter apart.

Sr. Lt. Kovietski darted around the side of the low cabin and shoved the small Vietnamese gunner away with enough force to nearly put the slightly built man in the water. "Get away from there," Kovietski growled in Vietnamese. "Let me have that gun."

Alexi Kovietski cut off five rounds before the badly worn, overworked machine gun jammed. The falling, green tracer told him how far off target he had been. The KGB *resedentura* yanked open the receiver and looked inside. Eyes squinted as though in terrible pain, Kovietski pounded a helpless fist against the mangled casing that had stuck in the chamber, receiving the nose of another round in its base so as to make clearing the weapon a job for an armorer. All the while he cursed the Fates, the American Hueys moved serenely away.

Once the choppers gained sufficient altitude, the interrogation of Phon Bai began at once. LCDR Barry Lailey wore the crew chief's big, plastic crash helmet, with boom mike in place. He had it set on cabin intercom and issued instructions to those with headsets.

"Bring that little fucker over to the door," he commanded.

Lailey then motioned for two of the three interpreters to take Phon by the ankles. They went to their knees and took secure holds on the thin shanks of the VC cadre, who looked on with an expression of bored disgust. Anticipating what Lailey had in mind, the two ARVN soldiers braced themselves with a foot against the bulkhead at either side of the open door. LCDR Lailey and the other interpreter moved in close to the Cong leader. Lailey stuck a set of headphones on Phon's ears.

"Now, you are going to answer some questions for me," he demanded through the interpreter.

"My name is Phon Bai. I am a prisoner of war and must be accorded the protection of such persons under the Geneva Convention."

"You are a goddamned guerrilla, terrorist, son of a bitch and you're going to answer me straight or else."

Kent Welby had a headset on and looked up in confusion at the rage that emanated from LCDR Lailey. The man couldn't be wrapped too tightly, he considered. He was skirting right on the edge of violating every international agreement ever written on the handling of prisoners. Doc Welby winced when he saw the smug smile crease the lips of Phon Bai.

"My name is Phon Bai. I serve the People's Liberation Army of South Vietnam."

Lailey's hand shot out and smacked solidly into the center of Phon's chest. Phon Bai spilled backward out the door, trailing the cord of his headset. Lailey crouched and peered out. A cold hand clutched at his stomach and his fear of flying nearly choked him out of the action.

"How many were to be at that meeting tonight?" he finally barked out.

"My name is Phon Bai..."

"One of you let go, just for a second," Barry Lailey ordered.

The Vietnamese holding Phon's right ankle released his grip. For a moment, the VC leader flailed wildly in the chopper's slipstream. Then the interpreter snagged his leg and drew him back against the fuselage of the Huey.

"I'm going to give you one more chance. How many ranking cadres will beat that meeting in Rach Gia?"

"My name... UH!... twenty-five." His change of heart came when he felt the grip of both ARVNs loosening. "Twenty-four without me," Phon added dispiritedly.

"What topics are on the agenda?" Lailey snapped, the last word swallowed in a gulp of fear when the helicopter entered a down-draft.

"I do not know," Phon toughed it out.

"Why the hell don't you? You're the ranking man, from what I hear. It's *your* meeting."

Phon compressed his lips and remained silent. Lailey

ranted and threatened, yet knew he could not allow the perfectly willing ARVN troopers to drop Phon from the craft. The man was simply too valuable to the intelligence net. Phon Bai remained that way, steadfastly refusing to talk, suspended outside the chopper from most of the journey back to Tre Noc. Only when they came within visual range of the base did LCDR Lailey give the order to haul their prisoner back inside.

When the choppers grounded, Tonto Waters saw that the professionals had come down for the formal interrogation of Phon Bai. Jason Slater was there, in wash-faded Levi's jeans and jacket, his pearl gray Stetson now sporting patches of a fuzzy jungle growth. Along with him was another spook that none of the SEALs had seen before. Before reporting for debriefing, Lt. Marino asked to talk with LCDR Lailey in private. Tonto decided it would be a good idea to have another set of ears in on this conversation so he hung close enough to pick up on their short, harsh exchange.

"What is it, Marino?" Lailey snapped impatiently.

"It's about the way the prisoner was questioned aboard the chopper, sir. I know that Marvin the ARVN goes in for that a whole lot. Usually with multiple prisoners, so they can toss out one or two to make the others talk. Thing is, sir, it's against regulations for us to do the same. It also violates every convention on the treatment of prisoners of war. If Phon convinces those spooks that it was done to him, we could all be in some deep shit, sir."

LCDR Lailey put on a mocking expression of dismay. "You're worried about *me*, Marino? I'm touched. It's not that you've never done anything that violates regulations, of course. What about those extra radios you have? That refrigerator in the platoon bar? And, we still have Saigon with us, don't we?"

Lt. Marino wanted very much to ask how Lailey had learned of that incident, but considered it wiser to remain silent. Lailey accurately read the expression Marino affected and tore into it with malicious glee.

"I have my ways of learning of your escapades. Particularly your jumping the chain of command, and even going outside the Navy, to whine to General Belem." His small, beady eyes narrowed. "I would advise that you keep your mouth shut about my interrogation of Phon Bai, if you don't want to end your military career cleaning the officers' head at the Naval Station in Iceland."

Not without a hell of a lot more clout than Barry Lailey had, Pope Marino thought angrily. Rocks and Shoals (Captain's Mast) was about all their Saigon escapade merited. No way there was a general court in his future.

Lt. Marino forced a smile. "Not to worry, then. They won't get any corroboration from me, sir. I don't trust those CIA pukes as far as I do *you*, sir. Now, if you'll excuse me, sir?" Before Lailey could blare out any outraged rebuttal, Marino pivoted on one heel and walked off to the debriefing shed.

With the debriefing completed and after-action reports filled out, a yeoman came to invite Lt. Marino and Chief Waters to the small, windowless room where Slater and the other CIA cowboy were working on Phon. Slater had apparently warmed up to his subject, but broke it off to greet them warmly.

"You did a great job. Nailed this little sucker cold. I hear nobody even took a hit. Good work." Slater produced a sheepish grin. "To tell you the truth, I don't know what makes this turkey tick. I'd like to take him apart to see if his mainspring is wound too tightly." Jason Slater swung back to Phon Bai and snapped a question in a harsh tone.

"When is General Hoi's offensive scheduled to begin?"

In a tired tone, made more weary by the strain of hanging upside down out the door of the Huey, Phon Bai answered again, "My name is Phon Bai. I am a peaceful teacher in my district. I know nothing of what you ask."

"We know your name, you little prick," Slater barked suddenly in Vietnamese. "We also know you are the Secretary General of the Communist Party in the Delta, and the leading cadre for Charlie Cong. Now, Mr. Phon...or do you prefer Colonel Phon?" Swiftly seizing on it, Slater acted on the fire that glowed in Phon's eyes for a moment. "Proud of that rank of colonel, aren't you? So, tell me, Colonel Phon, when does your 'master' intend to send his little brown men against us and run us out of the Delta?" His voice dripped denigrating sarcasm.

"He is not my master. We are comrades, equals." Pride betrayed Phon again.

"Except in rank."

"Yesss," Phon hissed, hating himself for opening up even this slight bit. "Except in rank."

Over the next half hour, Jason Slater continued to prick Phon Bai with such little barbs and innuendoes, poking him in his one vulnerable spot, his ego. Tonto Waters grew to appreciate the fact that Jason Slater was far from the poseur the SEALs imagined him to be. Even Pope Marino took advantage of a momentary break to whisper his observations in Tonto Waters' ear.

"This guy has to be one of their best. Slater's a highly skilled interrogator. He's not some ding-a-ling wannabe who's elevator doesn't run to the penthouse."

Tonto nodded silent agreement. Then Jason Slater put aside the glass of chilled mineral water he had been sipping from and began again. The tidbits kept coming, but over all they got less than sterling product out of Phon Bai. At last, Slater signaled that he had completed his preliminary go-around.

"We'll take him back to Saigon, wring him out, chemical debriefing, all that shit. Sooner or later we'll have it all. We'll work on what we've got and there'll be an intelligence briefing for your platoon after noon chow."

When all four squads of 1st Platoon had assembled in the briefing room — a partitioned off section of one of the metal-walled machine shops, Jason Slater gave them the analysis he and his fellow CIA man had made of what Phon had given. It was, by his own admission, spotty. Which prompted Doc Welby to remark in a stage whisper that as far as he could tell, "Military Intelligence is an oxymoron."

"An oxy—what?" Archie Golden asked when the snickers had died down.

"Oxymoron," Doc Welby explained patiently. "That's a condition or situation that is the exact opposite of what the words imply, something that simply cannot happen."

"Hey! You got that one right, Doc," Archie chortled.

A shadow fell over the two SEALs. They looked up to see Jason Slater and Lt. Carl Marino standing over them. "Pope, here, has convinced me to allow your squad to have a little go at our friend, Phon Bai. See what you can get that we didn't?"

"Okay by me, Mr. Slater," Archie gulped to cover his moment's embarrassment.

"Fine with us, sir," Doc Welby added, aware that he had once more allowed himself to engage his mouth before his brain was in gear. "We—ah—might need half an hour, say, to figure out a new approach."

"You've got it, sailor," Slater snapped, showing not the least annoyance at the by-play.

When Lt. Carl Marino, Chief Tom Waters, YO/1/C Kent Welby and MA/1C Richard Golden entered the interrogation chamber half an hour later, Archie held a contraption that had definitely sinister properties. It appeared to be two blocks of plastic explosive, taped together, with a chemical time detonator stuck in the top like a birthday candle. This he sat on the center of the table in front of Phon Bai. He took a seat at a right angle to the VC leader. Pope Marino took the chair opposite. Lt. Marino cleared his throat and began to ask questions.

Phon Bai remained motionless, though he sweated profusely, and refused to answer. After five minutes of this fruitless endeavor, Archie reached in to one baggy pocket of his BDU's and produced another time pencil. He waved it under Phon's nose and hung a lopsided grin on his freckled face.

"I'm sure you know what this is? Well, in case you don't, I'll tell you. It's a Mark IV, chemical time detonator, manufactured by Dow Chemical Company," Archie chattered on, his words translated by the interpreter, who cast repeat nervous glances at the object in Archie's hand and the device on the table.

"It's activated like this..." Archie gave a twist to the upper quarter of the flat, black stem. It made a grating, crackling sound. "When the mix of the two chemicals in here reaches the right potency, it generates an electrical charge that sets off the detonator....which, in turn, sets off the explosives. Believe me, those folks at Dow can make these remarkably precise. They claim up to plus or minus one second. This is a three minute one. We're going to find out in just.."Archie consulted his diver's watch, "two minutes and thirty four seconds how accurate it is."

He picked up the explosive package on the table and lay the chemical detonator in its place. Gingerly he carried the bomb to the far side of the room. No one said a word as the time ground agonizingly slowly toward the climax. Archie kept looking at his watch, nodded in satisfaction and planted a broad grin on his face. The interpreter moved away from the table. Lt. Marino and Doc Welby did likewise. Phon Bai began to run rivers of sweat.

He could not take his eyes off the deadly timer. The

seconds seemed like eons and it showed in his face. He knew only too well how the Czech and Soviet models worked. When two minutes and thirty-three seconds had been consumed, there came a bright flash, a sharp crack and a puff of acrid smoke from the detonator. It's shattered pieces flew to the edges of the table. A blackened hole still smoldered where the firing tip had rested when Archie came back and placed the taped package directly in front of Phon Bai.

"This one is a ten minute timer," Archie explained in his irritatingly patronizing tone, throwing a glower at the ARVN interpreter to insure he repeated every word. "I'm going to set it and you are going to start talking. Answer every question honestly and we'll get rid of the bomb. As you should have noticed it is made from some of the Symtex we captured. It's enough to turn this cinder block building into a mound of gray dust. And you, my friend, will be a red, wet memory."

Lt. Marino took over again. "What is the date of the offensive?"

Phon sweated away a whole minute of his ten then gulped and gasped out a reply. "Two weeks. Men are already gathering."

"What are the specific targets for the troops?"

"This base, of course. And all other American foreign devil bases in the Delta. Any village that has aided your cause."

"Name them," Marino barked.

Phon shot a long glance at the silently ticking package of death and licked dry lips. The spew of Vietnamese names rattled out of him in an endless rush. Suddenly something occurred to him. If the building would be destroyed, these men would die also. His litany dried up.

"Of course, we'll be long gone before the ten minute mark," Archie prodded, correctly reading Phon's new source of reluctance. "Keep talking."

Phon became downright frantic in his effort to convey

all he knew of General Hoi's plans. He named the units of NVA troops in transit. He was panting and his voice had become a sob when the timer neared the nine minute, forty second point. Still he poured it out. He was in mid-sentence when time ran out.

Crack!

Smoke roiled up from the small hole the detonator had blown in the taped-together blocks of Bondo crack filler. That's when Phon Bai knew that he had been had.

Chapter 24

YO/1C Kent Welby had not been in the compound at Binh Thuy since their return from Saigon. He had come to pick up the intelligence analysis and area photos for the final search and destroy mission, to which they had been assigned. The first thing he saw was the thick cluster of new buildings, modified versions of double-wide modular homes, that had sprouted in his absence. He tried to visualize the use to which they would be put by the staff, and failed. Accustomed to the loose-as-a-goose, Spartan structure of the SEALs, he could not imagine the need for so much space, contained within walls. Sea, Land, and Air were the elements that made up the acronym SEAL. The out-of-doors was the realm of the SEALs.

Had he really thought that? he arrested his runaway philosophizing to consider. Was he really all that ballsy? He knew he had changed since coming to Vietnam. Had it been that much? Doc Welby felt his cheeks grow warm from a deep blush. He had conquered it, though, by the time he entered the G-2 office. The orderly room stood empty before him. He knew the way to LCDR Lailey's office, and so went past the chief's desk and down the short hall. He found the door open and was about to knock on the facing partition when he heard Lailey's voice from inside.

"Good to hear from you, Ralph," Lailey stated affably. A silence followed, during which Doc Welby recognized this as a phone call. "Yes… it is a damn' shame. Right now there's little can be done about it… Oh, yes, I've been sticking his neck out for him all I can. That upstart little puke must be bullet proof. . No, sorry I can't do anything more for you. Oh, there is a big op laid on. Marino will spearhead it, naturally. Best chance of an accident I can see... What? No, I don't mean anything like that, Ralph. Why, that would be cold blooded murder." A soft chuckle came then.

Doc Welby drubbed his memory for anyone named Ralph. Whoever, it was obvious that Ralph and LCDR Lailey were on the best of terms.

"Yes—yes, you're right about that. It could be traced back too easily. D'you have any CID types assigned to your office?"

That's it! That Army major, Harkness. Doc Welby's mind raced beyond the bounds of common sense. Could that fight have been a set-up? Something plotted by these two? Doc took tight rein on his galloping imagination. That was nonsense. Where or how could they have met before, to be in a position to trust each other in such a bizarre plot? Yet, it sure was obvious they both had it in for Pope. Doc Welby filed that for future reference, cleared his throat and knocked loudly on the door jam.

LCDR Handley, the NAVSPECWARV G-3, had come down to Tre Noc for the final briefing. He paced on the small raised platform of nailed-together ammo cases as he outlined the operation order to the SEALs of 1st and 2nd Platoons. He had given the departure time, the coordinates of the AO, course and altitude to be followed by the Hueys during the extraction, and jump-off time. Hadley carried a long pointer made of polished mangrove, with a spent 7.62mm slug for a tip and the casing as a base. With it, he pointed frequently to the islands in the Bassiac that the SEALs had previously verified to hold supply bunkers.

"First Platoon will spearhead the operation, with first squad taking the lead. You will begin at the far south bunker and work your way north. The four squads of First

Platoon will secure the area around each of the targeted supply dumps. Establish perimeter defenses and hold them from the enemy while the squads of Second Platoon, reinforced by counterparts from ARVN, will destroy the contents of the bunkers. Then First Platoon leap-frogs beyond its own northernmost element and you do it all over again, until the supplies are all eliminated."

"If I may, Chet?" LCDR Lailey interjected, "Now, one thing to keep in mind. No matter what the numbers, First Platoon personnel are to deny the VC any access to the surrounding terrain, or to the islands, until sapper charges are attached and the fuses running."

"In other words, keep Charlie out until if he rushes in after you pull out, it will be to die," Handley simplified with a light laugh. "Now, the entire action is to take no longer than two days and two nights, taking out eight supply caches each night.

"On your handout maps, your ROD sites and RPs will be marked. You will be inserted by PBRs, and extraction will be by helicopter. The LZ will be marked on the maps of each officer and lead petty officers. Set your watches to Zulu time. The whole op will be run on that. Orient your maps the moment you set foot on land, unless, of course, you are under fire at the time," he added with a ghost of a chuckle. Handley went on with the myriad of details that seemed to get hung on any op order devised by a higher headquarters, usually non-SEAL.

At last the Operations and Planning officer asked the inevitable question. "Are there any questions?"

Pope Marino had one. "If we're to deny the terrain to the enemy do we follow the standard rules of engagement?"

Handley gave him a long, cool look. "This is just between us chickens, "he said at last. "According to our intel, you will be facing the largest concentration of Viet Cong that has ever been assembled in the Delta, augmented by at least three battalions of NVA regulars. You are to kick ass, kick-ass, and keep on kicking ass. Don't waste time taking names. This is so critical that we have even managed to get the Air Force to agree to lay on close air support. They'll have 20 mike-mike mini-guns, fifties in the wings, air-to-surface missiles, even napalm if you call for it. To put it bluntly, Lieutenant, you are to throw the rules of engagement out the fucking window." He received no other questions.

"We won't be needing a sniper, Doc. There'll be no time for finesse," Lt. Marino announced as he handed Doc Welby a Stoner. "Think you can do all right with this?"

"Aye-Aye, sir, it's my second best weapon," Doc reminded his CO, relieved to have the greater volume of fire at his command.

"Oh, and link up another two hundred rounds," Marino made his parting shot.

"I thought we had cans of belted ammo, sir?" Welby asked uncertainly.

"We do. And the Riverine guys are taking them to our AO right now. They'll be cached at our Rest Over Day sites." He made a wry face. "Although I doubt we'll be doin' much resting, if that brass hat from G-2 has it right."

Tiny tendrils of the old doubts began to seep into Kent Welby's consciousness. This was the biggest thing they had taken on so far. Maybe the biggest they'd ever be involved in. He made an effort to push the uncertainties back. He'd come through everything so far, hadn't he? Besides, outside of himself, what did he have to go back to? Betty was history, or soon would be. Then, unbidden, visions of Francie Song rose behind his eyes.

Francie, smiling and laughing, her eyes sparkling with the pleasure the expensive — by her lights — dress he had bought for her, which she now wore to dinner. Francie, pensive, chin in one palm, looking out at the rain falling on the mud river the street had become. Francie, singing to him and no one else, caught in the single bright cone of light on the stage at Mi Flower. Francie, her amber skin glowing with the contentment of intense lovemaking. Doc Welby managed to stifle a groan before it could free itself and be heard by his teammates.

"Thinking about your Oriental squeeze?" Archie Golden asked accurately.

"Yes, damnit," Doc snapped. "Francie and what kind of heavy shit we're going to run into out there."

"Hey, if it happens, it happens. And I'll sit *shiva* for you. Anyway, *sei gesund*, Doc."

Lt. Marino had taken in their little exchange and added his own encouragement for Doc. "Maybe what he needs, my Hebrew philosopher, is something more positive than a wish for good health. Perhaps *l'chaim* would be appropriate?"

Archie grinned up at the stocky officer. "'To life,'" he quoted. "Yeah. I like that, Pope. We could all use a little of that."

"What is this?" Tonto Waters asked, swaggering over under the weight of his usual shotgun and an M-79 grenade launcher. "You three buyin' into the gloom and doom shit just because we're goin' up against the whole Viet-fucking-Cong?"

Their tension broken, Pope Marino laughed openly. "Now there's a man with an attitude."

"I'll 'attitude' you, Pope—er—sir. Anybody in this platoon gets to feelin' lower than whale shit — which is on the bottom of the ocean, by the way — just stick by the ol' Chief. I'll drag you through by your boot straps if I have to."

Archie elbowed Doc in the ribs. "Now there's a man who never lacks confidence."

"We're all going to need a dose of that before long," Pope Marino reminded his men, his mood sober again.

"Yeah. Take two aspirin and call me in the morning," Tonto quipped.

PBRs took the SEALs to their area of operation as usual. For some reason the VC had not uncovered that the river patrol boats were used to transport the Men with Green Faces. They would stumble across it eventually, and some new security ruse would have to be employed. For this operation, Lt. Carl Marino would be needed to coordinate both platoons, so Ensign Wally Ott set off with 3rd and 4th squads, while Tonto Waters commanded 1st and 2nd. Dusty Rhodes led the second platoon, which would come in an hour before dark and start on the task of destroying the supply dumps. For the first night's mission, Pope Marino would stay aboard one of the PBRs to stage manage both units.

He had come up with enough hand-held radios for each squad to have one, with two channels each: one for inter squad communication and the other for forward air control. Command and control base communications would be handled by the RTOs on the Prick-25s. Tonto Waters grumbled over the exigencies of command that took him out of his usual point position, Truman Oakes replacing him in that post.

"I should be out there," Tonto muttered under his breath.

From close at his side, Repeat Ditto asked, "What, Chief?"

"Nothin'. True Blue's a good enough point man, but... it's what I live for. Never mind. We're takin' the farthest cache, got that?" Command responsibilities weighed heavily on Tonto's shoulders. "Stick close, you hear?"

"I know my job, Chief," Repeat pouted.

That got to Tonto Waters. He forced a grin. "Sure you do, kid. It's me. I'm not used to runnin' the show."

Chad Ditto produced a sunny smile. "You'll do all right, Chief."

It had been worked out at the briefing. Rather than try to occupy a small island with the enemy, and later elements of second platoon, they would stay on the west bank of the Bassiac. True Blue led the squad along the river bank to the target and they set up in the trees and underbrush along a stretch opposite the largest island. It would have been better, Tonto reasoned to himself, if they had the river between them and the bad guys. But the stated purpose of the mission was to deny access to the enemy. So, instead of watching the island, they peered into the shadowy illumination of the jungle. Grateful for all the lessons in patience they had received in UDT/R school, Tonto Waters let time roll past him without feeling the weight of its heavy feet.

Not so for Kent Welby. Doc missed the comforting feel of his 700 Remington. He even longed for the false sense of security afforded by his sniper's bench. To banish those disquieting thoughts, he let his mind drift back to the same familiar sore spot; Betty.

"I don't *care* what you do," Betty had snapped at him on Monday of their last week together. "Just so long as you do it here with me."

Dense. Stupid. He had not seen it as a warning sign. In agonizing detail he reexamined every word either had spoken, considered what he thought at the time to be the reason behind each argument. It all added up to a single thing. He had never truly known Betty. And, considering her foot-dragging on getting the divorce papers, he doubted that she actually knew herself.

"Don't you realize what this is doing to me?" she had wailed on Tuesday.

"It's my life, isn't it?" he has growled back like a spoiled little boy. "It's a career choice I have to make, right?"

"What about your wife? Doesn't she have any say in your future?"

"No—no, you really don't That's up to me. . and the Navy."

Talk about insensitive, Doc Welby chided himself while he kept watch for Charlie. It was a cop-out, denying the woman's side in such situations. Or so he'd been told by other team guys who had gone through similar experiences. *Where were the VC?* They had to be out there somewhere, coming to the river by the hundreds, maybe the thousands.

"Why won't you make an effort to understand me, Kent?" Betty had pleaded Wednesday.

"I have," he had answered, feeling helpless. "Believe me, I know this is difficult for you."

"How could you possibly know what it's like?" she changed themes.

"I thought you said I should make an effort to understand you?"

Oh, hell, he'd said the wrong thing again. Betty fled from the room in tears. Women, he thought bitterly, while his gaze roved across the terrain in front of him. You can't live with them.. and you can't live with them. And suddenly, there was Francie right in front of him.

"Don't you see, Kent Welby, it is my future. I have to get a job working for your Americans."

It jolted Doc Welby to realize that she had used almost the exact words he had in order to justify his position. With a start, he thought he knew how Betty had felt. He sensed, rather than saw, movement to one side and cut his eyes that direction.

"It's not just your life you're risking, it's both our lives," Betty had wailed on Thursday.

They had not made love since the first of the month, when Kent had told her that the Team was getting orders to 'Nam, and that first and second platoons would be going. Was that a VC out there? Doc used the trick of looking all around an object, rather than directly at it, until it moved again.

Son of a bitch! Their in-country orientation briefing had informed theSEALs that normally these creatures never ranged this far west. Hardly ever left Cambodia. But there he was, the biggest fucking tiger Kent Welby had ever seen. And this time without bars to separate them. With only the slightest sign of caution, it padded out into the grassy swath between the riverside trees and the jungle proper.

It's head was bigger than a bushel basket. Yellow-white fangs protruded below the lower lip. The big nose twitched as it sniffed the air. The air seemed to vibrate with a low rumble. That couldn't be a growl. The beast showed no other signs of finding anything out of order. It...had to be—purring.

"Go away, kitty," Doc Welby whispered under his breath. "Nice kitty, go away."

It had to have been driven ahead of the advancing VC, Doc reasoned. Now, if it only kept on the move, without finding any of them, all would be well. Watching the magnificent animal move with perfect grace made Doc a little giddy. Suddenly he was reminded of the old joke about the British soldier in India who was afraid of snakes. He had confided his fear to the Brigadier reviewing the troops, who had advised that the thing to do with snakes was to slowly put one's hand around its body, slide upward, with thumb extended and, at the last moment, give a quick jerk to snap it's neck. Several months later, as the story had been told to Kent at UDT/R training, the Brigadier had once more been reviewing the troops. He came upon the herpetophobe and stopped in astonishment. The man was all torn to hell, bandaged and walking with a crutch.

"What happened my good man?" the Brigadier asked.

"Well, sor, beggin' yer pardon, sor, it was them snaikes, sor."

"How ever did a snake do this to you?"

"It's like this, sor..." and the private went on to describe a night patrol on which something had coiled around his chest. It was long and round; a snake sure enough.

"So I did exactly like yez said, sor." He had run his hand up the round body, thumb extended and when the snap came, all hell had broken loose, as he explained in the punch line:

"An', beggin' yer pardon, sor, but have yez ever found yerself wit' yer thumb up a tiger's arse?"

Doc Welby caught at the laughter bubbling up in his throat and held it down, along with his breath, while the gorgeous orange beast strolled across the open ground and faded into the mangroves along the Bassiac. The slurping sound of something large lapping delicately at the water came to Doc's ears. Then, a moment later:

"Oh… my… God!"

Sounded like Archie Golden had found the tiger. Doc Welby looked around him and noted how time had shifted while he examined his fiasco with Betty, and viewed the tiger. A look at his watch told him local time was 1823 hours. He rummaged in a deep pocket of his utility jacket and brought out a C-Ration can. "Beans and Wieners in Tomato Sauce," he read off the label. Not too bad, as C-Rats went, he considered. A P-38, taped separately from his dog tags opened it quickly and he replaced the beaded chain down the front of his green T-shirt.

Doc ate with the tip of his K-Bar knife. The beans and so-called "Sauce" he drank down, washed it with a sip of halizone tablet-flavored water, and settled in to watch night fall.

It came rapidly, as it always did in an equatorial jungle. When a glance at the softly glowing face of his watch told Doc that the time had come, he reached for his set of IR, night vision binoculars and turned them on. Slowly he searched the jungle to the west, then pivoted his body so he faced the river. Subjective lenses to his eyes, he scanned the low mound of tropical growth on the island in front of him. Sure enough, there stood Charlie. And ten feet away, another VC. Beyond them, three more. He marked their position by the dark shapes of inanimate objects around them, then lowered the glasses and took up his Stoner.

Once he opened up it would blow his natural night vision all to hell and gone, but he would have time to recover on the way to the next objective. Doc's thumb slid the selector lever to full-auto and he touched finger to trigger.

True Blue Oakes opened the dance with his SAW. The M-60 rocked and rolled at 600 rpm, chopping the island flora into ragged stalks. A blinding wall of yellow-white wavered before Doc's eyes as the Stoner belched out a five round burst. He shifted to another target and cut loose again. One by one the others in the squad opened up. Screams came from the guards on the island, then utter silence.

Nothing for it now but for someone to go take a look. Verification of his estimate came a moment later as Tonto Waters spoke softly from close at hand.

"Good shootin', True, Doc. I think we got them all. You wanna go over and check 'em out?"

Chapter 25

Kent Welby replaced the drum magazine on his Stoner with a fresh one, unsure as to how many rounds he had fired. He opened the feed cover and carefully inserted the link belt of ammo, lined up the first round on the feed tray and closed the cover. That was the trouble with full-auto fire, he thought. They ate ammo at a hellish rate, with little guarantee you hit a damn thing, even in daylight. His full lips pulled into a grim line, Doc Welby rose from his position and worked his way down the bank of the river. Weapon at the ready, he began his crossover.

On the island he went from one to another of the guards. All had been turned into bloody sieves. Only one remained alive, although unconscious. Doc Welby bit his lip as he held a momentary debate with himself over killing the VC or leaving him for 2nd Platoon. A soft click came as he changed the selector to single shot. The flash and bang lasted only a fraction of a second. Next he made a quick check of the bunker.

Doc waded back and gave the all clear, having found the bunker empty of any human life. Tonto Waters rose out of the shadows. "All right, ladies, time to play leap-frog. I think you all know why you never play that game with the Greek army. Let's go."

They hadn't made it twenty meters when Doc Welby heard the noises made by 2nd Platoon's men as they moved in to place the explosives. There would be one hell of a lot of big bangs this night, he reckoned. And that would bring the horde of enemy troops down on them tomorrow with a vengeance.

Sampans had already reached the next island when the SEALs of 1st Squad came upon it. The Cong had all heard the gunfire and worked feverishly to load on the munitions they were to distribute to their comrades waiting a short distance away. At a signal from Tonto Waters, all of the VC were cut down mercilessly.

Hard to believe the whole night would go like this, Tonto thought as he sent True Blue off on point toward the next target. Tonto set a fast pace, silence meant little now that the enemy had been engaged. Still, he urged Truman Oakes to exercise due caution on point. Wouldn't do to run into some of the people coming to get this shit.

Ten minutes later, True Blue Oakes did just that, however. He smelled the VC before he saw them, and dropped low into the shadow of a fan palm. With a twist of his torso, he sent a thin beam of light back down the trail, flicking the sign for enemy in sight. The SEALs knew exactly what to do. No confusion, no delays.

By the time the last of those VC who waited for the weapons on the island streamed past True Blue, an ambush had been improvised. Unconcerned at the added weight, Archie Golden had brought along half a dozen claymores. He expended two of them on this ambush. He rigged one to fire straight down the trail, on his command, and the other had a trip wire and aimed at a right angle to the pathway.

Oakes moved then, off to the same side he knew the claymore would be placed. It was a good thing he did, too, because the first one went off with a flash and a roar only seconds after he faded from sight behind a tree. Little steel balls came howling down the trail, those that had not embedded in VC flesh. Those behind the leading six or seven leaped to the side of the path, which activated the trip-wire and set off the other mine opposite them. Six more of Poppa Ho's hardcases went off to Buddha in a repeat of the bright light and terrible bang.

In the wake of the ear-bruising explosions, the light spat of small arms fire sounded like lady finger firecrackers — those tiny, old-fashioned cylinders of red paper and flash powder designed to be safe to detonate in the gloved hand of a proper lady. A couple of stray rounds slapped into the tree where True Blue had taken cover. He winced with each impact. That was the trouble with automatic weapons, he thought. They ate ammo at a hellish rate, with little guarantee you'd hit a damn thing, even in broad daylight. Then he saw darker shapes moving against the background of starlit night. He stepped out onto the trail and sawed them down with his Stoner. He heard the soft *bloop!* of an M-79 and dove for the tree again.

Shreds of shrapnel slashed the bark when the 40mm grenade went off. It drew instant reaction from Truman Oakes. "Hey, you loony-tunes, it's me!"

A long, two second silence followed. "Sorry, True. Thought it was an RPK," Tonto Waters replied.

"You did that? You done that to me, Tonto?"

"C'mon, True. Shut up and move your ass. We've got another island to visit."

First Squad moved out once more. One hell of a long, rolling fire fight had broken out ahead and behind, and to their right as they trotted along the river bank. When the came to their third target, they found that two of the guards had crossed over from the island. True Blue drew their fire before he saw them, and he went down like a felled ox. One of the Cong rose from the underbrush to verify their kill. Mistake!

True Blue cut him in half with a burst from his Stoner. The dying VC's comrade tried to rectify the mistake, only to suddenly begin a frenzied dance of mortality as Chad Ditto blasted him from the AR-15 barrel of his XM-148. Excited voices jabbered in Vietnamese from the island. The surviving guards knew they could not go anywhere, and they had no idea how many Americans they faced. They would soon find out, as Tonto Waters signaled the SEALs to spread out and hit the mud mound in the river.

Repeat Ditto and Tonto Waters rained scalding pee on the heads of the Cong on the island with their 40 mike-mike grenades. The angry snarl of AR-15s, Stoners, and the roar of Tonto's shotgun added to the misery being received by the VC. The M-60 in the hands of MA/2C Dave Kimball joined in and it didn't take long. When the fusillade slackened for a moment, a voice in English called from the far bank.

"Hold it, hold it! They're all dead. We've got to rig this island and haul ass."

"You got it, buddy," Tonto Waters saluted his counterpart in 2nd Platoon. Only one more to go for tonight.

That the four squads of both platoons moved rapidly on their night's tasks could be readily verified by the confusion among the enemy. Several VC company commanders reported by messenger and/or radio that they had come against a large American force, estimated to be of battalion size or larger. Their panicked chatter crackled in one voice on top of one another in the radio room of the Delta command post of Sr. Lt. Kovietski. He had chosen to move there during the critical distribution of the weapons and munitions for the offensive and listened to it with growing disgust. At last he grabbed the microphone from his radio operator and shouted down one of the terrified captains.

"*Yeb Vas!*" he snarled, then repeated, "Fuck you! It is not a major offensive by the Americans. You will find that it is nothing more than their Navy's SEALs. Both platoons perhaps, more likely only one. Get control of yourself and your men. Push on toward the river. Keep your unit integrity at all times and attack, attack, attack. You will drive them into extinction that way."

A stunned silence followed, then, in a tentative voice; "Bu—but, you do not command us, Comrade. We were only reporting as ordered."

In a dreadful, deadly, barely controlled voice, Kovietski replied. "My orders are the orders of General Hoi. Now, do as I say, *vi pizda idyot!*"

Calling the rattled captain a pussy idiot might be too strong, Sr. Lt. Kovietski pondered a moment, then dismissed it. If they did not pursue these invaders vigorously, the whole offensive could be brought down in ruin. Of that he had no doubt. The years he had actually spent in Spetznaz before entering the *Komitet* had qualified him to judge that. These soft-handed majors and captains had sat around too long reading their self-inflating propaganda, sipping tea, and fattening themselves while other men did their fighting. They had to find their balls and fast, because the SEALs had to be utterly destroyed.

At their ROD site, the SEALs of 1st Squad resupplied with ammunition and spent an hour resting. Those who wore them changed socks. Everyone dug out fresh shirts and skivvies. Third Squad arrived then and they exchanged war stories for another hour. Any thought of actually resting over a day quickly vanished at O7OO hours.

"What the hell?" Archie Golden gulped coffee to exclaim. The coffee had been heated on a Sterno-like contraption he had made from a C-Rat can and a thin slice off a quarter pound block of C-4. For all its explosive ferocity, the stuff burned nicely, with a hot, clean flame.

Another rip of gunfire came from the direction from which they expected 2nd Squad to appear. "Sounds like Charlie has decided to come out and play in daytime," Tonto Waters said dryly as he reached for his shotgun.

"Maybe we ought to go have a look-see?" Archie suggested.

"Yeah," Tonto agreed. "Mr. Ott's with them. We wouldn't want to lose the smartest Ensign in the Teams."

The volume of fire had increased to what could be platoon size. Ensign Brooks, who had come with 2nd Squad, uncoiled and came to his feet. "We'll swing around to the north and take the Cong in the rear."

"Sounds good," Tonto agreed. "After all, the mighty LCDR Lailey made it clear we were to deny them the terrain."

He said it with a straight face, though his voice oozed sarcasm. It hadn't taken long to savvy the Chief on LCDR Barry Lailey. Already, Tonto worked at stuffing spare shotgun shells in his BDU pockets. Both squads saddled up in less than three minutes. By then, grenades had been added to the fracas.

First Squad made the initial contact. Five Japs had broken off from the VC detachment in a flanking attempt. One of them didn't even have time to register surprise before Repeat Ditto blew him away with a three round burst from his AR-15. Two others made futile attempts to dive for cover.

Tonto blasted one into Nirvana with a load of No. 4 shot. That left a startled pair with slightly more smarts than their comrades. They stared in shock at the camouflaged faces of the SEALs, popped a couple of quick rounds from their Type 53 rifles, then turned tail and ran like all the demons of hell had come for them. They'd made five high-stepping paces when a grenade from Tonto's M-79 caught up to them and burst two feet overhead.

Showered with bits of metal, they went down screaming. Not for long though, as Kent Welby ran to them and finished them with a single shot each. Tonto waved the squad forward. An increase in the volume of fire from second squad informed Tonto that the guys were holding what they had. A minute later, True Blue, on point, made visual contact with the little brown men in black pajamas. He signaled, the squad spread out, and slashed into the flank of the VC platoon. Taken by surprise, the Vietnamese guerrillas tried to turn their front to take on this unwelcome force that, to their frustration, they could not see. That brought more fire from the seven men they had pinned down.

Only eight of the enemy had managed to change position when they came under attack from behind. Kent Welby looked over the sights of his weapon and saw the wide-eyed features of a kid who could hardly be more than seventeen. The Cong had a bayoneted rifle, though, and charged directly toward Doc's position. Welby flipped the selector and tumbled his target with a five round burst. Another Charlie jumped into sight and Doc pinwheeled him with a tight burst in the center of the VC's chest. The dying man jolted and staggered a moment, while the bullets tore out a large chunk of his back. Then his legs went rubbery and he fell in a heap.

Doc Welby took surprised note that he had not the least shred of his usual anxiety over his own well being. The siren song of combat hummed in his ears. He saw movement to his right and swung the barrel of his Stoner that way. His finger eased off the trigger just in time as he recognized one of the guys from 3rd Squad. Man, they covered ground in a hurry. Suddenly the fury of battle dwindled to a few random shots.

"Mop-up time," Tonto Waters called out. Then, raising his voice, "Mr. Ott, you over there?"

"Johnny on the spot, Tonto. But, I should say that's what you are."

Drolly, Tonto Waters told him, "You missed morning chow."

"I guess we did," the young ensign responded. "Think we have time to take care of that now?"

Tonto had walked over to where the youthful officer stood, back supported by the bole of a gnarled old mahogany tree. "Naw. It's gonna get too hot, too soon around here. Clear your supplies out of the ROD site and we'll have to find someplace else."

"You ask me, we won't be doin' any resting today," Ensign Ott opined.

With a lopsided grin, Tonto agreed. "You got that right, sir. Charlie's gonna be madder than a whore at a fag convention."

They spent the rest of the day dodging patrols. Not *patrols*, exactly, Doc Welby decided. There had been varying sizes of units, moving purposefully through the jungle. Not on a random search for the SEALs who had disrupted their supply efforts, more like with a specific destination. Those same supplies, of course. New rifles, AKs to replace the old, worn Chinese communist weapons they now carried.

"I wonder if the brass really believes there's going to be a big offensive real soon?" Doc Welby asked Repeat Ditto.

"I'd say they did. We wouldn't be out in the bush destroying their supplies if they didn't have some idea what was going on. But, how do you figure there's going to be something going down here?"

Avoiding any mention of what had come from the interrogation of Phon Bai, Doc told him of his day-long ruminations. Chad Ditto might be small, with a boyish look about himself, but he was damned smart. He nodded agreement to every part of Kent Welby's hypothesis. Then made his own contribution.

"That gook big-shot we brought in must have spilled all about it."

Doc liked that, a bright kid, and contributed another. "I'd say ol' John Wayne Slater already had some idea that Charlie was fixing up something for the Delta before we went after Phon Bai. But, right now, all I care about is maybe ten or twelve hours of stacking Zees and filling my belly with *real* food." Doc changed the subject once again. "Our new AO should be right around that bend up there."

"That close? I wonder where the VC are?" Repeat asked, giving the terrain a nervous, though thorough, once-over.

Doc Welby perused the green wall of jungle with equal care. "If they were out there, we'd know it."

After hours of evasive action to avoid contact with the enemy, the SEALs had returned to a roughly northeasterly course, parallel to the Bassiac, around 1620 hours. The idea was to reach the next chain of islands shortly before darkness fell. They all knew that the moment a fire fight opened up or a bunker got blown, it would bring down the VC in fearsome numbers. Doc's gut tightened at the reminder. Doc recalled a staggering element of the operation order.

"Sixteen bunkers to be destroyed. If they're all as big as the ones we found, that could start one hell of a war."

"I don't like thinking about it," Repeat Ditto replied. "We get in enough tight spots as it is. In the last letter I got from my Mom, she said to be careful. My Dad said to give 'em hell. He was in Korea. He don't like communists one damn bit. Especially Oriental ones."

"Was he in the Navy?"

"Naw. The Army. Started off in the 40th Armored Division, California National Guard. They got activated, sent to Fort Lewis in Washington, then off to Hawaii, Guam, and Japan. Went into Korea when MacArthur took command. Dad don't like to talk about it much. He says it was a shitty war." Chad Ditto grinned. "First time I heard him cuss in front of us kids. I was eight at the time. He said it right out at the dinner table one night when my older brother asked him about Korea. He said it was a shitty war."

"This ain't any picnic, you ask me," Doc Welby returned. "From what little we get to see of the newspapers, it seems the politicians don't want to turn us loose, I mean all the services, and let us win this war."

"Politicians suck," Repeat said shortly.

"That your idea?"

"Well, sort of. I got it from Dad. He always said politicians sucked, that they always got in the way of a man doing what he knew he could do. It was politicians that stuck it to MacArthur. And, just you wait, it'll be politicians who stick it to us this time around."

"My God, Repeat. I never knew you were a philosopher."

They both had a laugh over that, then grew silent and ultra-cautious as they neared the final screen of trees between them and the river. Any time now they could be jumped by Charlie Cong. Doc Welby checked the selector setting on his Stoner and hefted it to get a feel for how much ammo he had in his snail drum. Too much to change now, he decided. Let Charlie come. He felt more ready than ever before.

The squad had settled into position opposite their first island target and eaten chow before the first of the VC showed up. They came by sampan and debarked on the island. A bit more cautious than those of the previous night, they did not chatter among themselves as they grounded their fragile craft and set about opening the bunker. The next party of enemy to arrive came from landward.

A low, harsh bark of command alerted 1st Squad of the VC presence behind them by not quite thirty meters. It must have been an order to shut up, because not another sound betrayed their positions to Tonto Waters and the SEALs he now, reluctantly, commanded.

Tonto shifted ever so slowly, until he could see clearly

to the rear. For a long count of heartbeats, nothing moved. Then he caught sight of a cabbage palm that fluttered in an unnatural manner. Had they been seen? Tonto wondered. No, definitely not. There would be a whole lot of shooting going on if those jerks had seen even one of the squad.

Maybe not, the cautious side of him argued. They could be sneaking up to take the SEALs without a lot of ordnance going off and endangering their comrades on the muddy bar in the river. A cluster of bamboo directly behind Tonto rustled violently and a little black pajama-clad figure stepped out. Tonto melted even lower into the clutter of vines and brush that shielded him.

Slowly the line of enemy troops drifted into sight. They advanced with stealth toward the SEALs. *Would there be more of them coming behind?* Tonto Waters weighed that possibility while the VC came even closer. One of them stumbled over a trailing liana and caught himself with an open palm against the trunk of the tree, at the base of which Tonto Waters crouched. He came within an inch of planting his sandaled foot on Tonto's hand.

Chapter 26

From that vantage point, after his recovery from the near spill, the youthful Viet Cong could see the island in the Bassiac. He could see his comrades working to remove crates from the underground bunker. All seemed peaceful. He peered beyond, to study the far bank. No sign of the evil American foreign devils. He cast a quick glance left and right along his own bank. Nothing. He turned slightly to call out to his superior, his sandal sole brushing the tips of the fingers of Tonto Waters.

"All clear, comrade Sergeant. Our comrades are at work on the island, awaiting us. There are no Americans on either side of the river."

"Go on over and let them know we are here," came the reply.

The young guerrilla moved to the lip of the bank and descended, and Tonto Waters breathed again. Then the rest of the VC came forward. Their weapons looked old, badly worn, barely safe to fire. One passed behind Tonto and out of sight. Suddenly the brush where he had gone thrashed violently and he let of a startled yell, followed by an excited jabber of Vietnamese... Then utter silence.

Off to his left, Tonto heard the abbreviated sputt of a hush puppy and another body fell in the brush. The sergeant called out inquiringly and thrust his way through the hanging vines that masked Tonto's position. His expression of puzzled anger changed rapidly to one of complete horror as he put meaning to the impossible presence of a pair of totally human eyeballs in the green and black shadows at the base of the tree. A fraction of a second later, Tonto Waters blew the sergeant's face away in a hail of buckshot pellets.

Pandemonium erupted. Short bursts of automatic weapons fire shred the twilight. Screams of the dying echoed off the lower canopy of the branches overhead. Muzzle flashes prolonged the afterglow of the setting sun. On the island, the VC setting out stores went down before even one could reach his weapon. On the west bank of the Bassiac, the stunned, thoroughly sandbagged Viet Cong platoon put up only slightly more resistance. After a furious six minutes, the firing abated.

Only an occasional shot came from the VC. That freed the squad to move and roll up the survivors. The meaty smack of a knife being delivered with enormous force in the chest of a VC reached Tonto's ears. Then, *Plink!*

"Ow! I took a hit. Oh, shit, I'm bleedin' to death." It was Kent Welby.

"Take it easy, Doc," Tonto urged at a conversational level. "Where are you?"

"Th-thirty feet from that tree you've been hugging."

"Be right there. I'll bring Saint Nick with me." Right then and there, Hospital Corpsman First Class Filmore Nicholson received his nickname.

"Yeah, you do that. I could use some of that stuff in his bag of toys." When Tonto and St. Nick reached Doc, he blurted an observation that had dawned on him only a moment earlier. "We fired too early. Second Platoon won't be here for a while."

"You're right, Doc, only we didn't have any choice." He nodded toward the fallen sergeant. "Charlie Cong there didn't give us one."

"Am I hurt bad?" Doc asked St. Nick.

"Where are you hit?" Filmore Nicholson asked the supine Kent Welby.

Doc's face flamed. "In the... in the... backside."

"Oh, for God's sake," the medic grumbled. "Roll over." It took little time for him to make sense of what he saw. "Your *haemorrage* is from your canteen. The slug went all the way through. I'm gonna have to get it out of the way before I can tell how bad you're hurt. Hang loose, Doc."

"Sure. Great. Easy for you to say, St. Nick. It's not you who is shot in the ass."

"You might not be, either."

"Tell me I can't feel what I *can* feel?" Doc flared.

"Cut the crap and let me get us regrouped. We have to hold the place until the sappers get here," Tonto growled.

"I'm trying, I'm trying," Nicholson appealed to reason.

He unhooked Doc's canteen cover and pulled it away from the area of the wound. He found a circular smear of red, with a black spot in the middle, on the tiger stripe shorts Doc Welby wore. Fil pursed his lips and frowned. "Looks like the bullet didn't penetrate very far. I think I see the base of it in the entry wound. Let me check it out."

"Can't you give me something first?" Doc asked miserably.

"Bite on a stick. Isn't that what they did in those old Westerns?"

Apprehension and pain raised Doc Welby's voice an octave. "That ain't an arrow, and I ain't John Wayne."

"Oh, all right," St. Nick Nicholson grumbled. "I have some local I'll use. Procaine. It'll numb the area. Gotta save the morphine for somethin' serious."

"This isn't?"

"Not from where I'm sittin'. Hang in there, Doc. Just a little jab, a couple of minutes to numb you out and then I can probe."

"I don't like the sound of that word... *probe*."

"Nothin' to it." Nicholson's hands went swiftly to his task.

He produced a small syringe, and a vial of a yellowish liquid. He drew up 2ccs of air and shot it through the diaphragm into the vial. Then he carefully tilted the glass bulb and pulled out two ccs of procaine. A jab here and another there, and a third at the top of the entry wound, and the job was done. The medic got busy with a squeeze bottle of Physohex and a wad of gauze, washing the wound field for his exploration.

After several seconds, St. Nick tapped the area around the entry hole, an angry purple mass of pierced flesh. When Doc showed no response to the touch, Nicholson took up a pronged wound probe and a set of forceps. Doc raised a hand to hold him back.

"Where's Tonto?"

The medic looked around. "He's gone on to organize the guys."

"Okay. This is bad enough, without having him look over your shoulder while you do it."

St. Nick had barely inserted the probe when the voice of Archie Golden came from near by. "No kiddin'? He took a round... *there*?"

Doc Welby groaned. "Everybody's going to know I got shot in the tail."

Fil Nicholson shrugged. "Not something you can exactly hide."

"You're so full of cheer. Do your digging, ghoul and leave me in peace."

"You'll be in one piece, all right, don't worry about that. Humm," he concluded as the probe chose that moment to make contact with the base of the bullet. "All right. In less than two millimeters. Hang on, Doc, out she comes."

Doc tried to stall. "Now hold on, Fil. Is it absolutely necessary to do it here and now?" As a kid he had hated every visit to the doctor's office, and the dentist absolutely filled him with panic.

"It is, unless you want to get gangrene and lose your whole butt! Hang tight." Following the course of the probe, St. Nick inserted the forceps, spread the jaws, and clamped onto the bullet. It made a little sucking sound as he extracted it from the wound. Immediately he stanched the flow of dammed up blood with another gauze pad and tore the paper seal from a packet of antibiotic, which he dumped into the small hole in Doc Welby's buttock.

Following that with an adhesive field dressing, he rocked back on his heels and waggled the offending chunk of metal in front of Doc's eyes. "Here it is. Want it for a souvenir?"

"God, you're sick, Nicholson." Then Kent Welby though on it a moment. "Yeah, sure. Why not? Get it drilled and wear it with my dog tags."

From the direction of the other squads came a spatter of gunfire. Medic and sniper exchanged glances. "Oh, shit, it's starting again," Fil Nicholson blurted.

"Good," Kent Welby replied in a harder tone that he usually used. "Let's get it the fuck over with."

Captain Thuy Mi had been given a second chance. Visions of a firing squad still danced in his head, his reprieve having come from the Soviet Spetznaz officer, who reasoned that combat leaders who had actually encountered the American SEALs were too valuable to dispose of for failure. In gratitude Thuy Mi had provided, at the senior lieutenant's request, copies of all after action reports and patrol summaries even before sending them on to his own headquarters. Now he had an opportunity to redeem himself.

Gratitude, being one of the "soft, capitalistic" emotions, had supposedly been driven from Thuy in hours of "self-examination" sessions. As a good communist, Capt. Thuy accepted this as necessary. Yet, what he felt toward the Russian, if not gratitude, had to be the next thing to it. He would not let him down this time.

Hardly larger in stature than an American boy of 14, Capt. Thuy drew himself up to his full height as he addressed his men regarding their current mission. "They are back. The Men with Green Faces. This is not a cause for alarm, comrades. They have come to spoil our months of planning and preparation. We must not allow that to happen. Already, platoon-sized units from the company of Capt. Diac have engaged the SEALs, with unfortunately poor results. Losses have been high. But, we have encountered this enemy before and most of us have survived.

"We are wiser, then," he went on, pacing back and forth in front of the semi-circle of junior officers and noncoms. "We know a secret that will make us victorious. Think on that a moment." Thuy paused, allowed a small smile to spread on his thin lips. "What is their greatest weakness?"

A slightly more preceptive, newly promoted lieutenant raised a tentative hand. "They are few in number. The Green Faces do not have the strength to stand up to a large, disciplined force."

Thuy beamed at him. "Absolutely correct, Comrade Lt. Troc Minh. Did you hear that, all of you? We are moving into the Delta in battalion strength. Many battalions. By sheer force of numbers we can overrun these American barbarians, smother them, utterly devastate them. We are to advance at once toward the Bassiac, rather than wait three more days as our orders first stated. We are to sweep the Green Faces into the river and exterminate them. Go now and tell your men. Let them know that the Men with Green Faces can, and are about to be, defeated."

Now, three hours later, Capt. Thuy Mi had some serious doubts about the accuracy of his prediction. The entire company had been fought to a standstill. Advance elements had insisted that the enemy strength could not be more than twelve. Yet, every time they tried to advance, *someone* hit them on the flanks. And all the while, the steady roar of huge explosions told a tale of more lost supplies. Nothing for it, but to go forward and see for himself. Capt. Thuy left the command post in charge of his senior lieutenant and headed toward the sound of fighting.

"What's going on up there?" he asked a wounded man, making his way to the rear, his rifle used as a crutch.

"Comrade Captain, these Green Faces fight like tigers. I had my leg shattered by a grenade, thrown by a man I believed I had killed a minute before. They do not die," he wailed. "They do not die."

Capt. Thuy struck him with a backhand blow that popped like a shot. "Enough of that, you fool. Do you want to start a panic?"

Face greenish pale, except for the imprint of Thuy's hand, the youthful VC fought for control. "No. Of course not, Comrade Captain. I am unworthy," he added, his head bowed until chin touched chest, in lieu of the full bend from the waist he would have executed in formal contrition.

"Then get a hold of yourself. Report to the medical tent, next to my command post. They will care for you there."

"Yes, Comrade Captain."

Thuy pressed on. A popping sound in the leaves above his head proceeded the stutter of automatic weapons fire and a shredding of green that filtered down on his shoulders. The front was farther away from the river than he had believed it to be. Bent low, he moved with greater caution now.

When he reached the front lines, it looked like any other part of the jungle. Only a narrow, shallow stream divided friend from foe. Spread out behind a low berm formed by the bank, his company had been brought to a standstill by a handful. Only one way to end this stalemate, Capt. Thuy knew.

Raising his voice, he began to exhort his troops. "Comrades, we are here to fight the enemy, not be cowed by them. Our lives are meaningless, compared to the thousands who will enjoy the freedom of our liberated homeland. Rise up and strike down these white devils. I will lead you!"

His AK-47 at the ready, Capt. Thuy Mi put deeds behind his words. Rising, he let off short, angry bursts with the assault rifle as he surged forward. Reluctantly at first, then in growing numbers, the men followed him. Then the grenades sailed through the night toward their ragged line. Blasts, the odour of burnt TNT, and the screams of the wounded filled the air.

White phosphorous followed and, in it's illuminating side-effect, silhouetted the attacking VC. Tonto Waters brought his Ithaca into position and began cranking off rounds. One flechette charge took a Cong in a green uniform jacket full in the chest. Immediately claymores detonated, shredding a dozen VC and leaving twice that number screaming in agony. Losing heart with the loss of their leader, they broke and ran from the glaring white light. A fury of bullets and grenade fragments accompanied them.

After the last Cong disappeared, a long silence followed. Tonto Waters went with others to check their body count. He bent over the corps in the green jacket. He rose, exhibiting his trophy.

"I got me a big-shot. This one carried an AK."

Thus ended the heroic efforts of Capt. Thuy Mi. Not in glory and praise, rather in excruciating pain, and as a provider of trophies for a SEAL warrior far fiercer than himself.

On board PBR 324, with the name painted on the outer bulkheads of the cabin combing, port and starboard, Lt. Carl Marino listened as voices crackled from several speakers at once. The four whip antennas on the stepped cabin roof had been augmented by eight clip-on antennas of the AN/PRC-25 radios brought aboard by SEAL RTOs. For the moment it put Pope Marino in mind of the Tower of Babel.

."Eagle One, there's a hell of a lot more people out here than expected, "came a plea from second platoon.

"Raintree, can you give covering fire to Jockey One? Over." Fourth of the First, Lt. Marino identified.

At the time the op order arrived, even before the briefing, Pope Marino had wondered why the Riverine force had not been given the assignment of destroying the supplies. His immediate suspicions centered on the bad blood between himself and LCDR Lailey. He dismissed that as being paranoid. A lot of good men, valuable for themselves, as well as the cost and extent of their training, could be lost if the vindictive Lailey saw this as an opportunity to end his vendetta. Marino put that aside as he framed his reply to Dusty Rhodes' remark.

"You know what has to be done, Eagle Two. If the situation demands, detach one squad to act as security. Eagle One, out."

Pope Marino heard the tight disappointment in the voice of Lt. (jg) Ruther, who commanded the - *Mary Lou*. "Negative, Jockey One. We are to stay on station until your extraction begins. We'll hose the whole area then. Raintree, out." He turned to Lt. Marino. "I don't like this a bit. We usually have more options."

"'Ours not to reason why,'" Pope quoted, not thinking it the least bit flip.

"Your guys are catching hell in there."

Pope Marino considered that a moment. His reputation marked him as a man willing to take any chances for his men. Well, then, why the hell not? "Do you think that if you took a little throttle off those engines we might drift close enough to provide fire support for both Eagle Two and Jockey One?"

A broad grin brightened the face of the twenty-three year old officer. "Right you are, Marino. Reckon if we accidently drifted into the fire zone, we'd have to bust a few caps just to get out safely."

"Then let's do it."

"Jockey One, say your coordinates, over."

"What the hell?" Chief Jim Wilkerson blurted as he yanked the radio handset away from his ear. Then he spoke softly. "Is this Raintree?"

"Roger. Give us your coordinates, and those of the other three squads."

Wilkerson did so quickly. Ten seconds later, the trees overhanging the river lit up with the flicker of an enormous blaze of gunfire. Half a dozen Cong died on the receiving end. Another outrage to human hearing came from the PBR, this time aimed at the island that housed another bunker.

"Raintree, this is Jockey One. I'd say everything is suppressed, out."

Silence came for about five minutes, then the hellish bedlam repeated. Engines roared briefly and died. A third cataclysm unleashed on the jungle, gouged huge holes in the vegetation and the Viet Cong, then ceased. The engines sounded again. By then, Chief Wilkerson had his people on the move. They had three more targets for that night.

First of the First had just reached their second target when the prow of a PBR nosed around a bend and the engine rumble died to an idle. Tonto Waters tapped Archie Golden on the shoulder. "Everyone get your heads down. From the sound of what's been happening I think we've got some help coming."

For a fourth and final time, the awful firepower of the PBR joined that of the SEALs. Mortar rounds caught a platoon of VC in the open, too committed to an assault on first squad to take shelter in the trees in time. Feeding the 81mm tube with all practical speed, the Navy gunner rained hell down on the vulnerable Cong. Then, when the shelling and the brutal fire from three .50 caliber MGs ceased, to their utter astonishment, the small force they thought they had surrounded counterattacked.

Stoners stuttering, the SEALs drove into the remains of the VC platoon. Tonto Waters pumped the action of his Ithaca, over and over, grateful for the clever machining of the shot dispenser made for him by a River Tiger machinist mate. It sent a horizontal spread of deadly shot over an area that measured ten feet at twenty meters. The first time he had used it, he'd cut down two Cong with a single shot. Now he wouldn't part with it for a thousand blue chip shares of General Motors.

It looked like the bill of a duck with seasickness, but oh, did it do the job. "Atta boy, Platypus," Tonto praised the bastard device as he took out another Charlie. Then, loud enough to be heard in the silence that abruptly fell, "All right, guys. Clean it up around here. We got two more to go."

Chapter 27

General Hoi Pak received the first reports of the disaster in the Delta at about the same time Tonto Waters led first squad away from their second target of the second night. Fire bloomed in the general's belly. Absently he reached for a clove of peeled garlic, crunched on it and washed it down with tea. No mere ulcer would defeat him.

But it looked like a handful of sailors, these American Navy SEALs, were well on the way to doing just that. Sailors did not fight on land. He had been taught that in the French war college he had attended. Oh, they could manage a shore party, to secure a downed comrade, or such, but not protracted battle that had bled the ranks of his Viet Cong subordinates by more than a battalion in strength. Unheard of. Impossible. The ulcer flared again. Damn the doctors, this called for some Wang Fu.

"Vang Li, bring me some wine," he shouted to his orderly, crouched in waiting outside the general's office. While he waited for it, he summoned Col. Nguyen Dak.

Col. Nguyen arrived first. "Yes," the ascetic intelligence officer remarked upon entering and seeing what the general studied. "It is everything gone bad that possibly could, and worse."

"You're philosophical enough about it, Dak. How could this have happened?"

"I am an intelligence officer, not a seer, old friend. "I would suspect that we were not apprised in a timely manner of everything known to certain parties."

"Kovietski!" Gen. Hoi exploded. "That *gua'lo* Russian pig. He has withheld vital information? Is that what you're saying?"

"Gently, gently," Col. Nguyen urged as he crossed to

the desk. "Our Soviet ally has ears everywhere. If I am right, he is much more than he appears. And he certainly has more rank than shows on his shoulder boards."

"What are you implying?" Gen. Hoi demanded.

Col. Nguyen dreaded the words almost as much as the entity they described. "The KGB."

Outraged by this, Gen. Hoi pounded a fist on his desk and felt an answering flame from his gut. "That is unconscionable. This is our country. We run it's affairs as we see fit."

Col. Nguyen cocked his head to one side. "Only so long as Moscow approves of what we do, I sadly fear. There are two realities for any client state of the Soviet Union. The reality that the client wants to believe in. And the reality as seen by the Russians and everyone else. Do you think that the Cubans would be receiving all the favors they get from the Soviets if Castro would have refused to allow those missiles to be put in place? No, I didn't believe you would. Bad enough they had to remove... some of them. Yet, Cuba enjoys a very favorable status with the Soviets. And why? Because, my friend, they proved their loyalty and obedience to Moscow. We will have to accept whatever comes out of this, bide our time, rebuild, and try again. Perhaps I can get some ears in Kovietski's operation."

Clinging to that slim hope, Gen. Hoi calmed himself, rapidly drank three cups of wine and went back to his gloomy contemplation of the reports from the Delta. He would make it his personal, all out undertaking to eliminate the American Navy's SEALs.

True Blue signaled and everyone went to the ground. The squad's leapfrog maneuver would take them another half a klick to the third target. Only, how could they do it undetected with so many VC swarming around. Everyone found a chunk of vegetation and made themselves into its likeness. None too soon, they discovered, as a file of twenty Viet Cong wended along the trail the SEALs had abandoned.

When the enemy drew nearer, the faint starlight revealed that they all carried some sort of poles, yokes and harnesses for carrying away supplies. They would be on the island, packing their loads, by the time the squad reached their position. Thanks to some screw-up by the brass in how they planned this search and destroy mission, Doc Welby thought furiously as the Cong padded past in their ubiquitous sandals. He accepted that it would be foolish to jump them now. No time had been allowed to lay out an ambush. Their numbers alone argued against it. He settled in and narrowed his eyes to slits.

When the last man had passed out of earshot, Tonto had the squad on their feet and off down the trail. A word of caution insured that True Blue Oakes would not blunder into the rear man.

In the end, it could not have worked out better. The newly arrived VC set their weapons aside and began loading the contents of opened crates into their carry systems, while more went into the bunker to bring out additional supplies. Many of those were marked with the symbol that assets had assured the SEALs indicated medical supplies. Well and good, Tonto Waters thought. Exactly what they needed to knock out. Viet Cong medical facilities were generally believed to be minimal at best. Any cut in essential items would further cripple the ability to recuperate wounded Cong.

That would happen Tonto felt certain when the squad located only three men left on the river bank to stand guard. They were taken out with suppressed S&W hush puppies, which opened the door for getting the rest. When the squad spread out to take firing positions, Tonto designated Archie to join the SAW in opening the ball with a grenade.

Archie, as usual, got over-anxious. With a flash and

bang, the grenade went off a fraction of a second before Kimball, the squad automatic weapons man, set his M-60 to chattering. VCs went down like wheat before a combine. The two 40 mike-mike grenade launchers dropped deadly pills into the open hatchway of the bunker. When they went off, sympathetic detonation left little work for the SEALs of second platoon.

It looked like the whole island raised up three feet, smoke and dust boiled together, while ammunition and explosives underground cooked off in the growing conflagration. Bodies whirled through the air to splash in the river. After three minutes of saturation fire, the fusillade ceased. While the reverberations of the last shots rolled along the river, no one moved. Then a figure appeared on the opposite shore.

"Didn't your mother ever tell you to leave something on the platter for others?" came a Texas drawl.

The swift ferocity of the attack, and the utter destruction of the bunker, did not give the VC time to send in a counter force. Second Platoon's men set their charges and faded into the jungle. First Squad of First Platoon moved out two minutes later. One more to go.

Doc Welby didn't like this one at all. The local anesthetic had worn off and the wound in his ass throbbed. Worse, there had been too much whanging and banging going on this night. This would make the sixteenth and last of the bunkers that had been located and identified. Enough shit, he had heard the G-3 say, to equip a regiment. Perhaps a light brigade, LCDR Lailey had suggested.

That left him no doubt as to the importance of what they had been assigned to do. Only, the way they had gone about it, so openly, exposed for so long a time, no proper rest. He felt the latter most, he admitted to himself. As a SEAL, he had no illusions about his own abilities or limits. If his body protested this much, and his mind swirled in this dense a fog, so would those of all the others. A second later, a single, sharp, *craaak!* jolted him out of his daze of fatigue.

Near by, Dave Kimball, a man with only two months with the platoon before coming to Vietnam, went down with a soft sigh. His continued movement, feeble thrashing, told Doc that he still lived.

"Get St. Nick over here," he whispered harshly from where he had gone down.

Damn, it just wasn't the same with Tonto not on point, he thought a moment later. Good as he was, True Blue had not even seen a sign of the enemy. When the black SEAL's Stoner snarled a second later, Doc knew True had found them now. A flurry of muzzle flashes winked in the jungle ahead. Doc Welby counted fifteen. This was going to be one bitch kitty. A grenade flashed loudly in line with two of the flares.

Good old Archie. Two more M-26s went off as fast as Archie could pull the pins, arm and throw them. Doc Welby heard the cough of an M-79 and knew Tonto was alive and well. Fil Nicholson showed then and Kent Welby pointed him toward the fallen Dave Kimball. Damn! Doc suddenly realized that Dave had been carrying the M-60.

Deep in the core of his mind he didn't want to move, expose himself to all that steel-core ammunition flying around. The rest of him knew he had to. In a low crouch he set off in a rush to make it in one try. He beat the medic to where Dave lay.

Quickly he retrieved the light machine gun, extended the bi-pod and rested it on a sturdy coconut log. A swift check of the belted ammo and he began ticking off three and five round bursts, right by the book. Wood and dirt exploded around him in a furious onslaught. Nothing like a machine gun to expose a guy. Everyone wanted to get a piece of him now. Gnawing his lower lip, Kent Welby stuck to the gun as he kept up a steady stream of jacketed 7.62 rounds into the enemy position.

It had the proper effect. Charlie kept his head down, while Tonto did a quick reshuffle of the squad. When they opened up again, it confused and disoriented the VC. Some, Doc Welby reckoned, must believe there were more of us out here than they had expected. The last of the belt slid over the back of his left forearm. Quickly he reached for another, which Kimball had wrapped around his upper torso.

Doc didn't find it there. Instead, it sat, neatly coiled, on a palm leaf at his side. He cut his eyes to St. Nick. "You're welcome," the medic mouthed silently. When the last casing spat from the ejection port, Doc lifted the cover latch at the right flank of the feed cover. He raised the cover and fed the linked belt onto the feed plate, links up, with the first round positioned in the feed plate groove. He checked to see that the second round was properly held in place by the feed plate retaining paw and then firmly closed the cover. He slid back the cocking handle and repositioned himself behind the weapon.

In less than a full minute he had the gun back in action. The VC quickly regretted his efficiency. They made their displeasure known by another blitzkrieg against Doc's position. That decided the young SEAL. He stopped firing and waited for the enemy to concentrate on something else. Then he slung the link belt over his left shoulder, draped a loop of it over his left forearm and bolted for another position.

Darkness remained an ally. Doc's departure went unnoticed by the guerrillas eager for his blood. A sniper's instinct led him to a far better position, almost flanking the Viet Cong, with the river at his right. Doc Welby raked the entire front of the VC position at the M-60's low cyclic rate of 550 rounds per minute. When he opened up this time it seemed as though Tonto Waters had read his mind.

Five M-26 frag grenades took to the air as one, followed by the distinctive cough of the two 40mm launcher tubes. Confusion, panic and terror erupted in the badly mauled ranks of the VC. Lighted by explosions and muzzle flash, Doc Welby saw better than a dozen of the little men in black pajamas melt into the jungle. They fled for their lives. And wisely so, for the force had been reduced to a reasonable quantity to allow Tonto to order a charge on the position.

One wide-eyed Cong rose to challenge Tonto with the bayonet on the end of his Type 53 rifle. In a brief moment, Chief Waters wondered if he could have his shotgun fitted with a bayonet lug. It would beat having to waste a round on such an easy target. He shot the man anyway and pushed on into the final line of trees at the water's edge. On the island, a Czech version of the Soviet RPK opened up.

Doc Welby shoved his way through the undergrowth and brought the M-60 to bear. One five round burst later, three bodies sprawled around the bi-pod-mounted LMG near the bunker. None of the enemy left on the island showed any desire to replace them. By then the rest of the squad had obtained clear fields of fire on the supply cache and opened up. When the last Cong fell, they turned about and concentrated their diminished night vision on the jungle, in search of any more unfriendlies who might be around.

Ten long, tense minutes went by before the first SEALs from 2nd Platoon showed up on the far side of the Bassiac. Tonto Waters used a red-lensed flashlight to signal the all-clear and the explosives boys moved in. Sporadic gunfire came from the areas where the other three squads of 1st Platoon held the ground for the sappers. The area around First Squad remained quiet. Ominously so.

Radio contact had been established for a brief while in late afternoon between the headquarters of Gen. Hoi Pak and the ranking VC District Commander, Tre Fon Lok. DC Lok had been on the point of hysterical rage. He demanded that Gen. Hoi give a go-ahead on releasing all available troops in the Delta area in a desperate attempt to save at least some of their supplies.

"Nearly half were destroyed last night," the district commander snarled over the radio link. "The Americans must have a battalion out there. Damn these white barbarians. We thought we had rid ourselves of the last of them when we threw out the French."

"Ancient history, Comrade," Gen. Hoi responded dryly.

Face purpled with fury, Tre Fon Lok growled like a hungry mastiff. "History that is coming back to haunt us, Comrade General. I must be able to deploy my men effectively. All of them. The situation is getting entirely out of hand. If the supplies are destroyed, the offensive is terminated. Also, I can no longer guarantee control of the Delta... day or night."

Gen. Hoi sighed heavily, more in regret than surrender. "Very well. You are the commander in the field. Do what you think is necessary. As of now, I am leaving the Delta situation entirely in your hands."

Now, with fresh troops pouring into the threatened areas of the Delta by the minute, Tre Fon Lok thought back on that conversation and fumed silently in his mobile command post, a highly prized gift of high technology from his Soviet friend, Sr. Lt. Kovietski; a BTR-5O, amphibious tracked APC. Although nearly a decade old, the armored personnel carrier served remarkably well for the purposes of Tre Fon Lok. It also gave him tremendous face. He, alone, possessed more power than Phon Bai, who had unfortunately been kidnapped by the Americans. The

BTR-5O had cost him a lot of favors owed, and many already paid, to Sr. Lt. Kovietski, but the status that accrued to the owner of the vehicle made it worth it.

Some time ago, Tre Fon Lok had come to believe that Sr. Lt. Kovietski was not what he seemed to be. Although a giant by Vietnamese standards, with seemingly inexhaustible strength and stamina, his youthful blond hair close-cropped and lacking any gray, the lines around Kovietski's eyes betrayed a greater age than he admitted to, certainly more than suited the rank he supposedly held. No, the Soviet officer undoubtedly held higher rank, and in the KGB.

A communist more by chance than by conviction, Tre had joined the Viet Minh to get what he most wanted; power. The son of a wealthy Saigon merchant, he had no need for more money. Tre's father had died of a heart attack while the struggle against the French raged on. Tre had secreted his new riches in a Swiss numbered bank account and declared his conversion to the cause of Ho Chi Minh. He rose rapidly. Through his fortune, he was able to perform numerous favors for his superiors, which won him their support. At last invited into the communist party, Tre blossomed.

He had been among the first to be made a cadre of the newly-formed Viet Cong. Tre worked diligently over the years to improve his position. When he had been elevated to his present exalted position, several among those who had aided in his ascent had paid for their kindness with their lives. Tre had learned well the lessons of Lenin and applied them in a purely pragmatic way. Then the Americans had come.

Tre Fon Lok saw them immediately as a threat. Not only to the eventual victory of the Viet Cong, but personally. The current situation only heightened his sense of extreme peril to his individual agenda. That higher headquarters believed all this destruction had been at the hands of two tactical units of twenty-eight men and eight officers only fueled his fury. So, he ordered out the massed forces under his command, with only one, specific order: "Find these SEALs, and kill them to the last man."

Chapter 28

A little under a klick separated the SEALs from their LZ. With everything in readiness, Tonto Waters formed the squad into a loose column and prepared to move out. Then the soft rumble of a PBR's engines reached his ears. A moment later, the *Mary Lou* nosed into the bank and a figure climbed over the gunwale. Tonto had no difficulty in recognizing the shape of Pope Marino. The muscular young lieutenant trotted up to his waiting SEALs with ease.

"To hell with these boat rides. Second Platoon is clear of the area. I'm going out with you," Lt. Marino announced.

Relieved to be free of the burden of command, Tonto Waters popped the OIC a white flash of smile. "Am I glad to hear that, sir. Now I can get back to point, where I belong."

"Do that, Chief. I imagine that'll make True Blue happy."

Puzzled, Tonto blurted, "How'd you know I put him on point?"

"Simple, Tonto. He's next best to you out front."

Two minutes later, the last SEAL disappeared into the jungle, their course being set by Tonto Waters, using the wrist compass he wore right handed. Following behind them would be Second Squad, then Third and Fourth. They would be picked up on a staggered schedule from four of six pre-selected LZs. In theory it would reduce the odds of a surprise from the VC. For the first time during the two frantic nights of roving battle, Tonto Waters took a deep breath and released the heavy burden of command strain.

For the first time, also, the mosquitoes and other flying insects came on them with a vengeance. Thicker than usual, if that was possible, the biting, stinging vermin swarmed into ears, nostrils, and mouths. Those that landed on lashes or the corners of eyes netted curses and soundless swats from the SEALs. Fifteen meters ahead of the column, Tonto Waters had mentally counted off four hundred meters when the next wave of Tre Fon Lok's vengeful Viet Cong came into view.

Tonto's signal given, the SEALs melted into the tropical forest. *With the charges all set, there ain't any reason to deny them the terrain*, TontoWaters thought.

Lt. Carl Marino must have shared the thoughts of Chief Tom Waters. Not a SEAL fired a shot as the Viet Cong forced their way through the jungle, spread out, four abreast. Five ranks passed within an arm's reach of several SEALs. Tonto Waters made a quick count and came up with thirty. Then the other side of the coin appeared to him.

That could put us between two enemy forces, with the LZ beyond that! Nota comforting thought. They waited, tensely, for the prescribed time. Before it had been reached, though, the sky behind lit with a hellish glow and outrageous explosions slammed at their ears. The ground shook beneath the feet of every SEAL. Following that came the blast wave and, borne upon it, the screams of the dying and injured. Maybe they wouldn't become a SEAL sandwich, Tonto considered.

Charlie had been stupid this time, Doc Welby thought. The VC had gone onto the island and tried to disarm the satchel charges left behind. It hadn't worked. But, would that bring more of them? Doc thought not. There would be nothing for them to do or see. He let relief roll through him when Tonto flashed the signal to resume the march.

On the fringe of the meadow designated Alternate Landing Zone One, Lt. Marino gathered the men. "Let's recee the area and make certain Charlie hasn't decided to keep watch on the place."

"Aye-aye," Tonto Waters agreed readily. He left the M-79 with Fil Nicholson and relieved Blue Chip Reno of one of the hush puppies. That and a knife would do a lot better. He had his own ideas of what to do if they discovered an ambush. With a quick nod to Archie Golden, the two SEALs set off to circle the meadow.

Truman Oakes took Kent Welby with him, to recon the opposite direction. Between them, he and Tonto would find any Cong who might be observing the LZ. True Blue hadn't gone twenty meters when he came upon the first Viet Cong. Sucking in a silent breath, the black SEAL brought up the Smith and Wesson .38 Super and sighted in. Naw, too long a shot, allowing for the suppressor. Exercising all his stealth, he crept closer.

Doc Welby watched, his lower lip caught between his teeth. One mis-step, one broken branch or rustle of palm frond and the whole squad would be compromised. Only a few yards closer, then. . ,

Pheewhut!

Not even the cycling of the slide or the fall of the expended casing could be heard beyond five yards. The VC would never hear it. His forehead and eyeballs bulged outward, then erupted with a spray of blood and pulped brain tissue. His legs shot out and jerked wildly on the ground until True Blue rushed forward and sat on them. Doc Welby watched in a sort of horrified fascination while the torso heaved upward, trembled, and went slack. Without a word, the two SEALs moved on.

Over on his side, Tonto Waters had the same method of dealing with an in-place ambush. He found his first VC some twenty-five meters inside the screening jungle. Whoever had set up this ambush lacked imagination, Tonto decided. He had gone exactly by the book in setting up a box ambush. Three sides covered, with the base facing the open end, the sides positioned at an oblique angle to give clear fields of fire. After disposing of the first man, the one furthest from the field's base point, with the suppressed, .38 autoloader, Tonto signaled for Archie to follow him.

The Chief came upon the second man sooner than expected. With the hush puppy shoved into his harness, Tonto Waters had only a split second to act effectively before the enemy shouted a warning that would spell an end to the squad. He swung the butt stock of the Ithaca at the head of the gaping man. The butt-stroke downed the VC, but not before the classic bayonet movement had been played out.

Automatically reversing the weapon and lowering it, Tonto jammed it forward, adrenaline adding power to his muscles. The duckbill shot spreader concentrated the force of the thrust onto two relatively thin surfaces. As a result, the device drove deeply into the soft tissue of the Cong's gut and did terrible damage to his liver. Face contorted with agony, he slipped soundlessly to the ground.

It was not what Tonto Waters had expected, surely not what he had counted on. Yet it did the job, in a wet, messy way. Feeling somewhat like a deck hand in his first storm at sea, Tonto wrested his weapon free. The duckbill came out with a soft plop and a fetid hiss of intestinal gas. Oblivious to the coppery-sweet smell of blood and putrid odour of feaces from voided bowels, after sustained combat over two months, Tonto's expression did not change as he wiped his shot disperser clean on the pajamas of his kill.

Instead, he jerked his head in a signal to move on. Ten meters further along, two VC shared a relaxed moment at the ambush site to wolf down some rice with slivers of fish from a coconut shell bowl. Tonto motioned for Archie to circle and use his knife. When he saw the slight movement of the underbrush that indicated Archie was in position, he took aim to shoot one of the Cong between the eyes.

Not unusually, he missed, though not by much. Tonto's round hit low and destroyed the man's lower jaw. The two fingers of one hand, that formed a rice scoop, jerked spasmodically and the soft, brown grains went flying. In the same instant, Archie leaped on the back of his target, yanked the head toward his own chest and the keen edge of his K-Bar bit into the exposed throat.

Meanwhile, the first VC tried to scream in pain and alarm while he choked on blood and rice. Cursing his poor marksmanship, Tonto shot him again. This time the slug smacked into the crown of the head. The Cong soldier went rigid, vibrated violently for a few swift seconds, then toppled to one side.

Archie had finished his target also, so they moved on.

Tan Tho Bac had been pressed into service with the Viet Cong at the age of fifteen. He hated it. He hated his sergeant, he hated the cadre, he hated the self-examination sessions, and most of all, he hated what he had to do to the people of villages that refused to cooperate with the Viet Cong. He hated it all with the intensity engendered only by a 16 year-old. So, when he caught a slight movement from the corner of one eye, he swiveled his head to look directly at the object.

Tan Tho's eyes widened when he made out one of the

Men with Green Faces. It made up his mind instantly. Slowly he laid down his Type 56 rifle, raised his hands, palms out, and waggled them. He accompanied that with a strong negative shake of his head. Then he rose to full height and pointed insistently at the jungle in a direction away from his comrades. Washed with relief, he watched the terrible apparition form a slow, wide smile.

He, too, pointed to the jungle and nodded affirmatively. Tan Tho Bac wasted no time at all in disappearing into the sheltering trees. The farther he got from his hated comrades, the faster he ran.

"Now why'd you do that, Tonto?" Archie Golden whispered in an ear of Tonto Waters.

"He was just a kid. And scared to death, to boot. Didn't have any love for his buddies out there, either."

Archie nodded. "I've heard our ARVNs talking about how the VC treat those who don't join them voluntarily." He shrugged. "The kid got lucky."

"The rest won't," Tonto vowed.

Doc Welby watched as Truman Oakes shot another VC with the suppressed pistol. How many could there be? He had counted seven men killed so far. Given the same number on the other side, this had to be the grandaddy of all Cong ambushes. And that didn't take into count those left along the base line.

They had reached the far end of the meadow and turned in toward Tonto Waters, who would be approaching from the opposite side. Nothing mattered so much to Doc than to get this ambush cleaned up and bring in the chopper. He would be one happy SEAL when he saw the buildings of Tre Noc again. True Blue Oakes motioned to him on and Doc broke that chain of thought to peer ahead carefully for the next VC.

Kent Welby didn't find the next man. Charlie found

Doc. The call of nature had acted upon the youthful Viet Cong, which caused him to stand and turn toward Doc as he came around a tree. In the second it took them to react, the Vietnamese' eyes widened and he opened his mouth to shout.

Unwilling to fire a noisy shot, Doc Welby grabbed at the knife on his battle harness. It came free while the VC filled his lungs for a shout. Doc dropped his Stoner and grabbed the smaller man by the front of shirt, then drove the blade to the hilt in the exposed chest.

"Heee-yiiiii!" the Cong screeched in the instant before the keen edge of Doc's K-Bar sliced through the right ventricle of his heart.

"Oh, shit, now you done it," True Blue Oakes complained from ten feet away.

Excited voices jabbered questions in Vietnamese from ahead of them. There came a muffled oath and the roar of Tonto Waters' shotgun. Two Type 56 rifles answered him, then abruptly stopped firing as True Blue and Archie got their suppressed Smith and Wessons into action. Silence followed for a heart-stopping minute. Then the platoon Chief and redheaded Archie came into view from behind two trees.

"Musta been the last of them," Tonto Waters opined.

"Am I glad of that," True Blue gusted out. Then he rounded on Doc Welby. "Why the hell did you let him make any noise?"

Kent Welby wiped the emotion from his face and assumed an expression common during UDT/R training. "No excuse. But I've got an explanation."

Still funneling his fright into anger, Truman Oakes snapped, "This had better be good."

"I didn't know he was there. All at once he came at me from around that tree, with his dork in his hand, and..." Doc broke off his response and stared at his team mates in baffled surprise. They were laughing. "What's so funny?" he asked.

Through his nervous chuckles, True Blue choked out a reply. "Thought he was trollin', huh?"

For a moment, that put Doc off balance. "What'er you talkin' about?" Then he recalled the taunt given to weenie wagglers in his Junior High School days. "Oh, yeah, sure. That's what it was, all right. Can't let those trollers get away with it."

"Speakin' of getting away, that little fire fight just blew this LZ for us. Best get back to Pope and set up another."

Training took over, the four SEALs sticking to the trees instead of taking the short way through the open meadow. When they reached the rest of the squad, Lt. Marino was already on the radio.

"Bluestreak Two-niner, this is Eagle One. Do you copy? Over."

"Roger, Eagle One. What's your problem? Over."

"We want to abort Alternate One. I say again, abort Alternate One. We're gonna have a hot LZ here any time now. Meet us at Alternate Two. Over."

"Second-first's on the way there now, Eagle One. Over."

"Roger. I know that. We've got to *didi* and will link up with them there. Over."

"Roger. I copy that, Eagle One. Over."

"ETA is twenty minutes, Bluestreak. Eagle One, out."

That twenty minutes became the hairiest time First Squad had spent in the bush.

Attracted by the gunfire, the platoon acting as security for the mobile CP of Tre Fon Lok advanced toward the meadow, the BTR-5OPK lumbering along behind. They would have to swing to the south to reach it. Which gave them an excellent opportunity to intercept the squad.

Unaware of this, Lt. Marino led First Squad through the jungle at an oblique angle to the meadow. They maintained a loose diamond formation, with plenty of distance between each man. That brought them into contact with the extreme left wing of the Tre Fon Lok's company.

"Holy shit, there's more of them," Archie blurted when he saw Tonto Waters signal of an enemy in sight.

Archie blended into the vegetation like the others and watched anxiously while Tonto made a count of the VC and flashed the number back. A dozen of them. They had just taken out eighteen. Archie made his hands busy reaching for grenades.

With a 14-plus ton tracked amphibious armored personnel carrier along, progress had been slowed to a crawl. Tre Fon Lok peered from the commander's hatch of the Czech-modified BTR-50, fuming with impatience. First thing he would do, once they had absolute control of the Delta, would be to order a massive road-building project that would provide a network for the proper deployment of armor. Every minute lost going around a tree too big to simply push over made his rage grow blacker. It did allow for a more thorough search, that he admitted. Captain Xeang was below him, seated in the troop compartment. He monitored progress of the search for the Americans. Tre Fon dropped down to speak to him about it.

So it happened that only the driver, operating the APC with the remote controls in his cupola, was the only one to die when Archie's pair of M-26 frag grenades clanged on the sloped glacis of the BTR-50 and went off. The driver's head disappeared in a red spray. Shrapnel spanged off the 10mm armor plate while bits of gore from the decapitated operator sprayed the interior.

"We're under attack!" the surprised Capt. Xeang squealed as he wiped a chunk of brain matter off his left cheek.

"Of course we are, you idiot."

"Bu—but they should not be doing that. We're the superior force."

"We do not know that, Xeang," Tre Fon replied calmly, his face covered by wet, crimson freckles. Inwardly he raged at the effrontery of the Americans to try an ambush on such a powerful force.

Xeang gripped the handset of the radio until his knuckles whitened. When the man on the other end completed his report, Xeang turned an unbelieving expression on his superior. "Comrade Colonel, there is firing at every sector of the line. We have walked into a trap."

Tre Fon Lok gave him a wintry smile, only too familiar with what had no doubt happened. "Are your lieutenants certain that your men aren't firing at one another?"

Xeang's face went blank. "I had never thought of that."

"Then you had better advise them of it and get this stopped. Then concentrate on killing the Americans."

Chapter 29

Unaware that the replacement ammunition they had come for had been destroyed, the VC fired wildly as concentrated bursts came from the jungle around them. Grenades crashed and men screamed. The cough of grenade launchers frightened the newer men. Driverless, the controls fortunately in neutral, the BTR-5OPK stopped a moment before it slammed into a thick mahogany tree. Another fusillade slashed into the VC platoon. And then, silence.

The SEALs had pulled a hit and run. They had no choice, considering the strength of the enemy. Eight men could keep out of sight a lot easier than thirty. They had another klick to go to reach the LZ. Everyone sweated buckets from the exertion, although the sun had barely risen. Tonto Waters set a fast pace, eyes constantly roving in search of any random booby traps the VC might have left behind.

In back of them, Col. Tre Fon Lok and Capt. Xeang worked desperately to restore order and get the platoon off in the direction taken by the fleeing Americans.

"Hornets sting, Captain," Tre Fon told the excited junior officer. "But one usually finds that they are few in number." He was yet to find out that the "hornets" to whom he referred were soon to join up with more of their kind.

Tonto Waters broke through into the stand of bamboo at the edge of the LZ. He took a careful look around for any sign of second squad. They would, he realized, most likely be waiting right inside the tree line. Five minutes went by, then Pope Marino and Repeat Ditto joined him in the sibilant concealment.

"Time to call in the cavalry."

"Roger that, Pope," Tonto agreed. "Do'ya think those A-Sixes are on hand, just in case?"

"If I know Lailey, we can forget about them. He'll have them flying cover over Second Platoon and our third and fourth squads, if he has them at all."

"Don't sound like you have much faith in the lad."

"Is the Pope Catholic? We'll be lucky if we can scare up one gunship," Marino replied sourly. He turned to the RTO. "Get me Bluestreak."

"Aye-aye, sir." Chad Ditto made the connection and handed the handset to the lieutenant.

Pope Marino made it short and sweet. "Ten minutes," he announced. "Second Squad's across the way from us. Their Slick will be in first and pull 'em. Then we go." He turned back to survey the terrain over which they had come. "I don't like it, Tonto. Too many of those nasty buggers out there."

"We don't have to like it, Pope. But, we sure's hell have to live with it." Faintly, in the distance, Tonto Waters could hear the growl of the V-6 inline engine of the BTR-5O. "They're gnawin' on our tail, Pope."

"I hear. Better get on the squad radio and tell those guys from Second we're on our way over there." He put deeds to his words. "They said we could make it there in five if we cut straight across."

"About half the time before those SOBs reach us," Tonto observed. "Then, as that Tel Aviv Irishman, Golden, would put it, we're gonna have a darlin' little donnybrook."

No sense in avoiding the short way, now they knew the position of the nearest the enemy. Cutting across the clearing, First Squad reached the second in time to turn around and prepare to stand off the approaching Viet Cong. Lt.

Carl Marino spoke urgently into the Prick-25.

"Negative, Bluestreak Four. We have a hot LZ. Hold your position and we'll call back. Eagle One, out."

Tonto Waters positioned himself behind a mound of earth that had once been a large mangrove tree. He meticulously laid out rounds for the M-79 and spare cartridges for his Ithaca. They had barely had time to arrange scant defenses when the first of the VC broke out of the trees across the meadow.

Eager and inexperienced, they sought to take advantage of clear movement. The SEALs' squad automatic weapons opened up, spraying them with 7.62mm death. Tonto's grenade launcher chugged, joined by the XM-148 on Repeat Ditto's AR-15. Bursting projectiles taught the neophyte troops the error of their way. When the Stoners and the rest of the two squads' weapons opened up they broke and ran for the trees.

"Well, that bought a little time," Kent Welby observed as he fitted another belt in the M-60 he had inherited from Dave Kimball.

"Not much, though," St. Nick Nicholson observed as he pointed to the phalanx of trees.

Roaring at max revs, the V-6 diesel engine of the BTR-50 forced the tracked APC through the lesser growth and into the open. The armored personnel carrier had been modified to accommodate a Chinese Type 56 machine gun in the commander's cupola. A young private manned it, while those below in the passenger compartment handed up cans of ammunition. He opened fire in long, staggered bursts that slashed into trees, vines, and shredded leaves. None of the bullets hit human flesh. He had seen what happened to the driver and it made him nervous.

"What I wouldn't give for a TOW right now," Kent Welby said wishfully.

"Hell, even a LAW would help," Archie Golden remarked. "At least it might scramble their brains a little."

A believer in the "bigger the bang the better" theory,

Archie Golden had little respect for the underpowered Light Antitank Weapon which had replaced the 3.5 rocket launcher of yesteryear. In his bitterest moments, Archie professed that the reason the more powerful antitank weapon had been replaced was because it worked.

Emboldened by the presence of the BTR-5O, some of the VC came out to advance along side of it, using the armored side for cover. Both grenade launchers fired and Tonto Waters uttered a muffled curse when his round fell short by twenty feet in front of the square front of the APC. He opened the breech and extracted the spent cartridge, sliding another of the fat, stubby, blunt-nosed grenades into the chamber and closed the weapon.

That one arched nice and high, a clean flight that dropped it to explode a few feet above the heads of the sheltering troops. Three went down without a sound, the other four uttered cries and screams of pain and fled back to the safety of the trees as the two squads unleashed a withering fire.

"I wonder if those A-Sixes are for real?" Tonto Waters cast an eye Pope Marino's way, as he studied the steady advance of the BTR-5O.

"Yeah. I was thinking this would be a good time to find out." He consulted a page in a small, spiral note-book, then took the handset from Repeat Ditto. "Hotel-Sierra leader, this is Eagle One. Do you copy? Over."

Static answered for two long seconds, then, "Roger, Eagle One, this is Hotel-Sierra Three-One. We copy five-by-five. Over."

"Hotel-Sierra Three-One, we have a target for you. Over."

"What's your authentication, Eagle-One? Over."

Fuck that, Pope Marino thought heatedly, then checked the note pad again. "Sierra-Echo-Alpha-Lima 4-7 X-ray. Over."

"We're on the same frequency, pard. What are your coordinates? Over."

Pope Marino read them off. "Good enough, we can be there in three," came the pilot's reply. "What have you for us? Over."

"Sierra Three-one, what stores do you have aboard? Over."

"Eagle One, we have a full load for the wing guns and mini-gun, that's M-97 HEIs for the mini, one rocket pod of 2.75s, a rack of 5 inch Holy Moses', and one — I say again — one Red Dog 500 Anti-PAM on the belly. Those do you some good? Over."

"Roger that, Sierra Three-One. Here comes your fire mission. Target Number One is a BTR-50 APC at coordinates…" Pope Marino calculated the distance the APC could cover against the fire from the two squads and read off the anticipated position. "Target Two is the tree line directly behind Target One. Hold your Anti-PAM for there and give us some crispy critters. Over."

"Roger that, Eagle One. One pass or two? Over?"

"We'll let you know. Over."

"Can't do it that way, Eagle One. We have to know up front to be able to turn the right way. Over."

"Make it two. Over."

"Will comply, Eagle One. Pop green smoke to show us your front. See you in a short. Hotel-Sierra Three-One, out."

"They're on their way," Pope informed the squad.

It began as a shrill whine, which developed to a burgeoning roar as the three A-6 close support turbo-prop aircraft rammed in at full throttle on the required heading to reach the beleaguered LZ. The wedge-shaped formation slashed across at altitude, made a rolling turn and a sharp descent. They began their run at treetop level. A hundred pounds of .50 caliber machine gun and 20mm mini-gun ammo spewed from flaming barrels. A twinkling stream of empty casings spat from the belly. Puffs of smoke came from the starboard hard point and a pair of 2.75 inch FFAR Mighty Mouse rockets sped toward the BTR-50. Each aircraft in turn fired on the exposed target.

The first pair struck to either side of the lumbering vehicle. The second pilot put one on the glacis and the other a yard off the nose. The last man in the flight overshot and his projectiles detonated over the frightened VC troops who made a desperate dash for the presumed safety of the jungle. Both the driver and gunner had abandoned their cupolas at sight of the birds. They came back up after the flight had passed over, right in time to have the backs of their necks warmed when the lead plane turned to make a pass and lob a cigar-shaped, 500 pound, thin-skinned aluminum bomb loaded with napalm into the trees.

Black-tinged, the red-orange, roiling trail of fire spread in an elongated teardrop shape that engulfed everything it touched. Trees burst instantly into flaming beacons, the lianas disappeared in a puff of smoke, air plants winked out of existence even faster, and screams of pain and terror got swallowed up in the infernal roar of the fire storm. The flaming, jellied gasoline sucked air from lungs already tortured by yells of alarm. Then the second A-6 came on point and made a sharp turn to port. An instant later the pilot released his Anti-PAM cylinder.

The third aircraft maintained the attack heading and released straight into the trees behind the enemy front. Then all three began a spiraling climb to altitude, formed up and streaked back to their attack heading. Hotel-Sierra Three-One, the flight leader, had better luck this time. He put one Mighty Mouse into the track, which blew off chunks of tread, bogies and rollers. The other struck the front of the driver's cupola, which blew off the head and shoulders of the machine gunner, who after many shouted demands had returned to his weapon.

All three aircraft fired machineguns and rockets into the burning trees, then waggled their wings and sped away to re-arm and cover someone else in need. For the next ten minutes all that could be heard was the crackling of flames. Tonto Waters wetted his throat with a swig from his canteen and licked his lips.

"Wow! Fourth of July in the Mekong Delta," he stated huskily.

"Navy guys," Archie Golden said with a tone of awe. "They knew how to put that shit on the enemy instead of us."

"Bluestreak One, Bluestreak Four, this is Eagle One. LZ is now clear. I say again, LZ is now clear. What's keepin' you guys? Over."

"We copy, Eagle One, LZ is clear. On our way. Bluestreak One, out."

Green smoke billowed at the edge of the LZ, with a third canister sitting atop the damaged BTR-5O, the living occupants of which had fled the moment the rocketing had ended. They ran, dodging bullets, at an oblique angle to the burning napalm, toward the jungle. No harm would come from that angle, Pope Marino had decided.

He did not know, so he would not take into account the outrage of Col. Tre Fon Lok. Considering the air assault a personal affront, he stubbornly remained with his wounded status symbol. Tre Fon Lok cursed the Americans, consigning them to the hottest corner of the Underworld in a manner that would have horrified and saddened his Buddhist monk teachers from his youth. Clearly they had failed in teaching the "gentle way" to this pupil. He crouched over the radio, in a futile attempt to make contact with any of the surviving platoon. After seven fruitless minutes, he did raise a faint voice from another patrol in the area. Unaware that the external antenna had been sheared off, he incorrectly assumed that their distance made them incapable of assisting him, until the platoon leader made a startling reply.

"We are at the Quan Tre crossing of the Bassiac, Comrade Colonel."

"What? Get your men here at once. Forced march. We

can capture or kill these American swine if you hurry." It would take no more than five minutes for help to arrive, Tre Fon Lok considered. Then he would make these Americans pay.

Whopping rotor blades announced the arrival of the Huey Slicks. They came on in a "line of ducks" formation. Tail rotors fishtailing, to line up with the littered meadow, the pilots compensated for a slight crosswind. This would not be a skids down extraction. The lead pilot, a warrant officer, had never met Eagle One, so he gave scant credit to the declaration that the LZ was no longer hot. It could just be entirely too damn hot for his liking. He'd lower to three or four feet off the ground and hover as best as the crosswind would allow.

From the bend of the smoke, he'd judge it to be a brisk ten miles an hour. Nothing that could be considered other than a text book hover evolution, given the size of the clearing, and provided that no one was out there shooting at him. Too damn bad about that APC in the middle. He noted the location of the two smoke grenades by the trees and swiveled around his own axis to line up between the jungle and the APC. That would give them some break.

"Eagle One, Bluestreak. Mount 'em up, partner," he spoke into the mike.

A dozen of the raunchiest characters he had ever seen began to stream out of the jungle and choggie toward the two Hueys. No, make that nine. Three of them carried another figure draped over a shoulder in fireman's grip style. White grins flashed in grizzled faces of mottled green, black, and brown that made them look like something out of the Age of the Dinosaurs. And they carried enough fucking armament to outfit a full-strength company. Yellowish flickers at the edge of the pilot's peripheral vision drew his attention.

"Aw, shit," he barked into the intercom. "In-coming. I see in-coming. Get those people on board ASAP. Double time."

A tin roof rattle on the thin skin of the tail boom told him that they had been hit.

Mortar rounds fluttered over the helicopters and landed long in the jungle. Tonto Waters looked beyond their way home to see the flicker of small arms fire. "I don't fucking believe it," he grumbled. "Those flyboys should have toasted every last one of those gook shits."

Pope Marino exploded into action, waving an arm over his head. "Get moving, get on board. Move, move, move!"

More mortar rounds came in, short this time, between the choppers and the APC. It took no added encouragement to hurry the SEALs to the Hueys. They tumbled through the open doors by pairs. In less than a minute only Pope Marino, Wally Ott, Tonto Waters and True Blue Oakes remained outside. Marino pointed at Ott.

"Get on."

"You go first," the young Ensign countered.

"No, goddamnit, get in that Slick."

"You, too, Tonto, True."

"No, sir. You goin' first," Truman Oakes insisted as he ticked off a burst from his Stoner.

"He's right, Lt. Marino, sir," Tonto growled warningly. "Haul ass," he added in determination.

Lt. Carl Marino shrugged and swung onto the lip of the door a moment behind Wally Ott. A second later, Tonto Waters joined him. He looked back to see a short burst of machine gun fire lace up the torso of Truman Oakes from crotch to shoulders.

"Jesus! Hold the bird, hold the goddamned bird!" Tonto shouted at the crew chief as he jumped from the deck to the ground.

When he heard the approaching helicopters, Tre Fon Lok came out of his despair. The platoon had reached him in time. Not only would they slaughter these invaders, they would destroy two expensive airships as well. He had removed the corpse of the gunner earlier, and now climbed cautiously into the cupola. Through the observation slit in the armor, he watched the enemy stream from the jungle and run toward the waiting helicopters.

He could not believe they were so few in number. Tre Fon Lok's eyes narrowed when he recognized the one who had to be the leader. A stocky man with black hair and nearly colorless eyes. He stood in the open, directing men toward the hovering craft. Gradually Col. Tre Fon Lok eased himself into position behind the Type 56 machine gun. It had not been damaged beyond the ability to fire. He remembered the platoon waiting in the trees behind him and bent down to snag the microphone. He spoke crisply and rapidly.

"When I open fire, put the mortars on them. Then sustained fire for one minute and advance. To the glory of Ho Chi Minh, Comrade!"

"Glory, Comrade," came the flat, toneless reply. All the haggard platoon leader wanted was to get out of there and find a bottle of rice wine.

Col. Tre Fon Lok took aim on the leader and squeezed the trigger. Green tracers smoked their way to slash a line of holes across the tail boom of the nearer helicopter. *By all the black dragons of the Underworld*, Col. Tre fumed. The sights had been damaged. He swung the weapon while he listened to the chug of mortars behind him. He sighted by triangulation, like a duck hunter. More bullets tore the ground, a good twenty meters in front of his target. Col. Tre made another adjustment. All of the men had boarded, except four, who stood talking to one another, by the time Col. Tre touched the trigger again.

Over the distance a gruff voice came to him. "He's right, Lt. Marino, sir."

His target was moving. In the desperation of total commitment, he swung the machine gun to where he thought the man would be. Instead of hitting the leader, the 7.63mm slugs ripped into a black enemy who jerked and spun before he sank to the ground.

"Hang in there, buddy. Hold on, True. I've got you, guy," Tonto Waters shouted in the ear of True Blue Oakes.

He tossed Truman Oakes over one shoulder like a hundred pound bag of potatoes and dug in with the soles of his sneakers. Powerful thigh muscles launched him into a staggering run for the chopper. Eager hands reached toward Tonto, to relieve him of his burden. Already the chopper wavered and hitched upward in preparation to lift off the suddenly hot LZ.

"Here! Here!" Doc Welby shouted at Tonto Waters.

"I've got him," St. Nick Nicholson bellowed in Doc's ear.

Tonto surrendered his burden and dove up and through the door. "Lift it, Mr. Baker. Lift this son of a bitch outta here," the crew chief shouted through the intercom.

The loaded Huey fought its way lopsidedly clear of the clutches of the earth. Tonto Waters turned back then and sighted his M-79. The weapon blooped out a 40mm grenade and it sped toward the target. It detonated on the side of the BTR-5O. Then the pilot swung their craft tail-on to the clearing and added throttle. Slowly, the jungle faded away.

Suddenly, while he shook a fist and cursed at the escaping Americans, shards of wire shrapnel from the 40mm grenade slashed into his face and shoulder. A deep cut in the right cheek of Col. Tre Fon Lok opened up and revealed white teeth, then the bit of metal cut his tongue also. Oddly, he didn't even care. He didn't feel any pain. He had a name now, a most hated name for certain. Lt. Marino. His pale-eyed, black-haired nemesis had a name. One that he vowed would soon be placed on a grave marker.

Chapter 30

Chad Ditto knelt at one side of Truman Oakes, while Filmore Nicholson prepared a line for an IV. Tom Waters held True Blue's head in place between his knees, wincing in sympathy for the imagined damage caused by the chopper's vibration. Chad pleaded with the black SEAL and his maker in an emotion-choked whisper.

"Hang in there, True. Please, God, let him hang in there. Everything is going to be okay. Stand tall, sailor. You can't resign from this outfit this way, man. Stay tough, True, man."

IV in place, Fil Nicholson watched large bubbles rise once, twice, three times. Then nothing for several seconds. Small, pinhead bubbles trailed upward in the plastic sack. Fil Nicholson bent forward, handed the IV bag of plasma to Archie Golden and bent to feel for a pulse.

None in the wrist. He tried the carotid artery. None there either. A tight lump formed in his throat as he looked up at the ring of worried faces. Swallowing with difficulty, he shook his head in the negative.

Chad Ditto wept openly now, as he rocked back and forth on his heels in the throes of sorrow over a lost friend. He felt this loss as deeply as if Truman Oakes had been his birth brother. Kent Welby looked away, his own eyes streaming. Even the vision of Tonto Waters blurred with moisture. Abruptly Tonto cleared his throat roughly and touched the talk button on his headset.

"Let's get this fuckin' thing back to Tre Noc."

Battered, bloody, and exhausted, the First Platoon of Team 2 returned to Tre Noc. They were met by LCDR Jorgensen of the Riverine Force and Capt. Stuart Ackerage, Area CO of NAVSPECWARV.

"You have pulled off a spectacular coup against the Viet Cong," Ackerage stated enthusiastically as he grabbed Pope Marino's powder-grimed hand and wrung it with energy. "You've set them back at least six months, according to our intel. We'll have a clearer picture with your after-action report." Ackerage changed the subject abruptly. "After your debrief, you'll have a lot of writing to do."

"How's that, sir?" a dazed Marino asked.

"Commendations, citations for valor, purple heart applications," the AOIC explained. "Believe me, these men deserve them."

"Yes, sir, I'll do that," Pope Marino answered vaguely. He went off to the debriefing.

For the first time, Lt. Carl Marino learned that 2nd Platoon, under Dusty Rhodes, had taken five wounded and two KIA. With one killed in action and only four wounded, 1st Platoon had come out of it a little better, but Pope Marino considered the point to be moot. He ached for all his losses. These were *his* men, and he felt that he had let them down.

One thing he could do, Pope decided, recalling his conversation with the AOIC. Although it seemed to be more symbol than substance, he would put them in for every medal he could think up specifications for. Ackerage had made it almost certain he would put them in for a Unit Citation. Then, ofcourse, there were the letters to be written to the families of those killed and wounded.

The SEALs had a system worked out for that. Depending upon the team involved, the letters would be sent to the base on Coronado in California, or at Little Creek, Virginia, where friends of the wounded would pay discreet calls on parents or wives to inform them. In the case of those KIA, officers and sometimes their wives would pay duty calls, along with the chaplain, on the survivors. In part this was a security measure. No one was to know exactly how many SEALs were in-country, and the number of casualties had to be kept absolutely secret. It was a Psy Ops thing, they had been told before leaving for Vietnam. The enemy had to believe that the SEALs were invincible, that none ever died and none suffered debilitating wounds.

It was believed in some circles, and quite correctly, that there were some Americans who willingly rendered aid and comfort to Hanoi and the Viet Cong. Their activities were suspected to not be limited to Agit-Prop (Agitation and Propaganda) and financial contributions, but that some had gone beyond the pale and actively gathered information which would be rendered into intelligence data. If these borderline traitors could not produce casualty lists, there would be a large blank spot in the enemy's knowledge of American activities and their cost. Lt. Carl Marino highly approved of the idea.

Accordingly, after the debriefing, he took the bottle of Johnny Walker Black, pressed upon him by LCDR Jorgensen, and barricaded himself in his small office to work on letters and specifications. He would put Tom Waters in for a Silver Star, and one posthumously for Truman Oakes, also three Bronze Stars for other platoon members. He had briefly spoken with Cy Rhodes and gotten his recommendations for 2nd Platoon; one Silver Star, six Bronze, and all of the Purple Hearts. Pope allowed himself two days to complete the task. They wouldn't be pleasant ones.

Tonto Waters finished the last half of his third beer in thirty minutes in a single draw. He gulped air, belched and crushed the steel cylinder in one large, square hand.

"Damn, I needed that," he declared to all around him in the platoon bar.

"Tonto, who do you think we'll draw as replacements for True Blue and Dave Kimball?"

Kimball was being med-evaced out to first Saigon and then possibly to Japan or Okinawa. His wound had been worse than he or Filmore Nicholson had considered it. A sucking chest wound, it had lost him a lot of blood and developed an infection, courtesy of the jungle climate.

"I don't know, and right now I don't give a shit." Tonto's dark mood had lasted over the two days since their return. He blamed himself for the death of Truman Oakes and saw how easily it could have been Pope Marino. Had that happened, it would have torn him completely loose from his moorings.

"C'mon, Tom," Archie Golden urged, using Waters' given name to reveal the depth of his own feelings. "We've got sort of a —whadda ya call it? —vested interest in this. I'm sure Pope would listen closely to any recommendation you made. Why don't you ask for Ted Spence and Yingle Bells Olsen?"

That jerked Tonto out of his black pit. "What! Those two loonies are about as nuts over explosives as you, Archie. I need them in the platoon about as much as I need a dose of clap."

Archie shrugged and raised both arms from the elbows, palms up. "Hey, what can I say, *bubbi*? Misery loves company, right?"

Tonto thought that over a bit. "You can be miserable without the both of them. I will suggest Yingle Bells to Pope so you have someone else to help with the big bang when we need it."

"You're a prince, Tonto."

"Aw, shove it, Archie." Tonto slammed a hand on the table. "I say this calls for another beer. You're buying, Archie."

"*Gevalt*, you'll make a pauper of me," he wailed in mock pain as he rose to comply. From the bar he threw over his shoulder. "Scuttlebutt is we'll be goin' out again real soon."

"I doubt that," Tonto said confidently. "There's nothing to go out after."

Early the next morning, Lt. Marino hitched a ride with the mail chopper to Binh Thuy. There he visited the office of the G-1. Personnel and Records held an arcane position in the military establishment of the United States. Some of the bright young boys in the Pentagon argued that the function of maintaining records on men assigned to any given unit could be as easily done by the G-3, thus more easily coordinating the activities of Plans and Operations.

Traditionalists urged the maintenance of the status quo. Separate entities insured a smooth flow of the necessary paperwork through which the Army slogged and the Navy sailed, albeit not as easily as before everything had to be filled out in quadruplicate. But, then, there were some among the Brass Hats that still doubted that a mechanized tank would ever successfully replace the horse in the Cavalry. Or so it was said. The G-1 also had been graced with the task of processing commendations.

When Lt. Carl Marino was ushered into the office of Captain Buckner, he got right to the point. "Sir, I was wondering at the delay in being notified that the commendations for our unit's action in Operation Full Sweep had gone forward."

Capt. Buckner looked at Lt. Marino with open sympathy and understanding. "That's because they have not gone forward."

"Why's that, sir?"

"As you know, every staff member reviews the citations and attaches his endorsement as an annex. Your commendations have so far received endorsements from all but a single staff member."

Pope Marino had no need to ask whom. "LCDR Lailey," he stated positively. "Sir, has he written a negative endorsement?"

"No. To date, he has refused to approve or disapprove. I'm sure you are aware that if they are not submitted in a timely matter that, at least for the present, they die for lack of our endorsement."

Pope Marino fought to contain his sudden flash of anger. "That does not apply to the Purple Heart."

"That's correct. And they have gone forward promptly. Along with the recommendation of a Unit Citation. I'm sorry, Lieutenant, there's little else I can do. Except I can lean on LCDR Lailey and urge him to sign the endorsement.

Lt. Marino stiffened to a position of attention. "Aye-aye, sir. I appreciate that. Thank you, sir."

He left the office feeling not the least bit better than when he had entered. Somehow there had to be a way to pressure Lailey out of stone-walling.

The Marine SP at the gate handed a folded sheet of paper to Kent Welby. "Got a note from your girlfriend," he advised with a smirk. "She's sure some looker."

Francie had written him? Doc Welby felt a surge of relief, followed immediately by a flood of anger-tinged guilt. Betty had not written him a single thing. He was still a married man. His anger came from the knowledge that so long as the divorce had not been granted, Betty would still receive the quarters allowance, have BX privileges, medical and dental care. Could she be so petty as to try to get back at him by hanging onto those service benefits? He tried to banish such thoughts by opening Francie's note.

It read simply:

"Kent Welby, We have to meet."

Well, he was headed for Mi Flower anyway. He would see her, find out what this was about. Expectation put a lightness in his step, although he still limped slightly from the soreness in his right buttock. When he reached the laundry and bar it became obvious some of the guys had told Francie Song of the wound Kent Welby had suffered. She sprang up from the table occupied by First Squad and rushed to him in the doorway.

"Oh, my poor, brave warrior. Does it hurt you badly?"

"Only when I sit down," Doc Welby quipped. That got a blank look from Francie. Doc felt disinclined to explain. "The bullet didn't go in too deep. It's healing nicely."

"I am so glad, Kent Welby. Come, sit with me."

They took a table apart from the others. When Momma Throh brought them beers in person, the smiling Mammasan arched an eyebrow and quipped in her fractured English, "I hear you get shot in butt, Doc Welby. Is that right?"

Color rose in Doc's cheeks and he suppressed a groan. "Yes, I'm sorry to say. It was just a little bullet."

"Little bullet... big butt. You not hurt so bad, then, I think," Momma Rose quipped.

Doc ground his teeth. "I could have gone all day without hearing that, Momma Rose."

"You be nice now, Doc Welby." Rose Throh waggled a finger under his nose.

After she departed, laughing hugely, Doc turned his attention to Francie. "I got your note. What's so important."

"I wanted to tell you I am so sorry about angry words I spoke to you before you left. When I hear you are shot, I am afraid I will not have this chance to tell you that."

"It'll take a lot more than a little slug like this to stop me," Doc boasted as he took the chain that held his dog tags and the .32 caliber slug from inside his shirt.

Francie's eyes grew large. A hand, tipped by brightly scarlet nails, flew to her face. "That is not so little. It scares me."

"It can't hurt anyone now. So, you wanted to apologize. You have and it is accepted. I wanted to tell you how much I regret getting so angry with you that… last time."

"It is forgiven. I cannot stay angry with you, Kent Welby."

"I'm glad. Otherwise, how are things?"

A small frown put a vertical grove between Francie's eyebrows. "It is the same. I still need most badly a job in the compound."

"Why, Francie? Why is it that you are so obsessed with taking a job in the compound?" Doc put up a hand to stop her answer. "No, don't answer yet. I want you to know that when I was shot, I made a promise to myself, to you, that I would do everything I could, and at once, to get you the job you want. I'll keep that promise, but I think I deserve a more direct answer than simply that you have to have a secure future."

Francie considered a long moment, her eyes straying to the rattan baby-seat beside the cash drawer, then back to Doc before she answered. "You know Thran Giat, yes?"

"Momma Rose's baby? Sure. We all do. What's he got to do with it?"

"He does not belong… he is not the child of Rose Troh. Thran is my baby. His name is Thran Giat Song. I have to be able to support him and see he has a better life than I have lived." Tears streaked the light touch of color and powder on Francie's face and turned her mascara into black ribbons. "Now do you see why I need that job?"

Stunned, Kent Welby stared at his beloved. "Yes, I—I understand. But, why didn't you tell me before?"

"I was afraid you would not like me."

"That's nonsense. Of course I like you, with or without a child. What about... his father?"

Pain registered on Francie's face. "Gone. He was French. He would not marry an Asian. I—I.. you can understand I do not like to talk of this, Kent Welby?"

"Of course I do. And, I'll see about introducing you to someone who can get you a job first thing tomorrow."

Overcome with relief and more powerful emotions, Francie Song flung a squeak of thank you at Doc Welby and fled to the sanctuary of the single restroom in the establishment. She left behind a very puzzled young man. For some reason, Doc Welby could not dismiss the small suspicion that remained in his mind as to which side Francie gave her loyalty.

Eloise Daladier returned to Tre Noc the next morning. She found Tonto Waters in the platoon maintenance shop, going over radios with Repeat Ditto. "You have created quite a stir in Saigon. Your unit is the talk of the town among all the journalists." Eloise paused to emit a throaty chuckle. "For some of them, they find it difficult, if not impossible, to turn your victory into a defeat." She sighed and continued. "Although I suspect they will worry it like a terrier with a rat until they invent something."

Perplexed, Tonto Waters took her by one elbow and walked her away from the table. "Is it really that bad?"

"Oh, yes. And worse. I have heard that certain of your American journalists have received orders from their editors not to file any stories that do not put your American forces in a bad light."

Tonto's face darkened and he growled his remarks. "I'd like to know which ones."

"So would I," Eloise said tightly. "Then I could expose them as being enemy sympathizers."

"Enough of that. Can I buy you a drink at the hotel?" Tonto asked expectantly.

"I'd like that. It's not exactly the Carousel Lounge, but it will do."

Tonto Waters had visions of a leisurely drink or two, a light lunch, then take a room for an afternoon of delightful love. Eloise Daladier had the exact same visions.

LCDR Barry Lailey could not hold back the AOIC citations for bravery for long, Lt. Carl Marino kept reminding himself. The word would get out and Lailey would be in a hot spot. Over at Binh Thuy, while Marino tried to satisfy himself with that thought at Tre Noc, time ran out for the foot-dragging Lailey.

The telephone on the desk of Capt. Stuart Ackerage rang brightly shortly before 1000 hours of the morning Eloise Deladier landed at Tre Noc. When he answered, the voice that rattled down the line from Saigon had the tenor of a constipated bear.

"This is General Belem. What the hell are you doing down there, sitting on your hands?"

"I—ah—don't understand, sir."

"I would like to know what the status is on the citations for bravery and commendations for First and Second Platoons of SEAL Team Two? Why the hell weren't they on my desk two days ago?"

"Ah—hummm, well, General, we have one staff member who has been reluctant to sign an endorsement."

"Barry Lailey," Gen. Belem stated as a fact. "Tell that obstreperous asshole to get off the dime and sign *right now!*" the general growled. You sent notice of intent to nominate First Platoon for a Unit Citation. I expected you to follow it up. Please to do so at once, or tell Commander Lailey to expect my immediate...and personal displeasure."

"I'll do so immediately, sir." *Damn that Lailey and his petty feuds*, Capt. Ackerage thought furiously as he hung up the phone. He would have Lailey's signature before noon chow or take great pleasure in making every day of Lailey's career miserable.

Half an hour later, LCDR Barry Lailey sat in a state of shock at his desk. Nothing like that had ever happened before. Not even when he had lost those men in Central America. Admiral Washburn himself, the commander of NAVWARV, had called on him in person and given the most vicious ass-chewing Barry Lailey had ever heard. His fingers burned as though ignited by the pen he had touched to the endorsement papers. Stu Ackerage had been with Washburn. Lailey recalled the expression of utter contempt on the face of his former classmate at Annapolis.

Well, he had signed, hadn't he? He had no choice, his mind mocked him. All Marino's fault. Marino was behind it sure enough. Must have gone sniveling to Ackerage at Special Warfare. Just his style. Fury rose hotly in Lailey's throat, thick enough to choke him.

By God, he'd not take this. Marino's first platoon had been back only three days now. And they had a short roster. He would send them out right away, only minimal warning, little time to prepare. Put them in harm's way again and again until Marino cracked and made a physical assault on his own person. Or got himself killed. He had other ways of getting even at his fingertips, too. Barry Lailey began contemplating them.

Hot words came down the radio net for *Starshii Lortyant* Kovietski, from General Hoi. The Vietnamese officer dispensed with any form of the usual courtesies exchanged between Asian officers. His voice sounded choked with fury.

"Only yesterday I received a report from you, based on information you say you developed from reliable agents in the field. Today I find that you possessed this information for nearly two weeks."

"An oversight, General, I assure you," Kovietski responded smoothly, wondering who was the leak in his organization.

"Oversight? I say that, for whatever motives, you deliberately withheld this intelligence on SEAL activities in the Delta until it resulted in a disaster. Tons of supplies have been lost, the ranks of the Viet Cong have been devastated, and my own decimated. And this by two forces of twenty-four men each. I consider your conduct in this matter to be reprehensible, bordering on treasonous. Can you give me one single reason why I should make a complete report of this to your superiors in Spetznaz?"

Alexi Koviestki nearly lost it, infuriated at being talked down to by Hoi. His eyes narrowed to thin, icy slits, knuckles white on the handset, he spoke with the sibilant hiss of an enraged reptile.

"Yes, I have, you..." He choked it off before adding the words that leaped through his mind, "inferior, Asian barbarian." Starting again, his words quivering with outrage so much that he nearly revealed that he was KGB and not Spetznaz. "I am not... You seriously misread me. It is the Soviet Union that commands the Worker's Revolution throughout the world, not North Vietnam. It is we who set the agenda. What has happened here is a minor setback. Speaking for my superiors, I can say this: You should be able to recover in record time. Instead of carping at a representative of your Socialist Big Brother, you should be forging ahead as we speak. I can guarantee you that the matter of the SEALs is under control. My agents will find a way to put and end to the cursed SEALs of 1st Platoon, Team 2, and a certain Lieutenant Carl Marino in particular. And it will happen damned soon."